SHATTERED SECRETS

KAREN HARPER

SHATTERED SECRETS

HARLEQUIN® MIRA®

DOUBLEDAY LARGE PRINT HOME LIBRARY EDITION

ISBN-13: 978-1-62953-136-6

Shattered Secrets

This Large Print Book carries the Seal of Approval of N.A.V.H.

To the staff and board of the Ohioana Library Association, which does so much to promote and preserve the work of Ohio authors. Especially to my friends, former director of Ohioana Linda Hengst and current Executive Director David Weaver. Don and I appreciate all you do.

SHATTERED SECRETS

1

Tess Lockwood drew in a sharp breath. She'd buried her memories deep, but the sign for Cold Creek, Ohio, brought the terror back. To face everything again—to relive it—no, she refused to do that. But they kept cropping up, tall as the cornstalks crowding the roads in this area.

She told herself that Cold Creek was a charming, quaint town but started to shake when she saw a sign stuck in the ground. Reelect Gabe McCord for Sheriff. It was with a few other local political ones, including a fancy poster to reelect Reese Owens, still mayor here after all these years. She'd tried to prepare herself for the fact that she was going to see people who reminded her of the past. But Gabe was the worst and she'd do everything possible to avoid him if she could.

Selling the family house she'd recently inherited was her immediate goal or she wouldn't have come back at all, especially at this time of year. But the day care center she wanted to buy would go to someone else if she didn't get some money fast. Her life's desire was to purchase the Sunshine and Smiles Center for preschool kids in Jackson, Michigan, where she'd worked for years. She planned to live upstairs and redo a lot of the space downstairs where she would teach and protect her young charges. The timing was doubly right since her renters in Cold Creek, her cousin Lee and his family, were moving out. Her mother had wanted to sell their house years ago, but it had no fields attached, and people hesitated to buy a place where a tragedy had happened. They had managed to rent it though, and were relieved that their cousins could live there for a while.

"Wow, four traffic lights uptown instead of one," she said aloud, thumping a fist on the steering wheel while she was stopped at the first light near the gas station. She needed a fill-up, but it looked pretty busy right now and she wasn't ready to run into familiar faces. "Like Gracie said, this place is so much bigger!" It felt comforting to talk to herself, as if she had someone with her, someone who really cared what happened.

Of course, she still had two sisters who cared about her, though Char and Kate were understandably upset that their mother had left the house only to her. On her deathbed Mom had said she owed Tess something for what had happened.

The Cold Creek Community Church they used to attend was at this end of the commercial district. She saw they had put on an addition. Piles of pumpkins adorned its lawn with a donation bucket out front for people to leave some money. Even in Jackson, you'd never seen something like that. Please Make Your Own Change, the hand-printed sign read. How she'd like to make a lot of changes in her life, banish the nightmares and the fear.

When the light turned green, Tess drove slowly to read the store signs. The doctor's

office was still there but with a new name
stenciled on the window, not Dr. Marvin,
who had tended to her immediately after
her kidnapping. The tiny storefront library
they used to visit between times the
bookmobile stopped by was still crammed
between the hardware store and the bank.
On the other side of Main Street she saw
the Kwik Shop, where they used to buy
groceries. She'd brought milk and juice—
and two bottles of wine—in her big cooler.
She also had cereal, bread, peanut butter
and jam, so she wouldn't have to stop
anywhere, at least right now.

Cold Creek had seemed huge when she
left at age six, but she knew that was just
because everything seemed big to little
kids. Still, from the keep-your-chin-up
phone calls from Lee's wife, Gracie, over
the past few years, Tess had heard all
about the recent growth of the town and
its influx of wealthy retirees and
weekenders.

She wasn't sure how people would react
to her return. Although eighteen years had
passed since she'd set foot here, would

people still stare and whisper? They might not recognize her at first, but how quickly would word get around? They might give her those looks so full of curiosity and pity it made her feel ashamed, despite the fact that her mother, Dr. Marvin, that investigator Agent Reingold and the sheriff had said over and over that what happened wasn't her fault.

But was it her fault? After all, she'd run into the back cornfield and tried to hide when Gabe, their teenage next-door neighbor and the sheriff's son, had told her to cut it out and called her a crazy tomboy. That was where and when it all began. And maybe Gabe was right, because she'd felt a little crazy ever since.

In the space where the sheriff's office had been, she saw a gift shop, Creekside Gifts, its windows decorated with Halloween costumes, wooden black cats and corn shocks. Farther on beyond the tiny town square, a brick sheriff's office had been built next to a new volunteer fire department. The American flag and the Ohio state flag flew from a big pole between the two buildings. A police vehicle with Sheriff emblazoned on the side was parked in the small lot, but she saw no one around. Rod McCord had been sheriff when she lived in Cold Creek and his son, Gabe, held that position now.

He would be thirty-one now, because he was thirteen when her family left town. Gracie said Gabe had bought his parents' house, directly across the roadside cornfield from the Lockwood homestead she now owned, so they'd be neighbors, just like when they were children.

The third traffic light turned red and she came to a stop again. Gracie had told her about "the great divide," but now she saw it for herself. The west side of town belonged to the outsiders, the new folks who had invaded and kept pretty much separate from the townies, except on market day. Well, what did she care? Tess told herself as she frowned at a new restaurant, a tearoom, some shops—and an English pub, no less, in rural Falls County.

Her stomach clenched as she turned

onto hilly Valley View Road. "You can do this, Tess," she said.

But as she drove down the two-lane road lined with tall, thick cornfields, she wasn't so sure. Especially when she passed the McCord place as the sun began to set atop the darkening Appalachian foothills and her family's old farmhouse crept into view. It seemed to leap at her. Even with the car windows up and the doors locked, she was certain she could feel the cornstalks clutching at her, rustling, whispering. She suddenly recalled being told to be quiet or the ears of corn would hear her. Who had said that? Mom or Dad?

"You're fine," she told herself. "You'll be just fine."

But she sat stock-still in the car at the bottom of the gravel driveway with the motor running until Gracie burst from the front door of the house and windmilled her arm to wave her in.

Falls County sheriff Gabe McCord left his cruiser about twenty yards outside the tall wooden gate of the Hear Ye Commune and walked closer. The place gave him the creeps, but the thirteen families of what he'd call a far-out religious sect had broken no laws and kept pretty much to themselves except on Saturdays when they had a big table of their produce at the farmers' market.

He'd received a complaint from Marian Bell that someone had seen a child at the Hear Ye market stall who resembled her lost daughter, Amanda, so he had to check it out. Gabe's theory was that the girl had been snatched by her father and taken abroad when the Bell marriage broke up, but Peter Bell had been impossible to trace. Amanda's disappearance didn't fit the pattern of the child kidnappings that had haunted his father and now him, but he was following all leads, desperate for any break in the long-standing case.

Although no one had disappeared on his watch, he still got heartburn over it in more ways than one. Worse, he was convinced his father had suffered two heart attacks running himself into the ground over the abductions. The so-called cold case of Cold Creek was always on the front burner for Gabe.

"Lee, how you doing?" Gabe greeted his former neighbor as he was walking across the grassy ground outside the fenced compound of meeting house, family buildings, school, gardens and workshops. Lee Lockwood was holding a forked willow branch straight out while pacing the grassy knoll. "Looking for water—or buried treasure?" Gabe asked. Most folks in the area knew Lee was a water dowser, which some in the area called a water witcher, as if it was evil or demonic.

"Oh, hi, Sheriff. Didn't see you coming. Usually we got guards out. You know, greeters who watch for strangers or gawkers. Got a lot of kids here to protect, including my two, now. And I really get into dowsing when I do it. Yeah, looking for water. Don't you go believing that buried treasure stuff you hear, nor the old wives' tales about locating ancient graves with a dowsing branch neither. It's just we could use another well since the water pipes don't come out this far from town yet. Been looking most of the afternoon though, and no go so far. I figure when cousin Tess gets back, I'll have her help me. She's got the gift too, you know."

He pointed the tip of the willow wand toward Gabe. Lee looked really nervous about his presence, but then some people were. The usually reticent man was trying to cover his unease up with talk.

Lee rushed on, frowning so hard his forehead furrowed. "Least Tess used to be good at it when she was a little kid. But I 'spose she don't want to be reminded of any of the old times."

"No. Me neither, but it's still an open case. Grace told me Teresa—that is, Tess—is coming back for a while to sell the old place. But aren't you going to miss living at the Lockwood house? Grace said your kids were doing fine in the public school, so why shift them here after only two months this year?"

"There's lots of benefits here. Protection from the world. Closeness to God through

Bright Star, other things."

It was getting dark as the sun sank behind the tops of the hills where rain clouds were gathering. Gabe wanted to get this over with, but he stared into the face of the earnest young man and hesitated to get him involved. He was a first cousin to Teresa, now called Tess, Lockwood, the first child taken in the two—or maybe three—kidnappings of young girls.

"Brice Monson has everyone here calling him Bright Star?" Gabe asked.

"Those who trust his guidance. 'You do well to heed a light that shines in a dark place until the day dawns and the morning star rises in your hearts.' That's the way we look at Brice. The bright morning star in a dark world."

Gabe decided not to get into it with his former neighbor, who had just moved out last week. He'd seen Grace was still there, sweeping the front porch, waiting for Tess at the very house where the first kidnapping had happened when his dad was sheriff. That afternoon Gabe was supposed to be watching several neighbor kids. Thank God Tess had come back alive, because the other two—if Amanda was one—had not come back at all.

"See you later," Gabe said. He headed for the gate to the compound.

"Oh, hey, forgot to tell you," Lee called after him. "Everyone's down by the creek picking up walnuts to sell at the farmers' market, even Bright Star. He let me stay here because we need a new water well, like I said."

The compound did look deserted. Gabe walked back toward Lee. Was the man shaking or was that willow limb quivering in his hands of its own accord?

"You tell him I'll be back tomorrow morning a little after ten," Gabe said, hoping Lee was listening. He looked transfixed, staring at the ground where the stick seemed to point like a skinny, crooked finger. Was Lee putting on a show for him? Gabe didn't really believe in dowsing any more than he believed Brice Monson was some sort of modern-day messiah. But Lee looked so amazed that

Gabe could only hope he'd remember to pass on his message.

As he strode back to the cruiser, Gabe couldn't help thinking Monson had picked a weird time to order everyone down by Cold Creek to pick up walnuts. Darkness setting in, a rainstorm coming. Gabe had helped his dad collect walnuts down there once. His hands were stained brown from it, and he'd run around the house pretending it was spattered, dried blood until he caught heck from his mother. "Blood on someone's hands is not fun and games!" she'd scolded him.

Did Lee actually have to get Monson's permission to stay behind? he wondered. This place was starting to sound worse than boot camp. Gabe was glad he hadn't mentioned what he wanted here. Monson might not agree to bring all the girls about Amanda's age for a lineup to see if the girl in the photo Marian had given him resembled her lost child. But Gabe was hungry for anything to make progress on these kidnappings—any lead, any hint, any clue.

As he got into his vehicle, he heard a rumble of thunder echo from the hills. It reminded him of things that made him uneasy when he needed to be in control, because it sounded like distant 155-millimeter howitzers, **boom, thump, thump.** Thunder often took him back to the day in Iraq when his Explosive Ordnance Disposal Unit disarmed a huge bomb in a Kirkuk market before it could detonate. Even as they succeeded, other IEDs went off in the distance, echoing, killing some of the men he'd sent to another site.

After he fastened his seat belt, his hand darted to his chest. Sometimes he almost thought he could feel his army-issued pistol in its cross-draw holster from his duty days. Today he wore his weapon on his equipment belt. From his inside jacket pocket he pulled out the pictures of Marian Bell's daughter and the Hear Ye girl. One was a close-up first-grade school photo, the other a grainy, more distant one of the child in question, standing by the commune's market booth. He stared at the photos side by side in the graying light. Again, he vowed he'd somehow finish what his dad had left undone: find the phantom Cold Creek kidnapper, who took little girls and, but for Tess Lockwood, made them disappear.

"Ooh, I think it's raining, and I hate to drive in the rain," Gracie told Tess as she looked out the window toward the road. "It's turning dark early. I had to get special permission to wait for you and I don't want to get back late."

After an affectionate welcome from her cousin's wife, Tess had toured the house at Gracie's insistence. Tess had tried to buck herself up to face the place alone, but it was good to have her here. Tess and Gracie were almost the same height, though the similarities stopped there. Gracie had long red hair, amber eyes, a round face and plump body compared to Tess's blond, chin-length hair, blue eyes and lithe frame. She'd never questioned why Gracie had taken such a liking to her, as if she were the Lockwood cousin instead of Lee. But then they had all played together as children. Gracie was one of the distantly spaced neighborhood kids, and their mothers had been friends. Back then, everyone in Cold Creek had known each other, or at least had seemed to.

"I'm sorry we sold most of our furniture, but I hope we've left you enough to get by for the couple of weeks you're here," Gracie said. "The houses in the commune are pretty well set up already."

"But your family will still be together, right?" Tess asked as they stood inside the back door while the rain rattled against the windows and Gracie scrambled into her slicker and pulled up its hood.

"Together when it matters, though Kelsey and Ethan will now have lots of family, lots of mothers and cousins in the faith."

Gracie didn't notice, but Tess shook her head, surprised that her friend had accepted Lee's new religious ideas so easily. But Gracie had a kind, sweet personality. How many girls who married into a family would keep in touch with someone who had moved away when Lee himself didn't seem interested? How many young women—Gracie was twenty-eight, four years older than Tess—would care so deeply about her? Why, at times Gracie seemed more of a sister to her than Char or Kate. She'd seen more of Gracie over the past five years, before Lee turned into such a religious man and they stopped visiting her and Mom in Michigan. The last time she'd seen them was at her mother's funeral just last year.

"I can't wait to see how big Kelsey and Ethan are now," Tess told her. "I love kids that age, same as the ones I work with. And just the ages I want to care for when I can sell this place and buy my child care center back home."

"Back home," Gracie said, giving Tess a quick goodbye hug. "Isn't back home really here? Well, I know about the bad things, but you have the strength to put it all behind you, and we wish you'd stay around longer."

"One week, maybe two max, but we'll make each day count. And when I get my place back in Jackson, you can come visit."

"Well," Gracie drawled, "don't know about that with our new commitments and all."

Tess frowned and looked out the kitchen window at the rain falling. The security light flooded the backyard with brightness. Her mother had put that in after Tess was taken, even before she found her way home.

As Gracie opened the back door she said, "I'll bring the kids to see you tomorrow, if it's allowed."

"Why wouldn't it be allowed?"

"Their school and work schedule. I'm not sure."

"Work? They're four and two years old."

"They learn to work during play!"

"Okay, okay. I'd love to meet with their teachers. We can exchange ideas."

Gracie hesitated between the inside wooden door and the glass storm door. Tess sensed she wanted to change the subject. "You still might want to rent out this place," Gracie said, her hand on the knob. "Real estate's not moving well around here."

"Two things I've decided for sure. One, I'm going to advertise and sell it myself so I don't have to pay a Realtor commission. And two, I don't want to rent it. I want it gone with the bad memories because I'm making only good ones now. And you've helped a lot. Thanks for cleaning the place. And for the cider, cheese and apple crisp in the fridge. See you tomorrow!"

They hugged again, and Gracie darted out into the rain. Tess watched the overhead light in her old black car pop on, then her headlights as they disappeared down the driveway. Slanting rain and gray gloom swallowed the two red taillights like a wild animal's eyes closing.

Tess glanced out the back window again at the place where the nightmare had started—and at this time of year. She had to fight the memories. The cornfield lay so close, so vast at the edge of the backyard, then curled around the house to join the field between the Lockwood and McCord houses. The day she'd been taken was a sunny one but with rain clouds threatening from the distant fringe of blue-green hills.

She'd run into the field, hiding from Gabe, who'd agreed to watch her and two other kids when her mom had to pick up Kate and Char at school and take them to the dentist. They were all just playing in the backyard. Gabe had watched them before for short periods. There was no problem....

Tess stood frozen, lost in thought. Unlike her sisters, she'd always had perfect teeth and she was so young, they had not taken her that day. After her father left the family, there was never any money for things like an orthodontist. Both of her older sisters ended up paying for their own teeth straightening as adults.

"Lots of folks around here have natural teeth, Claire!" she remembered her dad shouting at her mom. "We come from good Appalachian stock," he'd said more than once, "not those fancy folks starting to buy land over by Lake Azure who get their teeth fixed and face-lifts!"

Strange that the little Tess recalled of her father he was always shouting. She figured that bottled-up anger—his blaming Mom for not taking his "terrific, terrible Teresa" with her the day she was kidnapped—was the reason he'd left them. Several months after Tess came back home, he'd moved to Oregon, had remarried and hadn't seen his three Midwest daughters since. Char and Kate said he wasn't worth so much as a free weekend cell phone call or a Tweet, but Tess wasn't so sure.

Before she could keep a lid on the past from starting to spill out like worms from a can, she remembered another voice shouting. "You darn little, crazy tomboy, get out of that corn, or you'll get lost!" That's what Gabe McCord had bellowed at her that awful day. And then, even standing there, staring out at the field, her memories stopped, just like someone slamming the lid back on. **Thank God,** she thought. Because if her thoughts got loose, they turned to nightmares filled with monsters, turned to terror.…

Tess strode from the back door to the front one, checking the locks again, then tested all the windows to be sure they were bolted. Her mom had had the locks installed to protect Char and Kate after Tess was taken, though nothing bad ever happened to them. Tess nearly stumbled over her suitcase, then remembered her food sacks and the cooler she and Gracie had carried in. She'd better unpack for her short stay.

She jumped as headlights slashed across the dining room windows from the driveway. Was Gracie back already?

Her heart thudding to match the thunder outside, Tess peered out the dining room window. It was very dark for not being that late yet. A black car, not Gracie's, killed its lights. She certainly wasn't going to answer the door, but the man who got out had seen all the lights on, so she could hardly hide.

She gasped as she saw light catch the silver and gold printing on the car door as it opened. A man, broad-shouldered and tall with a brimmed black hat, got out. She heard the car door slam. She realized it must be the last man on earth she wanted to see.

2

The badge on the man's jacket glinted silver in the outside floodlight as he approached the back door and knocked. The sound rattled Tess. But she stepped forward to unlock it, then opened only the inside door so the glass storm door was still fastened between them.

"Sheriff Gabe McCord, Tess. Just wanted to welcome you back," he said in a loud, deep voice that carried well over the rain and through the glass barrier between them. His big-brimmed hat shadowed his face, and his jacket was slick with rain.

She knew she should ask him in. But she had the feeling that if she opened the door, she'd be opening up so much more. No, she had to be sensible, stay sane. This was the here and now, not two decades ago. She unlatched and opened the storm door.

"I appreciate that," she told him, relieved her voice sounded steady. "Do you want to step in?"

"Thanks. Just for a sec. Grace mentioned you'd be here today. Sorry to lose them as neighbors," he said, sweeping his hat off his head as he entered the kitchen, making it seem so much smaller. "I see you've got a sign up in the front yard already."

"Yes, I brought it with me. I put it up when Gracie and I were unloading my car."

She took two steps back. Gabriel McCord was so much taller and sturdier than the skinny kid she remembered. Unlike most people of Appalachian descent, Gabe was black-haired, although he was blue-eyed. She could see the young boy in his features but barely. He seemed all hard lines and tense angles— the slash of his dark eyebrows; the sharp slant of his shadowed, clean-shaven cheekbones, his square chin with a scar, his broad nose, even his solidly built body. His hands, which held his hat, were big with blunt fingers. He had a deep, commanding voice that, even when he spoke quietly, reverberated through her.

She tried not to stare, to say something light and polite. As he quickly assessed her, she felt frozen, yet she turned hot under his steady, probing gaze. He probably saw her as exhibit number one, the girl who came back alive and yet could remember nothing of her ordeal.

"I heard you'd be fixing to sell this place," he said.

"Yes, I really need to. I need the money to open a day care center for preschoolers back in Michigan. That's home now."

"A day care center sounds great. That's something folks around here could use, both those whose kids need a head start, besides what the government provides, and the Lake Azure folks."

"They're not all retirees in that community?"

"There are some well-to-do younger people who want to escape city stress, get back to nature, raise their kids away from crime and all that, though we have our share. Well, besides what happened to you, I mean. Meth labs, marijuana plots up in the hills, domestic disputes, drunks busting things up or shooting off guns. Especially this time of year, we get outsiders trespassing on the grounds of the old mental health asylum, vandalizing and worse. But I didn't mean to unload on you. I just wanted to say if you need anything while you're here, I'm just across the cornfield, at least at night. Don't hesitate to call the station or my phone next door. Grace said she'd leave the numbers for you on the fridge."

"Yes. Yes, she did," Tess said, glancing at the piece of paper under the magnet that advertised **Gabe McCoy for Sheriff.** "Thank you," she added. "So, how is your mother? Gracie said your father died."

"Yeah, at age seventy-two. A heart attack, though they had some good years living in Florida after they left here. She's still there. Sorry to hear your mother passed away so young."

"She had a hard life, working to take care of her three girls—me especially, after everything. That's why she left this house to me. Kate and Char have more… high-powered careers than I do. Kate's a university professor in anthropology, and Char's a social worker. They both travel a lot, so I'm here on my own for this besides the fact that it's my house now." She hesitated. "Listen, Gabe," she continued, unclasping her hands, which she didn't realize she was gripping so hard. "I'm sure you know a lot of people here and I don't. Will you let me know if you can think of anyone who might want to buy an old house to fix up?"

"Sure. If you don't mind people knowing you're back, I can ask around, have them contact you. If you put up any signs around town, better give your phone number, but maybe not your name, not say you'll be here for a while."

She could tell he'd tried to word that carefully, but it scared her. Actually she'd planned her for-sale posters that way. But was he thinking that since her abductor had never been found and she was an eyewitness—maybe people didn't believe she couldn't recall a thing about her eight months away. Was she still in danger?

"Thanks," she repeated. "I'll remember that."

He said goodbye, put his hat back on and went out into the rain. As she locked both doors behind him, she recalled that her mother had said some people blamed Gabe for not watching her better that day. There were whispers that her being taken was his fault, that he'd disobeyed orders to keep an eye on them. Tess had never told anyone but the truth was she was the one who had disobeyed him that dreadful day.

"Get back here, you crazy tomboy!" he'd shouted at her when she stuck out her tongue and darted back into the cornfield where she was hiding from him. She'd always liked Gabe, liked to get attention from him.

And with that mere thought, images came flying back at her. **Someone was** in the next row of corn, pushing stalks away, bumping the heavy ears. It must be Gabe. A terrible face jumped at her—hit her. Had she smacked into a scarecrow? She turned to run, but a hard hand covered her mouth. Was the scarecrow alive?

The thing dragged her away from her friends' voices. She fought, went to her knees with the thing on top of her, pressing her down between two rows of stalks.

She tasted soil from the field, spit out straw. Something sharp stuck her in the side of her neck. It hurt more than a bee sting. Hard hands on her, pulling her up. She couldn't see. Something was shoved into her mouth, something pulled over her head. She wanted Mom. She wanted Dad! Dad loved her, his terrific, terrible Teresa. But there was no Mom, no Dad, no Gabe.

Reality struck her. No Gabe...of course there was no Gabe. He'd just left and she stood in the kitchen of her family's old house.

Shaking, heaving a huge sigh, she checked and relocked both doors and leaned against the kitchen counter until her heart stopped thudding. She shoved the waking nightmare away...had to get back to the here and now. She was going to put her things away but have a glass of wine before she washed up for bed. She'd take a shower in the morning when it was light. And pray she could go to sleep in this house at all.

The rain on the roof—and the fear of another nightmare—kept Tess awake most of the night. She felt revved up from seeing Gabe after all these years. She couldn't help wondering if he became sheriff just to follow in his father's footsteps or because of guilt that she was abducted when he was watching her.

Gracie told her that another child, Jill Stillwell, had been taken about ten years ago from a tent where she was sleeping next to her brother in her backyard, no less. **Could it be the same kidnapper who snatched me?** Tess thought about what had happened. Gracie said there was a cornfield behind the house where the escape must have been made. Not until the next morning, when the boy woke up and found his sister hadn't gone inside to sleep, was she discovered missing. Another innocent young boy like Gabe, left to feel guilty, maybe even more so, since Jill Stillwell had never been found.

Tess also tossed and turned and agonized over the fact that Gabe joined the army and went to war straight out of high school. She could sympathize with him wanting to get out of Cold Creek. But maybe he went to escape the war going on inside him.

A glass of wine before bed usually helped her to sleep, but her thoughts kept racing. She could tell Gabe had wanted to make her feel comfortable, yet she felt unsafe with him. She admitted to herself the reason was that he kind of got to her. He was really sexy and she hadn't been expecting that. With her thoughts on Gabe she finally fell into a deep, dreamless sleep.

• • •

Tess had just finished a late breakfast of cereal, banana, juice and coffee when another surprise visitor showed up, this time at her front door. She didn't recognize the overweight woman at first because she'd changed so much, but the bright blue lettering on the side of her white van tipped Tess off. Thompson Veterinary and Pet Cemetery, Crown Crest Lane. Keep Your Beloved Pet For Life.

About half a mile beyond the back cornfield was a big house, veterinary office and pet cemetery owned by long-time bachelor Dane Thompson. Grace had told Tess that Dane's widowed sister, Marva, who had lived in the area for years, had moved in with him not long ago. When Tess and her family left town, Marva Thompson Green had been trim and spry, very attractive. She'd been married to a small-field farmer. Tess remembered that Marva had cared for her and her sisters while her mother looked for a job after her father deserted them.

"Remember me, Teresa?" Marva called through the storm door when Tess opened the wooden one.

With a smile, she extended a coffee cake with pecans and brown-sugar glaze. It touched Tess to realize Cold Creek hospitality still ruled here. Yet she hesitated a moment before opening the storm door. Dane Thompson had been under suspicion off and on for her kidnapping. Obviously, nothing had come of the gossip about him.

"Hello, Mrs. Green," Tess said as she opened the storm door. "How kind of you. Can you step in?"

"Why, surely will, for a spell. You're looking pretty, though you could put a little weight on. All three of you Lockwood girls were pretty, you especially. Now that you're all grown up, you call me Marva. I heard you'd be back soon from your cousin Lee. He did some work for us— built a new fence around the cemetery since kids are always messing with things there, and Halloween's not far off. It's usually not us they bother but the old mental health asylum over on West Hill Road. Sitting derelict, you know, so the kids from far and wide break in there and scare each other, leave graffiti, you know what I mean, Teresa."

"I go by Tess now. But how is Dr. Thompson?" Tess inquired as she put the coffee cake on the only table Grace had left in the living room. She gestured Marva toward the two rocking chairs, but the white-haired, very tan-looking woman just shook her head and plunged on.

"Busy like never before with the Lake Azure area getting so built up. Dane's been able to afford real upgrades in the cemetery. Why, you should see it. Using digital technology, Dane can offer having QR codes implanted on the tombstones. You know, those little black-and-white grids that can speak to smart phones. Presto! A person can see that pet buried there romping, playing like when alive, and can link to family Facebook websites too. Oh, I'm sure you know more about all that modern stuff than I do."

"Actually my preschool students knew

more than I did about all that," Tess told her, forcing a smile. "It's amazing all the things technology can do."

"Well, it's a lot better than Dane's taxidermist friend just stuffing dead dogs, if you ask me," Marva said with a little sniff. She brushed at the sleeves of her denim jacket as if there was dog hair there. "But," she went on, "I have to get the van back to Dane. He makes house calls at Lake Azure now, you see. I run the tanning parlor—two shops beyond the English pub uptown. You'll love their fish-and-chips," Marva added as she headed for the door. "The town has probably changed from what you recall—if you do remember, I mean, because you left so young. And good luck selling your house and land, because my old place and the barn are still for sale. I don't know what I'd do if Dane didn't pay the taxes on it for me."

The state of property sales in the area depressed Tess, but she smiled and thanked Marva again for the coffee cake. It surprised her there was a tanning parlor in Cold Creek. She knew they were dangerous. And it was being run by Marva, the former farmer's wife. No way was this the Cold Creek Tess remembered. If the Lake Azure area folks had money to invest in having their dead pets stare at them from tombstones, maybe someone there would like to buy an old house, closer to town than Marva's, to fix up and flip or for an investment. Instead of avoiding the new area of town, Tess decided she'd better put some of the posters she'd had made over by Lake Azure too.

She waved as Marva drove off in the new-looking van. If only she could have kept her mother for life and not have to come back here to sell this place and face her fears alone.

Standing outside a run-down, old barn someone had made into a makeshift meth lab before clearing out, Gabe put through a call on his police radio to Jace Miller, his only deputy. There were a few places in the hills that even satellite communications didn't work, like odd no-man spots around here. The best sites were near the

Lake Azure phone towers the residents had insisted be put in. Even some smart phones were too dumb to trust in these hills, but his call went through.

He'd figured that at least two people had been sleeping here, by the piles of smashed leaves on the floor of the barn. He'd found a scrap of old blanket once at another site and had sent it to a lab for fiber and DNA testing, but they'd found nothing except dog hairs, and he'd got nothing out of it but a four-month wait and a big bill.

"Jace, the place was another in-the-weeds meth lab," he said into his mouthpiece mounted on his shoulder. "Looks like a mom-and-pop setup, but they've been cooking the stuff up here for sure. Same old story. They managed to keep ahead of us and cleared out, like they knew their time was up. Or someone warned them, but who? Over."

"Copy that. If it's that fly-by-night bunch we've been after, they're probably already using another deserted barn or old hunting cabin somewhere. You want me to call our cleanup contact to get rid of the toxic stuff? Over."

"For sure. Tell them it's the usual. Drain cleaner, rock salt spilled, jugs and bottles. At least there's no sign that anyone's been held here against their—her—will."

"Gabe, you can't be on the old kidnap cases day and night forever."

"The hell I can't. Something's going to turn up when we're looking at something else, I know it is. Speaking of which, I'm going back to the commune to insist on getting a look at those girls to see if anyone matches the photo Marian Bell gave me. Over."

"She'll have you lifting fingerprints off those girls in the Hear Ye sect next. She's obsessed when we both know her ex took that kid."

"We **theorize** he did. Any and every lead."

"And you'll probably drive by your place again today to see if vic number one's okay too, won't you? Teresa, the one you were almost an eyewitness to her being taken."

"She goes by Tess now, and you roll out the welcome mat for her if she drops by or calls in. Who knows what she'll be able to remember now that she's back here? Worse, who knows who she'll stir up from fear she will remember something?"

Tess took the stack of eight-by-eleven-inch posters she'd made at home from the office supply store and went uptown. She knew a few spots to post them in what she was now thinking of as "Old Town," but she'd like to venture into some of the newer places too. The Lake Azure people no doubt had more money.

Even before Gabe suggested it, she'd decided to keep her name out of this, though some folks would recognize the place being sold as the Lockwood house. The poster only gave information about the house and her cell phone number. She'd included the color reproduction of an old picture of the place she'd found in Mom's photo album. Tess liked the picture because it was taken in the early summer before the corn grew thick and tall. It looked more spacious—almost safe.

She stopped for gas and they let her put a poster on the wall behind the cash register. The guy in charge tried to flirt with her, but she stayed all business. Without asking, she posted one on the crowded bulletin board at the Kwik Shop. She remembered standing there with her mother—or was it with Kate or Char?— reading signs about used bikes and a mini trampoline for sale. How they'd wanted any kind of trampoline.

Relieved no one had recognized her as people went in and out pushing grocery carts, she walked a few doors down into the small, storefront library both Mom and Char had loved, though they all got books there. To her surprise, Etta Falls, one of the community pillars, was still behind the small checkout desk. Miss Etta came from **the** pioneer family in the area, once successful farmers who had money, compared to most around here. Miss Etta was obviously surprised to see her too, because she jumped right up, whipped off her reading glasses so they dangled by a cord and clapped her hands over her mouth for a second.

"Well, I'll be! Is it Teresa Lockwood? I heard your mother died and wondered if you girls might come back to sell the house."

"I'm sure you remember Kate and Charlene more than you do me, Miss Etta. They were older and more avid readers."

"Yes, my dear," she said, hurrying around the counter, "but you were the one we were all pulling for, praying for." Still as thin and energetic as ever, she put her strong hands on Tess's shoulders and, stiff-armed, seemed to examine her. "You look just fine, Teresa. You all live in Michigan, so I hear."

"After Mother's death, it's just me. Kate and Char have careers that call for travel." Then she blurted out a big lie: "I don't think about the past, only the future."

"So good to hear. But, you know, it's hard to forget some things…. Now, I'll bet I could pull a few books for you to give you strength, cheer you up. I tried to give your kin Grace and Lee Lockwood self-help books on brainwashing and the like, but they are convinced that man who leads their group has all the answers— and I'm not even sure anyone in the compound even knows the questions," she added with the hint of a smile as she released Tess's shoulders.

Tess had forgotten how low-pitched the woman's voice was, so perfect for a lifelong librarian. She remembered how Miss Etta always tried to help everyone by suggesting books that would fit their interests or problems. In a way, it was nice that, just like Old Town, the woman—she was probably at least sixty-five now— hadn't changed much. Yet this close up, Tess could see her brown hair was streaked with gray, and tiny wrinkles like spiderwebs perched at the corners of her eyes and mouth.

"Do you still take the bookmobile out?" Tess asked. "We all loved to see it coming when the weather was bad or we didn't have money for extra gas after Dad left."

"I take it out for several hours when things are slow here. It's still a one-woman show, because the Lake Azure party house has book clubs galore run by their social director, and so many of them prefer to order their books out of the air—you know, online for digital readers," she said with a sniff and a roll of her eyes.

"And your mother?"

Miss Etta's head jerked in surprise. "You remember my mother? But she's been a recluse for years, still is."

"I only remember **about** her, that you take good care of her and that you're from the Falls family that was the first to settle in this area."

"Yes, that's right. Most folks think this county is named for the waterfalls over by the quarry, but it was for my ancestors. My great-great-great-grandfather Elias Falls was the Daniel Boone of this area. As for my mother, she's doing as well as could be expected. You never met her, did you?"

"I don't think so. Unless I was really young then. Oh, I came in to ask if I could post a for-sale sign about my house. And I go by Tess now, not Teresa. My mother didn't like it, but when I hit high school, she let me change it just to shut me up."

"And, no doubt," Miss Etta said, "because she loved you dearly, especially once she got you back."

With a firm nod, Miss Etta took the poster and used four thumbtacks to align it perfectly with other announcements on the neatly kept bulletin board with signs recommending books of all kinds.

Sometimes Tess wished she was as book smart as her mother and sisters, especially Kate. Mostly, Tess liked to read out loud to little kids, not spend her time on adult books about crime and suspense, thrillers, not even family sagas or passionate love stories—trouble, trouble, trouble. Children's books were so comforting, unless they were by Maurice Sendak, with all those grotesque, fanged night monsters, but she refused to read those to her kids.

Suddenly there was a strange roaring in her ears. **She was being dragged through the corn, then carried away from her house but closer to the noise.**

Dizzy, crazy, couldn't think, trying to stay awake because the scarecrow was going to feed her to the other, bigger monster. She knew it was in the field, big and green with a voice like the waterfall. It would chop her to pieces and eat her up like corn, but she was too scared to cry....

"Welcome home," Miss Etta said as Tess fought to thrust away the waking nightmare. The librarian brushed her hands together after hanging the poster and hurried to her desk to pump hand sanitizer on her hands from a big plastic bottle. Tess walked toward the front door and managed to wave to Miss Etta, who called out after her, "Remember, my dear, I'd be happy to give you a temporary library card if you aren't staying long."

On the sidewalk, Tess stopped to steady herself and breathe in the crisp autumn air. She'd been afraid Cold Creek would magnify her day or night bad dreams. If only she could get the broken, terrifying memories out, maybe they'd all go away! Meanwhile, she knew she had to stay busy, had to stay on task.

She decided to hit the barbershop and Hair Port beauty salon to leave posters. Then she'd visit the new part of town, even try the firehouse and police station, maybe drive out to Lake Azure just to look around. She liked the idea of some things being changed or new here, not like the parts of town that looked the same way as the year, the month, the very day she was taken. Tomorrow—the anniversary of her kidnapping—would be a tough day.

3

"Of course we want to cooperate with the outside authorities, but please run that by me again before I say yay or nay about parading our young maidens before you, Sheriff McCord," Brice Monson insisted. He had agreed to meet with Gabe that morning in the deserted common room of the largest building in the Hear Ye compound. Monson raised one eyebrow as he examined the photo Gabe showed him.

Gabe had to admit that "Bright Star" Monson's looks alone could make someone think he was from another world. The man was pale with hair either bleached or prematurely white, and eyes the hue of water. His face was gaunt and his torso thin as though he lived on alien food in this area of homegrown goods. He always wore loose-fitting, draped outfits that reminded Gabe of something a swami would wear—or was that a guru? It was hard to tell the man's age. His long hair was pulled straight back in a ponytail, which accentuated the shape of his skull. He wore a strip of leather tied around his forehead as if a dark halo had slipped.

"You're aware, Mr. Monson, of the abductions of two—possibly three—young girls from the area. The most recent loss was of a six-year-old, and that photo of a child in your group greatly resembles her. I'm accusing no one of anything and I realize blonde girls that age can look somewhat alike, but the mother of the missing child is adamant that I look into this, which I'm sure you understand."

"But all our young maidens are with families," Monson said, handing the photo back. "I assure you, if someone in our flock had taken such a girl, we would be smitten with confusion and rebuke because we had forsaken the light. But yes, to comfort that mother's heart, we will allow you to step into the room where that child is, maiden Lorna Rogers. There are two other daughters, if you would like to meet with the parents or their other girls."

It suddenly seemed like such a wild-goose chase that Gabe almost backed off. But since he thought some sort of mind-control game was going on with the clever, charismatic Monson, he followed him into what looked like an old-fashioned schoolroom at the back of the building. About a dozen girls of the approximate age he'd requested were weaving baskets into which their adult mentors—**craft teachers?**—were placing bouquets of bloodred bittersweet boughs.

"For our market booth uptown on Saturday," Monson whispered. Darned if the guy's voice didn't make Gabe think of the serpent whispering to Eve in the garden. Did he command control of this place by talking in that low voice instead of yelling?

Once the teachers caught sight of them, they and their young charges stood and bowed slightly to Monson, because Gabe knew it sure wasn't to him. The girls were all dressed in similar navy blue or brown dresses and reminded him of reruns of **Little House on the Prairie.** All had long hair pulled straight back from their faces with black cords similar to the one around Monson's forehead.

"Please, return to your games," Monson intoned with a single sweep of his right arm. The girls, without a grin or giggle, settled back to their tasks.

Games? Gabe thought. Right away he spotted the girl Marian Bell had been so riled up about. She did resemble Amanda Bell, but, this close, he noticed differences right away. Lorna Rogers was shorter and had not one freckle, while the Bell girl's nose and cheeks were dusted with them. Still, driven by his need to turn over every rock, he approached the child and the others with her.

"Is that weaving hard to do, Lorna?" he asked.

Her eyes widened as she looked up. She stared at his uniform, especially his badge.

"No, sir," she replied quietly, still not looking him in the eyes. "It's lots of fun, and I want to make more baskets for the walnuts too."

Aside from her distinct freckles, Amanda Bell had green eyes and an obvious lisp. This girl had neither. Gabe nodded and stepped back, realizing Monson had sidled over to hear what was being said. Did everyone whisper around here?

"Thank you for your time and patience," he told Monson as he started out of the room. "Sorry to have bothered you and the maidens."

"I'll see you clear out," Monson said, and Gabe noted the double meaning of that.

At least he'd learned some things today. Lee and Grace Lockwood were crazier than he thought for coming here to live, letting their boy and girl be part of this. And though Lorna was not Amanda, he definitely didn't trust Brice Monson.

Tess drove around Lake Azure, where the Lockwoods used to picnic and play as kids, when they were a family. The wildness of it seemed tamed now with manicured lawns and earth-hued condos set back in landscaped plantings of trees and late-flowering foliage. None of the residences looked the same, some two-story, some ranch, some A-frame. Part of the lake was cordoned off for swimming and paddle-boats. Canoes were pulled up on two man-made sand beaches edging the green water. A large, two-story lodge stood at the center of it all. This was a Cold Creek community?

Feeling she didn't belong there, she drove back into town. She'd already wandered along the new part of Main Street, reading the handwritten menu on the Little Italy Restaurant sign, peeking in Miss Marple's Tearoom and the Lion's Head Pub. She'd gone inside the pub because she could see a bulletin board, where she put up one of her posters. That board was a twin to the dartboard that was just inside the door.

"Want a pint or a shandy, luv?" came a very British male voice from inside. "Fish-

and-chips be ready straightaway!"

That all sounded good, but she made an excuse and went back outside. No one recognized her at the fire department. The dispatcher was alone since it was all volunteer, but he said the only postings allowed were for duty shifts and schedules. She knew she'd be allowed to put a poster up at the sheriff's office, so she headed next door. Despite the fact that it wasn't in the same place and, no doubt, had different people from those who had staffed it years before, her feet began to drag.

She found herself both hoping and dreading that Gabe would be there. Her stomach did a weird little flip-flop at the thought of him.

Inside, a young, pretty brunette sat behind the front desk. "Can I help you?" she asked with a smile.

"I was just wondering if I could put up a poster for a house for sale if you have a public bulletin board. I told the sheriff I'd be putting some up around town."

"Oh," she said, rising. "I'm his day

dispatcher, Ann Simons. Are you Teresa Lockwood?"

"Yes. I go by Tess now."

"Oh, right. So I heard. Sure, I got the idea Sheriff McCord wouldn't mind. You passed the board we use in the entryway there if you can find a place for your sign," she said, pointing. "I don't keep it very up to date, and please ignore the Most Wanted posters on it. We're glad to have you back for a little while, Tess."

"Thanks. People have been very kind." She headed for the corkboard, then turned around. "Ann, if you hear of anyone who needs a solidly built house just outside town, then—"

The front door banged open, barely missing Tess. A woman flipped her long blond hair back over her shoulder with a metallic clatter of bracelets. She wore knee-high boots with fringed cuffs, tight black leather pants and an orange brocade jacket. Her face looked too old for the hair or the clothes—or was her rough complexion just the result of too much sun? Tess wondered if maybe she was a regular at Marva's tanning salon.

"Is he back yet?" the woman demanded of Ann.

"No, but I'm sure you'll be the first to hear if there is anything to know," Ann replied calmly.

The woman huffed out a sigh as her shoulders drooped. "I'll wait. That's all I do now, wait. And study the other cases and find similarities despite the differences the sheriff's been preaching to me."

She collapsed on the pine bench in the waiting area, hunched over and swung her suitcase-sized orange leather purse between her legs. Tess watched her out of the corner of her eye. The woman looked Tess's way and exploded again.

"You're Teresa Lockwood, aren't you?" she cried, jumping to her feet. "I mean, of course you've changed, but I've studied the old newspaper pictures and articles in the library so long and— You are, aren't you? I don't mean to startle you," she said as she hurried toward Tess, "but my daughter's disappeared too. If you could just help me, I'm desperate for word of her. Here, let me show you her picture—I mean, you were younger when you were taken, but you are both blonde, and the sheriff—"

"Marian," Ann said, stepping between the two of them, "why don't you just sit down and wait for Sheriff McCord?"

"Because I said I'm desperate and I am! Surely this woman can help me find my girl if she can just recall what happened to her years ago."

"Come on now," Ann cajoled, tugging on Marian's arm. "Let's have some coffee and calm down. Deputy Miller or the sheriff will be back soon, and—"

"Calm down? I need to talk to her—to you, Ms. Lockwood," she cried, peering over Ann's shoulder.

Tess was shaking. Had her own mother been this berserk when she was lost? Her heart went out to this woman—Marian—even though she wanted to flee. She finally found her voice.

"I'm sorry," she told the woman, "but the sheriff, like his father before him, knows all I could tell. I came back, so I hope and pray your daughter will too, and then—"

"Amanda Bell. Her name is Amanda, and I'm Marian Bell. I live up in Lake Azure on Pinecrest if you recall anything at all— where you were kept, anything!"

"I don't," Tess whispered, more to herself than to the others. She didn't, did she? No, of course not. If she did, it would help find the other—now two?—missing girls. It could lead to Gabe's solving the case. It would end the horror that still haunted her like a monster just out of reach, trying to devour her. But, God help her, she could not recall a thing that would lead to anyone or any place.

Tess saw she still held the poster in her hand and quickly stuck it to the board between an announcement about a charity auction and a bank robbery in Chillicothe, the largest nearby city. She opened the door and went out into the brisk, sunny day, feeling assaulted, as though her soul had been shredded by that woman. Yet she forgave and understood her. Being recognized and interrogated like that—it was one of her worst fears about coming back.

Tess had started for her car when she heard a voice behind her.

"Hey, Tess, I thought that was your car. How's it going, putting up posters?"

She turned to face Gabe as he caught up with her.

"What's wrong?" he demanded, his piercing eyes scanning her face. He put a gentle hand on her arm. He wasn't wearing his hat, and the wind ruffled his mussed hair. "Were you in my office? Did Ann say something to upset you? I told her you might be in."

"Marian Bell recognized me. She's distraught, demanded I remember things I just can't."

"I'm sorry. She gets out of control, but I—"

"Understand why," she finished with him. "I guess I was thinking about how it must have been for my mother as well as me. One thing I'm sure of. I must have felt forsaken when I was abducted and gone so long, like I was abandoned. I never really thought how devastated my family must have been—only that they didn't come for me. I guess that was selfish."

"Don't think that way. You were a little girl. You were so young you might not even have formed memories into words at that point, and so you can't recall things in words now."

"Sounds like you've been reading up on it."

"Over the years. Especially lately. I'm sorry you ran into Marian or vice versa. I'm going to have to break her heart again, set her off on another tirade. I followed a lead she gave me today that didn't pan out. Her daughter, an only child she had late in life, was taken about four months ago and ever since, she's been seeing her behind every tree, so to speak. But I'll be sure she leaves you alone. I should have prepped her for you being back. If worse comes to worst, I'll get a restraining order on her. Let me walk you to your car. Were you leaving?"

"I am now. Thanks for everything, Gabe." She unlocked her car door, and he opened it for her. "Don't thank me for anything," he said, "unless I get the bastard who's been doing this." Despite his words, his voice was deep and quiet, even soothing. She felt as if she almost stood in his protective embrace since he had one hand on the car roof and one on the open door while she stood there. She sank quickly into the driver's seat, and he leaned down toward her.

Not looking at him but staring at her hands gripping the steering wheel, she spoke. "I want you to know I don't blame you for my being...being lost that day. You told me not to run into the cornfield, but I didn't listen, didn't obey, even though my mother told me you were in charge. I just needed to say it, because I'm not sure I ever told you or your dad."

"You remember that? I do too, but I still shouldn't have been so angry that I paid no attention to the little scream you gave. Even when I decided to just ignore your antics and you didn't speak again, I thought that was just the little tomboy next door carrying on, bugging me more.

Honestly, I don't think I've ever told anyone about our little argument either, including my dad."

"But— I did? I screamed? I don't recall a thing after you yelled at me and I ran through the corn rows."

"I'm not pressing you to remember more. Sorry, if Marian Bell's doing the yelling now. I'd better go in and break the bad news to her. Listen, call me if you need anything."

"And if I remember anything else?"

"Yeah, of course, but no pressure from me. Keep in touch, okay? And good luck with selling the house. I'll mention it to the mayor, since he sees lots of folks every day. He's been in office for years now. He knows everyone."

He extended his hand. She took it, and they shook. Despite the stiff, brisk breeze, his skin was warm, his touch strong. She needed that and gravitated to it when she didn't want to. She had steered clear of romantic complications in her life because she just didn't want to get close to anyone that way. And, of all people, for many reasons, Gabe McCord was way out of bounds.

He stood back and closed her car door. She started the engine and rolled down her window to say goodbye, even though they'd probably said all there was to say. She heard the crackle of his radio as words came over it.

He gasped and stepped back. "Gotta go. Marian Bell will have to wait," he said. She thought he'd head for his car, but he ran down the street toward the old part of town.

Tess sat stock-still, watching him in the rearview mirror. Tomorrow was the twentieth anniversary of the day she'd disappeared. And what she'd overheard made her want to cover her head, curl up and scream. "Jace here, Gabe. Four-year-old Sandy Kenton's gone missing from her mother's gift shop!"

4

Gabe felt as if a bomb blast had gone off close to his head. His ears were ringing, his head felt as though it would split, his lungs ached. In Iraq, he'd been thrown ten yards and suffered torn nerve connections from an explosion. Now his own blast of fury and panic propelled him down the street to the Creekside Gifts shop. He almost hurtled through the door. **Woo-ooo,** a haunted house automatic recording went off, followed by witchlike cackling.

He didn't see Jace, but the store manager, Lindell Kenton, Sandy's mother, was slumped over the checkout desk halfway back in the store. Gabe brushed aside fake cobwebs and two suspended mannequins dressed as witches. Lindell sat on a tall stool behind the counter. Her tear-streaked face tilted toward Gabe.

"It can't be," she said, and started to sob. Her face was red, her eyes swollen. "She was just playing in the back room, like always. She...she just disappeared when I answered the phone here. Win's on his way. This can't...can't be happening. Not now. Never!"

Gabe knew she was referring to the time of year. The two previous kidnappings had also occurred in October, though ten years apart. Tomorrow was the date Tess had been taken. He'd been planning to keep an eye on her and things in town. He'd always treated October 13 as a day to be careful—in short, be wary of copycats, protect people and places. But now this.

Jace appeared from the back room, shoving his way through two dangling ghosts made of sheets. "I've been up and down the back alley," he called to Gabe. "Next, I'll check all the stores and buildings on this side of the street."

"Go start that. I want Lindell to walk me through everything."

But he followed Jace to the back door, relieved to see he'd used rubber bands to fasten small paper sacks over both door handles to preserve possible prints. "And, Jace," he called after him, "check the alley Dumpsters and the creek out back. It's shallow enough there to see into. But we'll have to drag it to the east where it gets deep."

"Her mother says she wouldn't leave the building."

"But she did—one way or the other."

As Gabe hurried back into the front room, Lindell started speaking. "It was just a normal day." Her voice was nasally and thick with crying. Gabe put his hand over hers, gripped on the counter. "Normal—I mean that we do this two days a week when she's not at my sister's house with her kids. She plays here, helps me," she said, and dissolved into sucking sobs.

"Okay, Lindell, you've got to help me. We'll find her. Don't jump to conclusions," he insisted, though he was jumping to them too, despite the fact that the other girls had been taken more or less from their backyards. "There's a lot of stuff in here for Halloween and probably more things in the back. Could she be hiding? Could she have hit her head and knocked herself out? Come on, take me to the last place you saw her and talk me through it. Don't leave anything out."

Still shaking her head at his questions, she got up from the stool. Her cell phone on the counter rang. She jumped to answer it. Gabe moved closer to hear.

"Just a customer," she whispered.

"Tell them there's an emergency, and you're closed. Hang up but keep the phone on and with you."

She did what he said. Her voice quavered on the word **emergency** as she talked to the customer. "Maybe we'll get a ransom call," she said when she hung up. "I pray to God it's someone who wants to give her back for money."

Looking dazed, Lindell led him into the back storage room. It was a maze of stacked boxes, costumes and masks laid out on a worktable. He knew a lot of local folks would buy their costumes and candy at the big Walmart on the highway, but this was a popular place too, even with the Lake Azure residents. They always had a huge costume party here for Halloween, so, no doubt, a lot of people could have been in here and seen Sandy, cute, blonde, friendly, probably trusting.

In another area he saw shelves with small Christmas trees, cloth Santas and carved manger scenes. **Halloween isn't even here yet,** Gabe thought as he concentrated on what she was saying and showing him.

He'd known Lindell and her husband, Winston, for as long as he could remember. Elementary school and beyond; they were three years ahead of him in school. The Kentons had been high school sweethearts, prom king and queen. Win worked for the state park system; Lindell ran this shop. They had two boys in middle school, then Sandy, their baby. Damn, if this was another of the abductions that had haunted this place for twenty years. The sign on the road into town that touted the scenic nature and friendly folks ought to also read Home of the Cold Creek Kidnapper.

• • •

Tess knew she couldn't go home right away. Her thoughts were racing. It was almost the day she was taken. But if it was another of the abductions, this time it was from a gift shop in town. Perhaps this terrible event wasn't related to her abduction at all.

She forced herself to stop at the Kwik Shop, where she bought a sack of freshly baked donuts for Gracie and Lee, a box of chocolate chip cookies for Kelsey and animal crackers for Ethan. She had gifts for them at the house, but she'd have to deliver them later, because she could not face her house in the clutches of the cornfield right now. She didn't take the time to buy anything she needed for herself, but paid, got back in her car and drove straight past her house to the Hear Ye Commune about two miles down Valley View. She had to see little Kelsey and Ethan, put her arms around them, know that they were safe. That way, wouldn't she feel safer too?

When she turned in at the compound, she saw a hand-carved wooden sign that read Hear Ye, While There Is Yet Time!

A dirt lane led to a small parking lot outside the main fence. She turned in with the words echoing in her head. **While there is yet time.** If the young girl in town had been taken, how much time was left to find her before she was driven out of the area, spirited away to be gone for months, maybe forever? Gabe and his deputy must be looking for her in town, but wouldn't the girl's abductor flee for the hills or some rural place to hide her?

Without stopping, Tess turned the car around and drove right back out onto the road. There was surely safety in numbers inside the compound, where Kelsey and Ethan would be warm, watched, loved. But somewhere out on some road, there could be a child, taken away, hidden, a little girl, shivering and too scared to cry.

Tess knew she had to drive these roads looking for something—anything! And she was going past Dane Thompson's house and pet cemetery first.

• • •

As the minutes passed, Gabe could almost hear a clock in his head, one with an alarm clanging. Sandy's father, Win Kenton, had arrived and was pacing and shouting. Lindell was still crying. She'd gone berserk in the storage room when they found the Barbie doll Sandy always kept with her. Gabe had to physically remove her in case there were clues in the clutter.

In the past half hour, Gabe had called in the BCI, the Bureau of Criminal Identification and Investigation, from near London, Ohio, up by Columbus. They'd been helpful on the other cases, though they'd never found the abducted girls. But they could provide forensic help, which a small, rural district could not afford. He'd notified the State Highway Patrol, even though he had no clue what sort of vehicle might be involved.

Jace had said there was no sign of the girl in the creek, at least nearby. They had the volunteer fire department dragging the eastern part where it got deep. Jace was still talking to store owners and shoppers to find out if anyone had seen something suspicious. That helped to spread the word, including that the sheriff was forming a civilian search team of the area in one hour's time. The meeting place was the parking lot by the sheriff's office and fire department. It had not escaped Gabe that this abduction had taken place in the building that used to be the sheriff's office. Surely that had not been a perverted challenge or insult. But what if the kidnapper had chosen this site on purpose?

He walked away from the Kentons and called Ann on his radio. Before he could say a word, she blurted, "Marian Bell wants to offer a huge reward for any information leading to the recovery of her daughter and or Sandy Kenton. She's still here, refuses to leave."

"Better there than here, but it's too early for a reward. Listen, call Peggy in too, wake her up. You two are going to have to help each other on the phones over the next twenty-four hours in case any info comes in. And a BCI unit is on their way. I'll talk to the FBI later, but I don't want them taking over, and there's never been a shred of proof anyone's been taken across state lines. Actually Tess Lockwood coming back alive only about seven miles from where she was taken weighs in against that."

"I'll call my brothers to help with the search as soon as I get to Peggy," Ann said.

Peggy Barfield was Gabe's night dispatcher, an older woman than Ann. Poor Peggy had probably only gotten about four hours of sleep. But this was— at least it could be—war. He hated ordering Ann around so brusquely, and was reminded he'd done a dumb thing with her. They'd been dating, when he knew better than to mix business with pleasure. Worse, he wasn't that serious about Ann, but she—and her three local, redneck brothers—had it in their heads that Gabe should be proposing about now.

"Okay, Gabe, got it," Ann said. "I'll start

making lots of coffee. I've got the urns here for the charity auction. You take care of yourself, for the possible victim, the community—and me."

"Talk to you later. Let people wait inside if they show up early for the volunteer search."

For the possible victim, the community—and me, she'd said. Now there was a motto for a reelection poster, but that was the least of his worries right now. How about adding **For the first victim too—Tess Lockwood?** When she heard about this would she be stoic or distraught? Would it trigger any memories? If only he could be there to comfort her when she eventually heard.

Damn. He spotted Mayor Owens hustling across the street toward the store, looking really steamed. Having him around was the last thing Gabe needed.

Tess slowed as she passed Dane Thompson's house and vet clinic. She could see the fenced-in pet cemetery beyond the back lawn with its separate drive. Of course, the size of the cemetery had grown a lot from what she recalled. Once, before she was abducted, Char and Kate had taken her the entire length through the cornfield to read the tombstones—the names and quotes about the buried pets. There had been a few photos too, embedded into the marble monuments, but nothing like the electronic resurrection of pets Marva had mentioned.

Though she was trembling already, Tess shuddered at the memory of pictures of dead pets—some even after death, made to look natural, as if they were asleep. Or were they ones that had been stuffed and mounted by Dane's taxidermist friend? Pushing thoughts of dead pets aside, Tess wondered if the kidnapper was getting so desperate that he took a child from a store in town? And if Marian Bell's daughter was kidnapped only four months ago—she didn't know any details of that abduction—the crimes were a lot closer together than hers and the second girl, Jill Stillwell's, had been.

And why pick on one little town, one

small, rural area? It had to be because the kidnapper knew it well, probably lived here. So, did he keep his victims nearby? Why didn't he go to Chillicothe or Columbus, where there were more victims available and no one would recognize him? Her mother had said once that Gabe's dad had tried to check for similar kidnappings, but no other statewide or nationwide crimes had the same circumstances. Now, this missing girl's situation didn't match the first two either.

Tess saw that the same huge cornfield that backed up to her house still ended behind the Thompson property. Like many of the large fields nearby, it was owned and farmed by a wealthy local man using huge, mechanical planters and reapers. That deep, dark cornfield abutting the Lockwood property was one reason Dane had been on the list of persons of interest when Tess was taken. That and the fact that people just plain considered him a bit weird. He'd never married, had stayed out of public life and, with his close friend, a taxidermist named John Hillman, had always been fascinated by dead animals. And for some reason she could not explain, Tess admitted she had an instinctive dislike and fear of this place.

She didn't see the white van parked anywhere around, but she did see Marva raking leaves at the side of the house. Tess turned around at the next intersection and drove back. She wouldn't go into the house, the clinic, of course, especially not the cemetery, but she could drive in and chat with Marva. Indirectly, she could learn if Dane was home or where he was. It would be something to help Gabe, because she could never help him in the way everyone thought and hoped she could—by remembering any details about what had happened to her.

Her heart hammered in her chest as she drove slowly up the paved driveway. She reached for the sack of donuts she had bought for Gracie and Lee and got out.

"Oh, Teresa—I mean Tess," Marva called, obviously surprised to see her. She stopped raking. "Is this a return visit already, or do you have a pet who needs help? Dane's not here right now—house calls at Lake Azure and someplace else."

So Dane was out in his van somewhere while a new girl was missing. Gripping the sack in front of her, Tess walked closer. Dried leaves rustled under her feet. Did she remember this place? The farmhouse, the garage and clinic building? No, but she did recall being pulled through the pet gravestones here, didn't she? Or was that the memory of when Dane yelled at her and her sisters and they fled? What a shock it would be if she'd spent the eight months of her captivity so close to home.

"You were just so kind to bring me that delicious coffee cake, and I saw these fresh-baked donuts in town, Marva. After all, we are neighbors of the same cornfield."

"Why, yes, we are. I didn't expect one thing back in kind, but I thank you." She peeked in the bag. "Dane loves this kind, and coming from you, he'll be extra pleased."

"Why is that?" Tess asked, annoyed her voice quavered.

"Didn't anyone tell you that some

busybodies blamed him at first when you disappeared? This will mean to him that you certainly don't believe that false drivel and slander. Why, he's dedicated himself to protecting life, not harming anyone. Won't you step inside?"

Tess shook her head and stepped back a bit. She considered telling Marva that another child was missing, just to see her reaction. She should probably agree to step into the house, even to wait to talk to Dane, but she was suddenly filled with the need to get out of here.

She'd have to tell Gabe what she'd done and learned. Marva was outside as if nothing had happened, but Dane was out somewhere—and with his van. Perhaps someone had spotted him uptown today. Maybe he'd have an alibi. Guilt and fear aside, Tess knew deep down she'd be best staying out of all this, for her own safety and sanity. So what was she doing here on the property of the man many suspected was the Cold Creek kidnapper?

"See you later, Marva!" Tess called as she got back in her car.

She turned down one country road and then another, just driving, thinking. Finally, she found herself stopping at the spot where a man in a pickup truck had seen her walking dazed along the road eight months after she'd disappeared. **Eight months!** And she couldn't really recall one thing about her time away.

No cars were coming from either direction. Tess stopped and, sitting in her car with tears in her eyes, thanked the Lord for letting her be found in this very place—well, somewhere along here, Mom had said. And she prayed Sandy Kenton and the two other missing girls would be found safe and sound and soon.

5

"Is it true? Another girl gone?" Mayor Reese Owens shouted at Gabe as he ducked under the yellow police tape across the front door of the gift shop and exploded into the room. That's the way Gabe always thought of the man's entrances—explosions. Reese would have made a great national politician with his dramatic actions and shoot-from-the-hip comments.

"Sandy Kenton is missing—true," Gabe told him, gesturing for Reese to keep his voice down. "But by the same kidnapper as the others, not sure yet because of the different M.O." He put his hands on Reese's shoulders and backed him up to keep him away from the Kentons, who were huddled together at the checkout desk. He didn't want Reese lecturing

Lindell that this was her fault. Reese loved to play the blame game.

"Yeah, well," Reese said, not taking the hint to keep his voice down, "besides being desperate to get his hands on another one, maybe he wants to make a point about Teresa Lockwood coming back—like a warning to her to shut up or get out of here."

"It's been well publicized Tess—she goes by Tess now—has amnesia about her time away."

"So? People get over amnesia. She'll just draw media interviews—especially when this gets out, which it has. I already got a call from my wife and a Columbus TV station. I want publicity for the town, but not this again."

Reese was out of breath, but he was also out of shape. At least eighty pounds too heavy, he was all swagger and stuffing. Years ago, Reese had married one of the richest women around, Lillian Montgomery, whose grandfather had once been governor of the state, and that gave him instant clout. He owned the hardware store and a lot of property in town, not to mention he was one of the first Lake Azure investors.

In his mid-fifties, Reese had thinning auburn hair and a rising forehead—and usually a rising temper. Dealing with the man was one of the challenges of Gabe's job, enough to sometimes make him wish he still headed up a bomb squad in Kirkuk.

"Listen, Reese, I've called in outside help, and we'll have a civilian search party fanning out in about half an hour." He sat the man down on a bale of hay under an array of big yarn spiders and cobwebs, then perched beside him. "If you can handle the media while I head up the search, that will be a big help."

"Nothing's going to help if this is that same SOB again. I mean, what are we, rural rubes, can't track someone who's struck more than once at the same time of year, then disappears until he wants another kid? I know you're young and partly riding on your pa's reputation, only in your first term, but—"

Gabe interrupted him before he heard

the rest. The last thing he needed from this man was to be blamed for any of this. That cut too close to his own guilt feelings for losing Teresa all those years ago.

"That reminds me," Gabe said. "I've got to call in Sam Jeffers and his hunting dog. I swear his hounds can follow any trail." He dug his phone out of his utility belt and started skimming through his phone book on it. "Years ago, when Teresa was taken, the dog Sam had then got us partway across the field before the trail turned cold. And Sandy left a doll behind we can use to have him get the scent."

"I'll bet you and Jace have obscured that by now."

"Mr. Mayor—how about you leave this to me and you handle the outsiders?" Gabe said, trying to keep his own temper in check. He hit the phone number for Jeffers. No answer, no voice mail option. The guy was always out hunting this time of year. He'd probably turned his ringtone off so as not to scare his prey; so maybe he couldn't help. Gabe's gut fear was that maybe nothing could.

● ● ●

Tess almost drove into the Hear Ye compound again on her way home but decided she was too upset to see her family right now, especially the little ones. To her surprise, her cousin Lee was sitting on the front steps of her house with a bicycle leaned against the porch pillar.

"Lee!" she called as she got out and hurried toward him. He hugged her but didn't look her in the eye. He seemed distracted and upset.

"Is everyone all right?" she asked. "Did you hear what happened in town?"

"That's partly why I came to see you were okay. Reverend Monson announced it at the end of the church service."

"A church service on a Tuesday?"

"Whenever it's needed."

"I guess it would be good to have everyone together for an announcement like that, to pray for the child, comfort each other and all."

"Listen, you're invited to come visit us."

"Oh, that's great. I can't wait to see the

kids. I almost stopped there today, you know, just to be with my family," she confessed as he pulled the bike away from the porch and held it between them. It was an old one with fat tires and scraped paint. **He rode that here a couple of miles on these hills?** She wondered why he didn't use their car, but she didn't want to seem to criticize.

"And if you do come, can you help me with some dowsing?" he asked, his voice beseeching but his face worried. "I think I have a find, but I want to be sure if we're going to drill for another well, and your power was always better than mine, even when you were so young. Both of us, a gift from our grandmother—and the Lord, of course."

"But I haven't pursued water witching," Tess insisted. Tears sprang to her eyes. How could anyone talk about things other than the missing girl right now? How could life go on when she must be in mortal danger?

"Don't ever call it water witching," Lee said, giving his bike a shake when he probably wished he could shake her. "Water dowsing or, better yet, water **divining.** Like I said, a divine gift and not to be taken lightly. Tess, both your father and mine had the gift."

"My father quit doing it before he left."

"Yeah, well, it still meant something to him. His dried willow wands—branches—are still in a corner of the basement inside. That's like an omen, a sign from God, so quit stalling."

"They're downstairs? He kept them? But if I don't feel comfortable helping, does that mean I'm not to see your family?" she challenged, finally realizing she felt hostile vibes. She always thought that Lee had wanted Gracie to steer clear of her as phone calls and visits had waned over the past few years. And as Lee had been more and more sucked into the religious group that Gracie had evidently, finally embraced too.

"Sure, you can visit anyway," he insisted, frowning. "I just would appreciate your help with the willow wand, that's all. I'll still hold it if you just want to watch. A new well would benefit everyone, you know,

Kelsey and Ethan too."

He knew her soft spot for kids. Even as she agreed to help him tomorrow afternoon, she thought again of the little Kenton girl she'd never met, but—if she'd been taken—Tess's heart and soul were right there with her.

When Tess heard on the radio that a citizen search team had fanned out from the gift shop until dark, she cursed herself that she'd fled the town so fast. She would have helped with that, even if people stared or whispered or—like Marian Bell— asked her what she remembered. Then again, the radio and television people, no doubt, newspaper reporters too, would be around by now. Only a few times over the years had a reporter or a true-crime author located her in Michigan and wanted an interview, which she and Mom had never agreed to, even though they could have used the money.

As dusk descended, Tess stayed inside her house using only a flashlight to get around even when strangers knocked on her door, rang the front bell or called her name.

Unfortunately, her posters in town worked against her when word got out that her phone number was on them. Hoping it would be Gabe on the phone, she answered her cell only to hear it was a reporter from **Live at Five News** from as far away as Cincinnati. She hung up without a word.

She ate a cold dinner and drank cider—nothing tasted good—and sat with the curtains closed, huddled on the floor in a corner of the living room with her knees pulled up to her chin, ignoring the knocks on her front and back doors, her name being shouted by reporters. Then finally—finally—a voice she wanted to hear came from outside.

"Tess, it's Gabe! You in there? I've got everyone off your property. They went back into town! You're not answering your phone. Tess?"

She ran to the back door but peered out before opening it.

She undid the bolt, the locks, and swung

the door wide, only to have to unlock the storm door too.

"Did you find her?" she asked as he came up the steps and entered. He closed and locked the door behind him. She leaned against the kitchen counter. She had almost done the unthinkable, throwing herself into his arms and holding on tight like a kid.

"Wish I could say yes. The search and dragging part of the creek turned up nothing. Same story. Girl vanishes into thin air."

"Like me and Jill Stillwell—Amanda Bell too."

"Yeah. In broad daylight, without a cornfield, with her mother in the next room and while you and I were talking on Main Street."

"You...you don't think it was some sort of challenge or message to you or me. That someone else was taken so close to when I was?" she asked.

"No, I didn't mean that. I've been comforting her family and getting the personnel we need here to find her fast.

And it must have been someone she knew because she didn't make a peep, even if she was—is—a friendly kid. Tess," he said, stepping closer and taking her hands in his big, warm ones, "I gotta level with you. The fact that you came back home after being away for almost eight months, even if it was years ago, gives me a bit of hope for Sandy Kenton—Jill Stillwell too. There's a thing called a golden window, a very short period of time—usually three hours, I'm afraid—when young children are kidnapped that they are likely to be kept alive, but you came back after a long time away."

"Which is why people don't want to believe me that I can't recall anything to help. I wish I could, really, Gabe!"

"I believe you. Maybe we should finally let it out that you had needle marks in your arms, that you were probably drugged, maybe with some sort of amnesiac drug."

Her nostrils flared, and she sniffed hard. She was shocked. Why had she not been told that? In a way, it helped. She snatched her hands from his grasp and moved out into the living room, where she had all the curtains drawn. With Gabe here she felt safe enough to snap on a light, and then she collapsed, weak-kneed, into one of the rocking chairs.

"I should have been told about the drugs!" she said when he followed her and sank wearily into the other rocker. Their feet almost touched, but neither of them moved their chairs except to tilt them closer together.

"The decision was made, with your mother's approval," he explained, "to keep the drug thing quiet."

"And he was never caught, was he?" she shouted when she hadn't meant to raise her voice. If you raised your voice, people got upset and you could be punished; she'd learned that from her father—or was it from someone else?

"No, he was never caught," he said, tipping even farther forward in his chair with his elbows on his knees. "It's the great regret of my father's life. He started having heart trouble about then. But the failure to find you and then Jill—and the kidnapper—now may be my fault as well as my father's."

"I said before I don't blame you."

He nodded. "I want you to know, I told Marian Bell to steer clear of you. If she so much as glares your way, let me know. And I admit it would help if you could recall anything, **anything** at all."

"About back then, nothing but being dragged off through the cornfield—and yes, maybe that something stuck me in the neck. Maybe drugged, right away." She rubbed her arms through her sweater as if she could feel other needle marks there. She did remember tiny train tracks on her arms, that's what she used to call them, but Mom never explained, even when she could have taken the truth.

In a sudden surge of need to help this man and the lost girl, Tess said, "I can tell you at least that Marva Thompson Green was home shortly after the abduction today, and Dane wasn't. He was out in his van making Lake Azure house calls, according to her."

Gabe sat up straight. His rocking chair

jerked.

"How do you know that? Did you phone or see her? Did you see him or his van in town?"

"No, I stopped to talk to Marva at their place before I drove the back roads. I told her I was just returning her earlier visit and gave her some donuts since she'd brought me some baked goods."

"Right when you came back Marva came to visit? To kind of feel out what you remembered?"

"Maybe. At least my mother did tell me where I was found wandering around the day I was recovered—and I've never really recovered," she said. She stood so fast her chair rocked and bumped the back of her legs. "But I went there today."

"Look," Gabe said, rising too and stopping her with a strong grip on her elbow, "I don't want you on deserted roads or around Dane's place or letting him or Marva in here. You do know he was the prime suspect for a long time, don't you?"

"Yes, at least someone saw fit to tell me that."

"Tess, about the fact that you were drugged. It's common police procedure to hold back some vital evidence, some piece of insider information that will be valuable when questioning a person of interest or preparing a trial after an indictment."

"Don't you—didn't my mother—realize it would have helped me to know? If I was drugged, maybe that's why I can't remember, can't help Marian Bell, the Stillwells and Sandy's mother!"

"I didn't—and don't—want you to use that as an excuse. There can still be things you can recall, anything at all."

"So you're saying your offer to help and protect me was just a cover so you could hang close and see what you could shake out of me? Even before this poor girl was taken today?"

"I didn't say that. No, that's not true."

"Well, see, Sheriff McCord, here's my problem, one at least. I don't know what's true and what isn't about my nightmares. I have them, sometimes at night, but flashes of things when I'm awake too."

"What's in the nightmares and flashes?"

"Feeling lost. A horrible feeling of dread. Like I have to flee something, but I don't know what. Some kind of big machine, sometimes maybe a dinosaur, I think, and what sense does that make? Nothing I can clearly recall, and that's worse than if there was some bogeyman I could face and try to fight or conquer!"

To her amazement, though she wanted to strike out at him, hit him, instead she threw herself into his arms. Breathing hard, he held her close for a moment. Her belly pressed against his gun belt, her thighs against his. He felt strong and steady, but he must be using her. She pushed back so hard against his rock-solid chest that she almost fell.

"Tess, honestly," he said, grabbing for her arm again, though she shook him off. "Besides getting rid of the media mavens outside, I just stopped by to tell you that, even though I'm going to be working this new case day and night, you are not forgotten. Anyone bothers you, you let me know. Or if you recall anything in a bad dream or broad daylight. If you can't get right through to me, call Ann or Peggy on the desk. If you call 911, you'll get them too, and they'll get me. Got that? Promise?"

Tess nodded jerkily, kept nodding. She blinked back burning, unshed tears. The weight of having experienced things that could save others, things just out of reach, pressed hard on her heart. For one moment, she thought she heard a roaring noise, felt something awful flapping in her face, but then it was gone.

After a quick squeeze of her shoulder, Gabe hurried toward the back door.

"Lock up behind me!" he called back to her.

Without another word, she followed and did as he said. But could she really lock him out of her life anymore? The man meant a lot to her, much more than the boy ever had. She wanted to help him, but he stirred strange feelings in her that she feared almost as much as her buried memories. Need. Even desire. Instead of locking him out in any way, she longed to let him inside her defenses.

6

The first thing Tess thought when she woke from a fitful sleep was that it was the twentieth anniversary of the day she was taken. Most anniversaries were happy, but this one—now that another girl was missing—felt doubly cursed.

As soon as it was daylight and she'd eaten breakfast, she turned on the basement light, took a flashlight too and went downstairs. The basement stairs creaked as she went down. It smelled a bit dank down here. She thought she should buy an air freshener in case anyone came to look at the house. Should she accompany potential buyers down here, or could that be dangerous? Since her kidnapper might still be in the area, he could try to test her to learn if seeing his face again would trigger a memory. Or would he think she should be silenced?

She knew she had to be wary today, stay strong. But even if horrible memories came flooding back, it would be worth it if she recalled something to help the poor child who'd gone missing and the girls who had been taken before.

Lee hadn't exactly said where he'd seen her father's dowsing wands. She could picture his collection of green, slender willow tree boughs. She wondered why Lee had kept them, if they were dry. Since Dad had been so skilled at dowsing, maybe Lee thought they had some special power, or that it would be bad luck to trash them. And why hadn't Mom done that, especially after Dad deserted her?

Over the years Mom, Kate and Char had tried to explain to Tess that Dad's leaving wasn't her fault, though Dad had blamed Mom for letting a boy keep an eye on her, even if he was the sheriff's son. She remembered their terrible arguments. But Kate and Char assured her that Dad was just looking for an excuse to leave, and it was cruel and wrong of him to blame their mother for something no one could predict or prevent. **Could Gabe have prevented it?**

Tess found a pile of six willow wands behind the furnace. She shone the flashlight on them. Of course, they were not supple and green anymore but dried and dusty. Lee's father and hers, twin brothers, had possessed the gift to locate underground water by walking with a Y-shaped willow branch held out in front of them until it quivered in their hands. And most of the time, freshwater lay beneath.

She recalled her mother telling her about a sunny day, the Fourth of July the year she was taken, when her family was picnicking at a friend's house. At age four, she had picked up the willow wand Dad had brought to show people. She had imitated him, walked with it toward their friend's barn and felt the pull, a magnetism, making it quiver and tremble in her hands. Other times in the weeks of that late summer, Dad had tested whether her finds with the wand matched his, and they always had.

So, was that very willow wand among these? She touched them, stroked the top one. Some people thought dowsing was mere superstition or fakery, just chance finds or playing the odds. But others, especially older folks, believed it could find not only water but buried treasure, even lodes of precious ores. Some said it could point to graves, especially if the corpse had been buried with metal jewelry. If only, like a dowsing wand, she could find the thing that would point toward her buried memories!

She heard the ringtone of her cell phone, which she'd left in the kitchen. Taking the top willow wand with her, she dashed upstairs and grabbed the phone from the table.

"Hello?"

"Tess, it's Kate. I can't talk long. I've been making great progress on researching the Celts. I'm hopeful I can link their culture to the ancient Adenas of the American Midwest. Next time I'm home, I'm going to take a closer look at the burial mounds in our area because that could be another link to prove the Celts came to the eastern U.S. But I wanted to call you to see how you are. You know, especially today. I've been thinking about you. Are you back in Cold Creek to sell the house? How are you doing?"

"I'm here, and it was okay at first. But another girl was taken yesterday, like my coming back was a curse!"

"What? Taken from her backyard? Taken into the corn?"

"Taken from the back room of a gift shop uptown while her mother worked in the next room. It's a shop on the site of the old police station."

"That's terrible. Listen now, you call Char and let her talk you through this. She's better at that than me. And don't you go blaming yourself, or fixin' to hang around there to help."

Tess bit her lip. **Don't you go blaming yourself...fixin' to...** Her big sister was calling from England. Kate Lockwood, high school valedictorian, full college scholarship recipient, Phi Beta Kappa,

magna cum laude, professor and pub-
lished author, could travel the world to
study and teach ancient anthropology,
but when she got upset, she still sounded
like a southern Ohioan from Cold Creek.
And she wouldn't like to be reminded of
that one bit.

"Tess, are you there? How'd you find
the old place after Lee and Grace cleared
out?"

"It's pretty empty, but the ghosts are
still here, if you know what I mean. I've got
posters up all over town to advertise
selling it. And I just found Dad's old willow
wands in the basement."

"Witching wands, you mean?" she said,
her voice turning sharp. "He should have
taken them when he cleared out of our
lives. You know, I looked up a lot about
water divining once, even wrote an
undergrad paper on it."

"So what did you find out?" Tess asked,
stroking the cracked wood of the old
wand. At least that would get Kate off the
subject of the house.

"You're interested in dowsing? Okay,

here's what I recall…"

Here's what I recall… The words echoed in Tess's head. Again, she wished desperately she could recall who had taken her and where twenty years ago.

"So, besides dowsing appearing in artwork from ancient China and Egypt," Kate was saying, obviously in her lecture mode, "some claim that when Moses and Aaron used a rod to locate water in the Bible, that was dowsing. Martin Luther called dowsing 'the work of the devil.' In more modern times, Albert Einstein believed in it, and during World War Two General George Patton—well, he believed in the paranormal anyway—had a willow tree flown to Morocco to find water to replace the wells the German army had blown up. And that reminds me, the Brits used dowsing in the Falklands, and in Vietnam the Americans used it to locate weapons and tunnels."

"Your memory always amazes me, Kate. I'll have to tell Lee about all that."

"If he's still so gung ho for that whacked-out religious cult, he probably couldn't care less. But one more thing. I read that from time to time, some have used dowsing to track criminals or find missing persons. But don't go telling the new Sheriff McCord about that, or he'll think you've gone off the deep end. What's he like all grown up?"

"Very dedicated. Really intense."

"Intense? Tess, what does he **look** like?"

"Tall, broad shoulders. Icy blue eyes but dark hair. Black uniform. Strong but gentle…"

"Okay, okay. Intense about solving these crimes, you mean?"

"Yes, that's what I mean," Tess said, realizing she was sounding a bit shrill, as if she had to defend Gabe.

"So, is the town as diverse economically and socially as Grace has been telling you?" Kate blessedly changed the subject.

Tess explained the great divide in town and how that had changed things. But she told her how seeing Etta Falls at the old library made her feel as if she was in a time warp.

"She was so encouraging to me about reading and learning," Kate said.

"Especially the months you were—were gone—she tried hard to distract us with books Char and I would love, books for Mom on how to cope with loss, things like that. I remember our first-grade class went on a field trip to her house, because it still had one of the first pioneer cabins way out in the woods on their land. She showed us an old pistol and a family graveyard out back, but the tombstones were so old you couldn't read a thing on them. And that mother of hers is like a historic relic herself."

They talked too long, but Kate could probably afford it. Despite the great divide between her and her sisters—in education and ambition—she loved hearing their voices. Whatever her differences with them, she wished so much they were here to help and to hug.

Gabe recognized the older of the two BCI agents the minute he got out of the plain black car that had pulled in next to the blue-and-white mobile crime lab truck in the police parking lot. Despite it being two decades later, Gabe saw it was Victor Reingold, the agent who had worked with his father on Teresa Lockwood's abduction, though he hadn't been back to help with the second abduction nor had Gabe brought him in on Amanda's case.

Gabe hurried over to meet the agents. Reingold's shock of unruly hair had gone white, but his brown, hooded eyes looked as sharp as ever. He walked with a slight limp, and almost always dressed in black, like Batman without a cape, Gabe used to think. The man in the lab truck was a lanky blond wearing rimless glasses and a dark blue jacket with **BCI** emblazoned on the back. He looked as uptight as Reingold looked at ease and in control. Gabe thought the younger guy might as well have Forensics Techie tattooed on his forehead.

"Glad the posse's here," Gabe told them, shaking first Reingold's hand and then the other man's. "Sheriff Gabe McCord," he told them, though he guessed that was pretty obvious.

"Mike Morgan," the younger man said. "I

usually do lab forensics, so I'm glad to be out in the field, especially on this one. I have three young daughters, so I'm all in."

"Remember me, Gabe?" Reingold said as Gabe led them toward the building.

"I sure do, Agent Reingold."

"You were pretty young on that first case and pretty upset about being so close to it. Tough on you and on your dad as sheriff. He was a very good man, Gabe. My sympathies on his death. Glad to be back on the job with you to get this longtime pervert, but sorry it happened again. I was on special assignment in Washington, D.C., on the second abduction, but I kept up on things. So let's do this. And call me Vic, okay?"

"Thanks, Vic. Mike, you too," he said as he opened the door to the station for them. He knew the BCI agents liked to assess local facilities and staff before possibly calling for more help. He introduced them to Ann and Peggy, then, pointing things out, gave them a brief tour of the station.

As he walked them back to his office, he gave them the rundown. "The crime scene's a cluttered storage room of a gift shop, where we bagged the doorknobs."

"Good work," Mike said. "We can even track palm prints now. Ohio was the test case for that. And our databases for fingerprints use the automated APHIS system and are FBI connected."

"Outside of that storage room," Gabe told them, "it's a long shot, but I've got a local guy coming in, a tracker with a good nose dog to sniff the child's doll and see what that gets us. But I figured you'd want to fine-tooth comb the crime scene first. We did an exterior search with local volunteers beyond the alley that runs behind the stores near the creek, and dragged the water where it's deep. We found nothing—just like the other two or three takes."

"Or three?" Vic demanded, scrutinizing the huge map taped on the wall of Gabe's office. It was a site map he'd inherited from his father and had been updating. "I thought I'd read up on everything—but **three** previous to this Sandy Kenton?" Vic asked, turning to stare at Gabe.

"I think the possible number three, Amanda Bell, was a child snatched by her father, who left the country. He's hard to find but we think he's in South America. I've worked on the case, and the family has hired a private detective. The mother will probably be after you as soon as she hears you're around."

"Hard to believe it's been twenty years since that first abduction—my case," Vic said, turning back to the map and thumping his index finger on the site of the Lockwood house. "But Teresa Lockwood's surviving was pure chance, so I intend, just like you, to solve this fast."

"Teresa goes by Tess now and she's back in town briefly to sell her family homestead, the crime scene."

"Recall the place well, and her, when we finally got her back," Vic said, turning to look at him with narrowed eyes again. "Traumatized, drugged, been beaten, a real pretty little girl. Were the others blonde and good-looking too?"

"Not a common factor. I've got dossiers and all kinds of stuff on each victim you can look over."

"Great. You bet I will."

Gabe saw the man still had an unusual habit he remembered. He chewed wooden toothpicks to a wet pulp, then spit them out. If only these abducted kids had had some sort of habit where they left a trail, other than maybe a scent.

"Yeah, the dog on the scent trail's worth a try," Vic said as though he'd read Gabe's mind. "We could call in a K-9 unit, but time's of the essence. We'll just have to make sure you're with the guy, step for step. But remember, he ain't nothing but a hound dog, and we've got two leads right under our own noses. Number one, the abduction scene. Let's see the gift shop storeroom, where Mike can start working, but then let's you and me, Gabe, go pay a call on our ace in the hole, Teresa Lockwood."

Gabe's head snapped around. "She still has retrograde amnesia on the whole thing. Still delicate. I've been trying to establish a good relationship with her, but so far—"

"Then let's see if we can take it farther

than so far," Vic said and spit a chewed-up toothpick into Gabe's wastebasket.

Gabe stared the man down. "I think she'll bolt if we press her."

"You been trying another approach besides a frontal assault?" Vic challenged, coming closer. "You want one more try with her, using your method?" he said, raising one eyebrow. "If so, okay, but make it quick, before I go busting in. Ticktock, and you know it."

"Tess came back from her abduction after almost eight months away, so I'm hoping the others have been kept alive— are still alive for all we know. Maybe someone just wants a little girl to raise."

"Odds are against that, but maybe. Still, if the kidnapper's local, where are the girls? And since you once told me you wished you'd have rescued Teresa when she was snatched, I don't know if you're still feeling guilty about her, handling her—so to speak—with kid gloves. Take a little time today to try again with her, okay? Just a suggestion, of course, 'cause we're here to work with you, and you know the situation best."

Gabe just nodded, though he got the undercurrent of what Vic had said. Maybe the man did read minds, did sense how protective he felt about Tess. "I'll take you to the site, let you do your thing," Gabe told them. "This is the twentieth anniversary of the day Tess was taken, and I wanted to see if she's all right anyway."

"**You** all right, Gabe?" Vic asked. "You got a lot at stake here for the community, your father's memory, yourself—for Tess too, right?"

"Yes, I'm fine, just obsessed with solving these cases."

"Good, 'cause once we get this prelim work done, I got some other info for you, but first go talk to vic number one, okay?"

Tess sat on the top of the old picnic table in the backyard and glared at the waving shocks of heavily laden corn. Trying to dispel the bogeyman of memories—or lack of them—was something she'd wanted to do for a while. Besides, the cornfield had always haunted her. Those dark green, deep and long, straight alleys between the blowing stalks... The way you could get lost in there, especially if you were small as she'd been back then. Any cornfield could be a maze to a child.

She nearly jumped off the table when a man's voice spoke nearby.

"Tess?"

"Gabe! I didn't hear you. Did you find her? Any news?"

"We've got help from the Bureau of Criminal Identification and Investigation here—a forensics expert and an agent. The bureau's a lot more sophisticated now than it was then. As a matter of fact," he said as he came closer, "Victor Reingold, the same man who worked your case, is here."

"Really? But he seemed old then!"

"Only to a young girl. Listen, I need to drive up to the falls to check on some graffiti there. It will only take an hour. I hear there's something written there that may relate to this case. I wondered if you'd like to go along—to the falls. You could leave a for-sale poster for your house at the lodge there. I've got missing-child ones in the car that I'll leave."

"Oh, sure," she said, scooting off the tabletop. "I always thought it was so pretty there. So, Agent Reingold's here. I do remember him and things that came after—well, a while after I came back home. I should thank him for his help back then, even though it turned out I just came back on my own. If, that is, he understands I can't recall things to help with this case, but wish I could."

"Sure. I already told him that."

"I'll get my purse. Just a sec."

She darted inside. The old, dried-out willow wand lay on the kitchen counter, almost as if it was a gift from Dad to her on this day. He'd often done that—left their birthday gifts somewhere and made them search for them, not just handed them over. But if she could recall things like that, why were other things so far out of reach? If only she could do what Kate had mentioned, which she figured was pretty impossible—use that old dowsing stick to find the missing girl.

7

After they walked out of the rustic Falls Park Lodge, where they left posters on the community bulletin board, Tess noticed the distant roar of the waterfall again. It was a constant, breathless hum, partly blocked by the colorful autumn trees, yet it seemed to her a looming, unseen presence. It was kind of like her memories, muted, hovering, steady. It made her remember the howl of the local train on the edge of town, farm machinery in the fields. Was there something special about those sounds she should recall?

"You okay?" Gabe asked as they approached the cruiser.

"As ever, yes and no," she told him with a little shrug. "It's so strange to have places evoke so many memories. We had family picnics here. Yet other things I'm desperate to recall just won't come."

He opened the passenger door for her to get in, closed it and walked around to the driver's side. He closed that too but just sat there a moment, staring out through the windshield. "In the service, I commanded a squad that disrupted bombs—mostly erratic, homemade IEDs, at first in Afghanistan, mostly in Iraq. One went off when I was too close. The sound and shock waves stunned me, threw me twenty feet, whacked me out for a while. Most of my memories came back, but not when I was being hauled away by medics, then treated. And then in the hospital when I learned some of my guys had died—men I'd assigned to go defuse another bomb that same day in the Kirkuk marketplace—I kind of wished all the memories of sending them to their deaths were gone. They haunt me—their faces, that I called the shots that day."

They both sat silent a moment. She was stunned by what he had just shared. So he understood her memory loss, some of it anyway. But since he'd gotten his memories back, he probably expected her to do the same.

"I'm sorry, Gabe. But you were doing your job. You couldn't know what would happen, but others telling you about it could fill in the blanks, even if that brought more pain. And here it's **not** knowing that haunts me, especially now that Sandy Kenton's missing and Jill Stillwell and Amanda Bell haven't been found yet."

He only nodded and started the cruiser, and they drove along the curving blacktopped road toward the falls, past picnic areas, a kiddie playground and open-sided shelters for cookouts. She heard him clear his throat. Was he going to confide more terrible war memories? And could she manage to comfort him when her own past tormented her?

"Since you feel that way, and we're desperate," he said, "could you be brave enough to reenact the day you were taken? I mean, with me there, right beside you instead of across the backyard, beside you when we go into the corn. I got the feeling you were staring down that cornfield today. We could walk through it together the way you must have been taken. You just never know what that might trigger, and like I said, I'm desperate for leads. Tess?"

He pulled over on the deserted road but kept the motor running. As he turned to her, their gazes held.

Talk about bombs going off, she thought. Though his plan was enough to shock her, something huge leaped between them that had nothing to do with anything they were talking about. Once she'd stuck a fork into a toaster to try to get a piece of bread out and took such a jolt that her hair stood on end. It was crazy, but she felt that way now, like nothing she'd ever known.

"So, what do you think?" he prompted.

"I'll try. I trust you, and I want to help. Not only to save Sandy and Jill—maybe Amanda—but my own sanity, as well. Talk about your being haunted by regret about your fellow soldiers. I regret the fate of any abducted child who did not come back like I did."

"Kind of like survivor's guilt—like me." He reached over and put his hand on her knee, then withdrew it as if she'd burned him. He put the car in gear and drove around the next turn. The thirty-foot waterfall appeared with its frame of surrounding gray rock and trees hanging on to tiered ledges for dear life.

"See how people ruin beautiful things?" he said, and pointed through the windshield.

The Falls falls, as locals jokingly called them, were still spectacular, but she saw what he meant. With orange spray paint someone had scrawled a message in very fat, outlined letters on the face of the stone next to the white-green water spewing over the cliff above. Tess sucked in a deep breath. GIVE BACK THOSE TOWNIE KIDS YOU PERV OR ELSE!!! Then off to the side, though in different paint and writing, was AZURE ROCKS!

"Well, Azure rocks is a good pun," Gabe said. "Azure, referring to the new consolidated high school, not far from here. As for the threat about the 'perv,' a good thought, but delivered the wrong way."

"And in a different, more arty script."

They got out of the car and walked around the deep pool that was the source of Cold Creek and headed toward the cliffside path. The noise was so much louder outside the car that they had to raise their voices.

"I'd like to believe," he went on, "that message was also done by some kid from the school, where the Lake Azure students don't get along very well with the locals. I want to walk closer, see if I can find any discarded paint cans or something else to nail anyone. It's going to take expensive, dangerous sandblasting to clear that off, so it will be a felony, not just a misdemeanor for defacing state property."

"I heard that Sandy Kenton's father is a park ranger, right? Maybe someone who knows him or his family did this to get even more attention paid to her being taken. And we can figure Marian Bell didn't do this, because it only mentions townie kids and she and Amanda lived in the

Lake Azure area."

Gabe's eyes widened at that as they started on the path around the pool toward the foot of the falls. "The mayor insists we can afford only one deputy, or I'd hire you," he told her. "I think Amanda's father, Win Kenton, comes through here a lot, so who knows what a desperate dad will do? And it didn't hit me about Marian, but I'm putting nothing beyond her. Besides that, what's been worrying me is whether it meant anything that this latest victim was taken from the building that used to be the police station—like a challenge to the police, namely me."

The spray was drifting here but it felt good, cooling her flushed face. Just being with Gabe made her feel warmer than the climb did. She skidded on the path, cried out, and he reached back for her.

He grabbed her arm hard, held her steady, then leaned back against the rock face and pulled her against him. With her body pressed to his side, her head fit perfectly under his chin. His grip was strong around her, and she clasped his upper arms. His leather jacket was wet. She leaned her hip against his and lifted her head to say something as he turned his head.

They kissed. Tentative, gentle, then strong and sure, mutual. She felt his slight beard stubble, his warm flesh against her chin and cheeks as they moved their heads. She held to him, opening her lips. Was the entire cliff face moving?

"Aha," he said when they finally broke the kiss. Lips still parted, both of them seemed to breathe in unison. In the noise of crashing water, she stared at his mouth to read his words. "I didn't mean to do that, but…"

"I know. Me neither."

It was like a dream. They still held to each other, not moving, not saying more, pressed back against the solid rock. Tess felt strangely content. She liked heights— at least you could see everything around you. She sighed but that too was swallowed by the crash of the falls.

Finally, Gabe spoke, putting his lips close to her ear. "We're almost where the person with the paint must have stood."

"I can't believe I slipped," she said, almost shouting. Suddenly she had to fill the space between them with words, however loud the noise. "Where we grew up—after we left Ohio, I mean—in Jackson, Michigan, the big attraction was not a natural waterfall but a man-made one called the Cascades. Big, tall stairs, tumbling water, lit by colored lights," she went on, gesturing grandly. "You could go all the way up on side stairs. My sisters and I often did. But you'd get the spray if the wind was wrong, and the steps would be slippery running up and down."

"Tess," he said, turning back to face her. "I'm not sorry it happened, though—the kiss."

She nodded, maybe a bit too wildly. As he smiled, his features lifted, his eyebrows raised. His teeth were white and even.

She smiled back. For the first time in years, she felt good and—even standing on a slippery, lofty cliff path with thoughts about kids being kidnapped—almost safe.

• • •

After finding and bagging two discarded cans of spray paint and some wet cigarette butts, they headed back to town. Gabe didn't want to drop Tess off and chided himself for acting as if this was some date when it was a kidnapping investigation. He'd kissed her. Kissed her! And wanted more. Was he nuts? Mad-dog Vic would have a fit.

"I'll drop you off at your place," he told her. "I'll check with things at the station and crime scene, and then I'll come back and we'll walk through what we can recall from twenty years ago to see if anything hits you."

"Don't say it that way. But I know what you mean. Who is that honking?" she asked and looked out the back window. "Oh! I know that van. It's Dane Thompson's."

"Right. I was going to talk to him later, and here he is."

"It's like he's making a traffic stop on you."

"Yeah. Sit tight."

Gabe pulled over and got out. Maybe there was some emergency, but Dane was always a problem. The guy obviously believed the best defense was a good offense, but he evidently also liked being offensive. Ever since Gabe's dad had Dane pegged as Tess's most likely kidnapper, the guy had been on his case as much as the other way around.

Now Dane was yelling and shaking a fist at Gabe as they met partway between their vehicles.

"I hear that same state government agent's back in town!" Dane shouted. His thin face was red clear to his hairline. Spittle flecked his lips. Didn't he realize his demeanor made people dislike him? The man got along best with animals, maybe because he acted like one himself.

"Word travels fast to those who have a vested interest in a case," Gabe said, fighting to keep calm, because, like Reese Owens, Dane always got him going.

"Of course I'm interested, and not only for some poor child. How about my own situation getting worse again? Police harassment. Local gossip. Slander that can hurt the business I've built. Years ago I should have gotten a restraining order on both Mr. Victor-BCI-agent and Sheriff McCord Senior! Now McCord Junior's going to use the pick-on-Dane plan where they left off, I'll bet!"

"If I had any proof—so far—that you were involved, you'd be in the holding cell in the police station."

"So, have you got a suspect or a witness?" Dane demanded, squinting into the sun toward Gabe's cruiser. "You pick on me again, and you'll be sorry. Wait—is that Teresa Lockwood? My sister said that she was back."

Dane started to walk closer. "Hold it right there," Gabe said.

"What?" Dane rounded on him. "Like I'd hurt her now like I did before? Sheriff, if she got away from my place—which was searched, thoroughly, more than once in the months she was gone—would she have been found wandering a couple miles from town? No, she'd have been found closer. I just want to say hi, like my sister did. Teresa—I guess it's Tess now—reciprocated with donuts, just the kind I like. Come on, she and I are cornfield neighbors again, Sheriff, and I don't want any hard feelings, or wrong ones, between any of the three of us."

As Gabe and Dane approached the cruiser, Gabe saw Tess had rolled the window halfway down on her side, maybe to hear what was being said.

"Hello, Dr. Thompson," she said. She rolled the window the rest of the way down and stuck her hand out to shake his.

Looking surprised, Dane shook her hand and leaned down to talk while Gabe hovered. Something useful could come of this. Maybe Tess's facing this guy would trigger something in her memory if Dane had anything to do with the initial crime years ago. He had to admire the firm front she was putting up when she'd seemed shaky to him at times.

"Teresa—I mean Tess—nice to have you back, even if it is to sell and move away for good," Dane said.

"If you hear any of your clients—I won't

say patients, because my place isn't ready to go to the dogs yet—would like an old house, let me know," she told him.

"Oh, yeah, sure," he said, evidently undecided whether to laugh at her little joke or not. "I'll keep that in mind. I see you're very well protected, but I just wanted you to know that you or the sheriff are welcome to visit our place anytime. Marva loves company. She never had children and lost her husband, so we're getting on as best we can."

"She's been very kind."

Gabe took it all in, amazed as Tess chatted about the fact that she didn't have a husband or children either, but loved to be around kids, care for them and teach them. And about how good animals could be for little kids who were shy or afraid. She had calmed Dane down by the time he walked to his van and drove away.

But when Gabe got back in the cruiser, he saw she was shaking. Her hands were gripped so hard in her lap that her fingers had gone white. And tears were coursing down her cheeks.

"You remember something bad about him?" Gabe asked. "You carried on like that so he wouldn't know?"

She shook her head hard and sniffed twice sharply. "It's just that I thought he might be the one, so I tried to jolt something loose in my brain. Maybe he or Marva loves kids and so they take them, I don't know. He gave me the creeps, but I can't recall one bad thing about him. Sorry, Gabe," she said, wiping her wet nose with the back of her hand, "but I don't think I'm going to be any help at all, when I want to so bad. But maybe the cornfield trip will work."

He reached over to squeeze her shoulder. Then she got a tissue out of her purse and blew her nose. Tess's handling of Dane impressed him. Here he'd thought she was timid and broken, but the way she'd just dealt with a potential suspect—what a gutsy girl! He'd joked about making her a deputy, but he needed her, now in more ways than one.

8

After he dropped Tess off, Gabe drove to the crime scene. He parked on the street because he'd put up police tape in the alley. He'd finally contacted Sam Jeffers, who was bringing his dog, Boo, to track Sandy's scent—he glanced at his watch—in around ten minutes.

Going in the front door, he had to wade through a crowd of about a dozen people, two with news cameras on their shoulders, others thrusting cell phone recorders at him. He'd assigned Jace to do follow-ups on various vans that used the alley, food delivery for the Kwik Shop, the garbage collection truck, even the security vehicle that picked up money from the bank. Not that he thought they'd taken the girl, but what had they seen? A particular vehicle? Someone who didn't belong?

As the small crowd started to pepper him with questions, he held up both hands. "We're working on finding evidence and a suspect to lead us to the kidnapped girl. That's my only statement right now. There will be a press conference tomorrow."

"Anything different this time, since you've made no progress on finding the others? Is Teresa Lockwood back to help with your investigation?" a woman with horn-rimmed glasses, crimson lipstick and a pen stuck behind her ear demanded as she thrust her cell phone in his face.

Deciding not to give them a sound bite to broadcast, he said, "I promise a press statement at the conference tomorrow morning. Excuse me please."

The questions didn't stop. Gabe scanned the faces. It was common cop wisdom that some criminals loved to hang around the scene, fed off it, got high on it, but he didn't see any locals. No, there was one woman, a good-looking redhead who held up a large poster that read Hug Your Kids More! She kept trying to move behind Gabe to get on camera. Her name was

Erika something. She was the social director at the Lake Azure Community Lodge, who did a lot of activities for children there and was a friend of Marian Bell. He recalled that Erika drove in from Chillicothe every day.

"I know you don't have any kids of your own, Sheriff," she called to him. "So do you really think you can feel what the parents of the kidnapped girls are going through? Thanks to no progress on this string of abductions, people are starting to think Cold Creek is not a good place to raise children. The mayor's concerned it will bring real estate prices down lower than they already are. Little Amanda Bell and now this child are both—"

"Both getting a lot of attention to locate them. Local law enforcement is working with the cooperation of the state Bureau of Criminal Identification and Investigation, so, as I said, if you'll excuse me, we'll get back to that."

"Any new suspects this time—" a man's voice pursued Gabe as he ducked under his police tape, went inside, closed and locked the shop door. Ducking the flying witches, he saw Vic was sitting at the sales counter going through receipts.

Without looking up, Vic called to Gabe, "I'm not above doing grunt work. Been going over the civilian tips coming into your office, including from some psychics, and those are usually off-the-wall, but got to weed them out. Right now I'm checking credit card names of recent shoppers who could have seen Sandy, going back a couple of weeks. Glad you got through running the gauntlet out there. Man, you'd think a rural place like this wouldn't attract so many media vultures, but we'll have the national big boys in here if we don't turn something up fast. Get anything from Tess Lockwood?"

Gabe felt he'd gotten a lot from her, some professional, but a lot personal. "In about an hour, we're going to reenact her abduction on-site, what led up to it, see if we can spring some memory loose. She's all in to help. Your old **friend** Dane Thompson flagged down the cruiser and challenged me to lay off before I even went near him. He also insisted on saying hi to Tess, but she handled him great, even though she admitted he shook her up bad."

Vic finally looked up from his pile of papers. "Shook up because she recalled something about him?"

"Because she didn't."

"I swear, I sometimes wonder if Dane and that taxidermist friend of his could be in cahoots—John Hillman. I used to picture them mounting dead girls and hiding their bodies in one of those animal graves."

Gabe shuddered. "You should see Dane's house and cemetery now. Lots of money poured in. State-of-the-art."

"Oh, I will see it."

Vic was shaking his head as he went back to skimming sales slips. "I remembered that taxidermist's name because he was my number two like for Tess's kidnapper. So give me an update on Dane Thompson, your dad's top pick for the suspect."

"He's done really well since the Lake Azure community opened. Lots of pampered pets instead of outside-doghouse and barn cats to tend to, I guess. He's built a new vet clinic, redone his house inside and out, bought a new van, takes Caribbean cruises in the winter."

"That right?" Vic said, looking up again.

"About two years ago he asked his younger sister, Marva, to move in with him when she was widowed. She keeps his house, I suppose, but works at the spa uptown, which he might have money in too. She probably thinks she's died and gone to heaven because she was married to a small-time farmer with an old house and a played-out piece of land, which hasn't sold yet, by the way."

"I'd completely forgotten about her. We also checked out her husband's old barn and their house. I remember now sneaking around there after dark. Don't know why that slipped my mind since we thought Dane might have stashed Teresa there. We nearly got caught—maybe that's why I blocked it out."

"So all of us have memory problems, right?" Gabe challenged.

"Yeah, well, just be careful walking through this crime scene if you're meeting that tracker and his dog out back. Mike's been taking prints all over the place. I'll be out in a bit to take a look at Jeffers. Kids like dogs, trust people with dogs, you know—a real ploy to lure them away, then, zap."

"You're thinking Sam Jeffers could be involved?"

"Gabe," he said, glaring up at him, "I know you're part of this community, and that's your strength as well as your weakness here. I think **anyone** could be involved. Trust no one, okay? You said you couldn't reach Jeffers even on his phone right after Sandy disappeared, that he was out hunting in the woods somewhere. And he's a loner, right? Hangs out who knows where?"

"I know where. You want to go, I'll take you."

Gabe and his father had known Sam for a long time. Vic must have looked into him years ago, because it sounded as though he knew the man had several camping spots and crude hunting cabins. Over the years, Gabe's dad, Gabe and friends of his had been out hunting with Sam and he had always seemed like a stand-up guy. Gabe wanted to argue with Vic, but instead he stalked into the back room. He recalled now how Vic really annoyed his father sometimes. Hell, he might as well drag Pastor Snell in for questioning or longtime Mayor Owens, the little old librarian—his deputy or himself!

In the storage area, Mike Morgan was kneeling on the floor taking photos. If not for the strobe flash, Gabe wouldn't have located him among the piles of boxes and the table, masks and costumes.

"Hey, Gabe," he said, peering over the top of a carton. "I followed up on your deputy's Dumpster-diving in the alley, but they'd all just been emptied before she went missing, so not much to see. I called the waste management company that runs the trucks and told them the situation. I also processed and printed the Barbie doll if you want to let the dog sniff that. Hey, you look steamed. Vic lay his latest hunch on you?"

"Yeah, but I think it's crazy. Anything helpful here yet?"

"Lots of prints, probably mostly hers. I think she'd made a little dollhouse or play spot back here. Oh, yeah, I heard the dog out back a minute ago."

"Good. Here's hoping I'm not clutching at straws and his hound will turn something up."

"Speaking of straws, there's a really beat-up scarecrow thrown on the floor back here. Unlike the other decorations and figures, it's old-looking and dusty as heck. Can you phone Sandy's mother, ask her if it should be here? Everything else looks...well, better, like it could be for decoration or for sale, but not this."

"She may have just wanted something authentic-looking. But will do as soon as I see Jeffers work his dog."

"Sandy's Barbie doll is on the box by the back door." As Gabe took it in its plastic bag and went out, he saw Mike had debagged the doorknobs. "Hey, Sam, thanks for coming with Boo," Gabe greeted the man, and they shook hands.

"Always willing to try again," Sam said, but Gabe decided not to dwell on the fact that this tactic had not panned out when Tess was taken.

Gabe's mom had always said Sam looked like how she imagined Johnny Appleseed. And she'd said he was ageless, as old as the hills. Maybe now Gabe would have to check him out, age, background, possible motives, though he thought Vic was really overstepping with that theory. Sam was lanky with a full, graying beard that made him look older than he was. He wore boots, patched jeans and a dirty green-and-white Ohio University baseball cap on backward. His sharp blue eyes assessed Gabe as did the hound's sad-looking eyes.

"So, how's the hunting?" Gabe asked.

"Lots of deer. Trapping season too. Hope Boo don't smell like skunk. Last few days, we got us otters, beavers, coons, even coyotes, but old Boo got him a skunk this morning. Sorry it took me a while to get your message."

Boo, who did smell slightly of skunk, sniffed the doll Gabe took from the bag and held out to him. The hound was eager to be off from the back door of the shop. Gabe's hopes rose. The dog was following what must be a clear path, tugging Sam along on the leash. Gabe quickly followed, scanning the ground in case something had been dropped. There'd be no footprints on this blacktop.

After heading down the alley about twenty feet, the dog stopped behind the hardware store. Nose to ground, Boo went in circles, snorting, sniffing, then sat down and barked twice.

"What's that mean?" Gabe asked.

"Her scent ends here," Sam said.

Damn, Gabe thought. Just like when his dad used a tracker dog of Sam's in the cornfield and it lost the trail. "Can you move him out a bit, see if he picks it up again?"

They worked at that for nearly an hour, up, down the alley, near the creek. Nothing. Gabe swore under his breath, but they had learned something. The girl had walked—unless she'd been dragged, but not carried—out the back door and then had evidently climbed or been lifted into a vehicle behind the hardware store. Gabe wished that, like in big cities, there had been roof or pole cameras, but no such luck here. As he scanned the familiar area again, he saw Vic had come out and was watching, leaning against the gift shop door, arms crossed over his chest. How long had he been there?

Gabe thanked Sam and let him and Boo go. Sam ducked under the police tape, which Gabe went over to yank down in frustration.

"The dog's actions tell us something," Vic said, coming up behind him.

"Yeah, Sandy either knew the attacker and walked out a ways with him, or was intrigued by something enough to go outside without telling her mother and may have gotten in a vehicle parked out back—with or without help. So now I'll get Jace to focus on interviewing in more depth the hardware store staff and their customers that day."

"Good. Hardware stores are a magnet for men. Ordinarily, any hardware store customers park out back here?"

"Sure, especially if they want to load something into a truck or car."

"So there we go. I'll look through their sales slips that day too, see if I hit any matches with gift shop customers. Mike says you're going to ask Lindell Kenton about that scarecrow. Ask her if she'll come in and help me with matching hardware store names with her customers that day. And you, for now, focus on Tess Lockwood."

Gabe nodded. He was focusing on Tess Lockwood and not all for official reasons. It annoyed him that he couldn't get her out of his head.

Gabe and Vic watched Sam put Boo in his old pickup truck and drive away from down the alley where it hadn't been roped off. Then Vic helped him drag yards of yellow police tape toward the empty Dumpster behind the gift shop.

"I'll look into Sam too, but I'd vouch for him," Gabe told Vic. "You're thinking of him as a possible perp, with Tess's abduction too, right?"

"I didn't even consider Jeffers last time. It's bigger than that."

"So tell me," Gabe prodded when Vic seemed to hesitate.

"Don't like to admit this, but your illustrious mayor irritated me so much years ago when I was here on the Lockwood case I was tempted to slap him with obstruction of justice. Demanding things, ordering me around. Even told me to get out of town because I was 'bad PR.' So I ran a check on him. Not back then, but just a couple of days ago when I knew I was coming back here and found out he was still in office. Thought I might turn up a drunk driving charge, whatever. He annoyed your dad, and I'll bet he does you too."

"Got to admit he does."

"I'll show you the printout. Years ago, when he lived in Chillicothe, in his late teens, he was arrested for lewd acts on a minor child—a five-year-old girl—but the charges were dismissed."

"What? Man, you are reaching—but..."

"Yeah, but. Thought you might want to go yourself or send Deputy Miller to Reese Owens's old neighborhood where it happened, see if someone recalls the circumstances, because except for this item I stumbled onto, other references to it seemed just gone. I only found a memo where a court clerk had jotted down notes, including a notation that Owens's arrest and court records were either lost or sealed. They're still missing, Gabe. Reese Owens may be mayor of a small town, but he's got some big political heft and money ties through his marriage. Look, right now I'll stay here with Mike till he gets done so you can get back to Teresa—Tess. What's locked inside that pretty head of hers is exactly what we need."

Tess sat on the picnic table again, waiting, until she heard a car pull in the driveway. To her surprise Gabe was not in his sheriff uniform but jeans and a red-and-black flannel shirt. That's right. He'd been wearing something like that when it happened. She remembered that much. She hopped off the table, suddenly afraid, but still wanting to do this.

"You okay?" he asked, and waited until she nodded. "When we go into the field, we don't have to go clear over toward Dane's."

"I didn't know you meant to go really far."

"Let's just do what you think is best—is right—once we get going. Okay, so I was over there where there used to be a swing set, just sitting on a swing, keeping an eye on you and three other kids. I think it rusted out before Lee and Grace's kids got to use it. Anyway, you kept running past me, giving me a good shove in the back so I swung when I was trying to sit still. The other kids were playing in the sandbox like I asked, but—"

"But I didn't and even heaved a handful of sand your way."

He nodded but a slight grin lifted the corner of his lips. "I'll bet, even then, you were just trying to get my attention."

"So then," she said, wanting to tease him back but wishing even more to get this over with, "I started darting through the corn. I remember hitting the stalks to rock them, bounce them out of my way."

"I yelled at you about being a tomboy, to get back out here."

"A crazy tomboy," she added.

"I yelled so loud that the other kids quit playing and turned around to look at me."

"I think I went deeper in then, thinking you might come after me."

"I should have," he said, moving closer. "How about you go into the field, but I'll go with you, right behind you?"

She nodded but hesitated. What had crushed the full-of-life girl in her? Whoever had done it made her angry. They had no right to ruin her life, hurt her family, torment Gabe. Had there been a "they" or just one person? And who? **Who?**

She shouldered her way into the corn, ripe and heavy with ears that bumped her shoulders and hips. It was still taller than her but not sky-high as it had seemed then. Gracie had said the same man,

Aaron Kurtz, who lived down the road, still owned and farmed it. He'd been appalled, Tess remembered hearing, that she'd been snatched from his land. He'd sent Christmas gifts to them the year Dad deserted them. **Oh, thank you, Lord,** she prayed. Detailed memories were coming quicker, surer.

The rows of green leaves, some turning tan and dry, went straight away from the house at first, then curved to fit the contour of the distant, slight hill before leveling out again, reaching toward Dane Thompson's property. She heard Gabe right behind, his size making rustling noises louder than hers.

So that day, had her abductor been waiting, standing still in the corn, and she ran toward him? Was he tracking her through the corn by where she moved the stalks? Should she have heard him as she heard Gabe now? Had someone driven past the house and heard or seen they were playing in the backyard and come into the field to take one of the girls—any one of them? Or had she been the target?

It had to be a random choice of victim, didn't it? A crime of opportunity, as they called it? Or worse, had someone taken her because of something she'd done or who she was?

"Wait," she said, turning back to Gabe. "I'm going to stoop down, like it would have looked to me then."

"Missing, four-year-old Teresa Lockwood, blond hair in a single, long braid, wearing denim jeans and a yellow sweatshirt," Gabe recited. "That was the wording on your missing-child posters. **Pink plastic Princess Leia watch on left wrist. Blue-eyed, weight thirty-six pounds, height three and one-half feet.**"

She shivered. This memory probe might be as important to him as it was to her. She crouched a bit, her back to Gabe, staring up through the corn at the vast sky....

She heard the monster sound from decades of dreams. A muted roar, this time, not so close—but real! She stood, turned and threw herself against Gabe, holding tight. His arms came hard around her.

"What?" he demanded. "Tell me!"

"That's the sound. The monster!" she told him, blinking back tears. "Hear that?"

"Tess, it's only Aaron Kurtz's big harvester—his reaper. He's in the field beyond my house. He won't come roaring through here now, so—"

"No, I mean I heard that sound in this field that day!"

He held her tight. "And it scared you, and you ran farther from the house? Maybe toward Dane Thompson's or the side road?"

"The reaper—in my dreams, I turned it into a dinosaur or some sort of monster. But the reaper cutting in this field that day was louder. I think he sat so high in the cab that I saw his head go past. Yes, I do recall that now."

"My father questioned him, but he said he saw nothing unusual. You don't mean that he took you?"

"No! I mean, I don't think so. I must have ducked down, or got pulled down when he went past. When I screamed—more than the one time you mentioned—no one could hear me. Then I was too scared to scream at all. But I dreamed a warped memory of that for years, a big monster cutting and chopping me apart and taking me away."

"Away to where? Which way?"

She pulled from his grasp and looked around. She turned in a circle, again, again, trying to figure it out, until she got dizzy and Gabe grabbed her elbows to hold her up. She slapped her hand to the side of her neck as if something had bitten her there.

"I...I just don't know. Gabe, I still just don't know!"

9

Tess had just closed the curtains over the window facing the cornfield when someone knocked on her front door. Dusk had fallen. Gabe couldn't be back already. Besides, he used the back door.

Peeking out the front porch window, she saw a pretty, red-haired woman she did not recognize. Alone. She didn't look like a reporter. Her blue-green sports car was parked far down the driveway. Maybe she was lost. Tess opened only the inside door and kept the storm door locked.

"May I help you?"

"If you're Tess Lockwood, yes. I'm here to inquire about buying your house. I'm Erika Petersen, the social director at the Lake Azure Community Lodge. I drive back and forth to Chillicothe every day and I'd like a closer place."

Tess's stomach cartwheeled. To sell this place and be able to buy her own back in Michigan was just what she'd hoped for.

"Yes, won't you come in?" She unlocked the outer door for the woman. Erika brought a waft of scented powder with her that made Tess want to sneeze. When Erika took off her suede jacket, her emerald-green cashmere sweater was stunning. Her knee-high boots were fringed, just as Marian Bell's had been. This woman must be in her late forties, but her cosmetics were so carefully and subtly applied she looked years younger. She wore a big rock of a diamond ring next to her wedding band.

"Have you seen our Lake Azure area? So lovely there," Erika said as her eyes scanned the room before she sat in the rocking chair Tess indicated.

"Just to drive through. It was barely begun when I left the area. I suppose you know why my family left?"

"Yes. As I'm a friend of Marian Bell's, I can totally empathize and sympathize with what you and your family went through."

Tess doubted that, but at least this woman seemed reasonable, not distraught like Marian. And she was interested in the house.

Erika went on, "I don't mind the daily commute to Chillicothe when the weather's nice, but now that it's autumn again I've finally talked my husband into letting me get a place nearby just for the weekdays, when I'm here—social director at the lodge, great job, demanding…"

This was the woman, Tess thought, biting back a smile, Miss Etta didn't like because she ran book clubs that competed with the Cold Creek Library. Clubs, as the longtime librarian put it, where people got their books "out of the air."

"I'm sure that career keeps you busy and on your toes," Tess said.

"Oh, it does. Even though I have an assistant, there are a lot of weekends I need to be here too. I'd fix this place up, of course, my country pied-à-terre…."

Tess noted that, for a woman who worked with people all the time, Erika didn't look her directly in the eye. Her gaze darted around the room, but she probably wanted a tour of the house or was already imagining how she'd decorate it. Erika also had a habit of dropping her voice at the end of a sentence as if there were more to say, but it was a secret.

"May I give you a tour?" Tess asked.

"Oh, yes—but let's schedule that for another time, and I'll bring a friend with me. I need to head home. Promised I'd meet my husband for dinner at seven. There is something I need to tell you up front, a couple of things. I have a financial backer of sorts and it's not my husband. If you sell this property to me—for a very healthy price, I promise, cash up front— you would need to meet in private and in confidence with my friend Marian Bell to help her find her daughter."

Tess's hopes crashed. She almost burst into tears. Marian Bell was behind this and had sent a go-between this time. The bait was Marian's money. And the "in confidence" part of the bargain was, no doubt, to go behind Gabe's back. Why couldn't people believe she was telling the truth about not recalling her childhood trauma?

"Please tell Ms. Bell," Tess said, "that I would love to sell but not with strings attached, especially ones tied in knots. I do not recall my abduction details, my captivity or my captor. As you put it, I sympathize and empathize, but I cannot help her as she wishes, even for a bribe I would love to take."

Erika's back stiffened. "A bribe? Hardly that! Marian is kind enough to help me buy this house, that's all."

"Then, until either of you buys it straight-out with no hidden agenda," Tess said, standing, "tell her I'm so sorry about Amanda, but that's all I can offer her."

Erika didn't even put her jacket back on, grabbing it from the back of her chair and walking out. Had Gabe gotten a restraining order against Marian for bothering Tess so she had to send her friend? God forgive her, but it had entered Tess's mind that a few lies to Marian could help Tess have her dream and get out of here for good, but think how much damage that would do. No, she had to stay here longer to help Gabe, maybe even help find Amanda, Jill and Sandy.

As Erika's car roared off down the road—how could that small thing make so much noise?—Tess saw a vehicle she did recognize. The old white square truck marked CC Library Bookmobile pulled into her drive.

Though she was wiping away tears of disappointment, Tess almost smiled. It looked as if Miss Etta Falls had been stalking her book club competition.

"Miss Etta," she called, going out to meet her. "Do you know who that was?"

"By her license plate, CLBQN," she said with a nod and a sniff.

"What's that stand for?"

"Club Queen. Oh, I've had more than one discussion with that woman when she came in to see if we had the latest books—without a library card of her own. Not always the latest, but the greatest books, I told her."

"She was considering buying the house, but I turned down her offer."

"Good for you. You see I haven't changed the bookmobile one bit, don't you? Does it bring back memories of reading with your mother and sisters? Your father, I think, was interested in other things," she said with another sniff.

"Yes, I have those memories, at least."

"Well, I came by with several books I thought you might like. Can't say 'enjoy,' but they might help you. Not to recall the past, but just to cope with the present."

She pulled a book bag from the back of the van, slammed its door and started for the house. Tess, touched but hesitant to take on any books, followed. No one ever crossed Miss Etta, in the library or out.

"Now, these are books you can skim-read until something strikes you as helpful or personal," Miss Etta was saying as Tess held the door open for her. "Oh, my, bare bones in here, so you will have time to read—no need to be fussing with other things. And a rocking chair is the perfect place, right by a window."

Tess sat, feeling she was the preschool child and Miss Etta the teacher. The woman hauled out three books and gave a little summary of each, and as she spoke, Tess became more interested. One was **Too Scared to Cry,** another **Psychic Trauma in Childhood,** both by a woman psychiatrist. The third was **Unchained Memories: True Stories of Traumatic Memories Lost and Found.**

"If any of these help you—bounce something loose in that sharp brain of yours—you let me know. I've read all of these, just out of interest. So, if you need advice, I could talk you through some things, maybe go with you to the sheriff. You are working with him, aren't you?"

"I'd like to but I really can't help much."

"Well, don't fret. That specialist he has here from the BCI will find the girls, if they are to be found. And steer clear of Dane Thompson," she added as she got to her feet and picked up the now empty book bag. "He reads true crime," she said in a whisper. "And that cemetery of his is an abomination. Oh, here in the bottom of the bag—your temporary library card. I know you don't intend to stay long, so just bring that back with the books. I am sure you'll be more amenable to thinking about your situation than your cousin Lee and his wife were about theirs," she added with a shake of her head.

Tess waved to her from the front porch as the spry woman climbed up into the van, honked and drove away. One of the taillights on the old vehicle was out. She wondered if Gabe would ever dare to pull Miss Etta over for that.

At least some things never changed around here—good things—Tess thought. Maybe she'd take a look at those books. And Miss Etta's mentioning Lee and Gracie made her remember she still hadn't taken their kids the gifts she'd brought. First thing in the morning she was heading for the Hear Ye Commune. Seeing her cousin's family would cheer her up, after getting her hopes dashed for the sale of the house. And she'd have to tell Gabe about that.

Tess was surprised she had to wait in an anteroom at the Hear Ye compound to see if Gracie, Lee or the children were available. After about a quarter of an hour—she was getting bad vibes about this place—Gracie came in with Kelsey and Ethan. Four-year-old Kelsey, her blond braid bobbing, ran to give Tess a hug, but Ethan hung back until Gracie brought him over for hugs all around. It was only after chatting with the kids and reaching for the gift sack that Tess saw another woman had come in behind them and stood by the door. She was tall and big-boned. Her arms were crossed over her breasts.

"Oh, hello," Tess said, wondering if the woman could be a preschool teacher here. If so, she had a much too serious expression to encourage kids.

"Forgot to tell you," Gracie said. "This is Naomi, a friend. Since you mentioned you have personal presents for Kelsey and Ethan, she'll help distribute them."

"To whom? I brought gifts for them."

"To the others—their friends. I'm sure you teach your pupils to share, and we're real big on that here. You know, **Give unto others.**"

"I suppose the LEGOs could go far, but a doll—"

"A doll is wonderful," Naomi cut in, "to teach all the young sisters to care for others."

To Tess's further amazement and unease, even before she could lift the gifts from the sack, Gracie took it and handed it to Naomi.

"The children have to head back to school now," Gracie said, twisting the bottom of her denim jacket in her hands. Except for that, she wore the same style of dress as Naomi, though they were in different dark colors.

"Back to school? Preschool? But I just got here," Tess insisted. "Well, can I see their schoolroom, then?"

"Sorry," Gracie said, and rolled her eyes, either in an effort to subtly criticize Naomi and this place, or—was that some sort of warning? But about what? To agree to this? To back off?

Tess kneeled again to hug the children goodbye. It wasn't her imagination that Kelsey clung to her. The little girl no doubt recalled earlier gifts, the phone calls and recent visit for Mom's funeral. Maybe she'd even been told about or seen photos of the earlier visits to Michigan before Lee got completely swept up by all this.

"Don't worry about us—or think about us anymore. We're fine. Just fine," Gracie whispered, and, pulling Ethan along, followed the others out. Hurt and shocked, Tess stood there with tears in her eyes. They had left the door open as if she was to find her own way out.

As she strode from the room, down the hall she'd come in, she almost felt as if Kelsey and little Ethan—even Gracie—had been abducted. Her sadness mingled with sharp anger. Was that what the families of the victims of the Cold Creek kidnapper felt too? She could not recall her emotions when she was taken besides feeling so very lost.

Once she was outside, Tess saw she was being watched. The man at the gate who had let her in was still standing there, staring at her as she walked toward her car.

A scream pierced the air, carried on the chill wind. A woman's? A girl's? Where? Could that be Gracie, screaming for her to come back? Someone in pain or in trouble?

It came again, shrill, sudden. Tess turned back and started to run in the direction of the sound. She heard the man at the gate running after her. What if these strange people took in extra children by force? What if Gracie's rolling her eyes like that was some sort of signal? What if a woman or a child, maybe a young girl, kidnapped and new to this place, one who had not yet been brainwashed, was screaming for help?

"Wait! Hold it right there!" the man behind her shouted, but she kept going.

She heard no more screams, but she could see the building they must have come from. If she discovered an imprison-ed child, wouldn't that put her in danger too? Maybe she should get Gabe's help, come back. But what if they had hidden or hurt the child by then?

This religious compound had not even

been here when Tess was taken, though their leader, Brice Monson, had had a house here twenty years ago. She couldn't recall much about him, except people thought he was weird. Had they ever looked at him as a possibility for the kidnapper? He seemed to take people in by seducing them mentally, not taking them physically.

The guard snagged her arm and spun her around.

"Let me go! I heard someone scream!"

He released her but blocked her way toward the house. "I know who you are," he said, not yelling, but in a quiet, controlled tone she had not expected. "I'm Brother Silas. I can see why you'd react, but some children protest at first when disciplined."

"Disciplined? She sounded like...like she was being tortured."

"Look, this is none of your business. Chastisement is the only way to correct a wayward child, and it will **deliver his or her soul from hell.**"

Were they crazy here? Her own cousin Lee and her dear friend Gracie? As if she'd summoned him, Lee came running.

"Sorry, I was busy when you met with Grace and the kids," he told her. He was out of breath; his face was red. "And don't get all upset," he said, throwing an arm around her shoulders and propelling her away from Silas and back toward the gate. "That child has stolen things, and she was spanked by her own father."

Tess pulled away. "In front of others, to keep them in line?"

"Only in the presence of Bright Star, our leader and guide."

"Did she supposedly steal things that maybe once were given to her and taken away by everyone else?" Tess challenged, hands on her hips. Even if Silas and Lee had spoken softly, she was still shouting.

"Tess, listen to me. It's a good lesson, sharing. Caring for others. If we let kids run wild, they turn out wild."

Blinking back tears, Tess headed back toward her car. The gate guard had backed off. It was almost as if Lee was her guard now. And, curse it, she was going to tell Gabe about this and come back here.

After all, Lee wanted her help with dowsing. Of course, if she told Gabe everything— **anything** about today—he might not let her return. He and Vic Reingold might come in here with force, and the Hear Ye people might hide or punish her family— and maybe Sandy Kenton, if they had her.

"Okay," she said to Lee. "You're right about discipline for kids. Sorry I overreacted."

"Sure. I understand your protective instincts—being a preschool teacher and all. So, can you help me with the dowsing while you're here? The site is that knoll over there above the creek," he said, pointing. "We can use my willow wand."

That was her perfect excuse to stay right now or come back, and he'd set it up, she thought. "I have to leave, but I can come back later today," she said. "Besides, I want to try one of my father's old wands— and maybe yours too."

"Great. Appreciate it, Tess, and so will everyone."

Maybe not everyone, she thought as she waved and walked away, past Silas, through the gate to her car, hoping she hadn't seemed to agree too easily. Too bad that knoll was not in the compound itself, but maybe she could convince Lee to let her dowse the grounds inside too.

Tess knew Gabe would have a fit if she tried to check out this place without telling him first. Besides, she wanted to go uptown to see how they were coming with Sandy's case and whether she could learn the circumstances of Amanda Bell's abduction. She had to find the key to unlock her memories, even if those might make things worse than not remembering at all.

10

Tess ate a peanut butter and jelly sandwich for an early lunch, then did something she knew she shouldn't. While pacing from the kitchen to the living room as she had while she'd eaten, she poured herself a glass of wine and downed it fast. Then she realized Gabe would smell it on her breath, or if she drove erratically and he or his deputy picked her up—but no, they must be busy with the Kenton case.

She drove carefully, wondering whether to try the gift shop or the police station first. She should have called Gabe and let him come to her, but she didn't want him to think she'd remembered something big. Maybe the books Miss Etta had left would trigger something.

About ten media people more or less camped out near the gazebo on the town square with two satellite trucks parked nearby. It was enough to make her turn back, but she only ducked her head and hurried into the station—unnoticed, she hoped.

She saw Ann on the front desk again. Three strapping men in jeans and flannel shirts waited nearby, talking among themselves. Had Gabe found a suspect, or arranged some sort of lineup? Not for her to view, she hoped, but then they were all too young to have had anything to do with her abduction.

Ann got off the phone and spoke to the men. "You'll have to go without me, bros. Too much going on here. Hi, Tess. The sheriff's in the conference room if you need to see him again. How was the waterfall? It's one of Gabe's and my favorite places."

Tess could have fallen through the floor. Ann and Gabe—together—that way? She'd had no idea, but she could tell the three men did. Ann's brothers might be triplets since they looked like clones of each other. She overheard a few teasing remarks about Ann and Gabe, including something about "the sheriff of Hot Creek."

"I suppose," Tess said, suddenly having trouble forming her thoughts. "Did the sheriff tell you about the graffiti we went to see? If you would tell him I'm here, I'd appreciate it."

Ann nodded but narrowed her eyes. "These are my brothers, triple trouble. They work at the lumber mill just outside town, and they can't get it through their wooden heads I'm totally tied up with this case right now and have to miss our weekly pub lunch. Just ignore them."

Ann's brothers resembled Paul Bunyan-type lumberjacks. They hardly seemed the type for the English pub, but then appearances were often deceiving.

Tess nodded, but she could hardly ignore what she'd just learned. Gabe and Ann were seeing each other. Yet he'd kissed her, held her. Some sort of magnetic force pulled them together. But—had that just been her imagination? Or had Gabe been cleverly coercing information from her?

Frowning, Ann punched a button and spoke into the phone. "Tess Lockwood's here. Want me to send her back or have her wait? I figured. He's coming out to get you," Ann said even as Gabe appeared in the hall and gestured for her to come back. He met her partway and took her elbow.

"You okay?" he asked.

"I just wondered what you'd uncovered so far—if that might spark something in my molasses-thick thoughts. And Marian Bell's friend Erika Petersen stopped by with a cash offer for my house—if I meet with Marian to help her find her daughter."

"Clever move since I told Marian to steer clear of you. I didn't take out a restraining order but threatened to. But I still can't blame—"

"Me either. Blame her. I guess I'd move heaven and earth to get my girl back."

Tess thought again of Lee and Gracie in that religious group. They wanted to help their kids, but as far as she was concerned, they were actually endangering them.

"I kind of got the idea just now that Ann

considers you her very close friend," Tess blurted out.

"We've dated, but I'm not as close to any next steps as she—and her band of brothers—like to think."

"Oh," she said, sounding stupid to herself. This was not only the wrong time and place for that talk, but truly none of her business. Except for that kiss.

"Want to see Victor Reingold after all this time?" Gabe asked. "We were just going over things, so maybe you can help—and if not, fine. Anything else new?"

"I'll see him. Like I said before, though his hard work didn't locate me, I've always been grateful to him, and Mom was too. But nothing else is new."

She almost told Gabe about the screams at the Hear Ye compound. It was like lying to him not to, but she'd tell him later, if she was sure he and Agent Reingold wouldn't go in there like gangbusters. Or maybe they'd tell her something so that she could explain her suspicions to them. Maybe it would be better if she went back in there without law enforcement.

Gabe walked her down the hall, past his deputy's office and his own to the last room before the door that said Detention. It had a big lock and a grated window high on the door, so it must be the jail cell.

"Vic, you remember Tess Lockwood," Gabe said as they entered a big conference room.

"Sure do, but not looking like that," Vic said as he got up to come around the table.

It was what Tess could only call a war room. Kate had taken her to London for a week a few years ago, and they'd seen Winston Churchill's World War II war rooms deep underground. This was similar to what they'd seen there—wall maps with lines of yarn stuck in with pins on bulletin boards, piles of papers, strewn photos. But here, two laptops sat on the table.

Agent Reingold walked closer, limping. Had he always limped?

"Hey, my favorite survivor," he said, his voice gruff. The man had tears in his eyes. He held her at arm's length with his hands on her shoulders and studied her. "You look great, Ter—Tess."

"You too, Agent Reingold."

"Hey, no little white lies now," he said, making her feel guilty again as he pulled out a chair for her and Gabe sat beside her. Agent Reingold made his way back around the table. "We appreciate your trying with Gabe—to remember anything," he added hastily. "And you can call me Vic, since we go way back, okay?"

"Okay, sure. I don't mean to intrude, but I thought if I knew about Sandy Kenton's clues—disappearance—it might make me remember something, if, that is, it's not privileged information."

"What is privileged, we'll keep quiet," Gabe said, "but we've scheduled a news conference in about half an hour in the town square. You might want to keep a low profile until the media scatter—if that even gets rid of them. Then we could walk down the alley if you want to see the storage room the girl disappeared from, but it's a far cry from a cornfield."

A far cry, echoed in Tess's head. She heard again that girl's screams from that

Hear Ye building, even heard her own scream years ago before the monster came and darkness descended.

"That would be fine," she said.

"You can just wait here," Gabe said. "It does appear Sandy might have known her abductor, because she evidently walked a ways outside with him—or her—before getting in a vehicle. We figured that out from using a tracker and his dog. I'm not sure you ever knew this, Tess, but when you were taken, Sam Jeffers and one of his tracking dogs followed your scent through the cornfield. When the hound lost the trail, we tried to go by where the corn looked pushed aside or disturbed."

Disturbed. Why hadn't Gabe, her mother—someone—ever told her they'd tried to track her before? They'd tried to protect her when facing memories might have been better. She was desperate to face—and recall—them now.

"Also," Vic said, "when the dog lost your scent—probably because you were then being carried—we tried to lift the hound to see if he could catch your scent off cornstalks or hanging ears you might have brushed against. No go."

"A minute ago you referred to my abductor as him or her. Do you think it could have been a woman?"

"Standard procedure," Vic said. "We assume it's a man, but we don't know for sure. A young girl's taken, then people jump to conclusions. But you came back physically intact, Tess, and that's hardly ever the case if a man takes a young girl."

Not raped, he meant. Yet she'd been drugged and beaten. But how that happened or by whom was long gone.

Leaning closer to her, Gabe said, "You've got to realize if you sit in with us—which we both want you to—the talk gets tough at times."

"I understand. And you handled that very carefully—I was returned intact." **But I still feel like I'm in a million pieces sometimes,** she told herself. Then she recalled the reason she came.

"Gabe, about dealing with Marian Bell. Was there anything in her daughter's disappearance that could be a tie-in to me or the others who went missing?"

"Only that she was taken from her backyard, which Marian says is a big enough link," Gabe explained. Vic looked up from writing something down, long-hand, when a laptop was right beside him.

Gabe went on, "She was out there with her pet cat, which was left behind. Not a peep, not a sound. Did take her jacket though, which she'd earlier discarded. It was as if the abductor cared that she stayed warm and was not in a total rush to grab and go. No drag marks, tire marks, no trace, no witnesses, so basically that's the same."

"So why aren't you convinced Amanda could have been taken by the same person?"

"Her father took flights from Columbus to Miami to Rio the next day. No child was with him, but there was one who matched Amanda's description with a woman on an earlier flight to Rio. The child had a passport, of course, but not with Amanda's name. And then, even though her father had done business in Rio and had contacts

there, the trail—Amanda's father, Peter
Bell, the woman's and the child's—grows
completely cold."

"Poor Marian."

"First we worked with the police in Rio.
Now Marian's hired a private detective. I'd
bet my house Amanda's father is down
there under an assumed name with his
daughter and the woman he loves. He and
Marian were going through a bitter divorce
and they both wanted custody of their
only child."

A bitter divorce, like my parents, Tess
thought, though that similarity obviously
ended there. The order of her being taken
and Dad's leaving was the reverse of what
had happened to Marian and her daughter.
But, because Tess was a tomboy when
she was small and her older sisters were
more like Mom, Tess had always felt—
Kate and Char had too—Dad favored
Tess. But there was no way her own father
would have taken her, even if Amanda's
did.

"Jill Stillwell, the second girl who was
taken, and then Sandy—no problems

between the parents, right?" she asked.

"Not a factor," Gabe and Vic said, almost in unison.

"Good head on your shoulders though, Tess," Vic said. He looked back to what she assumed were his notes for the news conference.

Gabe, elbows on the cluttered table, said, "Let me go over with you what we do know and can share about Sandy's disappearance."

He talked about the child's play area in the back room of the store. He mentioned a well-timed phone call her mother took from a customer, which might have been part of a setup—a call they were trying to trace. The fact that the girl had never strayed on her own was noted. The chaos of the crime scene. The Barbie doll and the soiled, tattered scarecrow they couldn't account for.

Tess gasped. "A scarecrow?" Now, why, she thought, did that mere word make her stomach cramp? Had she seen one in the cornfield the day she was taken?

"Yeah," Gabe said as Vic looked up

again. "One Sandy's mother said had never been in the shop anywhere, though she had ordered some small ones that had not arrived."

"A scarecrow?" Tess repeated, frowning.

"So?" Gabe prompted.

"Nothing. It just seems weird. Maybe it's just the word **scare** I'm reacting to. Even though all this happened to me years ago, and I know I'm safe now, the whole thing still scares me."

"Let's get the scarecrow from the forensics lab in the truck and unbag it, get Mike to drive back here," Vic said. "He's only been on the road to headquarters about fifteen minutes. I agree the scarecrow's weird, but so is all of this."

"I'll have Ann call Mike," Gabe said. "He ought to make it back right after the news conference. Tess, you want to wait here for us? There's a smaller conference room, empty, that might be better next door."

"Yes, fine. You know, I was afraid I'd be spotted coming in."

"I'll have Ann tell Mike not to bring the

scarecrow in until you and I are back," Gabe told Vic as he escorted Tess out.

He walked Tess next door to a much smaller room with a regular door, a narrow table and two chairs facing each other. There was no evidence of the investigation in here.

"An interview room?" she asked.

"Multipurpose, but yes."

"With all those reporters out there, I feel like it's my safe room."

"I don't want you to feel that way—as if you're under attack, or we're grilling you." He put his arm around her waist as he pulled out a straight-backed chair for her and she sat down. One hand on the table, he bent closer to her. She could tell he'd had pizza or something Italian for lunch, but on his breath, it was enticing. She leaned slightly toward him.

"You really reacted to the mere mention of a scarecrow, Tess. Anything else that comes to mind then?"

"Fear. Something flapping in my face. Maybe being hit—smackings."

"Smackings? Is that a word your parents

used with you?"

"I don't think so. I can ask my sisters."

"If not, your using that term would not relate to anything in your own family, like a punishment or spanking paddle."

"Right. I really don't think my parents had anything like that."

"So that could be a memory of your time away that popped out. And once there's a trickle of memory, there could be a gush of it. Well, I read that in a book somewhere."

"Oh, Miss Etta gave me some books on childhood trauma I'm going to read."

"Let me know if something stands out."

She did think then of hearing that a Hear Ye girl was being spanked for stealing. Should she tell Gabe right now that she was determined to learn all she could about that girl, maybe to help her if she was imprisoned at the compound?

"Gabe, let's go!" Vic's voice came from down the hall.

Gabe squeezed her shoulder. When he moved away, his hand brushed through her hair, almost like a caress. But this was no time to imagine things, not about the past or the present. Especially since it seemed Gabe and Ann had something going on. And what did it matter to her? She wanted to sell her house and get out of here just as fast as she could, but if she could help herself or others in the short time she was here, then—

A voice interrupted her agonizing. Ann.

"Gabe said to bring you coffee and a donut," she said as she put the mug and a powdered sugar donut in front of her. "I'm going out to watch the news conference. My brothers are gone, but Peggy, our night dispatcher's, out front if you need anything."

"Thanks, Ann."

"Think nothing of it. But think about this," she said, her tone hardening. "Gabe's obsessed with this case—yours and the others, of course. But if you can't help him, you should clear out so having you around doesn't keep reminding him of his father's failures. You know what I mean. Maybe you should talk to Aaron Kurtz, who owns all those fields around your place. Maybe he'd want to buy your property, demolish the house and garage for more arable land. He's always trying to expand his holdings. You know, think outside the box to sell your house fast."

And get away from Gabe fast, was the rest of the message.

"Thanks for the suggestion," Tess said, gripping the hot mug between her hands.

"Yeah. Sure," Ann said. She almost ran from the room.

Think outside the box. Someone was still taking little girls, someone local, maybe right under their noses. So she was definitely going to take a closer look at the goings-on at Hear Ye. And maybe she should go talk to Aaron Kurtz, although, obviously, Gabe and Vic had crossed him off their list long ago. Both of those decisions scared her.

But what really churned up long-buried terror was the mere mention of a scarecrow.

11

Time crawled for Tess. One of those big, round schoolroom-type clocks glared down from the opposite wall of the tiny office. Not only did the minutes seem too slow, but the clock hands jerked with a strange sound not quite a ticktock.

Half an hour passed. Wasn't the press conference in the town square over yet?

She heard footsteps in the hall. Good! Gabe was back, but did he have the scarecrow? Surely it wasn't just that she'd seen a scarecrow the day she was abducted. No, it was something more than that.

She stood, facing the door, bracing her thighs against the edge of the table. When the door opened, it wasn't Gabe, but a man she knew even after all these years, though he was heavier than she recalled.

Mayor Reese Owens paused at the door, as if to see if she recognized him.

"Mayor Owens."

"Nothing amiss, Teresa. Or it's Tess now, I hear. The sheriff and Agent Reingold are still taking questions at the press conference. I made an opening statement. Ann told me you were in here, and I wanted to both welcome you back and suggest— Just a minute," he said, holding up a hand. He was out of breath and leaned over to prop his fists on the table. "Suggest you not stay long," he rushed on as he seemed to get his breath again. "Not stay long in town and the area, I mean. I know that sounds terrible here in friendly Cold Creek, but it's for your own good as well as the community's. You showed sound judgment in not attending the press conference. I hear your presence here has already stirred up reporters, and that doesn't do anyone any good. I'm thinking of you too."

"Then perhaps you've heard I don't intend to stay long. I only want to spend time with my cousin's family, sell my house and head back home. If I'm such a liability, you could buy my house and land—take up a community offering—to get me out of here quickly."

"Now, I know you've been through the mill, your family too. But as mayor, I'm charged with protecting the greater good. Sorry I came on so strong."

He edged around the table toward her. "I knew your father, you see. The day you disappeared he should have been sticking closer to home."

"He was working that day. Out of town."

He made a snorting sound. "I don't want you and Gabe to get so close you start thinking you're on this case too. Bad enough having Agent Reingold back in everyone's hair. Just keep clear of the investigation and Gabe. Those who don't pay attention to history are condemned to repeat it. This is police business and mine too."

"I see you make it your business to know everyone's business. And why, if you want this case—cases—solved, don't you want all the help you can get, Agent Reingold's, mine, anyone's?"

"Don't you go getting snippy with me," he said, shaking a finger at her. "Like I said, I'm thinking of you too. In other words, don't you and Gabe go repeating the sins of the parents, if you know what I mean."

"No, I don't know what you mean."

"Yeah, well, here's your daddy's phone number out Oregon way if you're so big on reunions," he said, digging in his jacket pocket. "And speaking of that, here's hoping that crazy Bright Star Monson doesn't suck you into his cult like he did your cousins."

Before she could tell him that he ought to find a way to get the Hear Ye community out of the area instead of her, he stopped shuffling toward her, cocked his head and backtracked.

"I hear the others coming and I want to know how they did," he said, and hurried from the room.

Tess slumped back in her chair. How had that man been elected, over and over, for at least two decades? He was obnoxious and kind of creepy.

She picked up the small piece of lined paper the mayor had tossed on the table. The phone number had her father's name, Jack Lockwood, scribbled in big, loopy writing.

Why did the mayor want her to call her father? Maybe her father wanted her to contact him because he was afraid to approach her after everything that had happened. Maybe he knew something that could help. But had the mayor suggested her father had done something wrong? **Sins of the parents?**

She heard muted voices down the hall and sat in her chair, waiting. Waiting for the scarecrow.

It was barely five minutes later when Gabe came into the room. He carried a large, clear plastic bag with him, but he kept it behind his hip. She gripped the edge of her chair seat and shifted back in it.

"Sorry if Mayor Owens bothered you. He says you were defiant and sassy—I like the sound of that."

Tess looked at him instead of what he held. She knew he was teasing—was he flirting?—but she was too upset to respond to that.

"He did bother me," she admitted. "I think he was implying my father knows more than has been said about the day I disappeared. He gave me his phone number."

"I have it and may use it. But if the man hasn't contacted any of you for years..."

"I just might let you call him, though I've thought of doing it myself many times. I'll talk to my sister Char. She's a social worker, good at those kinds of things... counseling and comforting. I meant to call her anyway."

"Tess, Mike brought the scarecrow back. Want to have a look?"

"Not really. But it's something important, I know it is. And I'm doing it for Sandy, Amanda, that second victim, Jill Stillwell too. It's not just for me."

"Okay," he said. He closed the door behind him. Maybe he didn't want the mayor or even Vic Reingold to hear her comments for some reason.

He came around the table and put the nearly two-foot-long bag down on it. Weren't field scarecrows a lot bigger than that?

He smoothed the plastic to show the scarecrow clearly. He watched her face. She bucked back so hard her chair nearly tipped over. "It's him! It's him!" she shouted.

Gabe put a firm hand on her shoulder. "It's who, Tess? Who?"

"Mr. Mean," she said, and burst into tears. "See his face? See how awful he is? It's not me that's bad, it's him!"

Gabe grabbed the thing, threw it facedown on the floor and kneeled beside her chair. He pulled her into his arms, and held her.

"It's all right," he said, rocking her as if she were a child. And that's what she felt like. A frightened child. The face on that thing—glaring eyes, frowning face, teeth showing. **But not huge teeth like on the green monster.**

"Tell me more about Mr. Mean," Gabe

said, his voice gentle. "He's the one who hit you?"

"Yes. Yes!"

"But who made him hit you?"

"I did. If I was bad."

"Tess, are you sure it wasn't your mother or father who had Mr. Mean?"

"No—ask Kate and Char."

"Okay, okay. But tell me about Mr. Mean." His voice was soothing, coaxing. "I won't let him hurt you ever again."

Suddenly, though she felt safe in his arms, she also felt silly. Exploding in tears like that. Almost using baby talk. Clinging to Gabe the way little Kelsey had clung to her at the Hear Ye compound earlier. She was acting like an idiot, when she had to keep control.

"Tess, are you seeing or hearing anything else? Did the scarecrow trigger any other memories?" Gabe asked.

She shook her head, then sniffed and sat up straight, wiping her wet cheeks with the palms of both hands. She wriggled out of his arms, and he helped her stand. Keeping her back to the thing on the floor, she moved a few steps away, fumbled in her purse for a tissue and blew her nose.

"Sorry I acted like a kid," she said.

"I'll bet you need to get back to that again to remember."

"Like I said—it's all I can recall."

"Smackings and Mr. Mean. It's a start. I know I'm asking you to go to a place you don't want to face, Tess."

"A place I **can't** face, not from fear, but because I just can't remember more. The helplessness, feeling abandoned by my family—I can't get more than that. But why was that thing left when the kidnapper took Sandy? Surely not to scare or warn me."

"I'd hate to think so. Maybe in hustling Sandy out the door, it was dropped, not deliberately," he said. "I swear, we'll go over this dirty, crude scarecrow with a fine-tooth comb."

"I can't believe I blurted that out—Mr. Mean," she said, wiping under her eyes. "I don't think it's the monster from my dreams. That one is bigger, louder—more like that corn reaper."

"How about you go with me to Aaron Kurtz's to take a close-up look at his harvester?"

"But he'd get suspicious. What if he did see something, if those presents he sent all of us that next Christmas were because of guilt? Besides, I was thinking of seeing him on my own. You might spook him."

"Tess, that's not a good idea."

"All I know right now," she said, "is that I need to head home. I'm glad you're going to take that scarecrow apart and maybe trace something."

"About Aaron," Gabe continued, "I usually have good instincts about people and I think he's a good guy. Vic and my dad looked at him, interviewed him years ago."

"Years ago..." she echoed as she headed for the door, giving the scarecrow a wide berth. "I'm going to get it all back, Gabe, whatever it costs."

After Tess left the room, Gabe picked up the scarecrow and looked at it closely. He knew it might take days for the BCI lab to check this out, and he needed something now. Tess's reaction when she saw the scarecrow had reminded him of soldiers with blast-induced trauma. In her cry, "It's him! It's him!" he'd heard shouts of "Incoming fire!"

The scarecrow had an orange, pointed cap. He might be crazy, but the stitching on it looked done by hand, not a machine. There was no tag on the cap. He squeezed the hemp-cloth head, tied with frayed cord at the neck. Nothing seemed to be secreted within except the stick it was on, spearing the body crotch to head. The hair was yellow yarn, the outfit black cotton, but even that color didn't keep the dirt from showing. The thing looked really old. And it was far smaller than the scarecrows he'd seen used to keep birds out of a garden or field.

It had no resemblance to the friendly-looking scarecrow from the **Wizard of Oz** movie that ran on TV every year. Yeah, Mr. Mean did look scary, as if he was made specifically for Halloween, perfect for this time of year. Some of the straw from the stuffed body stuck out where the wrists and ankles would be. It had no arms or legs, only smaller pieces of gray wood to simulate limbs that must be nailed to its wooden backbone. Swung hard, it could definitely hurt a child, be used as a paddle or weapon.

Looking closely, he thought that the pieces of straw stuffing poking out of the body looked fresh. But the wooden stick backbone looked old.

And then he saw what he was looking for—anywhere to start a search, find a link.

Just showing under the cloth of the body was a price tag still stuck to the wood. The machine printing was smudged, and there was no bar code, so the purchase couldn't be too recent. At the top of the tag, he could barely read the words. Mason's Mill. The local lumber mill, owned by his friend Grant Mason, was just outside town.

Tess was more determined than ever to get inside the Hear Ye compound. They had lots of gardens there, so maybe they had scarecrows too. Tess took her father's old dowsing wand and drove down the road to the small parking lot. What luck that Lee had said he'd needed her to give a second opinion on his dowsing site, so she had an excuse to come back. Even if she did not locate the girl who had screamed—and she knew how they guarded everyone here—maybe she could at least get more information and then tell Gabe.

She parked and walked up the gentle hill Lee had pointed out. From there, she gazed out over the fenced-in buildings to the fields beyond, stretched out above Cold Creek. Not a scarecrow in sight in the pumpkin patches or gardens with late tomatoes or dying pepper plants tied to wooden stakes. There was a small cornfield, probably just for the use of the community, since so many booths at the Saturday farmers' market uptown had corn. No scarecrows there either, though she did see a couple of tin pans attached to stakes by strings, dancing in the breeze to keep the birds or raccoons away.

She noticed a more distant field, where they had erected what some around here called hoop houses, plastic-draped tunnels that were unheated but could extend the growing season as if they were little greenhouses. No scarecrows were needed there, though the crops, hidden beneath what looked like long gravestones, would have to be watered.

The dried dowsing wand in her hand made her think of what Mayor Owens had said about her father. She'd wanted to call him for years, but she knew it would upset her mother and sisters. The mayor had warned her and Gabe not to repeat the sins of their fathers. For Gabe, perhaps he meant that he'd better not fail to solve the abductions as his father had. But for her, the warning made no sense.

"Hey, Tess!" Lee's voice interrupted her thoughts. He was running up the knoll, waving a dowsing wand. She'd figured the guard at the gate had announced her presence. As old-fashioned as the Hear Ye cult people dressed, did they carry cell phones or walkie-talkies to be able to communicate so fast?

"How is everyone?" she asked. "I hope Kelsey and Ethan at least get some time with the gifts I brought them."

"Oh, sure. Sure, they will."

It scared her to realize she didn't believe him, didn't trust her own cousin. Had Sandy Kenton learned the hard way not to trust the person who must have approached her in the familiar back room of the store, where she played so happily with her mother nearby? Had Tess herself known her abductor and was the shock so awful that she'd forgotten who it was? Maybe the drugs the kidnapper gave her also caused amnesia. But when the drugs wore off, why didn't her memories come back?

"Tess, don't look so upset. I'll see that the kids play with the things and remember who they came from. You'll see us all again. How about we do a family picnic down by the creek before it gets real cold?"

"That would be great. Lee, I was thinking

it would be optimal if you had the well inside the compound," she said, hoping to get him to take her there. "I see a lot of land there. How about we pace that off, then check out here after? If the same water source you think you've found up here could be located on lower ground, then—"

"My task is to be certain there is water here so we can drill outside the fence, not bring in outsiders to drill within."

Well, she thought, that ploy didn't work, but then she'd been naive to think walking around with this wand inside the fence would get her inside the building where she'd heard the screams. Annoyed at herself for her desperation, she held her father's old wand out straight-armed and began to walk the area. This wasn't what she'd wanted to do, to get back into something she considered kind of...well, esoteric, paranormal, despite Kate's lecture to her about people like Einstein believing in it. But maybe her try at dowsing for the first time in years would give her an excuse to phone her father, as if to ask for advice.

"I don't think this old wand is worth much," she called over her shoulder to Lee.

"Here, use mine," he said, and brought it toward her. "I don't want to influence you with what I found, but try toward me just a bit more."

With his wand, she walked the contour of the hill closer to where he'd stood. Nothing happened. Her arms began to tire. Perhaps as a child, when this came so naturally to her, she believed in it, but now—

The wand jerked downward, even pulled her hands down. She stopped, went back. It happened again. Chills raced through her, the nape of her neck to her stomach. She glanced toward Lee, who looked excited. Then she saw a pale man dressed in light blue, loose, flowing clothes coming up the gentle slope of hill toward them. His hair was stark white, and it seemed he had no eyes at all. Then she saw they were pale gray-blue.

"Bright Star," Lee said with a nod of his head that was almost like a bow. "This is my cousin Tess Lockwood and I believe she's verified the water source I've found.

Tess, our guide and leader, Bright Star Monson."

Up close, the man seemed to suck all the air toward himself despite the fact that they stood on a windy hill under open sky.

"Tess, the lost sheep who has been delivered," he greeted her. He extended his hand. She clung to the wand, then pulled one hand away to shake his. Dry, papery skin, cool to the touch. He held her hand. She pulled it back.

"Yes," she said, "I think Lee has found water here, but on a knoll it might take a deep well."

"I have been told by experts we are on a large shelf of shale here, but I know deep wells are the best for living water," Brice Monson replied with a smile. "And how wonderful to have that gift. Believe me, I understand a special gift from God. And I hear you were distressed by the cries from the justice session yesterday. I assure you the child is the better for correction. I can see, though, how that would deeply move a young woman who has suffered much. But we are all one family here, content in whatever state we find ourselves. Of course, we would be delighted should you join us for a worship service someday. Sheriff McCord has been to visit, and all are welcome who have pure intent."

Brice Monson's eyes seemed to bore into hers. Could he read her thoughts? Did he know her intent wasn't **pure?** Tess shuddered, but hoped the two men thought it was just the breeze. She had a strong urge to flee, but she tried not to show how repulsive Monson seemed to her. Surely she was not reacting to him the way she had done with the scarecrow earlier. Her instant, instinctive aversion to this man must be because she felt he was ruining Lee's family's future, not that she recalled him from her own past.

"Thank you for the invitation," she said. "And I wish you well with your drilling of the well."

As if she'd said something wildly clever, Monson laughed, displaying large white teeth and a pale tongue. Lee joined in. Tess said goodbye and made herself walk away slowly, but she really wanted to run.

12

With the scarecrow hidden inside two brown paper bags overlapping end to end, Gabe got out of his cruiser and strode from the parking lot toward the main entrance to Mason's Lumber Mill. The large, loud place was a fourth-generation, family-owned business. It employed a lot of locals and he knew there were plans to expand and hire more.

The sprawling sawmill was now owned and operated by Grant Mason, who had been a good friend of Gabe's since childhood. In second grade at the Cold Creek Elementary School, their teacher, Miss Sanders, had seated the kids alphabetically by first names, and he and Grant had been buddies ever since. Grant thought Gabe was nuts when he joined the service and was sent overseas and it had been a long time since the two of them had just cut out of town and chilled out somewhere together. They were both working way too hard without women or kids in their lives.

Gabe knew this place well since he'd had summer jobs here when Grant's father owned it. He'd swept up sawdust after everyone from scalers to debarkers to the guys who ran the big frame saw. He was familiar with the huge lumberyard with tall piles of stockpiled timber and stacked pallets of wood out back waiting to be processed after the big trucks hauled their loads in. Ann's brothers worked here now, three men he was determined more than ever lately would never be his brothers-in-law.

With a **screech, screech, screech** warning signal, a huge logging forklift started backing up in the parking lot. Gabe gave it a wide berth as he headed into the mill. He thought of Tess mentioning the corn harvester again. She might be right that it was a bad idea for both of them to go charging into Aaron Kurtz's place to look at the machine. Besides, the guy was a deacon at the community church and had been a solid family man for years. Gabe couldn't fathom Aaron not reporting seeing something strange in a cornfield, let alone snatching kids.

But then, since more obvious suspects like Dane Thompson, even Sam Jeffers and that taxidermist loner, John Hillman, hadn't panned out before, maybe it was also time to start looking at long shots, including Kurtz and even Mayor Owens. Was Reese really a nervous wreck each time a kidnap case was investigated by local and state law officers just because of bad PR for the town?

"Yo, Gabe!" Ann's brother Jonas shouted from his elevated position above the cutting line that fed logs into the debarker. He wore industrial earplugs that looked like earmuffs. A dust mask partly covered his face, but his voice was so loud the mask hardly muted it. "What's happ'nin', man?" Jonas shouted over the earsplitting din of the machine.

Gabe just waved and headed up the

metal steps toward Grant's elevated office from which he could keep an eye on the entire floor of conveyor belts and moving parts.

Grant was sitting on his desk, feet in his chair, working on a laptop balanced on his knees, probably so he could look farther down through his office's glass windows. How things had changed since Grant's dad used to oversee things with a pencil stuck behind his ear and a scratch pad in his shirt pocket.

Despite his dad's wishes he stay home and learn the business after college, Grant had gone out to northern California and Oregon, hung out with loggers, taken a job operating a big debarker in the field, not a mill. When Grant took over the business, his father had finally admitted a couple of years of roughing it was the right thing to do. It allowed Grant to mingle easily with everyone from environmentally minded CEOs to senators in D.C. to brush cat loggers in these hills.

Grant looked up as Gabe closed the office door to mute the noise. "Got something I want you to see—to ID," he told Grant, who put the laptop down and got up to shake his hand.

"Good to see you too," Grant said, his tone part teasing, part critical. "But I know you've been nose to the grindstone over this latest abduction. Anything I can do to help?"

"Help's exactly what I need," Gabe said.

In junior high and high school, they'd been so close they'd either finished each other's sentences or just answered without the other's question being asked. Though they were both tall, Grant was lanky and blond with blue eyes—the marauding Viking look—whereas Gabe was broader and dark-haired, but they used to feel like twins anyway.

"Could this have been made or sold here at the mill?" Gabe asked, dragging the scarecrow out of the sacks. "This center piece of wood was sold here."

"Yeah, for sure, that's our sticker," Grant said, looking through the plastic. "But it's obviously old. Dad used to sell those scarecrows years ago, but we don't carry anything like that now. We do, though, have bins by the door in the spring and winter of those squared-off stakes. People use them for staking up tomatoes, peppers, garden crops like that. In the winter, they string them together with wire to make snow fences. But the intact scarecrow for sale—not since about the time I was in college.

"But, you know," Grant went on, cocking his head, "this outfit—I have seen that too. I'm thinking my mom used to sew these for decorative scarecrows, other home-made figures with wooden bodies too, like Christmas angels that people could put in their yards, wooden Easter bunnies—her mad money back then, I guess. Some friends from church helped her make the outfits."

"Like who? Do you remember?"

"Ah, Marva Green, I think. Wanda Kurtz, for sure. Those two among all her friends were always tight. They used to kid about their names rhyming, and both were close to Mom. They did almost all the food at Dad's and Mom's funerals."

"Wanda—Aaron Kurtz's wife."

"Yeah, but we're talking at least twenty years ago. Sorry I can't help you more. So, what's the deal with the scarecrow?"

"Tell you later. You've been a big help."

"Don't tell me the idiots cooking up meth or getting high on bath salts are bootlegging them in old scarecrows."

"All right, I won't tell you that. Thanks, bud. See you," he said, clapping Grant on the shoulder, and made for the door, already stuffing Mr. Mean back into the paper sacks, top and bottom.

"If it's that important you have to take off," Grant called after him, "you owe me a beer somewhere!"

Gabe turned back as he opened the door, and the noise from the mill floor hit him again. It was louder than the rotor wash of a helicopter. "I may owe you more than that."

As he went down the stairs, he saw Ann's two other brothers staring at him from the catwalk across the big-toothed circular saw as it ripped into a huge log.

• • •

Tess drove directly from the Here Ye compound toward Aaron Kurtz's farm. She did not see or hear the big reaper in the surrounding fields, though Aaron owned or leased land far and wide, so he might be elsewhere. Perhaps Ann's pointed suggestion that Tess should sell her land to Aaron wasn't such a bad idea.

Tess was hoping the big-time farmer had gone home for a late lunch or early dinner. She passed fields he'd harvested, the cornstalks slashed low to the ground, leaving only stubble. As much as she didn't want to hear or see the big machine near her house, she wished those fields could be cut soon so she could see far out from her windows again, even if that brought Dane Thompson's pet cemetery into view. The thought of those huge projecting teeth that funneled the rows of corn into the belly of the beast, shooting cobs out into an open truck bed and chaff out the other way, really bothered her. Was she remembering that correctly?

Had she somehow memory-merged the reaper's metal teeth that protruded out the front with Mr. Mean's toothy grin? **Memory merge**—it was a term she'd seen skimming through one of the books Miss Etta had left with her.

She drove past the Kurtz driveway, turned around at the next intersection and drove back. Their place had always been so well kept and beautiful. The old white farmhouse sported neat black trim. The big red barn and other back buildings looked freshly painted, and tall twin silos stood like guards over it all. The yard displayed brick-lined flower beds and a spacious stretch of grass before the endless cornfields began. The wide-set property lines were edged by white fences.

Driving slowly, she turned in the paved drive, lined with corn shocks and pumpkins. She did not want to go out to one of those back buildings to see the reaper since they stood so close to the corn. But this had to be done. If Gabe was with her, it would look too official, too fishy. And besides, by asking Aaron if he wanted to buy her land, maybe she could suggest he cut the cornfields surrounding her house soon.

Again, as each time she drove past a farmhouse, even those abandoned and vandalized, lived in by poor people, or palatial like this, she asked herself if she recalled anything about it. The yard, the front of the house, the view—anything. But here, even with all those back buildings, she sensed nothing.

There it was!

The green John Deere harvester sat outside the barn next to a wagon hitched to a tractor. The wagon was full of shelled corn. She recalled it well, although she must have turned it into a monster of nightmares later. She viewed the elevated, glassed-in cab where the driver sat; the huge double wheels with yellow metal hubs; and the eight extensions thrust out in front that went between the rows so the cornstalks and cobs would feed in to be cut and shelled while the stalks were shredded for silage. She could see now why she thought of them as teeth when she was small, but at least she had clearly recalled something from the day she was taken.

She knew for sure that Aaron Kurtz and a machine like this one—or maybe this very one—had been in the field that day. So, had he seen someone or something amiss he had covered up for some reason? She knew he had been questioned about that years ago. Or had he done something he didn't want known?

"You don't listen, do you?" came a hard voice behind her. "Or can't obey orders for your own good."

She jumped and spun around, expecting Aaron. It was Gabe. Why hadn't she heard him drive in? She realized then she'd been hearing in her head the sounds of the reaper—this grim reaper—when here it sat, still and quiet.

"There's no law against my looking at this," she told Gabe.

"How about trespassing?"

"They wouldn't press charges—"

"How about impeding an investigation when I told you not to come here alone?"

He took her arm and steered her toward her car.

"Gabe, let go! Your presence will tip him off that something's wrong."

"Something **is** wrong! You are not formally on this case. We don't know who's responsible. Someone may get spooked or desperate if you're running around here and—"

"Oh, Sheriff, hello!" a woman's voice called out from the back porch of the farmhouse. "Is there a problem?"

"Hi, Mrs. Kurtz. No, there's no problem. I was just telling Tess Lockwood—she's a preschool teacher—that I thought a field trip for little kids to see some big, noisy farm machinery wasn't very smart, that she ought to stick to taking them to the firehouse to see an engine. Besides, they'd get a lecture from the fire guys about fire safety."

Tess was amazed at how quickly and smoothly he'd come up with those lies. Wasn't the job of a law enforcement officer to deal in the truth?

Wanda Kurtz came closer, wiping her

hands on an apron. "Tess Lockwood," she said, squinting into the afternoon sun. "Why, I heard you were back. And you're welcome here anytime. Are you helping teach the religious sect children down the road? Of course, we'd be happy to have them visit, if that's what you mean. I could have Aaron cut one of our back fields into a real easy maze for them to run though. He's not here right now, though. Had a doctor's appointment in Chillicothe."

Tess hemmed and hawed a bit to get out of the corner Gabe had backed her into. He might be angry with her, but she was angry too. She quickly said goodbye and started for her car. As she got in, she could see Gabe was showing Mr. Mean to Wanda Kurtz. What was he thinking? If Aaron was somehow guilty, wouldn't that tip him off?

Talk about a corn maze! She felt she was running through one, searching for someone or something hiding barely out of reach. She just hoped her desperation didn't trap her in a dead end.

• • •

Drinking some wine from the last bottle she'd brought from home and pacing from her kitchen to the living room, Tess was even more furious when Gabe didn't call or stop by to explain why he was showing the scarecrow to Wanda Kurtz. What had he learned? She knew she should tell him about the girl's screams at the Hear Ye compound. But she had to admit there was no way Brice Monson, however controlling and strange he was, could abduct a girl and keep her there with all those people around. And Monson had mentioned that Gabe had visited there, so he must be watching the compound too, and Gabe hadn't shared that with her. She thought that he'd wanted her help, but now he was critical and cold.

She wondered if she should get a Realtor to take over selling the house so she could get out of town faster. Yet, she'd started to harbor the hope that not only could she help Gabe solve the abductions, but that she might get her memories back too—

and be able to deal with them.

She considered her options now, since Gabe seemed to have turned hostile. She could call Char for some of her wise and warm sisterly advice. Call her father out west and try to learn if he knew something he hadn't told anyone about her being taken. They were her personal contacts, so Gabe could not object to family phone calls. She had to do something to keep from doing nothing, from just worrying and getting more upset. What time would it be in New Mexico and on the West Coast now? Char was usually out in some traditional hogan working with Navajo children, and Tess didn't want to talk to her dad's wife—she'd never met the woman—if he was at work.

She looked at the three library books Miss Etta had brought, which were piled in the rocking chair by the window. Maybe she should take another look at them to see if that triggered more memories. If she remembered anything, she'd just call Vic Reingold and tell him instead of Gabe.

She knew she was absolutely,

stark-raving crazy to have feelings for the sheriff, the son of the man who couldn't solve her case years ago. And even when she was so angry with him and couldn't wait to get out of Cold Creek, it was insanity to want to see him. It was terrifying. She shivered every time he looked at her. And when he'd kissed her, she'd felt she was not only looking at a waterfall, but going over it.

Gabe felt silly walking into the tanning salon Marva Green managed. It was feminine inside, but that figured. He couldn't think of too many guys around here who would patronize a place like this. Probably not many of the local women would use it either. Not that the Lake Azure women weren't local now, he reminded himself. It was just that, his having grown up here in the foothills of Appalachia, it was sometimes hard to get used to the more affluent lifestyle of the newer residents. But then, the Lake Azure folks had voted strong for him at their polling place at the community lodge, so he had no beef with them, unless they broke the law.

"Why, Sheriff McCord, what brings you here?" Marva asked, looking up from reading a magazine. Maybe it was a downtime for her, but that was good. He didn't need anyone but Wanda and Marva seeing this scarecrow right now. He was hoping it indirectly roiled the waters with Aaron or Dane, if they were involved with the kidnappings. He wanted to get someone real nervous so they'd make a rash move or a mistake and come out of hiding, though that was a risk too. He wanted them to make a move toward him, not Tess.

"I just came from Wanda Kurtz's, and she says you and my mother used to make these and sell them at Mason's Mill," he said, pulling the scarecrow out of the sacks. **Come on, Mr. Mean,** he thought, **rattle someone's cage besides Tess's.**

Marva gave a little gasp, then smiled. "Why, yes, we did, back in the old days when a job at an upscale tanning salon in Cold Creek would have been like something from that old TV show **The Twilight Zone.** The three of us cut and stitched those little outfits, stuffed the bodies and sold them at the mill and split the money. I wouldn't be surprised if more than one of your Christmas presents was bought with our profits when you were a boy. But why are you asking?"

"I can't say more than that it's part of the kidnapping investigation."

"Why, how can that be? But..." She paused and took a deep breath. "If it helps to clear Dane of the suspicion some folks still have of him, just because that cornfield joins his property with the Lockwood house, I'll be glad to help in any way I can. And thank you, Sheriff, for not rushing to bring him in or question him right away as your father did, because Dane has absolutely nothing to do with those horrible disappearances of any of those girls!"

"I hope to prove that's true, Marva. But let him know I will need a statement from him and he should sit tight."

"Oh. Well, he's gone hunting with Sam Jeffers and John Hillman—but only for overnight. Of course, I'll tell him. Actually," she said, leaning closer to him and whispering as the street door opened and a slender woman walked in, "Dane only went along because Sam said there was a wounded stag he could tend to that had a broken leg. Dane may tranquilize it and get the others to help him bring it back here. My brother is so tenderhearted, Sheriff. And if they find the stag dead—I'm surprised Sam didn't just shoot it, but he penned it in instead—John will mount it."

"That's quite a trio, isn't it?" Gabe said as he quickly stuffed the scarecrow back into its sacks. "An animal healer, an animal hunter and a dead-animal preserver."

"Well, yes, but they've been friends for years."

"Thanks, Marva," he said, and touched the brim of his hat to her and the customer, who already looked so tan her skin was leathery. Of everything Marva had said to try to put him off suspecting her brother, she'd actually given him a lot to go on.

Tess was engrossed in the books Miss

Etta had left for her and was making notes while lying in bed. She learned that memories of traumatic events could change over time, so machines could become monsters in dreams, when the monsters were really humans. And suppression was a common coping mechanism for someone with childhood trauma. She read about terror dreams, which were not recalled on waking, something she could have written a book on. But what really grabbed her attention was the story of one child victim who blamed himself for later kidnappings that were patterned after his.

"Do I do that?" she asked aloud. "Is that why I want to help Gabe so much even though I'm upset with him? I got away so the kidnapper is taking others?"

She heard something outside, and went to her bedroom window to see what caused the sudden noise. It didn't quite sound like car tires crunching gravel in the driveway. She'd instantly hoped Gabe was driving in, but she saw no headlights or vehicle below.

The outside safety lights went off and it was pitch-black. Just as she gasped, she heard a pop and the interior house lights went dark too.

Tess fumbled her way to the side window to see if Gabe's house lights were out. No, she could see light coming from his place.

Wanting to call Gabe, she shuffled to the back window and felt for her purse on the small dresser. It wasn't there. She knew there was a flashlight downstairs, but she'd have to be careful on the stairs. What if this blackout was set up by someone? She needed that phone now, needed Gabe! Why had she ever been angry with him?

As she dropped to her knees to feel for her purse on the floor, she glanced out the window. She could see a light outside, moving through the rows of corn below, coming closer.

13

Tess stared at the single light flickering through the corn. It moved steadily along the back of her yard, maybe only a couple of rows in. She tried to concentrate on the dark form carrying it. The person was holding the light low, maybe thinking it was hidden or so it wouldn't reveal a face. It was hard to tell the person's height from this high up. She was so scared for a moment she just stared, mouth open.

Then she scrambled to action, fumbling for her purse. She found it and reached inside for her phone. Its dim light almost blinded her. She had to ransack her purse, looking for her billfold, where she'd tucked the paper with both of Gabe's numbers written on it.

Her hand shook so much as she punched in Gabe's home phone number she misdialed and had to do it again. He had to be there. He could get in his cruiser, scare away or catch whoever that was. Could it be someone related to the kidnappings, who wanted to chase her away? Or worse, to silence her?

Gabe's number rang and rang. He told her if she dialed 911, his night dispatcher could reach him, so maybe she should do that. As his home phone was still ringing, she peeked out the window. The light in the corn was moving right through the area where she'd been snatched. She heard a voice.

"Gabe McCord."

"Gabe, it's Tess. Someone made all my lights go out, both inside and out. And someone's out in the corn in back with a light, kind of moving around, out by where I was taken."

"I'm looking out the window. Yeah, you're pitch-dark. Stay put in the house, and I'll be right there. I'm going to get a stun gun as well as my pistol and come through the cornfield between us on foot, see if I can surprise your visitor."

"But I want him gone! Can't you run the siren on the cruiser?"

"Tess, we want to catch this guy. I'll be right there, sweetheart, so don't be afraid."

Sweetheart? That word both comforted and frightened her, just like his plan. She crawled from the back window to the side one and crouched under the window, staring through the darkness toward Gabe's place.

She felt a sudden surge of anger. She couldn't just cower here, had to do something to help. Rather than just watch for Gabe, she returned to the back window so she could look at the light and maybe signal with her phone or shout to Gabe which way it went.

She couldn't let this monster control her. And she'd never forgive herself if something happened to Gabe.

• • •

Gabe strapped on his gun belt and grabbed the stun gun and a flashlight but didn't take time to throw on a jacket. Thank heavens he was here, not in town, not in the shower or in bed. It was only a little after ten. He'd been exhausted, planning to hit the rack for a couple of hours, but now adrenaline surged through him.

He raced out the side door, cursed taking the time to lock it, but he didn't want anyone to get inside to see what he had hidden in his spare bedroom. He tore past his parked cruiser into the field that stretched to Tess's house. He pushed himself hard. Ears of corn bounced against his shoulders and hips. He told himself to keep his toes pointed in, concentrate on not tripping over roots. Surely Aaron was going to cut these fields soon, though they'd been planted later than most in the area. At least asking when they'd be cut would be an excuse to interview the man. He didn't want someone being able to sneak up on Tess or him either like this.

Compared to when he used to run miles each day, he felt out of shape, sucking air. He slowed to avoid giving himself away with noise. It was so different from the way they'd handled problems in Iraq. They'd go in with a heavily armed convoy accompanying his blast-resistant Humvee with its four-hundred-pound doors. That let people know they were coming, that they could handle things, that the U.S. had power and might. But he'd also used remote-controlled cameras and robots to defuse danger. Here in Cold Creek it was hands-on and in-your-face.

As he neared the Lockwood edge of the field, he raised his flashlight and blinked it at the side of Tess's house, once, twice, just to let her know he was here. He strained to listen a moment to see if he had spooked the intruder. If the guy ran, he'd hear him rustle the corn, wouldn't he? Who among the suspects had the know-how to cut off the power to Tess's place?

Gabe heard her open her window above him. Did she think his signal meant she must answer? If the guy had a gun, she was about to make herself a target.

He vaulted out from the corn to yell up at her, but she called down, "He's moving away, toward Dane's place! I think he's almost halfway across, but I can't see his light now. He was in a row about where the swing set used to be, but he could have doubled back. Be careful!"

"Stay in there!" he shouted. He turned on his flashlight and, holding the stun gun, ran across the small backyard and crashed back into the rows of corn. Marva had said Dane, John and Sam were out in the hills tonight, but were they really? If there were three of them, he could be running right into a trap where he was outnumbered.

He switched off his light and went around to another row far from the area Tess had indicated. If this was a ploy to lure him away from Tess, to make sure he was out of the way so someone could not just scare her but hurt her, he wouldn't allow it.

Moving out of the field onto the side road, he headed back toward her house. Close to her property, he saw why her lights had gone out. A vehicle had hit the pole that carried those wires, and the whole thing was atilt. It was no accident, he'd bet, as there was no vehicle in sight. He'd have to notify gas stations and body shops in the area to watch for dents in fenders or crumpled hoods. Maybe Mike could get paint scrapings off the pole.

He cut across Tess's backyard, playing his light on the ground before him. Two eyes gleamed at him from the picnic table. He jumped back, transferred the stun gun to his left hand and went for his pistol.

But the thing—a dog—didn't move. Glassy-eyed. Dead. Mounted. Again, memories of Iraq haunted him. There had always been dead dogs in the streets, but what did this one mean? The scarecrow, now this. Either someone was leaving him clues, or this was meant to scare Tess away.

He shone the light on the dog. The shadows made it look even more frightening. This could be John Hillman's taxidermy work. But he'd never be so stupid as to leave it here, like a calling card, a come-haul-me-in-for-questioning sign. So who had left it here?

Through the back door, Gabe told Tess to stay inside, then he slumped on the picnic table seat. He called Vic.

Vic was staying in a motel out on Route 23 almost to Chillicothe. Gabe updated him. Vic said Mike had gone to BCI headquarters, but he'd get him back to look at the taxidermy work on the dog. Mike would also check for paint on the telephone pole. He said he'd see him first thing in the morning at the sheriff's office.

Gabe called Jace and asked him to call body shops in a wide area to ask that they be notified if someone came in with a staved-in or even dented fender. Then Gabe called the emergency line at the power company to get Tess's power restored.

"Can I come out now?" she called from the back door.

"No, I'll come in."

He didn't want her to see the dog. It was a pit bull, snarling and looking ready to leap, which was how he felt. As soon as he was done with the staff meeting in the morning, he was going to question John Hillman, Dane Thompson, even Sam Jeffers. They'd better have brought that stag back dead or alive to prove they weren't around Tess's place during the night. Could all three guys—loners and eccentrics, though the woods was full of them around here—have colluded on abductions over the years? Hillman was divorced, Sam a longtime widower and Dane a bachelor, so there were no mates or children in their lives.

"Oh! Gabe, what's that?" Tess cried, coming up behind him.

"I told you to stay inside."

"A stuffed dog! One that looks like it wants to attack. Obviously a warning to me."

"I called to get your lights back on, but it may not happen until early morning," he told her, getting up and facing her to put himself between her and the back cornfield. He snared her wrist with one hand to pull her away from staring at that dog. "Tess, please go in your house, grab a couple of things to spend the night at my place. You got any big plastic trash bags in there? Damn, I'm tired of hauling weird stuff around to show people."

"I saw you showing the scarecrow to Wanda Kurtz and wondered why. Yes, I have a trash bag. But can't you stay here instead?"

"We'd be sitting ducks in the dark. We're going to my place. I've got an extra room, a spare bed. You'll be safer there."

"We're going through the cornfield? What if that's his plan?"

"I think he—or they—only wanted to give you a good scare or warning. Just do as I say, okay?"

"All right, but you haven't confided in me, and not only about Wanda Kurtz. I hear you've been to the Hear Ye Commune, but then I guess I didn't tell you something too. I heard a woman or girl scream at the compound, but I kind of checked it out and got a reasonable explanation—if reason is any part of that place."

"What are you, my other deputy? Here, take my flashlight, go in the house, get your things now, or I swear, I'll arrest you for something and put you in the detention cell in town for safekeeping. I checked out Amanda's possibly being held at the compound. Brice Monson's weird, but he's got too many people around to be hiding Amanda, Jill or Sandy there. Now, do what I say!"

Obviously as frustrated with him as he was her, Tess grabbed the flashlight from him, went in, slammed both doors, came out, threw a trash bag at him and banged inside the house again. That all infuriated him too, but for one thing. She was not whimpering in a corner. It was kind of the spunky, younger Teresa again, animated, defiant, a fearless tomboy before trauma had crushed her.

Trying to keep his temper in check—it riled him especially that he wanted to put his hands all over her even when she was defying him—he worked the dog into the bag so he could carry it upright.

Tess came out with a full paper sack and her purse and thrust the flashlight back at him. "See, you've turned me into a bag lady," she said. "Like one you're taking off the streets because she can't care for herself. But I wasn't going through that field with my suitcase."

"Let's go. We'll set a timer and argue for an hour, then hit the rack, or since you're a bag lady, hit the sack. We're both exhausted, and I can't believe you'd even consider staying here alone tonight after this."

"Let's see, how to put this…" she said, her tone still sarcastic, as they walked toward the cornfield with him leading. "You can't teach an old, scared and traumatized dog new tricks, so Tess is going to ruin things if she tries to think on her own to help you out. She was misled at first because you said you wanted her to help, so—"

"I wanted you to remember what happened to you when you were taken twenty years ago, not take over now! Did you lock up the house?"

"Of course. Did you lock yours in your rush?"

"You bet I did. Look, I know you're upset and scared, but keep quiet right now. There's another saying that I've seen on signs in yards around here for years— Beware of Dog—and I think that's the message here."

"From that stuffed, dead dog or from

the top-dog sheriff?"

He turned back to face her. "Stop fighting me! Someone wants you to leave town or worse. Or if this dead dog is a message for me, I'm not sure what it means."

"I was just...just trying to keep my courage up, I think."

"Stick close, okay? Right behind me."

As he turned away to head into the field, he heard her sniff back tears. He knew he shouldn't have been so rough, but she really got to him. Maybe she was right on the edge of hysteria. Actually he knew the feeling. How many times had he beat down a screaming fit of fear when he'd had to dismantle a bomb by hand when the robot just wouldn't work?

"Yes, I'm staying close," she told him in a suddenly quiet voice that caught on a half-smothered sob as they headed into the tall, thick corn between their houses.

Tess drank the hot chocolate he fixed for them in his kitchen. She remembered how it had once looked, but it had all been updated, even to stainless-steel appliances. If she could recall what a kitchen looked like from two decades ago, why couldn't she recall more important things? She looked around. It was neat, not even dishes in the sink or drain rack. He'd pulled down all the blinds so no one could see in. She felt safe from anything outside now, but sealed in with him, newly alert as they faced each other across the wooden kitchen table.

"I can't take you to the early-morning meeting at the station with me," he told her. "But since you're so involved—and I didn't mean to shut you out except to keep you safe—I'll call you right after and tell you what the three of us have decided."

"I'd appreciate that."

"But I want you to stay here until the power is restored at your place."

She nodded. She was so exhausted her eyes almost crossed.

He went on, sounding nervous, "I'd better open up the extra bedroom for you so it heats up in there. I keep both extra rooms upstairs closed in the heating season. There's just one bath upstairs—a half bath down here, but you're welcome to take a shower or whatever. I'll get some towels out."

"Your mother would be proud of your hospitality and how great this place looks. She was always a good hostess."

"Yeah. Still is in the trailer park where she lives in Florida. Too good a hostess at times, I guess."

She didn't know what he meant, but a bath and bed sounded so good. And to sleep at night in security, to feel safe, as she never quite had in the old house the three nights she'd been back, would be great—safe from everything except her feelings for Gabe.

She followed him upstairs as he opened the door to a plainly furnished bedroom. It was his boyhood one, she was sure of that, though it had been redone. It was a bit feminine, maybe in case his mother visited. So he must sleep in his parents' larger one across the front of the house. But no, he tossed his windbreaker into the room at the back end of the hall.

"Don't you sleep in front?" she asked,

suddenly feeling awkward again as his eyes swept her. Oh, no, that over-the-waterfall sensation again. She'd been fighting it, but feelings flew between them like pounding spray.

"No, I keep that for my home office," he said, but he didn't open the door to give her a glimpse. "It's bigger. I'm down the hall. I can use the bathroom downstairs, so you just go ahead."

He got a set of towels and an extra blanket from a hall linen closet and piled them in her arms. "I'll be getting up early," he said. "Probably before six. If you want to join me for breakfast that's fine. Otherwise just get what you want, and don't go back to your house until you're sure the power's on," he repeated. "Don't answer the phone here either. Only use your cell."

He was so close she could see how thick his eyelashes were. Little flecks of gold swam in the blue irises of his eyes. He had a slight scar on his chin—from the war?

"I can't thank you enough," she whispered.

"Maybe sometime," he said. Then before she knew it was coming, he leaned forward to kiss her.

At first it was just closed lips, controlled, kind of sweet. But suddenly they crushed the stack of towels and the blanket between them, holding tight, clinging. When she clasped her arms around his neck, everything cascaded to the floor. They pressed together, chest to breasts, hips and thighs. His hands raced over her waist and back as they opened their mouths in a devouring kiss. He cupped her bottom with his hands, lifted her up against him, before setting her back, almost roughly. Both dazed and shaky, they stared wide-eyed at each other, standing a few feet apart.

"I don't mean to take advantage of the situation," he said, his voice raspy. "You have to be able to trust me. I made a big mistake once, mixing business with...with pleasure."

She was breathless too, but she managed to speak. "Dating Ann or someone else?"

"Yes, Ann. I should have considered her hair-trigger-temper brothers, as well as the fact that I wasn't that crazy about her. Besides, it hit me a few minutes ago that one of them—Jonas—raises pit bulls. I've been wanting to bust him for illegal dogfights. I think they have some sites in the woods, but I've never found the locations. And they're very protective of Ann. I've been trying to back off, even before you came back, but they all think I should be full steam ahead—like just now—between us."

They stared into each other's eyes for a long moment. Despite all those words—information—he'd put out between them like a barrier, she almost threw herself into his arms again. Instead she bent to gather the linens from the floor.

"Thanks for taking me in," she said as she forced herself to head for the bedroom he'd given her. He had taken her in, heart and soul, as the old song said. But she had to fight that sweeping need for him with all her might.

• • •

As exhausted as Tess was and as good as she felt after a hot bath in Gabe's big bathtub, she couldn't sleep. She prayed she would not dream of that dog, nor of the monster in the cornfield. If she screamed out in the night, would Gabe come running? She tossed and turned, thinking of her father, her sisters, the missing girls, Gabe.

She heard a voice, a young girl's voice, muted but close. Was she dreaming? No.

She sat straight up in bed. She heard a girl's voice coming from out in the hall.

Tess got up and wrapped the extra blanket around her like a robe. She was wearing her nightgown, but she'd forgotten her slippers. Her feet were cold on the wooden floor. Tiptoeing to the door, she opened it a crack.

Light bled from under the door of the room Gabe had said was his home office. And that's where the voice came from, definitely a young girl's. Could he have a TV on in there? Maybe he couldn't sleep either.

Tiptoeing closer, she put her ear to the door.

She could hear the words clearly now. "My name is Jill Stillwell. I love puppies and to camp out with my family. I love to read books. I can read now all by myself if the books are elentory, I mean easy enough, like in elentory school. I have an older brother, Jeff, who is nice to me mostly…"

The high, sweet, little voice went on. But…but Jill Stillwell was the name of the second girl who had been abducted, taken years after Tess's family had moved to Michigan. She sounded so real, as if she was just on the other side of this door!

Carefully, quietly, Tess turned the doorknob. She only meant to open the door a crack, but it swung inward with a loud creak. She gasped and gave a little cry at what she saw, just as Gabe turned around to glare at her.

14

"Tess!" Gabe cried as he jumped to his feet. He killed the sound track—he'd been sitting at a laptop—and came at her as if to block her from seeing what was here. Or was he going to grab her?

"I heard—I heard a girl's voice," she said, retreating into the hall. "Jill Stillwell's, one of the kidnapped—"

He grasped her shoulders in hard hands. "It's a recording her family gave me from their Facebook page. It helps me to remember."

It scared her how she recalled that some murderers kept relics of their victims. In the brief glance into the room, she wondered if it could be like a big memory box, a memorial to the lost girls. She'd glimpsed a large blown-up picture of a child who must be Amanda Bell, next to a map with all kinds of lines and other pictures. Were there things in there about her too?

Gabe gave a huge sigh that seemed to deflate his body. His broad shoulders slumped. "You're not dressed," he said as his eyes went over her. "And it's cold tonight. Go get something on so you don't distract me even more, and I'll show you what I've never shared with anyone. I do have some stuff like this at the office, but I've got more here—maybe it will jog something loose for you."

Hurrying, shaking, she did as he said and joined him in the big room that had been his parents' master bedroom. Two walls seemed dedicated to the two earliest victims, Teresa Lockwood and Jill Stillwell. He'd posted photographs of the kidnap victims and their families, with lines drawn out to what he explained was "a circle of acquaintances." On the next wall, narrower because of windows, he'd started to put up things about the Sandy Kenton kidnapping.

Each wall was a collage of evidence.

He'd written in times, places, even things like height and weight of the victims. For each, he'd posted an age-advanced photo of what she might look like now. Tess was amazed at how close to reality the one of her came.

Amanda Bell's area covered only the double-closet doors, but it included a big map of Brazil with cities and roads highlighted with a black pen. Sandy Kenton's wall shared space with a four-by-four-foot bulletin board with a map of Iraq. It was marked where, as Gabe put it, "those sites had victims too. We worked hard to disrupt bombs."

"Those red dots?" she asked, mesmerized by all that he was sharing, and still hesitant to look too closely at her own wall.

"No, the black ones. The red ones show where we didn't get there in time. Where the bomb went off. This one," he said, pointing at a dot nearly obscured by men's first names, "was where I...I lost my friends—and I was in charge."

She touched his arm, slid her hand down

to hold his. He gripped her fingers so hard it hurt, but he didn't look at her, only at the names.

Finally, she steadied herself to turn away and move closer to the wall dedicated to her. There were newspaper articles about her abduction, all laminated. From somewhere, probably her mom years ago, he'd gotten four photos of her, one alone, two with her sisters, one with the whole family. She stared at her parents, so young. What did her father look like now? And her mother was gone. Gabe had also posted a photo of his father in his sheriff's uniform. And down by the floorboard a map of the area with Dane Thompson's house and grounds diagrammed and labeled. She bent down to look at it closely. "So Dane really was your father's number-one suspect?"

"But he couldn't make it stick."

"Dane had an alibi?"

"That he was out of town at the time of the abduction, heading for a meeting in Chillicothe."

"A meeting?"

Gabe squatted beside her. "Yeah, with a woman, a colleague who still has a vet clinic there. She covered for him with a lie—at least Dad thought so. I have copies here of all the affidavits filed, the investigation files. I go over them, go over everything. It's kind of like looking for the missing link."

"But Sandy's and Amanda's disappearances are different from...from mine and Jill's," she said as they stood.

"Yep. No cornfield escape. But Jill was taken right out of a small tent she was sharing with her brother, near the cornfield that abutted their backyard. Why she didn't wake up and scream, we never figured out." He got up, walked across the room and pointed to a picture of a boy. "Mrs. Stillwell said both Jill and her brother were light sleepers."

"Maybe the kidnapper gagged her right away."

"Or used chloroform or some drug—jabbed her with a needle, since you'd been given shots of some sort. If we'd gotten you back in this day and age, they'd have run tests to pinpoint exactly what you had in your system instead of just having you treated by the small-town doctor your father insisted on."

"So the answers are still out there. And that's why this memory room."

"My real war room. I just didn't realize I had the recording with Jill's voice up so loud."

"You probably didn't. I have excellent—sometimes too-good—hearing. Sounds seem to stick with me."

"Like the harvesting machine sound you mentioned."

"Do you have the others'—our voices recorded?"

"All but yours. But yours, I remember. I was there not only when you were taken, but also when they got you back. I rode my bike into town when I heard they'd taken you to Dr. Marvin's office. I blamed myself for what happened to you. I had to see you, so I waited, but your father came out and told me to leave, to stay away from you. But then he saw my mother in the little crowd gathering, and he told her he was sorry for what he'd said to me, that he knew what happened wasn't my fault. They...hugged each other—hard."

Tess put her arm around his waist. He put one hard-muscled arm around her shoulders. "As I said a couple of days ago, Gabe, I don't blame you. And I understand you're partly so...so into this—"

"Say it. Obsessed."

"—because you're trying to finish what your dad started. You drive yourself hard for the victims, for his memory and for yourself too. But if you don't get some rest, you won't be any good to anyone."

He hugged her to him, sideways, hip to hip. When he spoke, his deep voice vibrated through her. "My mother would love you. 'Are you eating well, Gabe? Be sure you get your sleep and exercise even with all that's going on.'"

"Then she's still a good mother. She saw your father work so hard and tried to help him any way she could and now you."

"Yeah," he said, his voice hard again, but he sounded exhausted instead of intense. "She was a good mother, but he was gone a lot and that was hard—too hard for her sometimes as a wife, I guess. Let's get some rack time before the sun comes up, okay? And I'd appreciate it if you don't tell anyone about this room, including Vic Reingold or Deputy Miller."

"Right. I understand."

"You know," Gabe said, turning her to face him, "you do understand."

His blue eyes shimmered with unshed tears. Was he falling apart under the strain? She understood that too. He'd made a memorial here to all his tough times, his failures—including the bulletin board with his battle against bombs.

Maybe she should see if Miss Etta had a book that would help him—though she wouldn't say who it was for. Something about pressure on the job, stress, handling hardship. She desperately wanted to do anything possible, not only to help him solve the abductions, but to help him stay stable and strong. Strange, but worrying about him actually made her feel a little better about herself.

• • •

The next morning, Tess and Gabe had breakfast together, then she offered to clean up as he rushed out the door to head for his meeting with Vic and Jace. He also intended to have Ann check the stuffed pit bull into evidence. Washing up their dishes by hand, she thought about the difficulties of being married to a sheriff or any law enforcement agent. He might always be rushing out the door. Did Vic Reingold have a wife? If so, he had been gone from her for days. Jace Miller was a newlywed, so how hard was his job on his marriage?

And standing in Gabe's mom's kitchen she wondered about those long days alone when Gabe's father was working on her abduction case and then Jill's. It was a lonely life, but Gabe had explained at breakfast that his mother had friends, including Marva Green, no less, and Wanda Kurtz too. They'd even worked together sewing those small scarecrows to earn extra cash. Did the wives of law enforcement men ever hear about their cases the way Gabe had shared with her last night?

She went up to make her bed and looked out the window across the cornfield toward her house. There was an AEP electrical truck in the driveway. She'd promised Gabe she wouldn't leave until he called, but she couldn't wait to tell him that.

She cleaned up the room, then walked through the downstairs. Despite how tidy things looked, except for the kitchen, things were really dusty. So Gabe kept things neat—or had cleaned up the place once—but didn't manage the upkeep.

At seven-thirty, Tess got her cell phone out. She wanted to call Char in New Mexico and knew she'd have to phone her before she went out among the Navajos in their distant houses, some of them traditional hogans, which she visited as a social worker. But it was only five-thirty out there and she hesitated to punch in the numbers. Char would console her but question her too. She'd figure out how close she and Gabe were, then lecture her that she was crazy.

Holding her phone, Tess continued to pace in a big circle, through the kitchen, the dining room, the living room, around again. Surely, if she could just find the spot she'd been held prisoner, she would recognize it somehow, the house, at least. But the numerous places she'd driven past already, slowing down, staring, had not rung a bell. Even if she'd been kept inside all that time, she'd surely have looked out the windows. She must be able to recognize things outside, a barn, a field, a road—something. Maybe if she drove more of the roads around here, something would strike her as familiar.

Tess jolted when her cell phone rang.

"Tess, it's me." Gabe's familiar voice seemed to fill the house, to warm her, even though he sounded all business now. "I'm going to talk to Sam Jeffers, John Hillman and Dane Thompson, separately and on my own, so Vic won't spook them. I want you to stay put until you get your power restored and—"

"I see the repair truck in my driveway."

"Good. Jace is on his way to take paint scrapings from the telephone pole for Mike—he's coming back here today—before the repairmen handle it or climb it if they put it back up."

"Gabe, I think I should go with you to see those three men. If not, I'll drive to their places on my own, just to see if anything jogs my memory."

"What? No way you're heading alone to their properties! Tess, I'm not going for a good-time chat. I'm checking to see if they have alibis, at least for the time you were harassed last night, not to mention when Sandy was taken."

"Well, if I shouldn't go alone, I should go with you. We'll tell Sam Jeffers that I just learned he tried to track me with whatever dog he had twenty years ago and wanted to thank him. I assume you're going to show John Hillman the stuffed dog that was on my property, so I'd have a natural stake in that."

"Tess, I don't—"

"Of course, you're probably right that I

shouldn't go with you to see Dane, so we can compromise on that, and I'll just go on the first two visits with you."

"I'm trying to keep you safe and—"

"But last night shows I'm really not safe, not until we find whoever took me, Jill, Sandy—maybe Amanda. It's hardly some high school kids, even if they are the ones who put graffiti on the rocks near the waterfall. And I don't think my lights out and a dead dog are just someone's sick idea of an early Halloween prank."

She heard him muttering something. To himself? To Vic?

To Vic, she realized, as she heard his voice in the background. "Then let her go. Something's got to unlock her memory. She's still the best chance we've got."

Gabe sounded really mad—but controlled—as he spoke again. "I'll pick you up in about fifteen minutes. We'll stop to talk to the electrical guys, then head for Jeffers's place so you can 'thank him,' and we'll see how that goes. Then maybe you'll go with me to Hillman's taxidermy shop, his little house of horrors. You won't like it there, Tess."

"I may not recall where I was held when I was kidnapped, but **it** was a house of horrors. I'm sure it was, but I'm desperate to remember it—and I will! I'll be waiting for you here."

He didn't even say goodbye. He was angry with her, trapped into letting her help today, probably because of Vic rather than her arguments, but she thought she'd done okay standing up to him.

She got her things together in case he just dropped her at her house later, went to the bathroom, then paced in big circles again, waiting for him. Despite having her warm jacket on, Tess shivered. Had Gabe's mother paced just like this, right here, waiting for her husband? This house, any one where the family had loneliness and conflict, could be a house of horrors.

"About Sam Jeffers's place," Gabe said. They were heading out of town toward the southeastern foothills after confirming that her power would be back on line soon. "Other than his cell phone, the guy lives like the early settlers. His Appalachian roots run deep. He's here, he's there, he's everywhere around, has several small, old lean-to-type cabins in the woods, where he camps and hunts."

"I'm pretty sure I was kept in a house, not at some campsite," Tess said.

"We'll look at his main place, where he breeds and trains his hounds. He'll be there, I think, because, according to Marva, he, Hillman and Dane just got back from the woods, where they were looking at a wounded stag Sam had cornered but not killed."

"Cornered but not killed," she repeated. "I…I hope Sandy Kenton's being kept alive like I was. Jill too, of course—and Amanda, if she was kidnapped instead of snatched by her father. But why would someone take a third child if Jill was still…"

"Yeah. Assuming, of course, that whoever took Sandy out of the shop uptown in broad daylight is the same person who took you and Jill. But a copycat crime like this seems unlikely. I think we're still after one person, maybe with an accomplice. So far, no real leads from Jace's questioning folks who were in and out of that back alley when Sandy disappeared. Even our all-seeing, all-knowing veteran librarian didn't see anything unusual. It's almost like Sandy vanished into thin air."

"And, in exchange, someone left that scarecrow."

Gabe turned the cruiser into a narrow lane lined by buckeye trees. They always dropped their leaves early, so the bright autumn colors of the hills were muted to dry, brown foliage here. Some of the trees were even stripped of leaves, so it seemed their naked, crooked arms reached out. The narrow dirt lane twisted, climbed a bit.

"Oh, perfect," Tess said. "Like a scene in a scary movie. A mailman comes up here every day?"

"No, there's a box we passed down on the road. And, I'm surprised to see, a place for the Chillicothe newspaper. Can't believe a loner and wanderer like Sam keeps up with the news."

"Unless he likes to read about his handiwork."

"You know, you and Vic would get along real well. He suspects everyone, probably even the mailman and paperboy."

A one-story house with peeling paint came into view. It had a long side section that looked added on and was painted such a clean, new white it made the house itself look even dingier.

"That painted part is the canine wing," Gabe said. "Sam keeps his dogs under a roof. Sometimes I think he treats them better than people."

He pulled into a small, turnaround loop and killed the engine. The minute Tess opened her door, she heard barking. "I hope there's not a guard dog loose," she said.

"Hasn't been before. And probably not so a visitor doesn't get hurt, but one of his dogs. He's real fussy about who buys and adopts them."

Just as Tess closed the passenger door, she glimpsed the garbage bag with the mounted pit bull Gabe had put on the floor of the backseat. She imagined it was barking too. She knew he planned to show it to John Hillman but not Sam.

"Maybe he's asleep or not here," she said, surprised Sam didn't realize he had visitors with all the noise.

"I see his truck's in the old barn over there, but that doesn't mean—"

Sam came to the door and walked out with a single hound behind him. Tess was relieved to see he was unarmed. She had the funniest feeling about this place, even though it wasn't familiar to her.

"Hey, Sheriff. Heard you drive in. How you doin'? And that you, Miss Lockwood?"

They all shook hands and went through the usual greetings and small talk. In the old days in the hills, to "set a spell and get caught up" was essential before getting down to business.

"Tess wanted to come along just to say thanks for trying to track her years ago," Gabe explained since the talk had mostly been between the two men—also hill-country custom. "And I sure appreciate the effort with Boo the other day," he said, patting the dog on the head. "Hear you found a wounded stag up yonder."

"Did. Took John and Dane with me, but it died. John won out to claim it, though I get the venison. It was hurtin' real bad when we got there, so Dane used some of that pain med stuff to get it to stop thrashing around. You know, what he uses on people's pets in agony so he can set a leg and such."

As they talked, Tess glanced around. Surely she would have recalled yelping dogs if she'd ever been kept here. But was it at all suspicious that it took Sam a while to come out to greet them, as if maybe he had to hide someone or something first? He and Gabe were talking about trapping, but Gabe managed to get the conversation around to when Sam left the area with John and Dane and when they came back. He was probably going to ask the other two men the same to see if their information matched.

"You got time to come in and set a spell?" Sam asked Gabe, as if she weren't even there. At least that meant he had nothing to hide inside, didn't it?

Gabe turned him down, saying he had to get Tess home. "Someone hit her utility pole last night and her place went dark," Gabe said. "You old boys weren't out on the road after drinking last night, were you?"

How Sam found that amusing, she wasn't sure, but somehow Gabe conned his way into looking at the bumper of Sam's beat-up old truck out in the doorless shed he used as a garage.

Glad the hound Boo didn't show any interest in her, Tess didn't go with them but walked closer to the house. A slant-door of an old-fashioned root cellar with a padlock on it caught her interest. In this refrigerator age, root cellars were outdated, and people never locked them.

Checking to be sure the men weren't looking, Tess bent and knocked on the wood. The root cellar had been repaired with new boards, one with Mason's Mill stamped on it. She knocked on the wood again. Nothing. No answer, but what did she expect? Sandy Kenton to scream out that she needed help?

"Now, Miss Lockwood," Sam said when the men ambled back over, "I never would 'spect you trying to get to my best moonshine."

Tess blushed. He'd seen her. She'd made a mess of this, probably was wrong to insist Gabe bring her.

"I thought it was another place for dogs," she blurted, probably making herself look even more stupid.

"Bad dogs, you mean?" he said with a wink and a shake of his shaggy head. "Naw, it's not really moonshine, Sheriff, but I don't think you came lookin' for that. Keeps my beer cool, though. Want one, I'll bet, eh, Sheriff, but not when you're on duty?"

There was more small talk, all between Gabe and Sam, followed by some back-slapping. Tess walked ahead and got in the cruiser.

"Sorry I screwed that up," she said the minute Gabe got back in.

"Almost."

"No marks or dents on his truck, right?"

"Nope."

"Do you really think he uses that old root cellar for storing beer?"

"No way to know without a search warrant, and the Falls County judge I use would never give me one on what I know."

"I promise to keep even quieter—that is, say next to nothing—at Hillman's place."

"Tess, you did fine. But didn't you hear what Sam divulged about Dane? I can't believe it didn't occur to me before. The man uses veterinarian drugs. They not only cover pain, but could cause amnesia, I'll bet. Somehow I've got to find out what Dane uses, check into that."

He pulled out of the crooked driveway, and they started down the hill. "I see what you mean," she said. "A long shot, but—"

"But I'm desperate. And maybe it's not just that you were too young or traumatized so you didn't recall details of your captivity. I had a friend who had a colonoscopy—he was dreading it—but they gave him an IV that didn't knock him out so that he could follow orders, but it kept him from recalling the details of the unpleasant procedure afterward."

"And those needle marks on my arms, like I was some kind of junkie."

At the bottom of the hill, she almost thought she heard the barking of those dogs again. But there was some other sound, more muted and distant than her memory of the corn harvester, but—

She turned toward him, twisting in her seat belt.

"What's that?" she asked.

"What's what? That sound? It's just a train. Coal trains come through here real regular, you know that. Why? You look upset."

"Scared. I feel scared, and it's just a distant train. Sounds really stick with me, even when I can't get any visual memories. One of the books Miss Etta gave me about childhood traumas said smells or sounds could trigger a buried memory. Gabe, I think I remember the sounds of a train, and there's no tracks in earshot of my house here or where I live in Michigan. But I don't think the sounds from a train carry to Dane's place either."

"I'm starting to think we need a field trip to Chillicothe," he said as they turned out onto a paved road. "I need to talk to the vet who gave Dane the initial alibi, because I remember my dad saying she lived near a train track. I could ask her about vet drugs without quizzing Dane. And I've got something else to check on there too, looking into someone's past who has a record of molesting little girls."

"Someone who lives here now?"

"Yeah. Let's just save that until later. I don't want you to go to Dane's with me, Tess, but let's go see what Hillman has to say about that stuffed dog in the backseat. Just don't wander off if you see any buried rooms with padlocks and new wood, okay? Hearing the train narrows down where you might have been held around here to about fifty square miles instead of a hundred. Something's going to break these cases loose. I only hope it's not too late for the other girls."

15

Tess was relieved to see that John Hillman's driveway and house were a far cry from the creepiness of Sam's. Everything looked well kept and newly painted. The driveway was a short, straight one off State Route 104 to Chillicothe. A neatly lettered sign read Hillman's Taxidermy and had a stag's head on it. She wondered if Mr. Hillman would sell the new stag's head or keep it. Thoughts of mounted stag heads with those liquid eyes and that rack of pointed antlers made her uncomfortable.

But where had she seen mounted stag heads? She couldn't recall anything specific.

"When you said I wouldn't like this place—that it was a house of horrors—I pictured it back in the woods like Sam

Jeffers's house," she told Gabe.

"I didn't mean horrors linked to you. I just meant you might not like what you see inside, depending on what he's working on. Even though he hangs around with some of the backwoods boys, Hillman's a modern businessman. He advertises in the **Chillicothe Gazette,** and this location on a busy road helps promote his services too. People are in and out of here all the time."

Gabe took the mounted pit bull out of the backseat, got rid of the plastic bag, then held the dog under his arm as they went up to the side door with another Taxidermy sign hanging over it. He rang the bell. Tess jumped when the sound of it was not a chime but an animal's roar.

"Black bear recording," Gabe said as John Hillman, wearing a leather apron and goggles shoved up on his forehead, opened the door.

"Hey, Sheriff. And, Ann—oh, sorry, guess not," he said, squinting at Tess. "Hey—I was wondering what happened to that pit bull!" He reached out and stroked the dog's head. "Some jerk stole that right off my back porch when I had it out so the glue could dry. Glad you got it back for me. Come on in, both of you."

"John, this is Tess Lockwood," Gabe said, and made formal introductions, though the man seemed more interested in the mounted dog than her. "Someone left this in her backyard."

"That right?" he said, leading them into a large workroom. "It belongs to Jonas Simons, Ann's brother. It's one of his favorite dogs, named Sikkem, died real sudden."

"Sic 'em, huh?" Gabe said. "I don't see a mark on his fur. I'll bet you did a good job patching him up. One of his fighting dogs?"

"Fighting dogs?" Hillman echoed, looking overly dramatic, Tess thought. "Don't know a thing about that. But why would someone leave it in your yard, Tess?" he said, turning to her and narrowing his eyes.

"That's what we'd like to find out," she said, keeping her attention on him rather than looking around as she had done at first.

This place smelled strange, sharp, like turpentine, and the heads of dead animals peered down from all four walls. A large vat behind Hillman was making strange sounds, and he had a big, bloody pelt stretched out on the worktable behind him. Worse, a collection of what must be glass eyes stared at her from a clear vase on the table. Around the room, plastic carvings of different animals were displayed in great detail—including veins and muscle ridges—with various stages of their own hides pinned to them.

She had not expected to see carvings that looked almost like works of art. Nor was John Hillman what she'd expected. He was slim with a closely clipped beard unlike his friend Sam Jeffers's long one. He was younger than she'd expected too, maybe in his late thirties. Unlike Sam, he didn't "talk country" but sounded educated with a touch of a Southern drawl. What a weird trio of friends Dane, Sam and John made. Was the foundation of their friendship animals, dead or alive?

"So this dog belongs to Jonas," Gabe said. "Those Simons boys are pretty antsy about my relationship with Ann. All I need is them siccing a dog like this on me."

"Better watch crossing that trio of bubbas," Hillman said with a laugh. He looked at Tess again just as she noticed a shelf with a row of animal skulls, including one that looked newly scraped and cleaned. Either still wet or polished, it seemed to gleam.

"You don't use the real skulls," she observed.

"No. Even if there are antlers, they're preserved and screwed onto a plastic skull. Not to brag, but there's a lot of workmanship and even artistry that goes into shaping and carving the underlying forms. A lot of planning and care not to make a mistake. You're only as good as your last carcass, like we say. In sheriff lingo, that's you're only as good as your last case or capture, right, Gabe?"

Hillman sounded as though he was goading Gabe. Or rubbing it in that here he was, running down a stolen, stuffed pit bull instead of tracking lost girls. Or was she reading this all wrong?

"This is a piece of evidence, so I need to keep it for a while," Gabe said, when Hillman reached for it. "If someone's harassing Tess, I need to know who and why. I'll have Jonas stop around and fill out a stolen property form to get it back."

"He owes me for the work on it, and if he doesn't get it back, I bet he won't pay," Hillman said, sounding upset.

"Got you," Gabe said, and started for the door with Tess right behind him.

She was surprised to feel the tension between the two men when she had expected them to get along. Yet Gabe had acted as if it were old home week with Sam. Did he just play different men—suspects—different ways? Since he hadn't asked this man about his alibi for last night, she figured he must consider that new stag carcass proof of where he'd been.

At the door Gabe turned to Hillman. "Next time someone steals your property, report it, will you, John? Otherwise I have to assume you're the last one in possession of it when it turns up where it shouldn't be."

"I just got home this morning from a trip with Sam Jeffers and Dane Thompson," the taxidermist said.

"And that's when you saw this pit bull was gone?"

"No, it was gone a few days before, but the fact that I was on the overnight trip was why I didn't report it earlier. You got some agenda besides this dead dog, Sheriff? Like maybe kidnap victim number one here?" he said with a glance at Tess.

"When a kidnap case has never been solved, you trace any trail, whether one with a hound dog on it or a stuffed pit bull. I'll keep this until I talk to Jonas and then you two can work out the payment for the dog."

Hillman said something Tess didn't catch and closed the door pretty loud and fast behind them.

"Sorry that got kind of tense," Gabe said as he put the dog in the back of the cruiser again and they got in. "I needed to rattle a couple of cages, flush someone out by making myself the target, not you. Jonas may have taken his dog back without paying so that he could scare you off. If so, maybe it's because he thinks I'm more interested in you than Ann."

"As they see it, Ann's in love with you and the three of them are her protectors."

"Yeah. They aren't the brightest guys around here, but I don't want them bothering you or screwing things up. I almost hope one of the three musketeers put it there to get you away from here, instead of the kidnapper—yet I don't want to use you for bait."

"At least the Simons brothers are too young to have had anything to do with my abduction," Tess said as she fastened her seat belt. "Besides, I'm not to blame if they see you stepping away from Ann, because it's not that way between you and me."

"No?" Gabe said. It was not so much a question, more a challenge.

Gabe backed the cruiser out and headed

toward the road. He was frowning, but she was getting used to his moods now. She figured he wasn't angry but worried. Maybe just thinking. As she was. About them, but she couldn't face talking about that now. Until things were settled, a relationship was impossible. Even if the case was solved, the abductor found, it was still impossible. She just wanted to head home to Michigan.

Desperate for a change of subject when he kept shooting sharp looks at her that she felt clear down in the pit of her belly, she spoke. "Don't you think John Hillman is too young to have been involved in my abduction?"

"He's deceptive in more ways than one. I swear he's financing the floating dogfight ring the Simons boys run in the hills. I'd have found it by now if they didn't have someone with brains behind it, who keeps moving its location. Hillman's over fifty, just doesn't look his age, like he's been preserving his own skin and shape. He was a drinking buddy of your dad's way back when. He was such a ladies' man you wouldn't believe it."

"Hillman, you mean, not my father?"

"Yeah, right."

"But Hillman's being a ladies' man doesn't tie into kidnapping young girls, does it?"

"Nope. It's just that I don't trust him—or Sam, or Dane—and it really ticks me off I can't nail them on anything. I'm going to drop you at home, look around the place again before I leave you to head on over to Dane's. Later this afternoon, I'm heading to Chillicothe to call on Dane's lady-friend vet. I won't even fight you and Vic about not taking you. Her place is near the railroad tracks, and you have some memory of that, so I'll let you look around while I talk to her, see if her house jogs any memories. Then I'll drop you off at a restaurant or someplace safe while I do another interview I don't want you involved in. Deal?"

"Yes. Anything to help. And I feel safest when I'm with you."

He looked at her. Their gazes locked for a moment until he turned back to the road again. He started to say something, then evidently changed him mind as they passed Dane's house and headed for hers.

Tess glanced in the rearview mirror at the pet cemetery, but her gaze caught the snarling expression of the dead pit bull on the backseat as if it were chasing them.

Gabe didn't like leaving Tess alone, even in broad daylight, but after dropping her off and looking around her house inside and out, he drove alone to Dane's. After he parked, he had to wait for him to finish with a client. Jim Cargrove, the town banker, had brought in his new Great Dane pup to be neutered.

"Best breed around, Great Danes," Dane said, making a lame joke when he saw Gabe sitting in his waiting room after Jim had left. But Dane's eyes widened and his head jerked when he saw the stuffed pit bull in the next seat.

"Got a few minutes?" Gabe asked.

"A few. Busy day. My office is just down the hall where—"

"Mind if I just step in here with you instead?" Gabe asked and, without permission, the dog under his arm, entered an examining room. He quickly scanned the open shelves, but most were hidden behind cabinet doors.

"Just curious, Dane. When you knock a dog out for something like neutering, what do you use? Just straight ether or something else?"

"Things are a little more sophisticated than that today. Ether use began in the Victorian age. A variety of anesthetics are available now for animals, and certainly for people."

"I had a friend who just had a colonoscopy, and they gave him Versed, some kind of amnesiac. I guess with animals you wouldn't use something like that."

"Hardly. It was probably a sophisticated cocktail of drugs your friend had, and Versed was a part of it. We don't need or use such drugs for animals, only painkillers, not ones that kill the memory. So, where is this going?"

"Obviously nowhere," Gabe said, noting that Dane showed no particular reaction to the mention of an amnesia drug. "I actually came today to tell you someone's been harassing Tess Lockwood by putting one of John Hillman's taxidermy dogs on her back porch. It belonged to Jonas Simons. I just wondered if you ever treated this dog."

"The Simons boys—all three of them—don't get their dogs treated, neutered, nothing, though I have sewn up a couple of wounds from fights they had with coons."

"Or fights with each other?"

Dane shrugged and looked away. He started to straighten items on his counter, dropping scissors into some sort of sterile bath, his rubber gloves into a waste bin he opened with a foot pedal. He let the bin slam closed.

"I don't know about the dogs fighting each other," Dane said, obviously trying to keep his temper in check. That's the way Gabe liked it: let them get riled.

"But," Dane went on, gesturing more

broadly as if that would convince him, "I did not harass Tess Lockwood by putting a mounted pit bull on her back porch, if that's what you're implying. Sheriff, are you still on a mission to pull me into her case, or any of the others? You know I had an alibi from when Teresa Lockwood was taken, so give it up."

"I know both you and Dr. Linda Stevens said you were going to see her and that you arrived, visited awhile and headed back. A single witness, a friend or more than a friend."

"Just leave her out of this! And Marva said you went to see her at the spa. Make a case, Sheriff, or get out of my life. Unless you have a search warrant, and want to go looking for lost little girls in these drawers or cupboards, get out of my examining room!"

"Thanks for your cooperation, Dane. I'll be seeing you," he said, and walked out.

After Gabe called Tess to tell her to be ready in half an hour, he walked into the police station with the pit bull in his arms.

He put the dog down on Ann's desk.

"You tagged this and entered it in evidence," he said, "but forgot to tell me who owned it."

Her cheeks colored. She didn't meet his eyes, staring at her computer screen as if she'd read her next words there.

"If you mean it might belong to my brother, I wasn't sure. Lots of people have pit bulls."

"Recently dead ones mounted by a local taxidermist? I hear his name was Sikkem."

"I thought it might be, but I wasn't sure. You don't hire me to solve cases. You didn't ask. You haven't asked me anything of importance lately."

He ignored that barb. All he needed was her brothers tampering with Tess's confidence, complicating his investigation by leaving terror presents on her back porch.

"Are we adversaries now, when I need my entire staff to pull together at this time—all times, Ann?"

"I don't want to be your enemy. You're the one backing off, getting confused, getting too close to a witness and victim."

"She's helping me. I have to be able to trust you."

Ann started to say something else but shut her mouth and bit her lower lip.

Keeping his voice calm, Gabe gave her instructions. "Please phone Jonas and tell him I'd like him to stop by my office before work tomorrow morning. Ann," he added, putting his hand around her wrist as she started to write that down as if she would not remember it, "I'd like for us to be friends."

"Strange how that word can hurt—**friends.** And please take that dog off my desk. I hate dogs. I've always hated their dogs."

"It must have been painful to watch your brothers pit their dogs against each other."

"I don't know what you mean. And if I did ever see a dogfight, it wasn't as bad as when people fight."

He picked up the dog. "Tell Jonas he still owes John Hillman for his work, but, if he wants it, he has to pick up the dog here."

Gabe ignored whatever Ann was muttering as he walked back to his office with the dead dog in his arms. He felt he was getting nowhere fast, but at least he hadn't turned up any human bodies—yet.

16

On the highway to Chillicothe, Tess started to realize what else it meant to be a law enforcement officer, besides being on call all the time. Cars slowed down when they saw Gabe's vehicle, though they were going the speed limit. Even huge semis moved out of their way, as if Gabe had the siren and light bar on. It was a strange kind of power she'd never experienced, though she was familiar with the feeling that people were looking at her. Yet everything about being with this man seemed new and amazing. Since she felt safe bouncing her deepest fears off him, she'd decided to share something else she was agonizing over.

"Gabe, I found something disturbing in one of the books Miss Etta loaned me. It's called Stockholm syndrome. It means that sometimes hostages express sympathy and have positive feelings toward their captors. They're so grateful to be fed and kept alive that they come to need and like—even love—their abductors. Is that insane or what?"

"Sounds crazy, but it happens. Do you think it figures in what happened to you?"

"I'm not sure, but it makes me wonder if that could be a reason I can't remember things. Could there be someone I think well of now who took me and hurt me years ago? I like almost everyone in Cold Creek except Dane and Bright Star Monson—which I realize doesn't narrow suspects down one bit for you. And," she added, eager not to dwell on the subject, "I meant to tell you I called my sister Char out in New Mexico and asked her if Mom and Dad ever used the word **smacking** when they punished us. She'd never heard it and had no memory of a scarecrow either. She about had a fit when I admitted I'd been thinking of calling our father."

"I'm sure your mother and sisters were hurt by his desertion. As the youngest, you maybe don't remember too much about it."

"We were all devastated. I remember that. He must have been really upset or bitter about something to leave. I know he partly blamed Mom for not keeping me with her the day I was taken, but Kate and Char hinted it was more. I know all the jokes about traveling salesmen, but I never heard he had someone else. He met the woman he married out west after he moved there."

"Yeah. Well, it might be rough to talk to him after all this time. You might want to put it off."

She pulled her seat belt out a bit and turned toward him. "Gabe, he was never under suspicion for taking me himself to get back at my mother for something, right?"

Gabe looked as if she'd hit him. His eyes widened, his nostrils flared. He didn't look at her but kept his eyes on the road. "Vic Reingold and my father considered it. But they decided no."

"He had an alibi?"

"There were rumors he'd been out of town, but he'd gone for a walk near the falls. He took off work that day and wasn't traveling. He told Vic, who interviewed him, he had some tough things to decide about his marriage. The parents are always looked at immediately in abuse or kidnap cases, but Vic believed him."

"Your father did too?"

"Yeah."

An awkward silence stretched between them. She thought he was going to say something more, but he didn't, so she continued, "Anyway, it was great to talk to Char. She's always good at calming me down. It's the social worker in her. Kate says she's a bleeding heart. Kate's a lot more ticked off that Mom left the house to me alone, but they're both still supportive in their way."

"There are advantages and dis-advantages to being an only child, like me. The youngest kid, the middle kid, the oldest and in between can all have problems, but when you're the only kid, it's all on you. You're the firstborn, but you're always the baby too."

"You and your mother must miss each other."

"We're getting close now," he said, as if he'd had enough family talk. He turned the cruiser onto the ramp to downtown Chillicothe. "Let's go over this again. I'll drive past Dr. Stevens's house, then her vet clinic. They're not in the same area. The clinic's off Bridge Street near the hospital. Just take a good look at both places to see if anything prompts a memory. Behind her vet clinic, near the train tracks, she had an extension built out the back that's evidently not used. It's something my dad discovered and I've checked on periodically since. I'll interview her while you look around, and if you see anything at all suspicious, just meet me back where I drop you off, and we'll check it out together. Tess, are you okay? Got that?"

"I hear you. Agreed. It's all a long shot, isn't it? You have to just keep unraveling threads and hope that something really frays or tears loose."

"That's a sad way to look at police work, but I guess, at least in the case of the Cold Creek kidnapper, that's right."

She reached over to squeeze his shoulder. He covered her hand with his. At that smallest touch, her heart soared.

"This is certainly a surprise and, quite frankly, not a welcome one," Dr. Linda Stevens told Gabe as she sat across her desk from him. "I was barely beginning my practice here when your father came calling with cloaked innuendoes that I might have something to do with a kidnapped child when I only had contact with Dane Thompson for business."

The vet going on the offensive reminded Gabe of Dane's attitude earlier. He felt deflated that Tess had not recognized this woman's house or clinic from their drive-by, but he wasn't giving up on this interview. He kept thinking his only chance without a solid lead was to rattle each possible suspect's cage. It bothered him when there were so many caged animals nearby. He could hear the muted cries of dogs and cats, even with the office door closed. But he'd give about anything to hear a young girl's cries from her place of imprisonment, so he could rescue her.

"Each time there's another abduction," he told her, "we need to go back over all former evidence. These crimes may well be linked."

"But I gave no evidence, per se. I merely gave a deposition that Dane Thompson visited me the day of that first abduction for which he was wrongly suspected."

The woman lit a cigarette then inhaled deeply. It surprised him, but then he knew all kinds of doctors smoked. He took it that she was nervous enough to light up in front of him without asking if he'd mind.

Linda Stevens was a good-looking woman in an icy way. Her blond hair was pulled away from her face into a twist. A face he'd call classic or aristocratic with high cheekbones and arched eyebrows. He could see why it was his father's theory that Dane Thompson was interested in her for more than business reasons.

"So, what can I do to get rid of you?"

she asked, tapping nonexistent ash from the end of her newly lit cigarette into a cut-glass ashtray.

"Make my day. Admit you covered for Dane by giving him a false alibi that he wasn't in Cold Creek when Teresa Lockwood was abducted. You certainly won't be prosecuted for misleading statements to my father from twenty years ago, whereas withholding information now that would be useful—that could be a different story."

"All right, so I was seeing Dane socially at that time and didn't want people to think I was dating a possible kidnapper."

"I believe that much."

"But I don't think he was—a kidnapper."

"I should tell you, however, that all kinds of law enforcement, even media, may be swooping in here with our new emphasis on the investigation. And one way to stop that is to level with me about the drugs you and Dane use to sedate animals."

"What? Now, wasn't that a non sequitur!"

He hoped she'd be upset enough to go for his bait-and-switch tactic. Maybe she'd want to get him off the topic of her earlier lies in her deposition and instead give him info about sedation drugs available to vets. He saw her quick mind follow exactly what he'd implied. She stubbed out her barely smoked cigarette with such vehemence that her long fingernails went **rat-a-tat** against the ashtray.

"Drugs?" she said. "Ask him. Besides, all vets use sedation drugs. And yes, some are the same or similar to what would be used by doctors of Homo sapiens, if that's where this is going."

"A drug like Versed, for example?"

"You mean midazolam? That's for humans. It's an amnestic. With a dog or cat, unlike with a person, it isn't necessary to suppress memories of a medical procedure. We use pain or knockout meds for animals. However, I will say one other thing, if you keep it off the record." She hesitated, frowning.

He shifted slightly forward in his chair. "So far, this is all off the record."

"Dane, at that time, not now, was my source for drugs. Vet drugs, not recreational drugs or medical drugs for humans like midazolam. He had some source on the East Coast, got them cheap from some clearing house, nothing illegal."

That was intriguing, perhaps useful. But he decided to go for another quick change in topic. "Did he phone you to say I might be visiting today?"

She blinked, once, twice. "I don't see him anymore. Haven't for years."

"That's not what I asked. You want me out of here right now, answer the question."

She pushed the ashtray away. Her hand was shaking. He heard a distant train coming closer and thought of Tess. The tracks were barely a block from here. Would that sound trigger a memory that she'd been kept near here, even for a short while? He wanted to be with her in case her memories came back. The problem was, he wanted to be with her more and more.

"Yes," she said, not looking at him. "He phoned earlier to give me a heads-up you might stop by or that Reingold might. Look, Sheriff, I had nothing to do with the first abduction or this latest one of Sandy

Kenton or anything!"

He stood. Maybe that was why Dane was so confrontational. He was afraid Gabe would uncover his drug pipeline, whether for animals—or young girls.

"I see you're keeping up with details of the latest kidnapping," he said. "You know Sandy Kenton's name."

"It's been in the papers for several days, for heaven's sake!"

"Thanks for the information. I'll show myself out. And even though Dane phoned you, I'd advise you not to report this interview to him or take more of his calls, or it will look like current collusion, as well as twenty years ago. I'd advise you to steer clear of him."

He walked away and opened the door, then turned back. She looked as if she was going to cry. He'd probably overstepped, but learning Dane was a drug supplier was important. And that search warrant he was going to apply for would give him the power to comb the man's house and clinic for any trace of amnestic drugs.

17

"You won't like this," Tess told Gabe as he picked her up down the block from the vet clinic. "Despite that train going by—much closer than my memory of it—I looked in the windows of that wing she has built out the back."

"Tess, I told you—"

"I know, I know, but I want to help, and we've got to find those girls. I think it's meant to be a kennel for boarding dogs, but it's empty. Maybe she built it, then decided not to expand that way. Did she say anything to help?"

"She gave me a lead on some drugs Dane might have access to."

Tess rubbed her arms through her jacket until she realized she was trying to soothe the memory of injections she'd once had there. Gabe went on, "It will help me get a search warrant if there's any problem with that. Since the guy's supposedly such an upstanding member of society, the judge may balk. Would you do me a favor while I drive, partner, and look up a drug called Versed or midazolam on your phone, then read me the specs on it?" He spelled it out for her.

"She told you Dane uses that drug?" Tess asked as she leaned down to fish her phone out of her purse.

"Not exactly. It's another of my wild-goose chases, I suppose."

She selected Wikipedia, since it always covered the basics, while they drove through downtown Chillicothe, a city large enough to swallow twenty Cold Creeks. As she read aloud to him, she began to shiver.

"Midazolam is not a pain medication. The main effects are amnesia and patient compliance. Patients lose touch with reality, not knowing where they are or what is really occurring. Patients do not recall pain or a bad experience. Under the drug's influence they can carry on a conversation but will remember nothing once it wears off. It can open the door to abuse!" she went on, her voice getting louder. "Some patients, during a procedure or later, experience a distorted, nightmarish version of actual events and later feel abandonment and panic. Gabe, that's it! That's how I felt! Abandoned. I've felt panic, deep inside for years, especially when I hear or see certain things."

"Calm down. You're okay now, safe with me," he said, gripping her knee with his hand. "It's still a stab in the dark, but maybe one that will find its mark. Dr. Stevens said Dane had easy access to and sold vet drugs, which do not need the property of amnesia, but who knows what else he had access to?"

He put his hand back on the steering wheel, then thumped it with one fist while he spoke. "Tess, as long as I'm here in Chillicothe, I still need to check into something else."

"And this is about someone other than Dane, right?"

"When Mayor Owens talked to you at

the police station, how did he seem to you? Glad to see you? Upset?"

"In a hurry to get me out of town. At first he acted kind of creepy, almost like he wanted to scare me away. Is this something about Reese Owens?"

"He is alleged to have molested a young girl years ago when he was a teenager and the girl was five."

Tess gasped. "And when he started walking toward me in your conference room, I felt so…so oppressed. In danger. But how could he run for public office, even in such a small town?"

"Well, here's the strange part. As far as Vic Reingold can tell, the records for the crime have disappeared, except for one he found that someone had missed expunging. But I need to get corroborating evidence of what happened years ago before I question him on this. I'm heading to the neighborhood where he grew up. I'm going to ask around, see what people recall."

"Well, he did marry the former governor's granddaughter, so that might be why it was erased, not just so he could run for mayor. Friends in high places—at least as high as that hill near Lake Azure with the mayor's beautiful house on it," she said.

"My thoughts exactly."

He pulled onto a side street in an area that had seen better times, where the houses were night and day from the Owens mansion outside Cold Creek. In the distance the big paper mill loomed with its smokestacks stabbing the sky. The yards were small, the buildings close together. No garages, cars parked on the street. A couple of places had Halloween decorations, ghosts or a black cat cutout. A few garbage cans sat on the curb. Near dinnertime, it was almost deserted except for a couple of boys shooting baskets at a bare metal hoop attached to a pole. The moment the boys spotted the police cruiser, they disappeared.

"You weren't going to bring me with you here at first, or even tell me you were checking into Mayor Owens, were you?" she asked.

He was leaning forward over the steering

wheel, reading house numbers as he slowed even more, then parallel parked under a ghost tied to an old tree. It was made of a dirty sheet with a noose around his neck to make its head.

"I didn't want to spook you," Gabe said, "though I hate to put it that way, considering what's hanging over us. It reminds me of the gift shop where Sandy was taken."

He leaned toward her and looked at the dark green house out her side window. "Hard to believe Reese Owens grew up here," he muttered, and turned off the engine. "As much as his wife's a snob, I'm surprised he didn't have someone erase records of this old address too. Sit tight. I'm going to see if anyone's at his boyhood home, ask if there's someone in the neighborhood who's lived here a long time. Lock yourself in."

Tess watched as he went up to the door, rang the bell, then talked to a young woman whose face was obscured behind the torn screen. He came back out to the car, unlocked and opened her door. Arms on the roof of the car, he leaned down toward her.

"Maybe things are finally going our way," he said. "Mrs. Bowes, who lives right across the street, has been here for thirty years. The problem is, this woman says she's a bit of a gossip, so isn't that too bad?"

"I have a feeling I should not go with you," she said.

"Be right back. And I'm not sure it's a good thing you're reading my mind," he said, and winked at her. He closed the door, then motioned that she should lock herself in again.

It was a good thing, she thought, he wasn't reading her mind. No man had ever gotten to her the way he did. His glance, his voice, his touch, made her tingle and tremble and in the most delicious way— even when things were supposed to be strictly business, maybe life-and-death business.

The two-story, gray house had tired-looking lace curtains in the windows, upstairs and down. The narrow sidewalk was sunken and cracked, and the porch boards creaked under Gabe's feet. The two-seat swing on chains was atilt and moving slightly in the breeze as if ghosts sat there.

When he rang the bell, he saw the curtains twitch as someone looked out. He could hear a TV program blaring from inside. A short, elderly lady with some of her white hair on end and some matted down opened the door. The TV got louder. It sounded like some game show with a lot of applause. She must be hard of hearing. Gabe raised his voice.

"Mrs. Bowes, I'm Sheriff McCord from over in Falls County, just checking up on someone who grew up in this neighborhood. I understand you've lived here for years."

"Thirty-five with my husband, Bob, who worked at the paper mill, but he passed. My daughter says I'm getting forgetful, but not about the past, no, sir. Want to come in? I'm watchin' a rerun of **Family Feud,** but I can turn it down."

He didn't want to leave Tess alone, even

locked in a police car. "If you don't mind, I'll just ask you a question or two from here. It concerns the Owens family, and the boy was named Reese."

"Oh, him. Did real well for hisself, married up, he did. He's even a mayor now in some little town down yonder."

Gabe heard applause from the TV in the dim room behind her. It hit him that Reese might resent having to run such a small town, but in a way, he might be hiding out there. If Reese was mayor of a big town, that would bring more media attention, maybe a check of his past, hidden records or not. Maybe that's why he ate too much, taking out his frustrations that way. And maybe Reese took little girls to prove he was clever, or to feed his sick fantasies that had started here in his teens. There were no doubt plenty of places in that huge house on the hill to hide a child. The Owenses were childless. Maybe they wanted a compliant, sweet little girl— several of them.

"Yes, that's the man," Gabe said. "Mrs. Bowes, do you recall anything about Reese

Owens getting in trouble with the law?"

"Well," she said, drawling her words and rolling her eyes. "They tried to cover it up then and after."

"Who did?"

"His family at first. Then I'll bet his wife's people. You know who her granddaddy was, don't you?"

"Yes, I do. What sort of trouble was he in years ago?"

"I'll tell you, young man, but I don't want what I say showin' up in the papers or on TV. My Bob took good money for promisin' to keep quiet 'bout it once, though I was shopping at Kmart that day and never promised a thing. Just don't you go getting poor little Reese in trouble for something bad he did long ago. People change, you know."

"I won't get him in trouble for that. This is about something that happened more recently."

"Well," she said, leaning closer to the screen and glancing past him as if there might be others hovering. "He got hisself accused of lewd acts on a minor, a kindergarten girl lived over on the next block back then, Ginger Pickett. I remember her name, all right. The evidence was iffy, least we thought so. At first we heard he could be sentenced up to two years in juvie prison. Then we heard eighteen months. Then he got nothing for it, but they moved away. And that's the last we heard of him till his marriage—oh, not countin' when a man came here to talk to Bob and the neighbors to keep quiet and handed out good money for it too. We spent it on fixin' up things around the house here. You sure you don't want to come in? I'll turn the sound down."

"I really can't, Mrs. Bowes, but you've been very helpful."

"And what you're askin', I'll bet you couldn't look it up in the old court records, right? I mean, if they're gonna spend good money on the neighbors keeping a tight lip, they prob'ly wiped the record clean."

"Please tell your daughter that I think you are sharp not only about the past but about the present," Gabe said, touching his hand to his hat. She waved and smiled, showing one prominent gold tooth before the door closed behind her and the voices shouting on the TV stopped.

This was a good little field trip, he told himself as he walked toward the cruiser. Although he now had enough information to confront Reese Owens, he was going to target Dane again after all these years, just as his dad had done, but with new evidence. The drug connection was tenuous, what his father would have called "a blind hog finding an acorn." It was sheer, dumb luck. He'd like to believe it was a gift from God, but anyway, he was going to run with it.

As for Reese, if the powerful, political family he'd married into could wipe out court records, who knew what else they could hide? Vic would be pleased they now had two persons of more than interest to pursue.

It was dark when Gabe dropped Tess off at her house, so he went in with her and looked all over, including the attic and basement, before walking around the perimeter of the place, especially the backyard. Tess could tell he was anxious to see Agent Reingold, whom he'd called from the car to set up a meeting at the police station in town.

"I'll be home later," he told her at the back door. "Lock up. Get a good night's sleep, take it easy tomorrow, and I'll see you at the farmers' market on Saturday. Meanwhile, I'm going to serve Dane with the search warrant as soon as I can get my hands on it."

She looked at his strong, big hands on the doorknob. Feeling awkward, wanting to kiss him goodbye, she just nodded and closed the door after his quick exit.

Missing him already, feeling drained, she poured herself a predinner, calm-down glass of wine from the new bottle she'd purchased with some other supplies at the Kwik Shop. She sipped the wine as she walked through the house, checking again to see that the curtains were tightly closed. The glass of Chardonnay went down well, so she poured a second. It had been quite a day, not only turning up information Gabe could use but helping him, being with him for several hours. Even if it was strictly business, she loved just breathing the same air he did.

She grabbed a few crackers and cut some skinny slices of the cheese Gracie had left for her. She figured she needed some food with the wine because it was going to her head. She was starting to feel funny. Not dizzy but floaty, and it was more than infatuation with Gabe. She'd better fix some proper food.

When she bent to look in the small refrigerator to get more food, a wave of dizziness slammed into her. How strange! Even though the refrigerator was fairly empty, it seemed to be full of corn leaves.

She knew something was wrong. Should she call Gabe? No, she'd better call her mother. She must be upstairs. "Mom? Mom!" a woman's voice called nearby. Then she remembered her mother was dead. She'd seen her last alive sitting in a wheelchair in the hospital, waving after Tess had spent the afternoon with her.

Tess staggered against the wall, slid to

the floor. The door to the cornfield was still open, wafting out cold air. She had to hide, had to hide or they'd find her, take her back to the house, smack her with Mr. Mean.

Tess sprawled flat on the floor, moving her hands from her eyes to over her ears. She heard the howl of a train coming closer. A monster roaring. She screamed and cried. She could not breathe. She saw bodies in graves, tear-streaked, muddy faces staring up at her, gesturing with their dirty hands.

"Help us. Find us," they cried.

When the soil covered her face, Tess cried too.

18

Tess heard glass shatter. Shards clattered in the sink and flew across the kitchen floor to where she huddled under the table.

"Tess! Tess, are you all right?"

Dad was home. She'd meant to call him.

A man climbed through the broken window over the sink, stepped right in the sink! He moved the chair by her head, bent down and touched the side of her neck with two fingers. He kicked broken glass away, then gently lifted her out from under the table. It was Gabe. Why did he break her window? She would have let him in.

He sat on a kitchen chair and pulled her into his lap. She clung to him.

"Tess, what happened? Was someone here?"

He'd closed the refrigerator door, but the ceiling light was on. It was bright and hurt her eyes, but she was so glad to see him.

"I've got to get you to the doctor. I'm calling him," he said. He suddenly had a phone and started punching in numbers. She remembered that Gabe—no, it was his father then—had called for the doctor to look her over when she was found. But that wasn't now. She didn't recall anything except nightmares, wasn't sure why she was here on the floor. She must have fallen and hit her head.

He talked into the phone while she cuddled against him. He steadied her with his free arm. "Yeah, no, not poison, Jeff. She's conscious, looking a little better than she did a minute ago. It would take too long to get a squad out here to take her into the Chillicothe E.R. I know it's nearly ten, but can you meet us at your office? Yeah, her pupils are dilated. Keep her alert, right, okay. Listen, we'll need blood and urine samples, because there's an open bottle of wine on the counter, and she might have been drugged by something. Yeah, we'll be there in fifteen minutes. She can't just be drunk."

"I'm not drunk," she protested, but he ignored her as he called Vic and told him to get Mike over to take prints in the kitchen. She was able to concentrate a little better as he spoke. "No, I'll bag the bottle, take it with me, and we'll have the contents checked later. Can't let it out of my sight or someone could get in here before Mike does, try to remove the evidence. I know tox tests take a lot of time, but it's important we know what's in her since we might be dealing with Dane's drugs now."

It's important we know what's in her. The words floated through her brain as he kept talking. Tess thought about what was in her. Sadness and regret. Memories that would not shake loose. Fear because someone had done this to her. And the need and desire for this man was in her. She might have been back here only five days, but had she cared for Gabe for years? Wanted his attention even when she was little? Felt sorry he was blamed when she was taken? But taken where? Would she ever remember who did this to her?

"Okay, Tess, we're going to take another ride in my cruiser," Gabe said. "Talk to me, sweetheart. Stay awake," he insisted, rubbing her hands, one at a time, then lightly slapping her cheeks.

"The sheriff broke into a house," she said suddenly with the urge to giggle. "And now I'm going in his police car, under arrest, under duress...I don't know."

"How much wine did you drink or what else?" he asked, getting them both up, then sitting her in the chair while he found the top for the bottle, put a paper napkin over it and screwed it on. Still touching the bottle only with the napkin, he put it on the table. She didn't want to look at it, only at him.

"I can't exactly remember," she said, slurring her words. "I think I had bad dreams. So, what's new, right?"

"I want you to tell me every one of your dreams."

She felt giddy. "It means a lot when a gentleman caller asks a lady to share her dreams with him."

"Keep talking."

"Gabe, don't leave me!" she cried when he walked out of the room, but he came right back with her jacket and helped her put it on.

"Don't nod off," he ordered when she yawned. "Did you get the door locks changed when you took this place over from Lee and Grace?"

She tried to remember. She felt spaced out. Her thoughts were all gummy. "No," she managed to say, "but Mom changed them all after I was taken and then again after Dad left. I didn't think to do it."

"My fault not to ask earlier. You should have. Who knows who had keys when Lee and Grace were living here, including their dictator Monson? I'll have to ask them."

"If you can get near them. They have guards at Hear Ye." She was pleased her thoughts were clearing, but it almost hurt to think.

"I know. But they'll probably be at the

farmer's market uptown Saturday. Okay, now hang on to me. Upsa-daisy," he said as he lifted her to her feet and steadied her with his hands on her waist.

Upsa-daisy? Why did he say that? She didn't like that. It made her think she was a kid again and...and she did not want to remember that, even though she knew she had to.

"What good will it do to lock the door?" she asked as he made her take steps while he propped her up. He took the bottle along too. Maybe she should give up wine, at least in Cold Creek. Her legs were a little wobbly, but she was walking. "Someone could come in that window," she added as if he didn't get what she meant.

"I'll put police tape over it, and we'll get it fixed—and your locks changed—first thing in the morning. We're going to Dr. Nelson's. Then you'll stay with me again."

That sounded good to her. Though her head was clearing, her thoughts were dark. Whoever had done this wanted to scare and hurt her, maybe even worse than that.

• • •

Tess woke with a jolt. It was light. She saw an unfamiliar ceiling and room. She realized she was under a quilt on Gabe's couch, and he was slumped in a chair he'd pulled up close. She had no shoes on but was dressed in her clothes, which must be a wrinkled mess. She started to remember. She'd been to the doctor last night after...after she'd blacked out and then Gabe came. He wasn't dressed in his uniform now but jeans and a sweatshirt.

"You awake?" he asked the obvious when she looked at him. "It's eight. Friday morning. How do you feel?" His voice was gravelly, and his beard stubble made his face look dirty. His usually police-sharp hair was mussed.

"I feel tired. That train I hear in my head sometimes—I think it hit me." She scooted herself up to a sitting position, pulling the quilt up higher too.

"Dizzy, nauseated? Doc Nelson said you might be."

"Just hungry, I think. Wow, don't buy

cheap wine at the Kwik Shop."

"You giggled and cried last night. Talked in your sleep too. I would have taken notes, but you weren't making any sense."

"Nothing makes sense anymore."

"Can you remember anything after you drank the wine or during the night?"

"No. Maybe it was another amnesia drug. Maybe my kidnapper came calling again," she said with a shiver. "Did you get the search warrant for Dane's place?"

"At least your head's okay on what happened before you got blasted. Not yet. The judge was holding it up until she heard new evidence, but the fact that Dr. Stevens has perjured herself in a deposition means I should get it soon. The judge is obviously reluctant since the warrant my dad, 'the previous Sheriff McCord,' as she puts it, failed to pin anything on Dane when he served him with a search warrant twenty years ago. I told her double jeopardy should not figure in here, since Dane wasn't arraigned or tried before. She took offense since I was lecturing her about a legal matter, but I think she'll get me the warrant. The case is too hot not to."

"And are you going to talk to Reese Owens?"

"Thank God you're all right. We just have to keep drugs and booze out of your system. Stay right there while I fix us some juice and coffee. Oh, yeah, I'll talk to Reese," he said as he stretched his big frame, then went into the kitchen. "He's in Cincinnati until tomorrow morning, and I'm not doing that over the phone."

"I hope I feel better by tomorrow," she said, rubbing both eyes. "I'd like to go to the farmers' market. I want to see my family if they come with the Hear Ye people."

"Let's just see how you do with food and walking on your own today—you need some rest. Doc Nelson thought you might have ingested something like a date rape drug. They're short-term but made worse by being mixed with any kind of alcohol. I'll take you over to your house to pack up some things but you're staying here."

He came back with two huge glasses of

orange juice. A date rape drug? And then she'd spent the night here with him....

Thank God she could trust Gabe. Because there was obviously someone in Cold Creek who'd been watching her, who wanted her out of here one way or another. That terrified her but made her angry enough not to leave until they found Sandy Kenton.

After breakfast, Gabe shaved and changed into his uniform, they picked up some things at her house and he checked everything there again. Nothing else seemed amiss. He called the hardware store to order new locks and a window. He took her back to his house and left, returning for lunch, still stewing he didn't have his search warrant yet.

"You'd think there's someone pulling the strings for Dane, just like for Reese," he groused as he quickly ate the lunch she'd made, before heading back to the office. She felt as if she was married to him—and spending most of the time on her own. He said Vic was going to want to talk to her, but right now he was busy trying to locate a housekeeper who had recently worked for Reese Owens and his wife.

Tess locked up after Gabe left each time. She'd asked his permission to go up to his war room to look it all over again, hoping, as ever, to recall something useful. But she sat up there, studying the walls for an hour, while the wind kicked up and the house creaked. Feeling haunted, not by the house or even what had happened to her yesterday, but by the faces—her own and her family's included—staring at her from the walls, she went back downstairs to wait for him.

He called and said he'd be there in a while, just a little late. It got dark so early now. Though she hadn't heard his car, she jumped up to greet him when she heard him at the back door. She started to open it for him, then hesitated. No footsteps, no key turning in the lock.

When she tried to look out the window in the door, she saw it was blocked by a piece of cardboard or paper. She wondered if Gabe had done that to keep someone from looking in. But no, a crude drawing and printed words faced inward. Done in crayon, it depicted figures of three girls. Big tears dropped from the eyes of the smallest one. It looked so familiar. Suddenly she was certain she had drawn it. Was she hallucinating again? Were more memories coming back?

She read the words under the figures. YOU BAD GIRL! YOU CAN'T HIDE FROM ME!

She heard a voice from the past. She wanted to hide, had to hide! She rushed toward the closet in the hall, opened it to throw herself behind the hanging coats before she realized where she was. She took a deep breath. She was an adult, not a terrified child! She tried to recall more than her terror, but nothing else came, and she collapsed to her knees in tears.

Tess and Gabe stared at the drawing with the note he'd brought inside. "At first, I thought I might be hallucinating again," Tess said. "But I'm okay now, and I'm positive I drew that. I do remember drawing

Kate, Char and me many times, but since I'm crying here—I must have drawn that during my time away or just after."

"So you did drawings like this while you were in captivity?" he asked as they huddled over the paper at the kitchen table. "Your abductor evidently let you draw, gave you crayons and paper."

They had both collapsed in kitchen chairs. He'd scooted his so close to hers that their heads almost touched. She could hear him breathe, feel his deep voice when he spoke.

"Yes, I think so. But this possibly could have been done when I got back home. Mom got me some counseling through the church, and they had me draw what I remembered—which was only this. Me so sad and scared and missing my sisters."

"I didn't know about the counseling. Maybe we can find out who worked with you, contact them for memories. Can you recall anything else connected with this?"

"I sure as heck didn't write that message. Mike's going to have to get prints off this too."

"And I'd bet we're dealing with someone who's too clever to leave prints. Mike found none on the wine bottle but yours."

"And to think I could have seen who it was if I'd just looked outside at the right time!"

"Or if I'd driven in earlier. But it was already dark outside. Tess, don't keep beating yourself up," he said, putting an arm around her shoulders, "because someone else is trying to do it. I'm just grateful you didn't open the door when you thought it was me."

"Whoever it was probably comes out of the cornfield, does his dirty work in your backyard or mine, like he did twenty years ago, then runs back home, maybe with that light I saw moving through the corn the previous night. Can we beg or demand that Aaron Kurtz cut the field early?"

Gabe slumped back in his chair and sighed as his gaze met hers. "You know Aaron Kurtz's visit to the doctor his wife mentioned to us? It wasn't to Jeff Nelson here in town. He went into Columbus to see what the pain in his legs was, and he's flat on his back there for a while with a blood clot."

"So we can't bother him with that right now. Doesn't he have others working for him who could cut the field?"

"Other farmers will step in to help, but we've got this field for at least a week or so. It was planted late anyway, and Aaron's going to need the yield from it. Doc Nelson says he's always been so independent and in good health that he doesn't have much insurance. But listen, now that my place isn't even a safe house anymore, I'll understand if you want to leave town. You're not remembering what we need, and you're obviously in danger. I'll try to sell the house for you so you won't have to pay a middleman. Maybe you should head home—to Michigan—until this is all over," he said, taking her hand. Their grips tightened as their fingers entwined.

"I don't know. I'm scared, but I'm really angry now. You have enough to do without worrying about watching a house you're trying to sell. And who knows if the person who did this is desperate enough to follow me, where I wouldn't have you around. I want to stay at least over the weekend to think it over, go to the farmers' market to see my family, if I can get to them without Bright Star hovering."

"In that case, starting tomorrow, I'm going to ask Vic Reingold to move in here too. He has to drive too far to get here fast anyway. Taking turns, with my deputy's help, we can keep a better eye on you."

"And I still might remember something, even if I need to be jolted, like seeing that drawing. And those words—the 'bad girl' part. I know I was called that and I think it ties to being smacked with that stupid scarecrow."

Standing, then pulling her to her feet, he put both arms around her. She clung to him hard, her arms around his waist, her cheek pressed to his shoulder. Whatever horrors had happened before or were to come, his tenderness, his touch right now, made all that almost worth it.

19

Saturday morning, Gabe followed Tess as she drove into town and parked. He went to check in at the station before he walked down to mingle with the crowd at the farmers' market. Jace Miller was working traffic in the area and making an occasional sweep of the roads farther out, including driving by Dane's house now and then. Vic was moving his things into Gabe's, then coming to the market. In the BCI lab van in the police station parking lot, Mike was checking for fingerprints on the paper that had been taped to Gabe's back door. With all those allies around and in the crowd, Tess almost felt safe.

She was happy that a man from the hardware store had already put in a new kitchen window, changed the locks on her doors and given her the new keys. When

Gabe spoke around here, people jumped.

On Main Street, Tess strolled through the rows of tables and booths. They had sprouted overnight while through traffic was diverted a block away. It was quite a sight with autumn bounty piled high. A mix of townsfolk of all ages, some who must be Lake Azure residents and many outsiders who'd driven in for the market, were strolling and buying. Some ate baked goods or apples right on the spot. It seemed everyone was carrying cups or plastic jugs of cider. People walked their dogs while they shopped. Tess was glad to see that kids young enough to be in strollers were pushed by their parents while preschool and elementary kids were kept within close reach. Even in a crowd like this, children needed to be watched. The bustle almost made her forget how wobbly her legs had been yesterday and how much she had slept. Her thoughts were still a little fuzzy at times.

The earthy sights and smells helped her settle down, that was, until she saw the mayor glad-handing everyone who walked past. He'd plunked himself down on a bench that she did not recall being there before. She saw his wife, Lillian, too. What a mismatch they were. She always looked so put-together and stylish, despite the fact that she'd gained weight over the years. Marian Bell was standing over them, talking and gesturing. Tess wondered if Marian sensed they knew something about her child's disappearance.

Tess walked behind the bench so she wouldn't have to face them and strolled past tables with pyramids of gold and red apples and piles of squash. The Community Church had a small mountain of pumpkins set up for this event. She smiled when she read the sign. All You Can Carry, $2. Globes of red and white onions, brown and reddish potatoes, even braided garlic, smelled of garden-rich loam from being buried in the ground.

She stopped walking. The movement, the buzz of noise around her, seemed to stop. That thought—buried in the ground— almost triggered a memory in her, but it flew just out of reach. She looked around to see if anyone was watching. Blessedly, no. Everything was normal, busy. It felt so good just to be part of the crowd.

She strolled past a booth that offered late-blooming herbs, another with gleaming glass jars identified by handwritten labels: honey, maple syrup, molasses and sorghum. Several booths offered bakery goods, home-baked pies, donuts, cakes and loaves of bread. She bought some eight-grain bread, then couldn't wait to get home to eat it, so she tore off a chunk and started chewing.

She took a wide berth around the next table. Sam Jeffers was selling animal pelts he had spread on a table with a few attached to a Peg-Board with a crudely printed sign showing his prices. She found it hard to believe, but he had buyers too.

Tess studied the man's printing on the sign, but it seemed cruder than that on the stick figure drawing. Still, she walked even faster to get several tables away from him and those pelts.

She saw Dane's sister, Marva, had a

table promoting her tanning salon. It looked as if she was giving out nail files, which Tess could use, but she just wasn't up to talking to Marva. As soon as Gabe got his warrant, she figured Marva's friendship as well as Dane's phony kindness to her would go up in smoke anyway.

To her surprise, Miss Etta had a table with books and magazines spread out on it, though ever so neatly. And she had a huge plastic pump bottle there for browsers—and no doubt, herself—to sanitize their hands.

"Oh, Tess, come over here," she called, gesturing her closer. "This is just another of my endeavors to make learning part of this community, to get others to read. With some of the folks around here, if they so much as read a newspaper or a store coupon, it makes my day, but those little phones and tablets with picture screens are killing all sorts of real books. Now, most of these are discards, but if I give them away in trade for a new library card—" she leaned forward to tap a pile of temporary, paper ones "—maybe it will make a difference in someone's life. By the way," she added, gesturing for Tess to sit in the second chair she had behind the table. "How were those books I loaned you? Help ring any bells?"

"A few. They made me think, if not remember. I can't stop right now though, Miss Etta. I want to find my cousins if they're here with the commune people."

"They are, though I didn't see their children with them. It's all business on Saturdays for them to sell things, but how that group makes ends meet beyond those sales is a puzzle, though I heard a rumor they might sell their land for some sort of oil drilling. Their illustrious ruler," she added with a roll of her eyes, "doesn't like his subjects holding regular jobs."

The wiry woman turned away to extend a magazine with a motorcycle on it toward a couple of teenage boys slouching past. She tapped the sign, Free Reads for a Temp Card, and the boys stepped forward to sign up. Not much Miss Etta didn't think of. It seemed as easy as baiting a hook and fishing.

"You look peaked, Tess. Are you all right?" she asked when the boys drifted off, and the woman quickly pumped gel sanitizer on her hands.

"Just not sleeping like I should yet."

"Yet? I hope you don't mean since the tragedy twenty years ago. Well, you just stop by—or I'll bring the bookmobile past—and you can get a nonfiction book on relaxation techniques. You know, medical research has been proving that everything from weight loss to resistance to illnesses depends on getting a good night's sleep. On the other hand, dependence on something like sleeping pills can create new problems."

Tess made her escape when Miss Etta started to talk to two women about scrapbooking. She passed a man selling handmade birdhouses, and then, at the end of the row of vendors, she saw the Hear Ye people behind a series of oilcloth-covered tables.

Looking for Lee and Gracie, she skimmed over those working. Miss Etta had said they were here, but, with the Hear Ye members all having similar clothing and hairstyles, they seemed to blur together. **So much for American individuality,** Tess thought, although the bounty of their offerings was diverse. Beautifully woven baskets were filled with bittersweet, walnuts or wildflowers. Mesh sacks contained walnuts in the shell and there were glass jars of them already shelled. She looked at painted wooden plaques with sayings on them like **It is more blessed to give than to receive.** Tess wondered if that was a hint that people should give them a tip when they purchased something.

"Looking for Lee and Grace?" a voice behind her said.

She turned. Bright Star Monson seemed to have materialized from the crowd.

"Yes, I am."

"It's their turn to carry sacks of things to people's cars, a kindly gesture, going the extra mile. Now, let's see," he said, smiling as his eyes went over her, and he tapped an index finger against his chin. "If I ordered a plaque made expressly for you, it would say something like **For the Lord has called you like a woman forsaken and grieved in spirit.** And should you continue to feel that way, Tess Lockwood, you will always have a place with your cousins and with all the brothers and sisters of our flock."

She stood mute for a moment. Not only because he'd dared to think she would ever join them but because he'd spoken about a woman forsaken and grieved. Could he read her so well in the little time she'd been near him? Had Lee or Gracie told him much about her?

This man gave her the chills. If Dane Thompson or Reese Owens did not pan out as suspects, Bright Star Monson should be number three on Gabe's list, just for the bad vibe he gave off.

"I'll look for them later," she said, eager to get away from him. "I hope you have a good day selling things."

"Always," he intoned as she turned and walked away. In the crowd, she nearly bumped into Vic Reingold, who took her elbow and steered her along.

"I was keeping an eye on the mayor and him," Vic told her. "I can tell Monson bugs you. Is it because of the here and now, or does he ring any bells?"

"If he does, they're not conscious ones," she said, remembering how Miss Etta had used the same phrase about ringing bells a few minutes ago. "No one really rings my bell, and that's my problem."

"And ours too," he said. "Gabe's around here somewhere—everywhere, actually, he's good at mingling—but I don't think he'd mind if I got you off your feet for a while, after your bad experience Thursday night. How about the English pub while we get something to eat and drink—no booze for you. You, my girl, are on the wine wagon."

She forced a little smile. "All right. I was hoping to talk to my cousins, but it would be just like Bright Star to have hidden them from me. I'm still tired after what happened—being drugged, I mean," she said, wondering if he knew she'd spent that night at Gabe's house.

The man was chewing on a toothpick, which he spit out into a trash can as they walked past the police station toward the pub. If Vic thought he was going to get something out of her, she was hoping to turn the tables on him.

"Of course I'll be at the prayer vigil for Sandy at the church tomorrow night," Gabe told Pastor Snell. "Deputy Miller and I will be glad to provide security too. And my prayer is we'll have Sandy back by then. I've been meaning to ask you something, Pastor."

"Of course. If I can help with anything…"

"Tess Lockwood only recalled recently that after she returned from her kidnap ordeal, her mother got her some sort of counseling through your church. Would you know who spent time with her?"

"If I recall, it was Melanie Parkinson, not a child psychiatrist but she had a psychology background. Unfortunately she moved to Columbus a good time ago when her husband took a job there. I'm afraid I've lost contact with the Parkinsons, but I can inquire if others who knew her still have ties."

"I'd really appreciate that. And as soon as possible."

"I understand time is of the essence, if this ties at all to getting Sandy back— maybe the other girls—the way we were blessed to have Teresa returned. I'll try to locate Melanie as soon as I can and get back to you."

When they parted, Gabe walked through the cars parked in the church lot and spotted Grace and Lee Lockwood. He had no intention of telling them what sort of harassment Tess had suffered lately, but he did want to ask them who might have had keys to her house. As he got closer, he saw they were loading sacks of produce into an SUV for someone who looked like an outsider. He waited a row of cars over until the SUV drove out and Grace and Lee walked back his way.

"Hey," Gabe said, greeting them. "How are things going at the Hear Ye tables today?"

"Great," Grace said with a tentative

smile. She immediately looked toward Lee rather than saying more. She used to be quite a talker, he recalled.

When Lee only nodded and started in about the beautiful autumn weather, Gabe directed the conversation where he wanted it to go. "Listen, I told Tess for safety's sake when she sold the house she'd have to tell the buyers to get all the locks rekeyed. But for now, do either of you still have keys you could give her, or does anyone else have them? She'll need some extras if she decides to use a Realtor so she can get back home to Michigan."

"Oh, dear," Grace said. "If she's having trouble selling, I hope she doesn't leave early. I...I know she feels she hasn't had enough time with us, the children, especially. We probably do have an extra key, just in case she needed me again to clean, or whatever. I know I lost one once, but we had another one made. Lee must still have his."

"I think I threw it away when we left. After all, you gave her your set of keys. As for someone else—don't think so," Lee said.

Gabe sensed he wasn't going to get any further than that with them. And he wasn't sure he believed them. They were edging back toward the market, so he strolled along. He wondered if one of them had been asked to give a key to Monson. If so, they'd protect him at any price—maybe even before worrying about Tess's safety.

"I see Brice Monson's here himself today," Gabe said, still trying to sound conversational. "I never figured someone who chose the name Bright Star would be an early-morning person, unless he's the Hollywood kind of star instead of the night one."

Grace giggled until Lee glared at her. "He's someone who is available at any time if we have questions or need guidance. He prays and watches over us day or night," Lee said.

"But he takes his night walks alone when he prays for us all," Grace put in, and this time Lee nodded.

"Walks down by the creek?" Gabe asked, his mind spinning with possibilities of Monson taking walks at night. The

Lockwood house was only about four miles down the road, fewer with cut-throughs across the fields.

"Oh, I don't know," Lee admitted. "No one goes but him, under the stars, communing with the Great Star whose name he bears. We've got to get back now, Sheriff. Good to see you. Come on over to our tables and buy something."

They scurried off. Gabe leaned against a tree, thinking that if Dane didn't pan out, weirdo Brice "Bright Star" Monson deserved to be in a dead heat with Reese Owens for the next suspect. Tess said she'd heard a young girl scream at the compound, but where could Monson be stashing kidnap victims? Where could anyone be kept hidden in this tight-knit area, even if there were lots of hills and hollers and abandoned buildings? He'd been checking such places over the years, around and around, until he was dizzy with it all. He couldn't even find that damn floating meth lab.

Like a kid who'd been punished for something he didn't do, he kicked the tree, then walked back into the crowd.

As Tess and Vic walked down the busy street toward the pub, she noticed a table she hadn't seen before, maybe because she'd skirted around the mayor. Neither he nor his bench was there now, so had he spirited it and himself away? More likely, he'd hired a couple of guys to move it for him so he could hold court somewhere else in the market. Or maybe the buyers there were so thick she just hadn't seen it. The table she was surprised she hadn't noticed had piles of Halloween costumes, with others hanging from racks. The table also had decorations for sale under a sign that read Creekside Gifts.

"Oh," she said, "I'm surprised the Kentons came."

"They didn't. Friends offered to take care of it for them. Mrs. Kenton's not doing well, and the father, Win, is understandably mad as heck."

"I think that's how my father must have reacted, and at my mother."

"Yeah. I think you're right."

Tess noticed they'd also displayed baseball caps with bills that looked like tombstones. She suddenly imagined herself looking out a window, down at a small cemetery, the stones gray in the day or at dusk....

She must have been looking out a high window, maybe from the attic in Dane's house at the animal graves. And hadn't she had some nightmare about seeing people in open graves, maybe ones crying like in the drawing she'd done? Could Dane have threatened her by saying he'd bury her out there if she didn't behave, didn't stop being a bad girl? Had he terrorized her so that she, amnesia drugs aside, couldn't clearly recall much else?

"Sometimes I think I do remember Dane's house," she told Vic as they passed the police station. "I hope Gabe gets that search warrant soon. But the thing is, since Dane seemed the obvious culprit before, I don't want that to influence my memories. That can happen, you know. A child's memories become warped to fit something not understood. The big, noisy reaping machine turns into a monster, for example. I read about displacement in a book from the library here."

He held the pub door for her and waited until they were seated to answer her. "So the cemetery of your buried—pardon the pun—memory would be of a cemetery much smaller than what Dane Thompson has now, since he's really expanded over the years."

"Yes. Yes, exactly. I picture a smaller one."

"Then maybe we're getting somewhere, the beginning of a breakthrough. But Gabe and I'd better find something in his place like drugs that cause amnesia—or something like Rohypnol or Scopolamine, the so-called date rape drugs. I call them predator drugs, and that's exactly what we're dealing with in these abductions—a predator. Still, I don't think an interrogation and especially a court case can turn on vague, traumatic memories buried this long.

"But listen," he went on, after they'd

ordered Reuben sandwiches and soft drinks, "you haven't phoned your father yet, have you?"

"No, but Reese Owens told me to and gave me Dad's phone number, which I didn't have before. Their connection over the years strikes me as strange. So you're thinking I should call him?"

"Well, yeah, maybe with Gabe or me on the line in case he says something about Reese we can use."

"Or about himself? Vic, his phone number is burning not only a hole in my pocket but a hole in my heart."

"It's hard to forgive someone for desertion on top of unfaithfulness."

"Yes, he was unfaithful to leave us like that."

"I'll bet your mother partly blamed herself."

"For not watching me better that day. He accused her of that."

"He should have blamed himself for being gone so much for their marital troubles. Your dad must have thought your mother or Rod McCord wouldn't find out about the affair between him and the sheriff's wife."

Her stomach cartwheeled. And then all the missing pieces of things Gabe had said—and mostly hadn't said—slammed into place for her. He'd come so close to telling her more than once but had always changed the subject. Her mother had begun to tell her once that there was another reason her dad had left besides Tess's abduction. No doubt it was the elephant in the room her sisters knew about but never explained.

Now Tess understood some things. That her mother had tried to protect her too much. That Vic had assumed she knew about the affair because he felt she should be treated like an adult and not some child to be coddled. But Gabe didn't. He could not be trusted to tell her the truth she needed to know even if it hurt. It was almost as if he'd lied to her. She was going to tell him off and then go it alone. And if it came to it, she'd just sell the property long-distance.

"Vic, I'm sorry to be rude, but I need to

go find Gabe and talk to him right now. I'll cancel my order on the way out."

"Tell him about the memory of looking out at Dane's pet cemetery?"

"Yes. Those little tombstone hats back at the gift shop table..."

She was afraid she wasn't making sense, that he would see the hurt and anger on her face, but maybe she looked like that all the time. Except now she'd been betrayed not by a stranger, not even by her long-gone father, but by Mom, Kate, Char and the man she'd stupidly imagined she loved.

20

Blinking back tears, Tess stormed out of the pub and headed for Gabe's office. As she walked in, Ann looked up and frowned at her. "I wouldn't advise that you bother him."

"So he's here?" Tess demanded. "Alone?"

"Yes, but I'll just have you wait for him and let him know," Ann said, and moved to pick up her desk phone.

"I'm not waiting for him anymore," Tess said.

"Hey, just a minute!" Ann shouted as Tess strode back to Gabe's office. The door was ajar. He was on the phone, arguing with someone.

She pushed the door open just as he hung up. "That judge has dragged her feet too long," he muttered as he looked up at her. "Did you see Grace and Lee and their—"

Tess slammed the door in Ann's face. "Don't blame Vic for this, blame yourself!" she shouted.

"For wh—"

"Oh, it's my fault, of course! For thinking you were treating me like an adult. Vic let slip about our parents' love affair. Your bored, lonely mother, my angry, supersalesman father, right? Right? And you wouldn't tell me, not little Tess, who still can't think things through for herself. If I'm willing to face what happened to me when I was kidnapped, don't you think I can handle a family hardship?"

He put up his hands as if to hold her off, though she stayed on the other side of the desk. She was not getting near this man again, in any way.

"I was honoring your family's wishes," he insisted. "Since they hadn't told you, why should I? You're delicate enough, and I needed to protect—"

"Needed to use me to get what **you** wanted and needed! How can I trust you?

Though I sometimes feel trapped in my past, I'm not a child, Sheriff McCord!"

"That's obvious to me in more ways than one. My eyes—my entire body—are fully aware you are not a child, Tess. I thought protecting you from something that would upset you was the best way to go. And I guess I should have clued in Vic that you didn't know about our parents."

"No, you should have clued **me** in! Before you kissed me at the falls and at your house! Before you made me think you cared about me as more than just an eyewitness who could not remember one stupid thing! But now I'm starting to recall sounds and sights."

"Sights, like what?"

"See, that's all you care about! Like seeing a small graveyard out an attic or upper-level window."

"Dane."

"Probably. And I'm remembering what an idiot I was to think you cared about me."

"Tess," he said, slowly coming around the desk. "It's the wrong time to say this, but I not only need you to help me solve this—your case—but I need you in other wa—"

"No!" she shouted, moving out of his reach. "You need to find Sandy Kenton and Jill Stillwell, Amanda Bell too—so if I think of anything that will help, I'll let you know. Probably through Vic or Deputy Miller. Don't worry about me. I'll stay locked in my house at night until I decide if I'm staying or going from your Cold Creek kingdom!" She yanked open his office door.

Ann stood in the hall. She jumped back, knowing she'd been caught listening. Tess glared at her and walked out into the hall. No way was she going to run like a child.

"Gabe," Ann said. "Jace called, but I told him you were...occupied. He said Dane's driven his van into the Lake Azure area, but he didn't follow him farther since he'd be spotted. And a fax is coming in for you from Judge Wilson's office."

"Thanks. Call Vic for me and get him back here pronto."

Tess slowed to hear what was happening. She knew Gabe probably wanted to chase her, but he wouldn't with his precious search warrant waiting. She hesitated in the empty outer office, tempted for one moment to go back.

"And tell Vic," she heard Gabe call out to Ann, "as soon as Dane gets back on his property, we're going in. I want to shake him up when we serve the warrant and start to take the place apart. Who knows what he'll admit then?"

Tess went outside. She was working on her own now. It was nearly noon, and the farmers' market was winding down. Shoppers were leaving; a few tables were being carried by vendors to their cars.

She went to her car and drove away, thoughts racing. Dane wasn't home and Marva was still at her market booth. Gabe wouldn't be on Dane's property until the vet got back from Lake Azure.

She was going to go there herself on foot, through the cornfield, to take a look at the pet cemetery. It just had to trigger memories. And from now on, she was going to dig up her past not for the sheriff, not for herself, but for those lost girls. And any risk was worth that.

Tess dumped the contents of her purse onto her kitchen table, then took her new house keys and phone out of the pile of items. She put the two items in the child's backpack she'd brought from home, mostly because it reminded her of her students. She'd stenciled SUNSHINE AND SMILES on packs for each of her kids last year.

For the first time, she analyzed the real reason she was so dedicated to her job as a preschool teacher. She realized she'd been trying to recover from her lost, damaged childhood through her students. She needed to protect and comfort them. She desperately wanted to have her own day care center, to make the lives of children better, sweeter, safer.

She went to use the bathroom, threw on her dark windbreaker, pulled a scarf over her head and knotted it. As she slung the little backpack over one shoulder, her phone rang. She dug it out and checked the caller ID. Gabe. She let it go to voice mail.

She had to get this done quickly before Dane returned to his place or Gabe showed up.

She locked the back door and ran across her yard and into the corn. No more room for fear. No more clinging to Gabe or calling Char for counseling or hoping Kate called her again. As she shoved her way through the tall stalks and bumped into the ears, she thought she might phone her father once she calmed down. But how could she ever forgive him for having an affair with Gabe's mother, for daring to blame Mom for not keeping an eternal eye on his "terrific, terrible Teresa," then deserting all of them?

How many people in Cold Creek knew her father had been unfaithful with Mrs. McCord? She realized Miss Etta had alluded to it when Tess had first come back to town, but she hadn't caught on. "Your father was interested in other things," Miss Etta had said with a disapproving tone.

Out of breath, Tess stopped several rows from Dane's property. She was proud of herself for coming right through the field full of anger instead of fear. And she was just where she thought she would emerge, behind the pet cemetery with the east side of his large, old house in view. She stared up at the second floor and attic windows. Had she been held there for the eight months she was gone? Had she gazed out those small attic windows toward the then much smaller graveyard? She realized she would have seen her own house from those windows. Why couldn't she recall gazing out toward home?

She wanted to get closer to the house to see if it triggered any new memories. There were old buildings out behind Marva's abandoned, derelict farmhouse. Could she have been kept there?

Tess crept out of the cornfield and strode through the tombstones. Some of them were small, but most were square or rectangular, nearly the size of those in a human cemetery. But wasn't she picturing narrow, rounded stones? Embedded in these polished marble ones, pictures of dogs, and a few cats, caught her eye. She saw the little QR codes Marva had mentioned. If only there was some way to access stored images from her past.

Many epitaphs were sad, some funny. She was amazed that people had money for these elaborate memorials when so many others—kids especially—were starving or homeless. She paused before heading out into the open again. After looking around carefully, then glancing out onto the road, she ran across the driveway and pressed her back to the house between two windows. She looked back at the graveyard.

Vic was right, of course. It would have been much smaller twenty years ago, the stones not so elaborate or technology-enhanced. She did see a few toward the front, probably early ones, that were more modest. But she experienced no flood of thoughts, no buried fears unearthed. The cemetery triggered no memories.

She decided to check the death dates on the smaller stones to be sure they would have been here twenty years ago. She darted away from the house and into a row of them just as she heard the sound of a vehicle approaching. Dane's van turned into the driveway and parked in front of the vet clinic.

Tess ducked behind a gravestone and huddled there, waiting for him to go inside. When he got out of the van, he was talking on the phone. She heard him say something about a meeting. He carried a satchel with him, probably a vet bag with medical supplies. To her surprise, he didn't go into the clinic or his house but walked into the cemetery just a few rows from her.

She crawled behind another stone and put her back to it, sitting on the ground with her knees up to her chest. Not talking, but with the phone still to his ear, he walked past the spot where he could glance down and see her. Tess scolded herself for wishing Gabe was with her. He said he'd be waiting when Dane returned ready to serve him with the warrant and search his house, so where was he? Not that she wanted him to find her here meddling in his plans.

She wondered if Dane was heading for the cornfield. Could he be meeting someone there? Or what if he had something in his satchel to take through the field and leave in her yard? No, probably not in broad daylight.

She wasn't sure where he was. He could double back and see her. She debated making a run for the cornfield but it was a tall maze in there if she didn't go in the direction toward home.

She knew she should phone Gabe to tell him that Dane was here, but she was done working with Gabe.

She heard Dane speaking again. He sounded upset, but he was far enough away that she couldn't catch his words until he shouted, "No!"

A single bang sounded. Tess jumped so hard she hit her head on the stone she was pressed against.

Tess knew she shouldn't have come here on her own. She wanted to get out of here. Let Gabe and Vic take over. Dane's voice had stopped, so he must have ended the call, but that didn't help her pinpoint where he was. She decided she was going to make a break for it.

She got to her feet carefully and yanked the child's backpack up on her shoulder. Bent over so her head didn't show above the stones, she started toward the field, glancing at each cross row to be sure Dane didn't see her.

She'd made it to the last row of tombstones before the field when something caught her eye. Dane Thompson was sprawled on the ground with no one else in sight. Was it a trick to get her to come closer?

She tiptoed two steps nearer. It looked as though he'd hit his head. She saw blood on the corner of a tombstone. Could that have caused the sound she'd heard?

"Dr. Thompson, are you all right?" she asked from about ten feet away. When there was no response she crept closer.

There was blood on the bottom corner of the stone, but as she looked carefully she saw it was spattered all over it, even in the grass!

Horrified, she moved closer. A gun—some sort of old pistol—was in his outstretched hand. She didn't see his cell phone, but a scarlet-speckled note lay on the slick grass. As she moved around the bloody stone, she saw blood on his neck and shoulders, and half his head was gone.

21

Tess's hands shook so hard she could barely dial Gabe's cell number. After she'd said she was on her own, she needed him. Now. He picked up on the first ring.

"Tess? I tried to call you earlier. You home? Vic and I are almost to Dane's place to serve him w—"

"I came to look at the pet graveyard from his house. I'm here. He—he— I think he killed himself—in the tombstones by the cornfield. Gabe, there's blood everywhere."

"Don't move. We're close."

As tears poured down her cheeks, she heard a siren. Thank God they were nearby.

Although she'd declared her independence from Gabe, she did as he said and stood her ground, though she couldn't bear to wait near Dane's body. She'd disliked and feared him but had never wished for this.

The siren came closer and stopped. Two doors slammed, **bang, bang,** but not as loud as the gunshot. Why didn't she know it was a gunshot?

Gabe's distant voice called out. "Tess!"

"Over here!"

He and Vic came running but went straight to Dane. Vic bent over to look closely but neither man touched him.

"One shot through the forehead," Vic said. "Look at that old weapon. He collect them or something?"

"I don't know," Gabe said, "but we've got the warrant to find out. Suicide? He must have thought we were going to arrest him this time. But who could have told him about the warrant?"

"Stay here. I've got to check his house. Nobody move!" Vic said, then ran toward Dane's house and kicked in the front door. He returned moments later. "No sign of any girls inside, but we need to do a thorough search of the property."

"I've called in help," Gabe said. "See if you can read that note without touching it while I talk to Tess."

"Yeah, Tess," Vic said. "She's got some explaining to do."

Gabe approached Tess, who was frozen in shock. He put his arm around her waist and walked her a few tombstones away from the gruesome scene.

"It was suicide, wasn't it?" she asked them, her voice shaky, as she sat down on the edge of a tombstone.

"Gun's in his hand, but first impressions are never good enough," Vic said. "Got to be sure. The angle of the wound looks unusual for a suicide."

Gabe stooped beside her, his elbows on his bent knees. "Are you okay?" he asked.

"You need to tell Marva," she said.

"I know. But I don't want her to see him this way. I'll notify her, but it should be in person. Tess, tell me everything you saw. Did he see you, confront you?"

"No!" she insisted as he took out a small notepad and pen. "I looked at these tombstones from over by his house, trying to remember if I'd seen that view years ago, but nothing clicked. I saw him drive in, talking to someone on the phone when he got out of his van. He was carrying a satchel, like a medical bag."

"You sure?" Gabe asked. "There's not one near him."

"There isn't?" she said, craning her neck to look past him. Vic was still hovering near the body, but he stood and came closer. "Maybe he dropped it or hid it. But yes, I'm sure. That is, I thought that's what it was, but maybe it was a case for his pistol. The only thing I could pick up from his distant voice was something about meeting someone."

"Now? Later?"

"I don't know. He shouted 'No!' right before I heard the shot, but I didn't realize what the sound was at the time."

Gabe and Vic exchanged looks. They were both furiously making notes. Her stomach went into freefall. Surely they didn't think she had something to do with Dane's death—that she came here to confront him.

Gabe sat beside her on the edge of the tombstone. She wished she could hold Gabe's hand, but when she reached out to him, he didn't touch her. "Just keep calm," he said. "We'll have to test your hands—standard procedure. Go ahead. Anything else you remember?"

She shook her head and blinked back tears she dared not brush away. "That's all. Oh, after the shot, when I didn't hear him anymore, I was going to sneak back into the cornfield to go home. That's when I glanced down a row and saw him slumped. I went closer—blood, his head..." She gasped and started to hyperventilate. "But—about my hands," she said, "I didn't touch him, don't have blood on them."

"We see that," Gabe said. "It's for gunpowder residue."

It was like a punch to the stomach. More standard procedure, but it scared her, until she realized her hands would be clean. But she couldn't bear it if either of these men—especially Gabe—believed she could have killed Dane. Killed anyone.

Vic broke the tense silence. "I managed to read the note without touching it."

"What did it say?" Gabe asked, looking up at Vic.

"I got it exactly." Vic flipped back a page in his notepad. **"Sorry this is late. I know you won't forget, but can you forgive? Dane.** The bottom of the note's trimmed off as if there was something else. Now, who could he be apologizing to?" Vic asked. "Was he hoping someone would forgive him, someone who came here to meet him?"

Tess saw Gabe stiffen at that suggestion, but she wasn't waiting for him to stand up for her. "Not me!" she insisted. "I was angry with Gabe for not telling me about our parents' affair. I decided to come over here on my own, only to see if looking at this cemetery reminded me that I was kept here. Not to settle anything with Dane. I'd overheard Gabe say he wasn't here, so that's why I came."

"If he surprised you and you struggled with him and his gun, it would be self-defense," Vic said.

"Damn it, Vic!" Gabe exploded. "Don't try to put words in her mouth!"

"Sure, fine, but you both need someone who isn't emotionally caught up in this—and each other."

Tess jolted at that. Was it so obvious?

"And," Vic plunged on, "Tess took off from her meeting with me—and evidently you too, Gabe—angry and upset."

"At you two, not at Dane!" Tess countered.

Gabe stood, then helped Tess up, keeping his hand on her elbow. "Mike's got a lot of work to do here. But if he says Tess's hands are clean, we have her statement and she can go home."

"For now," Vic agreed. "I gotta admit, 'Kidnapper Kills Self in Remorse' sounds like a good headline for the papers. But the placement of that head wound tells me someone else shot that gun."

Tess cleared her throat. "Write this down, both of you. If someone shot him, it wasn't me. He did yell 'No!' and probably not at himself."

Vic finally nodded, instead of frowning

at her. "I didn't see any sign of his phone," he said, his voice not so strident. "Unless it's under the body or in his pocket. Tess, you mind if we take a look at what's in your backpack?"

"Be my guest," she said. She turned so she could shrug out of it without touching it. Vic looked through it, shook his head but didn't give it back.

"Maybe he called to say goodbye to his sister," Gabe said. "She tried to talk him out of it, he yelled 'No!' and bang. But you're right about the bullet placement. Male suicides often 'eat' the gun, and if not, shoot the side of their head, not their forehead and at an upward angle. I saw some suicides when I was in Iraq."

Despite the fact that Tess was still angry, her heart went out to him again. "If there's no phone and no sign of the satchel I swear I saw, maybe the meeting with the person on the phone was at the edge of the cornfield. When that person killed Dane, he or she took both items and ran into the field," she said, almost whispering.

"We'll have it searched as well as this

graveyard," Gabe said. "So, who has the motive to point a pistol point-blank at a man's forehead, stare him right in the eye and blow his skull apart? I say, not Tess Lockwood."

"Is his sister shorter than him?" Vic asked. "Tess was here—and if she suddenly remembered he was the kidnapper—she has motive."

"I said I didn't and I don't!" she shouted. "There are other suspects, and I wouldn't do something to keep us from finding the other girls if he's the one who had them stashed somewhere!"

"Maybe Mike will get prints off the gun," Gabe said. "But things like wine bottles and doorknobs have been wiped clean so far. As soon as we get this scene turned over to others, we'll hit the house. We'll have to ask Marva if he was talking to her and if she's seen that antique pistol before."

"Okay," Vic agreed. "After Mike checks Tess's hands, let's get her out of here until we get a formal deposition. The forensics posse will be here soon. I don't figure you for a flight risk, Tess, but we need your word you won't leave the area. Gabe and I have a lot to do, and I don't want to be fighting him on insisting we hold you for further questioning right now."

Tess looked Vic straight in the eye. "As scared as I've been ever since I've been back here, I'm not leaving the area. I'm in this to find out what happened to me twenty years ago, who is trying to scare me away now and more important, to help find those girls."

"I admire your courage, Tess. I just always check every angle." Vic turned toward Gabe. "After Mike dusts the weapon, I'm gonna take it and run it down—type, provenance."

Tess was amazed to realize that, despite Dane's bloody body and the grilling she just experienced, she was feeling stronger.

Vic tilted his head and craned his neck. "Two vehicles just drove in. Mike and your deputy. No, three. A silver car right behind them."

"That's probably Marva," Gabe said. "You brief Mike so he can check Tess's hands, and I'll talk to Marva, tell her she can't go in now because of the warrant. It's best she not see Dane."

"Gabe," Tess said as he started to move away. "Maybe I can help you break it to Marva. She's been good to me lately, friendly when I came back."

"Let's see how she does first," he said as he broke into a run. Vic went to brief Deputy Miller and Mike, who was toting a lot of gear. Tess leaned against the tombstone until Mike approached her. He explained that it was standard procedure to test her hands for residue—in case she'd picked up the gun. He produced what he called adhesive tabs and took samplings of her hands and wrists.

"I'll check these out in the van with my scanning electron microscope," he told her. "But I've got to photograph and deal with the body first."

A scream pierced the air. "No! No! He wouldn't!"

Tess hurried down a row of tombstones toward the driveway. Gabe was talking to Marva, bracing her with both hands on her shoulders. "If he's dead, someone killed him!" she screamed.

Gabe's low, steady voice sounded, followed by more shouting from Marva. "He wouldn't do that, he had lots to live for! Yes, he bought a few old guns lately, Civil War ones, a couple older. No, I didn't talk to him on the phone, haven't since this morning, and he seemed fine."

Marva saw Tess over Gabe's shoulder. Tess stepped forward, hoping to find words of comfort.

"What's she doing here?" Marva screeched, pointing at her. "Dane had nothing to do with her kidnapping, and this latest one's made it worse! All he did was live across the field!"

Startled, Tess stopped walking. Gabe kept his voice low as he spoke to Marva again, but she cried out, "I don't believe her! She's the one who put you up to this— new suspicions, a search warrant. She came here to spy on or accuse Dane, and who knows she didn't kill him?"

It was late afternoon and, exhausted and

frustrated, Gabe and Vic sat silent in Gabe's cruiser. They had searched Dane's house. Mike had run the test to be sure Tess's hands were clear of gunpowder residue before they'd let her go. They were still waiting for the body to be taken to the morgue for an autopsy. They planned to have volunteers search the entire cornfield for Dane's satchel and phone, but nothing had turned up nearby.

Mike had helped with the search of Dane's property; Jace too, after he had run Tess home and the coroner had taken over the crime scene. Gabe had been tempted to send Tess to the police station for safekeeping, but he didn't want her there alone with Ann. Marva's reaction to her had been tense enough, although the woman wasn't responsible for what she said right now. She'd been taken to a friend's house, and Dr. Nelson had sedated her.

And that, Gabe thought, was a good one, because they could probably have just taken a sedation drug from Dane's cache of them hidden in his attic. They'd scoured it and the basement for forensics evidence of Sandy Kenton, coming up with nothing. But they had discovered two key things. They found a lot of drugs, including a few for humans like amnestics and hallucinogens, all neatly labeled. It would take Mike and the BCI lab days to do the tox tests on all of them, maybe match one of them to what was in Tess's system when she drank the wine. They also found that Dane did have a small collection of antique American guns, two rifles and four pistols. When they'd shown the pistol in question to Marva, she hadn't recognized it as Dane's. But they could find no formal paperwork on it or on two of the other pistols, so it was impossible to know how many he'd had.

Gabe glanced in the rearview mirror again. He had it angled so he could watch for the body bag to be placed on a gurney to be wheeled out of the cemetery to the E.R. vehicle. It was starting to rain, perfect weather for this tragedy. Usually he loved the rain because he'd missed it when he was in Iraq, but today it only depressed him more. A handy place to die, a cemetery, Gabe thought. Marva said Dane had wanted to be buried there so it did make sense he'd kill himself there.

But the missing cell phone and satchel meant there had been someone else in the cemetery. It was looking like murder, not suicide, and that would complicate his investigation into the missing girls.

"They're finally done with the body," Gabe said when he saw movement. He and Vic got out to stand by their vehicle as the body bag was loaded, the doors slammed shut on a man's life. The E.R. vehicle pulled past them and drove out.

"Even if his death stops future abductions, we still don't have Sandy or the others back," Gabe stated the obvious as they got back in the car. They pulled out, following the E.R. vehicle at a distance.

"Yeah." Vic sounded as tired and discouraged as he felt. "Gut instinct—you think it was him who took the girls? Maybe in cahoots with someone else, like his sister?"

"You know that old saying, 'Two can

keep a secret if one of them is dead.' Someone would have let something slip over these years. I heard Marva always wanted children, but that's proof of nothing."

"Yeah. And in this case, I don't buy the copycat thing. I'm sorry I told Tess about your mother and her father. Honest, I thought she knew."

"She should have. I should have told her, since they didn't. I just have a thing— an instinct to protect her like I didn't do when she was taken."

"So I noticed. You definitely have a thing for her."

"I get what you're saying, but I'd stake everything that she was telling us the truth. She was furious with me, she runs over to see if Dane's house and graveyard come back to her and is just there at the wrong time."

"No coincidences in police work, remember? You're getting emotionally involved with her, Gabe, and—"

"And that's another reason I'm going to solve this. Hell, Vic, I'm emotionally tied to each of the kidnapped girls, even the ones I never met! You know, when I was assigned to defusing bombs, I had to have someone dress me in state-of-the-art armor every time. Eighty-pound Kevlar bomb suit, helmet with a shield over my face. But I'm feeling vulnerable on this case, terrified the bomb's going to blow in my face—that another girl will go missing or we'll find a body.... And Tess. I care deeply for the woman, and that traumatized, scared little girl still inside her—I've got to get back in her good graces so she can remember more, help herself and help me."

"Look," Vic said, gripping his shoulder hard, "it's gonna be dark soon. Drive me to the station. I'll get my car, go back to Dane's house, work with Mike on the forensics and look for more possible evidence inside. You eat something solid, get a couple of hours' rack time. I know you're gonna see if Tess is all right. Swear to me you'll take care of yourself, or you're gonna lose it—lose objectivity and control."

"Yeah, I hear you, about keeping my

head on straight about Tess too. I promise," Gabe said, grateful for the support. So why didn't he believe he'd keep that promise to Vic?

22

After Jace Miller dropped her off at home, Tess refused to just collapse. In a way that was what she'd been doing for years, either falling apart or hiding. So what if she was upset by Gabe and Vic's interrogation and by Marva's accusation? It was nothing next to what Sandy Kenton, Jill Stillwell, even Amanda Bell, might be going through.

If the kidnapper had been Dane, maybe Marva had helped him. Dane could have given the Greens money to keep them going over the years before Marva's husband died. Maybe money to keep their mouths shut or to house a kidnapped girl. Had Marva been faking her friendliness from the first just to keep an eye on Tess and what she remembered? Tess had been shocked at how quickly the woman had turned on her. But that seemed somehow familiar in the dark depths of her mind—someone who coddled her, then struck out at her.

Tess certainly wasn't leaving the area, as she'd promised Gabe and Vic, but she was going to pursue any memories that could help find the lost girls. One of the library books talked about cascading flashbacks. Once they start to emerge from the buried past, they supposedly couldn't be stopped, like a waterfall.

Since everyone was investigating at Dane's place she decided she was going to look at Marva's old place. If she saw the house, maybe she'd remember it. In case Gabe stopped by, she'd leave him a note explaining where she'd gone. She had agreed to give him an extra key when her locks were all changed, so she put the note on the kitchen counter, where he'd see it right away.

As she drove past the Hear Ye property heading for Marva's place, Tess tried to ignore the fact that it was starting to rain and getting dark. This would not take long.

She was amazed she could hear the muted roar of the Falls waterfall when she rolled down her car window near Marva's. She hadn't realized the sound would carry this far.

Tess pulled off Blackberry Road. The old Green farmhouse sat on a fairly sharp curve in the road. She drove past once. There was a light on in the place! Or was that the reflection of her own headlights on the turn?

The house was supposed to be deserted. She turned around and drove back but saw no lights this time. Surely that hadn't been her imagination. She'd have to go closer to be sure. There was no point getting Gabe or Vic out here on a wild-goose chase. They'd have her head for sure. What if it was kids or someone homeless passing through? She'd just peek in a window, then decide.

So she couldn't be spotted from the road, she parked in a narrow, grassy lane that had been a farmer's tractor entry to a field that was unplanted now. She knew

Miss Etta and her handicapped mother lived a mile or so farther down the road in their historic home, but she couldn't recall ever being out there. Behind the small woodlot between where she stood and the Green acreage stretched a barren, single field where Marva's husband had grown vegetables. He'd done odd jobs in the winter, hunted with Sam Jeffers sometimes, but that was about all she knew. That and the fact that the Greens had never quite made ends meet, so their house and outbuildings were in bad shape. They'd gone derelict after Marva left.

Tess muted her cell phone and got out of the car, carefully locking it, then securing her keys in her backpack. Again, she heard the roar of the falls, but, in a way, it was comforting, like white noise blocking out other sounds. She would take a closer peek at the house, then phone Gabe if anything looked suspicious.

She hiked off the road, going through the woodlot. The tree cover stopped the rain but made it darker. Such a place would have terrified her just days ago, but that had all changed now. She was willing to take risks for the stolen girls. And, despite her own denials, Gabe.

Just as she came to the fringe of woods, she saw a distant light move through the trees along the lot line. The light seemed to be dancing since branches were blowing in the wind. She sucked in a breath and pressed her back to a tree trunk. The light she'd seen when she drove by was not her imagination.

She looked carefully. The light itself was not moving, only the trees. Despite the fact that the rain pattered down when she emerged from cover, she crossed the grassy field and stood on the gravel driveway. The light was closer than she thought.

Darting from tree to tree, she approached the derelict house. The outside had been marred with graffiti. She wasn't sure, but the style looked similar to the graffiti that had defaced the rock wall at the falls. That was only about a mile away. Maybe whoever was inside was putting their handiwork there too or just getting out of the rain.

She stopped by a leafless bush near the front porch. The windows were boarded up. She'd have to go around to the side or the back of the house to try to see in. She looked at the floor of the porch. It would probably creak or cave in if she stepped on it. Even with the steady, muted roar of the falls, she couldn't risk that.

Her heart beat faster and faster. The run-down house looked like a decrepit face with blank eyes and tattoos. She tried to picture how it must have looked years ago. Did it seem familiar? She knew Gabe had checked the place more than once and found nothing. But she knew someone was here and now she could hear voices— up this close, she heard at least one man's and one was high pitched like a girl's.

Her gut instinct was to back off and phone Gabe. But if someone had Sandy, Jill or Amanda here, she wanted to know for sure.

It was bad enough that Tess still wasn't

taking his phone calls, Gabe thought as he pulled into her place. He saw there were no lights on in the house, though the outside safety lights were on. Her car was gone and it was getting dark and raining. Could she have driven to see her family at the Hear Ye compound? It seemed unlikely. Maybe she'd gone over to his house. He'd given her a key.

He drove past the cornfield and into his own driveway. The house was dark. There was no car outside. Vic wasn't even back yet.

What if Tess had decided to head for Michigan? If so, he'd call the State Highway Patrol, have her arrested for disobeying their order to stay in the area. He knew she'd been through a lot, but he'd been impressed at how she'd stood up to Vic's accusations. Gabe knew Vic had agreed to let her go home mostly because of her sticking to her story—and the fact that they both had soft spots for her. He didn't really believe she would take off.

He drove right back out of his driveway, turned on his bar light but not the siren and headed toward town. He auto-dialed Tess again and got her voice mail. He swore and pulled into his parking spot at the station. Vic's car was here; Ann's too.

Inside, he found both of his 911 dispatchers chatting over fast food at the front desk. Maybe Ann just didn't want to go home in the rain. With Dane's death, they'd had a lot to handle, especially with him and Vic out in the field. No doubt, the media mavens had sniffed the news out already.

"Too bad about Dane," Ann said. "Oh, the mayor called about five times and insisted he talk to you ASAP." She handed him a call slip. The neat way she'd cut it off across the bottom made him think of Dane's so-called suicide note. "I guess you left him a message you wanted to see him, but he's really upset about Dane's death. A couple of newspapers and TV stations called, so they may be back in town tomorrow. Agent Reingold's in your office. We've got an extra cheeseburger here if you're hungry."

"Yeah, thanks. I promised Vic I'd eat and

rest. I appreciate both of you working overtime through all this."

In a way he thought he shouldn't take the burger from Ann—take anything from her right now—but he suddenly realized he was starving. He'd last eaten at breakfast, hadn't thought of food when it was all around him at the farmers' market. Ann handed him the wrapped burger; it was still warm. He started to unwrap it and headed to talk to Vic.

"I told Agent Reingold the person in town to see about that antique pistol is the librarian, and not just because she knows everything," Ann said. "Just a couple of months ago, she had a small display in the library that had some of Dane's old pistols and some of hers. Hers, I'll bet, are ones her family owned— pioneer relics. Sometimes I think she's a relic. **Ebook** is a dirty word to her."

"I remember all that stuff about her pioneer family," Peggy said. "Sheriff, did you ever take that field trip to her place when you were in elementary school?"

"I must have missed that day." He took

a big bite of the burger.

"Well, I didn't miss it," Peggy went on. "She talked about her ancestors knowing Daniel Boone or something like that. You know, 'Kilt him a bar when he was only three.'"

"You sure that wasn't Davy Crockett, that Disney show?" Ann said, dipping her French fries in ketchup that reminded him of the crime scene. He quit chewing the burger. Couldn't they cut the chatter? A man had been killed today.

"Okay, thanks again for the food," Gabe said. "I'll talk to Miss Etta about that and get back to the mayor. And before I head home tonight, I'm going to drive out to Blackberry Road to take a look at Marva Green's old place."

Vic had evidently heard their voices and walked in from his lair down the hall. "So far, all I have on the gun is that it's an 1842 lock pistol by Derringer, no less. Made in Philadelphia, curved wooden handle, the whole nine yards—except who owned it and who fired it. Mike's driven back to BCI to use the lab facilities there instead of the ones in the truck, so I'm waiting until tomorrow to go back to Dane's house."

The desk phone rang, and Peggy answered it. Gabe said a silent prayer it was Tess. Peggy handed him the phone.

"Sheriff Gabe McCord here."

He heard a woman's excited voice, though not the one he wanted to hear. It was Marian Bell.

"Sheriff, you were right all along! Thank God—and you—I just got a call from the private detective we hired! He's located Amanda with Peter and the home-wrecker slut he's been living with in South America! I'm going to get a lawyer, and I'm going to get her back, but she's alive! She wasn't kidnapped here like the others!"

"That's great, Marian! Let's get our congressman and the state department involved. You'll need other kinds of help now. Call me if you need assistance from this office."

He was relieved, happy for her, but he still felt the loss of the others pulling him down. After he hung up, Ann and Peggy cheered. Vic even cracked a smile. But

Gabe knew he was the one who needed other kinds of help now. When he was in Iraq, his team had a superstition: if you got a gift when one bomb was a dud, you really had to fear what happened next.

Tess had to go clear around to the back of the old farmhouse in the rain. The side windows on the first floor were too high to look into without climbing on something.

The tall windows made her feel like a small child again. Was this place getting to her in another way—subconscious memories? Fighting that fear, she decided to move her position so she could hear more than a blur of voices muted by the sound of rain and the waterfall.

Her stomach cramped, but she'd come this far and she was going to look in. One peek, assess the situation, catch something said, more than what she'd overheard from Dane. Then she'd back off and phone Gabe, if there was more to report than kids who had to put their thoughts in black spray paint on places they shouldn't.

Under a sagging porch ceiling held up by two crooked pillars, the back door was open! Maybe they wanted fresh air or just hadn't thought to close it. Again, she heard a female voice and maybe more than one man's. There was a sharp, acrid smell drifting out the back door. Holding her breath, she edged closer and peered inside. She saw a kind of mudroom. The kitchen must be down a short hall beyond where the people were. To the right, she saw back stairs that went upward.

The voices were clear now, though she couldn't really follow what was being said—until she heard Gabe's name.

"Far's I'm concerned, McCord might as well be Barney Fife with one bullet in his gun," a man said with a kind of hee-haw laugh. "This whole place is like that old TV show **Mayberry R.F.D.** He's been lookin' for us for years, his daddy too, but we keep movin' the goods."

"Who's your daddy?" another male voice said. "If he ain't the sheriff out chasin' lost little chicks, he ain't nothin' around here."

Tess's stomach cramped. Could these voices belong to the kidnappers? Was that what they were mocking Gabe about? But what were they doing here? And why didn't the girl or woman speak again? Had they gagged her, drugged her? Tess could almost picture that as if it was happening to her.

She edged in the door, sidling toward the staircase in case she had to hide. Then, on the stairs above her, she saw a small circle of light. Maybe there was a window into the kitchen, a vent perhaps.

Holding her breath, she tiptoed up a step, then another. In the kitchen, they were making so much noise they didn't hear the stairs creak, and she had the waterfall and rain to thank for that too. The hole was where a vent must have come out into these narrow back stairs years ago, when there were wood fires in potbellied stoves.

Keeping her face as far back from the opening as she could, she peered into the kitchen. It looked as though they were cooking something on the counter and on a beat-up table. She saw no stove or refrigerator, but of course the appliances had been stripped out years ago. They were using a small generator that was making a low buzzing noise. No doubt the electricity in this place had been turned off when Marva left. These weren't homeless people making dinner somewhere they could find shelter. They'd said Gabe had looked for them for years, and they knew about the kidnappings.

She glimpsed bottles, a big funnel, Pyrex-type dishes and a blender. She gasped. These people were mixing and cooking up meth. It could blow sky-high if something went wrong. A petite but tough-looking woman moved into view. Tess glimpsed two men; she heard a third.

"We oughta go to the one-pot method," the girl said. She had dirty-looking hair pulled straight back in a long ponytail. "You know, shake-and-bake, toss the bottle out of the car when we're done with it."

"Too damn dangerous. You think this stuff can't blow? One wrong shake of the bottle, a little air gets in and fireball." The man clapped his hands together, and Tess jumped.

She had to get out of here. She'd call Gabe, but not about finding kidnappers. She was sure these people didn't have the finesse, the smarts, to pull that off. But this old house, the sound of the falls, even the back stairs, seemed somehow familiar, and she'd have to tell Gabe that.

Holding her breath, she began to creep down the steps to get out the back door. She froze when a phone rang, but it wasn't hers. She'd muted her ring, and that phone played "Dixie." One of the men stepped into the mudroom to take the call, blocking her escape.

"Yo, Jonas. What? She thinks he might be coming here? Now? Okay, we're outta here! Hey," the man shouted to everyone as he went back into the kitchen, "leave it cookin', grab what you can, 'cause we gotta go. Tip from Jonas that the law might be comin'. Chop, chop! Maybe this stuff will blow up in his face. I'm sick of him always being on our tails."

The light source went off. Tess heard

them run like rats off a ship as she huddled in the darkness on the stairs. At least Gabe was on his way. Terrified the stuff would explode, she counted to ten and tore out behind them right into the rough embrace of a big man.

"You want in on the action, honey?" he goaded, grabbing her arm and swinging her around toward him hard. He was the one who had taken the call. "You thinkin' to turn us in?"

"Hank, come now!" the woman shouted, running back toward them. Someone was driving a car out of the old barn. The headlights slashed across them. He held Tess in such a crushing grip her feet dangled off the ground.

"Let's take her with us," he yelled, starting to drag her toward the car. "Who knows what she heard or saw? I saw her shadow on the stairs and figured she'd bail out right behind us. This has been so clean before, and I don't want witnesses."

"No, you're not taking her!" the girl insisted, tugging at his arm.

"She can ID us!"

"Wait! I think I know who she is. That first one got taken by the Cold Creek kidnapper. Remember, Jonas told us about her."

The man swore a string of oaths, then put Tess down and yanked one arm up behind her back. "Yeah, we don't need in on that. Turn off them headlights, and I'll be just a sec. Gimme that flashlight," he shouted, grabbing a large one from the girl and turning it on. He checked Tess's pockets, then ripped her backpack from her and flung it into the darkness. He half shoved, half carried her toward the house. "The place goes up, good riddance to her and the sheriff if he's coming too," he yelled back at the girl.

Tess struggled as the man named Hank forced her back inside. He shoved her to the floor and tied her with rope and netting they must have used to carry their gear in. Her hands were behind her back secured to a table leg with the cooker hissing over her head.

"Hard way to learn a lesson, honey," he said. "Better say your prayers."

He patted her head, got to his feet and ran. Tess heard the car roar past the house, the squeal of brakes as it turned onto the road. Then there was only the sound of the gurgling, steaming stuff on the table over her head, which blended with the muted rush of the distant waterfall.

23

Tess soon gave up struggling to get free. The rope and netting were so tight they cut into her wrists. She was scared to try to kneel under the table, then try to lift it with her shoulder or back to maneuver her ties off the table leg. She might tip it over, make it explode even faster than it would on its own. At least Gabe was coming, but if he did, she couldn't let him be blown to bits too.

She could not believe her life could end with all her dreams and hopes up in flames. She would never know who had abducted her and ruined her life. Still, except for her father, she'd had a good family. No romantic love of her own, at least before Gabe gave her hope. And children—how she wanted children of her own.

Say your prayers, that horrible man had told her when he left. Would she be reunited with her mother in heaven? She wished she had called her father. She thought about Kate and Char. She loved them. She missed and needed them.

She tried sawing her wrist ties up and down against the edge of the table leg, but it would take hours to get free. She kept at it, however exhausted her shoulders and arms were, all the while picturing herself reading to her most recent class of preschoolers at the Sunshine and Smiles Center while they sat cross-legged on the floor and she used a low stool, so she could show them the pictures. Wouldn't Miss Etta have been proud of her for that? Little Cristelle wasn't paying attention, but her twin, Nanette, was. Those girls were as different as Tess, Kate and Char. Jacob and Ashley were really into the story of the pioneer boy's life.

She was about to lose her life. Her mind almost went blank with fear, but she forced herself to remember happier times. Her little redheaded student Jacob's name reminded her of hearing Jonas's name in this room. Ann's brother? Was he the one tipping off drug-cooking criminals that Gabe was coming? If so, was Ann his source of information? Would Gabe ever know what had happened to her? She should have told him that she cared deeply for him.

Tess was angry with herself for getting caught. The cooker over her head was rattling so fast and hard that it might explode at any time and her life too, just another girl gone.

Since it was dark, Gabe decided he could park fairly close to Marva's old place. He drove slowly looking for a spot to pull in. If Sandy Kenton was being held there—though he'd checked it before—he intended to surveil it from the outside before checking the interior.

Tomorrow was going to be a busy day, including questioning Marva again. Dane had lawyered up fast both when Gabe's father suspected him and again recently. Marva might too, but not, he hoped, before he saw her again. Even if she and Dane had nothing to do with the Cold Creek kidnappings, Marva, who had been poor so long, was sitting pretty for the rest of her life if she was Dane's heir. So Gabe knew he had to look into the possibility that she'd left the farmers' market, hidden in the cornfield to kill her brother, then come home later, faked surprise and shock—and tried to blame Tess.

He was also planning to catch Reese Owens when he came out of church around noon. At least the mayor wanted to talk to him too. Then Gabe planned to be at the evening church service, the candlelight vigil and procession to the gift shop, where Sandy Kenton had been abducted. As for today, Tess sure as heck better be home or at his place when he got back, because all he needed was to have to go check on her with her cousins at that weird Hear Ye compound after dark. He trusted Bright Star Monson about as much as he did a Taliban terrorist.

He parked on the near side of a woodlot not far from the driveway. The old Green house and outbuildings looked dark and deserted. Though he'd check them out now, he'd come back with Vic and Mike with a search warrant later—if he could pry another one from the judge. Before he got out of his vehicle, he muted the volume on his portable radio and drew his semiautomatic pistol. He pulled his flashlight from his duty belt but didn't turn it on.

He hiked across the driveway at a good pace until he heard the other equipment in his duty belt bounce. No need to make noise, even if the hushed sound of the waterfall covered some of it. He slowed to a walk.

The front windows were still boarded up with cheap plywood. No wonder this place hadn't sold. He'd buy Tess's house over this any day. The Green property did have more acreage than hers, though.

At the side of the house, he bent down and played his light through a broken basement window. Nothing much, except some chemical smell. Cleaning fluid? Maybe Marva had scrubbed the basement before she left. Mixing some toxic cleaning fluids gave off an acrid smell and could even cause a minor explosion. He knew Mrs. Taylor in town had gotten badly burned that way. But this reminded him of the stink of a deserted meth lab, like the ones he'd always come across too late to catch the cookers. At that thought, he walked even more quietly and carefully.

Around the back of the house, he slowed his steps. Would he ever get over the fear he'd felt before going into a small shop in a market or an Iraqi house, searching for a bomb?

He stepped up onto the small porch. The back door stood ajar. The smell grew stronger. He knew it was chemicals. He heard a strange sound, then a grunt or sob. Could someone still be inside?

He jumped away from the door to take cover, and his foot went through a board with a sharp crack. He sat down hard. His flashlight went spinning away, landing somewhere off the porch. Still holding his gun in one hand aimed toward the open door, he swore under his breath and tried to pull his foot back out. The broken boards scraped his shin. He pulled his leg free, scraping it more. When he stood, pain shot through his ankle. Throwing himself flat against the outside wall next to the door, he shouted, "Police! Don't move!"

"Gabe?" came a shaky female voice within. "It's Tess."

"Tess? What the h—"

"Get away! Don't come in. I'm alone. There's a meth lab here. The stuff is bubbling pretty hard, and I think it's going to explode!"

"Get out here!"

"They tied me up when they ran!"

In the dark, he stumbled through the door, into a small room, down a hall, feeling his way, following her voice.

"I lost my flashlight!" he said. "Where are you?"

"Gabe, go!"

"Not without you!"

But as he careened into the darkness, through an acrid stench that burned his eyes, he had a flashback. He thought he'd gotten over those long ago. Having to search a dark place at night, disrupt the bomb, feel the heat of the desert, feel the hate of whoever left the IED. He could see the detonation cord and the electrical wires within, the foam casing, the steel frags of ball bearings, nuts, bolts and nails all around it, meant to puncture body armor. Where were his armored gloves? He had bare hands, holding his pistol that would do him no good now, so he shoved it back in its holster.

"Gabe!" Tess cried, cutting through his waking nightmare. "This cooker they use—it could explode. They've been gone awhile. I'm tied here. You should go. I...I really care for you—love you. Please go."

He fell to his knees beside her, wanting to hold her but not having time.

"Gabe, please—"

"Shut up, Tess. Damn, you're trouble, but not more than you're worth! Where are you tied? Help me, tell me."

"Hands behind my back. Tied to a table leg with rope and some kind of netting. But there's a cooker on the table above my head, and one on the counter too."

He ran his hands down her shoulders to her wrists. His gut instinct was to tip the table away to free her and run, but disturbing the stuff could make it blow. He fought not to recall the earsplitting **BANG!** and fireball that had once tossed him like a toy soldier. And the one that had blown his team to bits.

He groped for his utility knife in his duty belt, slid it by feel between her wrist and the cords. "Pull your wrists toward me to give me room," he told her. He shoved the knife, sawed. She gasped once.

"Your legs tied?"

"No, just there—ah!"

He wasn't sure if he'd cut her, but she was free. He yanked her to her feet and dragged her down the little hall toward the door. His shin and ankle felt as if they were on fire. He lunged over the porch and pulled her with him. They hit the ground, rolled on the grass. He pulled her to her feet and, staggering like drunks, they ran into the darkness.

• • •

Tess knew her left wrist was cut, but she didn't care. As they limped along past a small, ramshackle back building, she gasped, "That's where they hid their car—one woman and three men."

"Can you ID them?"

"Two of them—a young woman and the guy who tied me up. His name is Hank. But they said someone named Jonas tipped them off that 'the law' was coming, and that's why they took off. I ran too, and Hank caught me—threw my backpack with my phone and car keys over there somewhere."

He swore under his breath. They finally stopped at the edge of the open field and sucked in breaths of damp air while the light rain seemed to wash them. They sank to the ground, holding tight, her sitting with her back to his chest between his spread legs. His trouser leg was torn. He tore her scarf in half. She wrapped his bloody ankle, then he tied the rest around her wrist.

"The walking wounded," he said, giving her a hug. "Tess, some good news in all this. Marian Bell's daughter's been found living with her father in South America."

"Oh, that's great! You were right about her! I'm sure Marian's ecstatic, even if she doesn't exactly have her child back."

"And that might be another battle," he admitted as he took out his cell phone.

Still shaking, Tess caught her breath while he called his deputy and told him to stop entry traffic on both ends of Blackberry Road, except for the fire trucks, and to tell people there could be a gas explosion in the deserted Green house.

"No," she heard Gabe tell Jace. "We're both all right and can walk out to our cars when the fire guys get here." He put his phone away. "If the meth lab doesn't blow, I'll need a BCI tox crew in the morning to clean it up, get evidence, so I'll call Vic," he said. "And that's bad news about the call from Jonas, if it's Ann's brother, because she'd be his source. As for you, coming here like this..."

"Don't start."

"I'm going to start, because it could have finished you. But maybe it was worth it to hear your confession of how you feel about me. It was probably only the fact that I have the same feelings that made me crazy enough to try to save you."

"You do? I thought maybe it was just that you need me."

"I do need you, and not just the way you're thinking."

"For getting me out of there—I'll never be able to thank you enough."

"When this mess is over, we'll find a way," he said.

"Maybe my so-called confession of love was just in the heat of the moment."

"Maybe there's heat in every moment we're together," he muttered, and turned her in his arms to hold her sideways across his lap. He tipped her head back and kissed her hard.

She threw her good wrist up around his neck and held his lips to hers. His mouth opened, moved against hers. His beard stubble rasped her chin and cheeks, but it felt so good. Her back balanced against his good leg, she held to him, breathing to match his ragged breaths, kissing him back. His hand gripped her waist, slid up her rib cage to cup and finger a breast, then dropped to squeeze her thigh through her jeans. She leaned into him, her wrapped hand grasping his back. It was the most beautiful, stunning thing that had ever happened to her, as if the entire world was on fire...golden lights...the noise in her head and heart pounding...

It took Tess a moment to realize the meth lab had blown.

They sat up, clinging to each other as orange-red flames belched into the air and heated their faces. They blinked and ducked in the sudden brightness, before Gabe pulled her down, flat in the cold soil of the field, and covered her with his body. But they were far enough away. The ground shuddered with a second blast.

Finally, when the explosions stopped, they watched the old house burn. He spoke loudly to make sure she could hear. "I'm cursed when it comes to preserving evidence. I came looking for a kidnap site and got this."

"There's no way this can tie to the kidnappings. Those people weren't smart enough to pull those off, I can tell you."

"Except there's the drug connection. I'd still bet on Dane for drugging his kidnap victims. Still, I suppose you could have had meth or some version of it in your wine to cause your hallucinations. And I never could figure how I kept missing the cookers by just a couple of minutes when I'd go to check a place. At least now I've got Jonas and Ann to interrogate, and they may give up names."

"Could Ann have tipped off Dane that you had your search warrant and were heading for his place, so he panicked and killed himself?"

"Everything's up for grabs. But panicked over what, since we found nothing in his house or the vet buildings? Ann volunteered to come in tomorrow even though it's Sunday, because so many people will be in town for the evening church service, candlelight vigil and march to the gift shop. I'll decide what to do about her then.

"Tess," he went on as they watched the flames dance and crackle, "I'm sorry if it puts you in danger again, this time with the Simons clan if they find out you're my witness. I swear, I'm gonna have to lock you up. I'd chain you to my bed, except I'm seldom in it."

He held her tight as they finally heard the distant sounds of the volunteer-manned fire engine. They sat, arms around each other, as if they were watching a big bonfire on an autumn night. Even when the rain got heavier, it didn't seem to calm the blaze. The old wood fed the fire like a giant torch in the damp, black night. But by that light, Tess saw something that convinced her even more that this could have been the house where she was kept prisoner.

In the flicker of the flames, off to the side, she glimpsed something she had not noticed in the dark.

"Look at those!" she cried, turning and pointing.

To her surprise, Gabe drew his gun. "I

don't see anything. Only old white man-made beehives. I think George Green once sold honey."

"But to a child—me—upstairs, they must have looked like tombstones! And I remember those back stairs I was hiding on tonight, I'm sure I do! This must have been the place. You can hear the waterfall from here, and there's a train track a couple of miles over, though I didn't hear one tonight."

"It's enough to give me more reasons to question Marva. Whether it was Dane or her husband behind it, she would know—"

"But what if it was Marva herself? Maybe she wanted children around. But then where would Sandy be held right now?" She shuddered and glanced at the burning house again. "I pray she wasn't upstairs.... Surely not in that tanning salon. The girls are still missing and so is a piece of the puzzle."

"Like I said, I'll start with Marva. And if Ann's been tipping off her brother, who then phones the meth cookers, maybe she's also been telling Jonas where I've been looking for his dogfight spots for years so he can stay one step ahead of me. What an idiot I've been with her. I may have to charge her as an accessory to these crimes—if I can nail Jonas. I hate to fire her, just when I need someone on the desk during the day. Want a temporary job?" he asked, giving her a little squeeze. "Peggy Barfield, the night dispatcher, could teach you the system."

"Are you serious?" she asked, turning to look at him in the dancing firelight. "It would keep me out of trouble, you mean. Sure, I could help for a little while if it comes to that, but—this old farmhouse, the layout of it, now these wooden-frame stacked beehives that look like tombstones... I think I've finally remembered the place where I was held."

"Walking into that house to get you tonight, I had a flashback to defusing bombs. Don't need more of those memories."

"But, as awful as they are, I need mine," she said in a whisper when they'd been almost shouting to be heard over the roar of the fire.

They both jolted when the farmhouse roof caved in with a crash just as a train screeched its warning in the dark distance. All the clues Tess could remember fit this place, coming together just as it disintegrated in its fiery death.

24

"Sorry to get you out so early on a Sunday morning," Gabe told his young deputy as they exited their separate vehicles. Dr. Nelson had taken care of him and stitched up Tess, though Gabe was still walking on a gimpy ankle. "But there's three Simons brothers when I don't even trust one of them anymore. I think we'll find Jonas alone at his place, but you never know."

"No problem about my missing church. Carolyn just said the memorial service tonight will count," Jace said as they started walking through the trees and up the hill toward the house.

"Not a memorial service. A prayer service and candlelight vigil," Gabe reminded him. "Memorial would mean Sandy's gone, and I hope to God she isn't."

"Yeah, I knew that. Gotta admit I'm nervous, going in on a big, shifty guy who's good with pit bulls and chain saws. You ever see that **Chainsaw Massacre** flick?"

"Save it. I'm hoping this will be a knock-and-talk at first, but I've learned to expect the unexpected, especially since I hope to arrest him. Just let me do the talking but cover me from a stand of trees where you can see us, like we planned. Even if he asks me in, I'll have him step out into the open. I'll give you time to get set."

Gabe left Jace and limped toward Jonas's large log cabin home. Ann had let slip that the new home's interior was beautifully finished and cost a lot. Then she'd tried to backtrack on the expense comment. Gabe figured that was because Jonas's job at the mill didn't provide a big paycheck even if he did get a discount on wood. He might not be only running illegal dogfights but also getting drug money from tipping off the meth lab gang through Ann. Gabe couldn't think of anyone else named Jonas around here, but there could be—though not with links to key information from the sheriff's department.

He had to get something out of Jonas before he accused Ann of anything. She was a lot smarter than her brothers, so, as tough as they were, Gabe was betting she wouldn't crack as easily.

The minute he stepped into the yard, about ten pit bulls behind a wire fence went wild, barking, snarling.

Jonas stuck his head out the front door, looking like death warmed over.

"Hey, Sheriff," he said, laughing and scratching his belly through a loose flannel shirt. "You come to ask me for Ann's hand? I'd agree to a shotgun wedding. Should I go get mine?"

Gabe moved closer but not too close. At least the man seemed to be in a good mood, but he knew it wouldn't last too long.

"Step out so we can have a talk please," Gabe called to him. "I'm here to ask why you didn't come in Friday morning to retrieve your dog. The one John Hillman mounted for you before it was stolen from the taxidermy shop. Ann did give you a quick call from the office as soon as she knew about it, didn't she?"

Gabe watched the big man closely as he stepped out of the house but saw no hint Jonas got what he was implying. Although the man really annoyed him, Gabe kept his game face on, as impassive as possible. He glanced around at the open door, the front windows, the side of the house he could see, in case Jonas wasn't alone.

"I heard the dog doc shot and killed himself," Jonas said, coming no closer than the edge of the porch. Gabe kept an eye on his hands. He could have a gun stuck in his waistband under that loose shirt.

"Answer my question, Jonas. I told you to be there on Friday. Dr. Thompson died yesterday. Since this is Sunday, you're a couple of days late."

"Didn't come in 'cause I had to work at the mill. And 'cause I didn't want to get questions from you like this. I don't have nothing to do with nothing. And I don't like the way you been treating Ann lately," he said, propping his fists on his hips, which at least suggested there was no hidden gun.

"You didn't want questions because you have something to hide?"

Jonas came down off the porch. Gabe stood his ground.

"You trying to say I'm fighting dogs again? You just go see if any of them look torn up."

"I would imagine you get rid of the ones who are injured. Bury them in the woods? No, I came to tell you that I have information you're tied to the gang of meth cookers."

"What? Says who?" he said, edging toward the dog cages instead of coming closer.

"Stay there. Stay put," Gabe commanded.

"You mean like 'heel'? I ain't someone you can order around, like Ann, just 'cause she works for you, is soft on you."

"You give me your contact's name in that gang—Hank's last name—and where I can find him, and things will go a lot easier for you in court."

Gabe saw the man's eyes widen when he heard the name Hank.

"You're nuts, man! You come out here, accusing me of...of what? You been tapping my phone? You can't prove nothing! How would I know anything about any meth lab gang? I can prove where I was last night!"

"Last night? You mean someone tipped off the meth lab gang last night, so that's when you need an alibi? I didn't mention last night, and you wouldn't have to be with them to tip them off. No, I haven't tapped your phone, but since you're innocent, how about you just let me check calls on your cell? I will tell you Hank and his friends are going to be charged with attempted murder when we arrest them, so you might want to come into the station and make a statement to help me locate them faster than I'm going to anyway. That would make it go easier on you and anyone else who is tipping you off so you can tip them off. And quit shuffling toward that dog compound. You loose those dogs on me, I'll have to shoot them. I'd rather not, nor would Deputy Miller, who has my back right now."

"You're bluffing."

"Really?" Gabe said. "Deputy Miller," he called, without taking his eyes off Jonas. "You there?"

"Fully armed, Sheriff!" Jace called out. He shot a single bullet into the air, which made Gabe jump as much as Jonas did.

Gabe put his hand on the holster of his gun. At first he thought Jonas would lunge to free the dogs, but instead he looked as if he was going to cry.

"Don't mind for me," he said, as if talking to the dogs, "but for Ann."

Finally, Gabe thought, he'd found Jonas's soft spot. "Like I said, your cooperation—and Ann's," Gabe said, "will go a long way in all this. How about you let me take you in, make a statement? She can too."

"I'm not friends with those lowlifes, Hank McGuffey and his crew, just could use the extra money. Mill don't pay enough, selling extra firewood neither. Don't need no bank foreclosing on my dream home here."

Again, the big man looked as if he was close to tears.

Gabe had expected a fight, was even, if those dogs got loose, prepared to have to climb a tree. With all this hitting him at once: losing Ann in the office, suspecting Marva as a possible suspect for the kidnappings, wanting to protect Tess but afraid he couldn't—in more ways than one, he felt he was up a tree whatever happened next.

"Jonas," he said. "I'm going to read you your Miranda rights and explain them."

"I'll cooperate. That should go a long ways with you and in court. Ann had no idea I was passing things on. Told her I was just interested in police work, and asked her stuff."

Gabe didn't believe any of that, and realized this might not be smooth sailing after all.

Sunday morning Tess fixed breakfast for herself and Vic, since Gabe was long gone. "The pancakes are great," Vic said, tucking into his second stack of them. "So much better than those toaster waffles and quick-fix stuff. I'm a disaster in the kitchen."

"I thought you were married."

"Was," he said, pouring on syrup. "Can't be married to a wife and the career I've had. I don't blame her for taking a hike. I was married though, when I was here for your case, and she suffered right along with me until you turned up. See," he said, his hands resting with his fork and knife beside his plate, "we lost our daughter to cancer when she was young. My wife was real happy when your mother got you back. Our Tiffany had neuroblastoma—rare but with only about a five percent survival rate."

"Vic, I'm sorry," she said, sinking into the chair across the table from him. Tears burned her eyes, but she blinked them back.

He sighed. "Well, yeah. Thanks. I think it's why I was really shook when Jill Stillwell went missing, and I was assigned somewhere else so I couldn't work that case. And now the Kenton girl. I might come off hard as nails, but I know how it feels to lose a young girl."

"Speaking of marriage under the strain of the man's career, it was obviously hard for Gabe's mother."

He started to eat again. "Speaking of obvious, I had no idea you didn't know about your father and Gabe's mom."

"It's best I know. I don't hold it against you. My family should have told me. But what you said about your wife too—no wonder Gabe has never married in his position."

He narrowed his eyes and stared straight at her. "He and Ann were done before he found out she betrayed him, you know."

"That's what he said."

"You thinking of the two of you—him and you?"

"Of course not. With all that's going on, and I've only known him—as adults—for six days, no way! I'm heading back to Michigan as soon as this is all over."

"'Methinks the lady doth protest too much.' That's Shakespeare—impressive, huh? Look, I can see you two care for each other. That's why he asked me to keep a good eye on you today at the church service for Sandy, the candle walk, all that."

"I'll be fine in the crowd."

"Because the person or persons out to scare you off or keep you quiet only come out of cornfields and we'll be uptown? Nope, I'm sticking by you today. You know," he said, with a shake of his head and slight smile as he poured more maple syrup on his last few bites, "I saw a tabloid newspaper when Jill Stillwell went missing that claimed 'the Hillbilly Kidnappings' were done by the same aliens that make crop circles in the fields."

"No kidding? What a joke! That's terrible—saying Hillbilly too! I'll bet Mayor Owens had a fit over that. But I guess, unless Marva confesses, aliens make as much sense as anything." She hesitated for a moment. "Vic, one other thing."

He looked hard at her as if he knew something bad was coming.

"I'm going to phone my father."

She thought that would surprise him, or

he'd speak against it, but he surprised her. "Take notes. Hey, I'll clean up here. You go call him. And keep your spirits up in case he doesn't want to talk. I tell you though, I'd give years of my life—my entire life—to talk to my girl again."

Gabe saw Ann jump up from behind her desk when he and Jace came in with Jonas in handcuffs.

"Gabe!" she shouted. "What? What?"

"He's agreed to answer some questions. Just call Peggy for me, get her out of bed again and tell her I need her in here on the desk."

"But what's the charge?"

"Ann!" Jonas said. "Get outta here and call us some fancy lawyer from Lake Azure, 'cause there's a bunch of them there."

"**Us?** Gabe..."

He took Jonas into the smaller conference room, uncuffed him and left Jace with him. He went back to Ann, took her arm and steered her toward her desk. "You said you were disappointed in me the other day for cooling off on you. But I—"

"Since Tess—"

"It's not her fault. I'm more than disappointed in you. Now, I'd like you to sit down at your desk and write out a statement. How long and how often you've been tipping off Jonas or anyone else about my comings and goings. Specifically reference the warning call to Jonas to tell Hank McGuffey and the other meth cookers last night, right after I told you that's where I was going. No wonder you didn't tell me who owned that stuffed dog, then tried to talk me out of linking it to Jonas. Now I know why I never could break up his dogfights, let alone the drug dealers he was tipping off."

She yanked her arm away and snatched her purse from behind her desk. "You're a loser, you know that!" she shouted. She rushed over to the coat pegs on the far wall of the waiting area and grabbed her jacket. "You—like father, like son—couldn't solve the biggest case this county's ever seen, and I'll bet the kidnapper's right under your nose! Meanwhile, you waste your time with petty things. I am going to get a lawyer."

He refused to shout like she did. He was hurt and furious, but she wasn't worth his emotion, let alone his passion. He spoke calmly. "You were right under my nose, and you've been caught. You and Jonas both. If you don't write out the statement right now, you can do it in a jail cell."

"He's an idiot to have told you anything! Excuse me—permanently—because I'm done wasting time and effort on you. Now I need to spend some of my hard-earned money to get a lawyer to protect me from something I'm not guilty of. By the way, Marva Green's done the same thing. I took a call from her attorney this morning." Her face puckered in a sneer; her voice was snotty. "He'll contact you on Monday, but you're not to see her without him present! Consider that my last duty and contribution around here!"

He snared her arm as she made for the door. "Take your hands off me!" she insisted.

Without a word, he marched her back to the holding cell, took her purse for Peggy to itemize and locked her in. He stomped back to her desk, got a pad and pen, and shoved them through the small food-tray opening at the bottom of the thick door. Through the grate, he said, "Jace will be right in to read you your rights and let you call a lawyer—unless you want to write out what I asked and leave to see a lawyer yourself."

Gabe went over and sat at her desk. He called Peggy to come in. Later, he'd go through Ann's records, phone log and computer thoroughly, but right now he just wanted to tell Tess one more time not to come uptown without Vic today. But her cell rang busy. After last night, maybe she needed counseling and comforting from her social-worker sister again, but he wished she'd just come to him.

Tess could not stop shaking, but she was going through with this. A man's voice answered the phone. The past hit her like a sledgehammer. For a moment, she couldn't say a word.

"Hello? Jack Lockwood speaking."

Afraid he'd hang up whether she talked or didn't, she blurted out what she wanted to say in a rush. "Dad, it's Tess—Teresa. I know this is a surprise but I've wanted to talk to you for a long time. I'm in Cold Creek to sell the house after Mom died. There's been a third kidnapping, so I just had to call you. I mean, it brought things back, and I'm trying to help Sheriff McCord—you know, Gabe's sheriff now—but I still can't remember who took me."

"Teresa. My terrific, terrible Teresa! I'd heard your mother died. I'm sorry. Really, I am...for lots of things."

She was crying now. "But who told you about her?"

"Reese Owens. The bastard calls sometimes. I think to make sure I'm still thousands of miles away. He once accused me of taking you, my own daughter. I wasn't sure you knew any of that. I guess Kate and Char did."

"Dad, was Reese Owens part of the reason you left, because he threatened to accuse you in public?"

"Yes. But I'd told Sheriff McCord—Gabe's dad—that he should take a look at George Green. The guy needed money because he was going bankrupt. Your mother said he'd been around that day before she left you at home with Gabe. George was peddling corn on the cob and said you were the prettiest child of the three. I loved all of you, Teresa, but you were such a feisty tomboy. I guess I'd hoped for a son, but I'm glad I got you, since you were most like me."

In a rush, Tess told him she'd changed her name, just to help let the past go—but it hadn't helped. She explained the possible Dane and Marva connection for the kidnappings. He told her he'd read about the Kenton girl's abduction. She explained that Reese Owens was trying to get her out of town fast too, though she didn't mention what she knew about Reese's once molesting a minor.

Instead she changed the subject and talked about her dreams of selling the farmhouse and buying a day care center;

about how Kate and Char were doing well in their careers and travels. She asked him about his family. He told her he had two sons, Josh, age seven, and Jerod, just turned five. Silently, secretly, she was glad he had sons but not more daughters. "I'd like to meet them someday. It's exciting to think I have two brothers."

"Teresa—Tess—I'm sure your sisters are still angry with me, but tell them it wasn't all my choice that I stayed away. A man more powerful than most folks in Cold Creek realize swore he'd make it bad for me if I came back."

"Sheriff McCord or Reese Owens?"

"Owens, honey. I must have been his ace in the hole if the sheriff ever needed someone to blame for your abduction. Besides the mayor's friend Dane Thompson."

Or in case Vic or Gabe's father suspected the mayor himself, Tess thought.

Her father went on, "Reese wanted the case solved and closed fast to get bad press away from his precious town."

Tess couldn't breathe for a minute. Gabe had said he intended to talk to Reese today, right after he came out of church. She looked at the time on her phone. The service would end in about ten minutes. She needed to let him know the things her dad had said. George and Marva Green might look bad right now, but Reese's actions were suspicious for sure.

"Dad, I have to go, but can I call again?"

"I'll call you. I've got your number here on caller ID. Ask your sisters if they'll let me talk to them someday. Sorry about your losing your Mom, honey. She's—she was—a good woman, just like you."

The minute she hung up, she sucked in a huge breath to steady herself then dialed Gabe's number.

"Hey, I've been trying to get you," he said. "I'm walking down the street to catch Reese Owens when he—"

"Gabe, I just talked to my father, and I have to tell you what he said. George Green was at our house that afternoon just before I was taken."

"I know, but he was questioned

thoroughly. No go at that time. He had alibis from everybody on the road where he'd stopped to sell corn. Like with Dane, I can't question the dead."

"But there's more about Reese Owens. Just listen to this."

25

The Community Church bells rang out twelve times. Gabe spotted Mayor Owens shaking the hands of the congregation as they streamed out after the morning worship service. Reese seemed to be greeting as many people as the pastor he was upstaging. Always a politician, and, sadly, they weren't to be trusted, Gabe thought. At least he didn't see his wife with him as the mayor finally headed toward the parking lot. Lillian Montgomery Owens reeked wealth, social class and self-appointed power more than her husband.

Gabe cut through a line of cars and fell into step beside Reese, who spoke first. "So, you heard I wanted to see you. You'll be doing security at the Kenton service and procession tonight?"

"I, and my deputy, and Agent Reingold, will be there. Are you expecting trouble?"

"Avoiding it. I called you yesterday to find out the details about Dane's death. A shame. And more unwanted notoriety for Cold Creek."

It annoyed Gabe that the mayor kept waving and calling out to others while they were talking. Did the man never stop campaigning? Gabe knew how to get his attention fast, but he didn't want to spring everything on him in public.

"I need to talk to you too," Gabe told him. "Let's walk down to my office, where it's private."

"I'll drive. Lily's staying here to oversee the ladies planning dinner for the Kenton family before the service this evening. You want to ride with me?"

"Sure. Fine," Gabe said, not wanting to let him get away.

"So, shoot," Reese said once they were settled in the black Mercedes. Gabe saw Reese could hardly get the seat belt around his girth. "Oops, shouldn't have used the word **shoot** when we're talking about Dane's death. I hear he left a note. Confessing, I hope, to the kidnappings. You're pursuing Marva for information? I heard she lawyered up."

"Word travels fast."

"When did it not around here?" Reese said with a little laugh. "I'd hate to think they were both involved in these abductions, but it would be a relief to have everything solved. At least I hear we got Marian Bell off our backs with her good news. But tell me about the investigation of Dane."

"He left a vague note, but there's evidence he might have been shot, not shot himself."

Reese pounded the steering wheel as he pulled into the police station. "What? You and those fancy BCI boys been sitting on that? You should have told me at once. It's a miracle outside reporters aren't swarming in here over that. That's all I need! A high-profile man murdered in my town and still no definitive answer about who took those girls!"

"Let's continue this in the conference

room," Gabe said. He got out fast enough to go around and open the mayor's door for him. Why a man allowed himself to get so heavy he had trouble getting out of his car was beyond Gabe. He walked ahead and opened the police station door for the mayor. The office was deserted. Tess was going to help fill Ann's daytime shift tomorrow until he could hire someone else, but that was the last thing on his list of things to do right now.

At least the fact that Jonas had fingered Hank McGuffey and his crew meant Tess didn't have to spend her time going through mug shots, though she would eventually have to testify against McGuffey for trying to kill her and against the others as accessories. But that meant he'd see her then—if she really was moving back to Michigan when this was all over.

In the smaller conference room, which didn't have all the kidnapping information on the walls, Gabe pulled out a chair for Reese.

"This is terrible, just terrible, about Dane," the mayor said, wiping sweat off his brow. He'd gone red in the face. Surely not just from the effort of walking in here, Gabe thought. "It opens the door to the kidnapper being someone other than him, or at least someone he was working with, namely Marva. Poor dead George Green— at least for the first two kidnappings, he could be guilty too. Nothing's been solved or going right around here, and I blame you."

"Mr. Mayor, the blame game won't help here. Jonas Simons has been arrested for working with a local meth drug ring, who were picked up this morning by the State Highway Patrol since they live over by Athens. But I provided them with all the information to make the arrests. Sorry to say that Ann Simons was also aiding and abetting the meth gang by passing on info she overheard from me. She's written a statement, been released on her own recognizance and hired a lawyer for herself and Jonas. Oh, by the way, the so-called gas explosion at the old Green place was really a meth explosion. The gang I just mentioned tried to kill Tess

Lockwood, who had stumbled on them. So, how about you do your job and I'll do mine?"

"Tried to kill her? Then maybe they're the ones you and your father failed to find."

"You don't let up, do you? They're young. They've been cooking meth all over the county, not abducting little girls."

"So that's small potatoes compared to the kidnappings. You need to concentrate on that."

"As a matter of fact, Agent Reingold and I have worked together to run down a very vocal, very involved local man who has a criminal record of child molestation. The man didn't live here at the time he committed that crime, but there was a large, ongoing attempt to cover it up."

The mayor's eyes narrowed and his upper lip went slick with sweat. "Such as Jack Lockwood, Tess's father?"

"He was thoroughly checked out years ago and was clean, although I understand you've been keeping him under your thumb. No, it's a man with a past criminal record, Mr. Mayor, although most of the information on that was expunged. But we have one record of it left and at least one Chillicothe civilian who remembers the details and the ensuing cover-up, including bribes."

Despite his satisfaction in seeing this man cornered and speechless, Gabe hoped Reese wasn't going to have a heart attack right in front of him.

"You can't be serious about that—that wrongful, old charge. A b-b-boyhood indiscretion. You—you're b-blackmailing me?"

"Hardly. I'm keeping you informed, just the way you like. And don't try to pull Jack Lockwood out of the hat again. Now," he said, trying not to revel in the moment and wondering if this long shot would ever lead to something useful about the abductions, "although we have a court record, I'd appreciate it if you'd just write out your recollection of the incident between you and the minor named Ginger Pickett, so we can clear you of—"

"Damn you, boy!" he cried, banging his

fist on the table between them. "I don't have anything to do with this, and it's a big mistake for you to be dragging up erroneous information from another place and time! These kidnappings are a whole different bag from that boyhood infraction. And Tess wasn't sexually molested, was she? So I bet the others weren't either, just taken for some other sick, warped reason. But since you're grasping at straws and you and your daddy never managed to solve this terrible case, I'm going to get a lawyer, one from Columbus, not these parts! You want to read me my rights?"

"You're not under arrest. You've merely been asked to help clear up a possibility, which an innocent man and the longtime leader of his constituency should want to do."

"Nice try. I'm getting a lawyer. One who will help me have your head for this outrage."

"Good idea to retain a well-known and well-connected Columbus lawyer," Gabe said, trying to keep from losing his temper too. "Marva, Jonas and Ann have already retained Lake Azure attorneys. Besides, a lawyer from the state capital will be within better reach of the national media you'll want to use for interviews. Nice working with you, sir," Gabe said as Reese rolled out of his chair and, pulling himself up by the table edge, rose to his feet. "I'll see you at the church service this evening."

"And you just keep your mouth shut. A couple of words from me and you'll get thrown right out of office!" Reese shouted.

"It could happen to the best of us up for election next month," Gabe countered. "I know you've been rubber-stamped as mayor for years, but I'll bet I can find someone to oppose you, especially if you run on your record—your real record."

He didn't open the door for Reese this time as the man stormed out of the room. Gabe kept thinking about how those pit bulls at Jonas's place had rattled their cages. He was like a pit bull now. And he was going to sink his teeth into whoever had hurt those little girls.

• • •

The town turned out in droves for the church service that evening. Sitting in the second row, Tess stared at the big, hand-painted banner with the words Sandy Kenton: Bring Her Home hanging below the screen with projected photos of the girl. She had now been missing for five days. Tess studied the images, memorizing Sandy's face, but it almost blended with her own early photos, despite their slightly different coloring. Sandy had blond hair and brown eyes. A wide space between her two front teeth made them look even larger in her small mouth. A shy smile, pert nose. There were pictures of her with her family, at a picnic, at a wedding, at a petting zoo with a fawn, being read to by her mother, playing in a princess costume with a magic wand.

Jill Stillwell's family sat in the front row along with Pastor Snell and his wife, Jeanie. Tess had spoken with them briefly. And she'd spent a lot of time on the phone with Lindell Kenton, Sandy's mother. Lindell had asked Tess to say a few words this evening, but they'd compromised that she would do a Bible reading instead. She had to admit she was a bit nervous about it, but she wanted to help—anything to help!

She'd read in one of Miss Etta's library books that Freud, no less, had defined mental health as the ability "to love and to work." Tess figured she was doing both, not just in longing to have her own preschool where she could care for kids, but in working on the investigation. She was going to help Gabe by answering his dispatch and office phone during the day for a while. And as fast as everything had happened here in Cold Creek, she was very sure she was falling in love with him.

She sat between Deputy Miller's wife, Carolyn, and Miss Etta. Mayor Owens and his wife sat with the families of the kidnapped girls. Although Vic was to be her bodyguard this evening, he and Gabe sat at the back to keep an eye on everything.

Lindell Kenton had given Tess a Bible with the short passage to be read clearly marked. Tess held it in her lap, stroking the pebbled leather cover.

"That's a book people don't read enough anymore," Miss Etta whispered to her, reaching over to tap the Bible. Her hand smelled of that sanitizer she always used. "They think the Good Book is in an old, hard language, but there are plenty of modern versions."

"I thought you might bring your mother tonight," Tess said.

Miss Etta looked surprised at first, then said with a smile, "Speaking of old versions, you mean? No, I used to bring her to church but not anymore. It's too hard to get her around. By the way, Sheriff McCord said he wanted to talk to me tomorrow about my antique gun collection. I'm going to look up the very gun that Dane must have used to do himself in. Also, I have a library book for Gabe to read."

"He's pretty busy."

"Yes, of course he is, and should be. But a book about stress on the job, that's what I'll recommend to him."

The muted buzz in the church quieted as Pastor Snell rose and went to the podium. He spoke a few opening words, said a lovely prayer, and then the organ led them, standing, through the hymn "O God, Our Help in Ages Past."

How well Tess recalled going to Sunday school downstairs and sometimes coming up to "big church" with Mom and Dad. How had everything gone so bad?

"O God, our help in ages past,
Our hope for years to come,
Be thou our guard while troubles last,
And our eternal home."

Tess knew Sandy Kenton must be thinking about home, longing for home, feeling frightened and abandoned right now. Thank God the child had not been hidden where Tess had been kept, which she was convinced had burned to the ground last night. The firemen and a BCI arson consultant were still sifting through the debris for bones, but Tess was sure there was some other place Dane and

Marva—or someone—had been keeping Sandy.

During the next prayer, she thanked God for letting her escape her captor or captors and asked for more memories, however terrible, to help Gabe arrest the monster.

When her turn came, Pastor Snell introduced her as "our ray of hope for both Sandy and Jill." He explained that Amanda Bell had been found alive in South America and that was an answer to prayer. "And now the greatest gift in all this grief," he announced from the pulpit, "our own Teresa Lockwood, who now goes by Tess, who came home to us years ago and is back with us again. Though she still bears the mental scars of her captivity, she is here with us today to read words to encourage our hearts. Tess."

As she walked up the three steps to the elevated platform, she was amazed that the audience broke into applause. It was too much. She teared up and sniffed hard. Even Vic was clapping. Gabe too, standing by the back door—her Gabe, who had been there at the time and was now her guard while these troubles lasted. She was surprised to see Sam Jeffers and John Hillman sitting together in the back left corner. It was wrong of her to judge them, of course, but she hadn't expected them to be in church.

She put the open Bible down on the podium and held up a hand to still the applause. When it quieted, though she'd meant to say nothing personal, she shared her thoughts. "It means a lot to me to be home. We have to face and recall the past to face the present and the future. And I'm trying, getting better and stronger. Now, Mrs. Kenton has asked me to read to you from Luke 15:4 about a lost sheep who was found."

Her voice caught several times as she read the passage. **"What man of you, having a hundred sheep, if he loses one of them, does not leave the ninety-nine in the wilderness, and go after the one which is lost until he finds it? And when he comes home, he lays it on his shoulders, rejoicing. And when he** comes home, he calls together his friends and neighbors, saying to them, 'Rejoice with me, for I have found my sheep which was lost.'"

As soon as she sat down, Win Kenton got up behind the podium and explained that tomorrow at noon they were going to have another search for Sandy, through bare fields and even those still filled with corn. He explained that Aaron Kurtz needed prayers while bedridden with a dangerous blood clot and that others would soon be cutting his cornfields for him, but that they wanted to search them now.

"Also," he said, his voice breaking, "we need to search the cornfields now so that when the big reapers come through, no one is in the way, no evidence Sheriff McCord or his assistants need to trace— to find Sandy..."

He meant, of course, her body could be out there. He choked up, just standing mute for a moment. "We need to find traces of her, not have them destroyed. Our family thanks you for your help and prayers." He hurried back to his seat beside his wife.

Again, Tess visualized the cornfield, the big reaper. Then someone had leaped at her, put a needle right in her neck—she was sure of it. She jerked at the memory, and Miss Etta put a steadying hand on her arm. At least, Tess thought, she was remembering more and more, like the waterfall of memories. And, strangely, she kept seeing a mounted deer head—a stag—with its glassy eyes looking down at her, as if to say, "Bad things can happen to you if you don't behave." She would have Gabe ask Marva if her house had once had a deer head on the wall. But she might lie. And what if Tess was just recalling how creepy John Hillman's taxidermy shop had been?

After they sang a final hymn and the pastor made an announcement about signing up for the new search, Tess stood to go. It was getting dark; people at each door were passing out pink candles with white paper drip guards. "Are you going to the ceremony at the gift store?" Miss

Etta asked.

"Yes. Are you?"

"I think I'd best get home to Mother. She spends enough time alone as is. I just hope everyone's careful with those candles. The gift store isn't so far from the library with all those books. I know I'm a worrywart and a perfectionist, but I just hope everyone's careful."

"Miss Etta, can I ask you a question?"

She looked surprised. "Why, of course, my dear."

"Were you ever in Marva and George Green's house, their living room?"

"I was indeed, delivering books there more than once when George was so ill. Why do you ask?"

"You have such a good mind for everything. Do you recall if they had a big stag head mounted on the wall there? It was over the fireplace, I think."

Miss Etta frowned, evidently trying to remember. "You know, my dear, I've been in and out of so many Cold Creek houses, I can't rightly recall. Why do you ask?"

"Just that either those books you gave

me or just helping Gabe is freeing up my memories a bit."

"I see. I'm relieved to hear it, and I shall look for more books to help you along. And you tell Sheriff McCord that I expect him promptly at ten when the library opens tomorrow morning to talk about that antique pistol."

Ever quick and spry, the old woman was out the door before Vic made his way to Tess through the crowd.

26

"I'll bet you never thought you'd be taking on bodyguard duties when you came here to help solve a kidnapping," Tess said as she and Vic walked out to his car parked behind Gabe's house. The wind was up today, and the cornfield was waving as if it was restless, waiting for the big search for Sandy this afternoon. Tess hoped they'd find the girl but not lying in a cornfield. She was proud of herself that the field didn't frighten her that much anymore. "But," she added as they got in the car, "I can see why Gabe doesn't want me sitting at the front desk when Marva and her attorney get there."

"We don't need another rant at you, and I'd just upset her too. Man, we need a break on this case. Even though Marva and Dane should be looked at, I'm still trying to track down that housekeeper fired from the mayor's house. Her sister said she'd be back in town today. But a side trip to the Hear Ye property is right up my alley. You can see your family, and I'd love to have a chat with Brice, aka Bright Star."

"No, you wouldn't. He's weird and he can make anyone feel guilty. That's what scares me about Lee, Gracie and the kids being there. Bright Star warps minds and lives. Anyhow, I'm glad to have you along. Gabe said he chatted with Lee and Gracie at the farmers' market, and they seemed as committed as ever. I'd rent them the house cheap again to get them out of there, but they'd never agree."

Vic drove his unmarked black car the few miles down the road to the cult property and parked in the small lot. As ever, a guard, another tall, muscular man, stood at the gate to the compound to stop free entry.

"Brother Lawrence is my name. How may I help you?"

Like Bright Star himself, he was

soft-spoken. "I'm here to see my cousins, the Lockwoods. I recently helped Lee find the location of a well here and would like to know how the project is coming," Tess said.

"Ah, yes, I know who you are. The well will be dug soon. But Monday means school for the children. Lee and Grace of God are at work."

"Grace of God?" Tess asked.

"She's risen from newcomer status to special, so to speak. If you'll wait here, I'll inquire. And you, sir?"

"Friend of the family. Victor Reingold."

"Ah. I do believe everyone is occupied, so perhaps I can get you an appointment for later. Of course, many of our members will be helping with the search for the recently missing girl this afternoon, so perhaps you can catch your family later at that event."

Vic said, "Not sure you'd know about the search, since you weren't at the prayer service for her."

"We had our own here for her—for all who are still lost. And we stay informed."

When he left them standing there, Vic said, "Nice hospitality here." He zipped up his jacket and hunched his shoulders in the wind. "Glad it's not raining or snowing so we could wait out in that weather. And I suppose all of them speak in that strange way that says nothing but seems eerily important."

"It's a scary situation. I wish I could spirit my family away from here—so to speak."

Vic walked up to the crest of the hill that overlooked the Hear Ye land. "No wonder they had the best vegetables at the market," he said as Tess joined him. They gazed at the neatly laid-out fields, mostly harvested, and long rows of white, plastic-domed covers to protect the more tender crops from early frost.

"See how strange that one looks?" Vic asked, pointing.

"Strange how? Everything's strange around here."

"I think that plastic in the middle isn't covering crops. See how it's low to the ground, kind of clinging to it? See that it's draped over two small, rectangular plots it outlines but completely covers?"

"Maybe there's something newly planted, and the ground sank in a bit."

"Yeah, that's what I'm afraid of," he said, starting down the hill. "If Brother Lawrence comes back, keep him busy. I'm gonna have a look," he called over his shoulder.

"Vic, you'll attract a swarm of people from the compound!"

But he kept going. It was obvious he was limping more than usual, which reminded her of Gabe's leg injury. She hoped things were going well at the sheriff's office with Marva and her attorney. If only Marva would answer questions that would help solve this.

When Tess heard the gate creak, she went back up toward Brother Lawrence. "It's a lovely view from there," she said, hoping he'd think Vic was enjoying it. But to her dismay, the man ran up the hill, so Tess followed. Vic was peeking under the plastic covering the two sunken areas. As Brother Lawrence hurried down the hill toward Vic, she recognized the voice behind her.

"Abomination!"

Bright Star had materialized from nowhere as usual. No wonder people thought he was more spirit than flesh and blood.

"He just wondered what was growing under that since it is so different from the others," Tess told him.

"It's the graves of two blessed infants who have recently passed beyond, and I have county permits allowing us to bury them on our property. Long-established religious groups have their own cemeteries, and we shall too."

Tess's mind raced. **Two infants? Or two dead girls? Surely not.**

Below, Brother Lawrence was arguing with Vic, who ignored him and came limping back up the hill.

"Bright Star says it's two infant graves," she called to him before he reached them. "And he has permission from the county to have them buried there."

"So I see—about the graves, since they have little stones with angels and lambs and names. All on the up-and-up, Mr.

Monson?"

"I could report you for trespassing, sir, but that would have to be to Sheriff McCord, and I know you are a confederate of his."

"That I am. So why hide the graves?"

"I ordered them covered, not hidden. It upset the grieving mothers and others of the flock to look down at them. It's like an extra cover in the bed of the earth on a cold day or night."

More like it upsets this man to have to admit babies could die in his supposedly perfect place, so he hides their graves, Tess thought. She wondered if they were born here or in a hospital.

"Miss Lockwood," Monson said, turning to Tess. "Your family can certainly spend time with you alone tomorrow, at noon, if you're available."

Despite the fact that she'd told Gabe she'd try to help by answering the dispatch phone and covering the front desk until he could get some permanent help, she knew he would understand, and who knew what else she might learn about strange goings-on. "Yes," she said to him. "I'll be here."

The man bowed, glared at Vic and walked away, followed by an out-of-breath but now subdued Brother Lawrence.

When they were back in Vic's car, he said, "If Gabe wasn't tied up, I'd phone him right now. I don't like asking for court orders to exhume graves, but it may come to that. That guy's arrogant, positive he can get away with anything. Like looking at the mayor, it's a long shot, but desperate times need—"

"Desperate measures," she finished for him. "Not Shakespeare this time?" she asked, hoping he'd calm down. His face was red and a pulse beat at the side of his forehead.

"'Thus do all things conspire against us' will have to do for Shakespeare right now."

"But I am starting to recall more things about my captivity. You know I've recalled a graveyard view—but surely not that one. It's true Brice Monson lived on this land years ago in a single house, but even a child wouldn't mistake those long, plastic covers for tombstones. I remember the scarecrow for smackings, of course, and a back staircase in a house—and I'm sure there was a stag's head over the fireplace."

"Good for you and for us, Tess. Now all we need you to remember is a name or a face."

● ● ●

Gabe was disheartened and angry. Marva hadn't given him anything he could use and was insisting he solve "Dane's dreadful murder." As if the best defense was a good offense, she'd turned hostile toward him and Tess. Her lawyer had insisted the suicide note had nothing to do with the Cold Creek kidnapper cases. He also continually counseled Marva to "take the Fifth." The whole situation made Gabe wish he could have a good, stiff belt from a fifth of whiskey, even this early in the morning.

And now he was late heading to the library to hear what Miss Etta had to say about the pistol that killed Dane.

As he headed toward the library, Gabe

saw several posters about the search for Sandy he'd help spearhead this afternoon. Jace was at the church helping the civilian organizers lay out grids for the volunteer teams to cover. There was a poster on the library door above an Open sign and one that read Come in and Change Your Life! **If only that was true,** he thought as he opened the door.

Miss Etta was shelving books from a rolling cart as two women he recognized were browsing the shelves. "Good. You came," Miss Etta whispered when she saw him. "One can't expect a busy sheriff to be prompt, and that's quite all right. Would you like some hand sanitizer?" she asked as she walked over to her desk to use it herself. "One can't be too careful with flu season coming."

"Ah, sure," he said, letting her pump some of the cool gel onto his hands. "Thanks for researching about the antique pistol."

"First of all, please tell me, how is Tess?" she said, taking a book from her desk over to a long wooden table. "Just let me know if you need help, ladies," she said to the two patrons.

Gabe sat in the chair beside her. The heavy oak furniture all looked antique, though the overhead lighting was modern and bright. There was an air of solidity about the place. As flighty as she seemed sometimes, this woman suited the place. She seemed unchanged over time, the bedrock of the community in a way Reese Owens would never be. She looked at him expectantly, waiting for his answer about Tess, then added, as if to prompt him, "I recommended some books on childhood trauma she's been reading. I hope they help."

"I think they have. Some things are coming back, and she's a lot more steady."

"Oh, good. She seemed that way at the church service, and she certainly handled getting up in front of all those people. You know, I hate to speak ill of anyone, but I always thought Dane was highly suspect, so perhaps he has meted out his own justice to himself." She leaned slightly closer. "He liked true crime and murder mysteries, you know."

"Not exactly proof, but—"

"But with Marva and George Green's help in the first two abductions—there you go. Dr. Dane Thompson, guilty as your father always believed. Now, here is a picture of that pistol your BCI friend Agent Reingold described to me on the phone. Have I found the correct one?"

"That's it," he said, looking closely at the sketch and then the two photos.

"Well, it's of the same era as a few I own. They came down through my family who founded this area. Elias Falls, born 1785, was my great-great-great-grandfather, a contemporary of Daniel Boone in these parts. No doubt Daniel wandered through southern Ohio."

Gabe was exhausted, but he tried not to let his eyes glaze over. No wonder kids recalled taking field trips to Miss Etta's house for her pioneer-days lectures. He barely remembered her mother, Sybil Falls, who must be up in her eighties now and had been a recluse for years. Sybil had married and outlived a man named

Vetter, which was Miss Etta's actual last name, though both she and her mother had always used the prestigious Falls name. Talk about the mayor's wife coming from Ohio "royalty." Etta Falls could take her on any day.

"As far as I know, that gun **was** Dane's," she said, which made him alert again. "He wouldn't let me include it in the display we had here because it was his favorite. So, if he did kill himself, I can see why he did it with that one."

"You've been very helpful, Miss Etta."

"And I have just the book for you," she said as he rose. "It's on occupational stress and how to cope with it. I'll just get it from my desk."

"I'll remember that when I have time to read, so—"

His cell sounded. He looked at the display. His office phone.

"Excuse me, Miss Etta. I've got to take this, and I thank you again. Sheriff McCord here," he said as he walked out onto the street.

"It's Vic, Gabe. I've got some good info

from going with Tess to the Hear Ye sect, but I also finally got a call back from Reese Owens's former housekeeper, Ruby Purtle."

"I'm on my way to the office, on foot. Be right there."

"Yeah, well, be prepared to get your gear and jump in your vehicle because this woman says Reese Owens has a cabin up on a place called Green Mountain that no one knows about, even his wife. And get this—he fired this housekeeper but gave her a big payoff and a good recommendation, she thinks, just because she heard him ordering furniture for it on the phone. Think we can find it?"

"As heavy as he is, it can't be far off the single road up there, and I know the area. Yeah, we'll find it!"

Gabe jogged back to the office. Tess was sitting at the front desk with Peggy. "Just teach her the basics, Peg, and we'll get some other help in ASAP," he said, hurrying past them. Adrenaline surged through him as he and Vic grabbed Kevlar vests, guns and clips from the small equipment room.

"I can't help thinking of this stuff as bomb-squad gear," Gabe said, double-checking items in his utility belt.

"This could be the break we need. Despite the fact that Reese Owens likes to fight with words, I think it's wise we go up there like this. If he's not there himself, he might have a guard for the place—and whatever he's got stashed there."

"As much as Marva's turned into a witch, I'd love to nail Mr. Mayor," Gabe said.

"And if not, there's a couple of hidden, child-sized graves Tess and I spotted on the Hear Ye property."

"You're kidding!"

"No. Bright Star claims they're the graves of commune babies who died and says he has permission for a graveyard there. The librarian any help?"

"Yeah, but I probably ticked her off by leaving before she could give me a book on stress."

"Get me a copy too."

Gabe looked up to see Tess standing in the hall outside the equipment room.

"Miss Etta tried to give me that book for you before," she said.

"Yeah, well, at lunch, maybe you and Peg can walk down to get it from her just so I'm not in her doghouse." He and Vic walked past her. Gabe gave her shoulder a reassuring squeeze.

Tess followed them into the front office. "Call Mike, Peg, and fill him in about our destination of Green Mountain, though we don't know the exact location. Tell him to keep an eye on everyone gathering for the search for Sandy," Gabe said. "I hope we'll be back by then, but I think that cabin's probably in a dead area for cell phones. We'll be in touch ASAP."

He looked back at Tess again. Wide-eyed, she nodded as if to encourage him. She'd come so far in such a short time, and his feelings for her had too. He hurried out behind Vic.

27

"I'm glad you didn't wish them good luck," Peggy said as Tess sat behind the reception desk with her after Gabe and Vic left. "They think saying that is **bad** luck."

"We need more than luck in all this," Tess replied.

"You got that right."

Tess thought Peggy Barfield—unlike Ann—had a great personality to work in a job that required both a friendly nature and firm control. Tess had only observed her answer a few emergency calls so far, but she'd handled them with ease. Now Tess tried to concentrate on Peggy's explanation about what appeared on the computer monitor when a 911 call came in.

But her mind—and heart—kept clinging to Gabe. Could she ever be the kind of wife who could send him off toward possible danger, as she had done just now? If she owned a day care center or had children of her own, she could probably keep herself occupied when he was so busy and under such stress.

Despite trying to learn all of the emergency processes Peggy was teaching, the morning dragged. Tess was anxious for a call from Gabe. If the trip to Green Mountain didn't turn up anything, it terrified her to think what no one had put into words yet. The two abducted girls could be in those two graves under plastic—if Bright Star didn't have them dug up and moved when it got dark tonight.

When Peggy told her to take a break Tess decided to carry a cup of coffee down to Miss Etta and get that book on stress for Gabe.

"I'll be right back," she mouthed to Peggy, who had just taken a call about someone bitten by a raccoon. She was telling them they had to see Dr. Nelson about possible rabies shots.

Out she stepped with a covered paper cup of coffee into the windy but sunny October day.

To Gabe's dismay and embarrassment after telling Vic he'd be able to find the cabin, they couldn't locate a pull-off spot on the single-lane dirt road up Green Mountain. It really wasn't much of a mountain, just another of the tall Appalachian foothills around here, but it did loom above the others nearby.

"Finally!" Gabe said as they spotted an area where brush had been cut back to allow access off the road. "Let's try it."

"No vehicle here right now, but I see ruts. Bingo!" Vic said when they got out. "Let's go in armed and all dressed up for a shooting party to check out Mr. Mayor's hidden cabin. Can't imagine he didn't tell his wife about it and fired Ruby Purtle because it's a lovers' nest. No way he'd be meeting his secret ladylove up here, not that guy."

"But remember to expect the unexpected. If he or someone else does arrive, the sheriff's vehicle's a dead giveaway, but it's not like there's alternative parking. Okay, let's go."

They donned their Kevlar vests over their jackets, took their weapons and hiked in. A path was soon discernible, even through falling, blowing leaves. Reese Owens always did drag his feet, but had he dragged something or someone else through here? Gabe felt his heart rate speed up. His mouth went dry. Something had to break on this case, but he was already dreading what he was going to find.

An elderly couple Tess didn't recognize, but who greeted her by name, were just leaving the library when she walked in. "See you at the search for Sandy," they said to her, evidently assuming she'd be there. And, even if Gabe and Vic weren't back on time, she planned on that.

Except for Miss Etta, the library was deserted, but then it was almost lunchtime and the volunteer searchers would be gathering soon. The librarian was busy shelving books.

"Miss Etta, I brought you some coffee— small thanks for the research you've done for Gabe and me."

"Tess, did you come alone? I rather had the feeling that Agent Reingold was keeping an eye on you."

"He's out somewhere with Gabe right now. I'm learning to answer the dispatch phones in the sheriff's office—just helping out for a while."

Miss Etta used the disinfectant on her desk, then, smiling, took the coffee from Tess. "I must admit I'm a tea person, but this is very kind. Nothing like good sheriff's office coffee when they are out trying to solve their big cases. I do think with Dane's demise, your own case may be resolved by his death and Marva's eventual admissions—you know what I mean."

"That Dane was guilty and she helped him? That could be, since I recall a small graveyard out behind the house where I was held, and Marva's house seemed familiar in several ways."

"Did it? Including its location on

Blackberry Road?" Miss Etta asked, sitting at her desk and rummaging in her lower drawer.

"Not that so much, but I recall the back stairs, the attic that looked out on old stacked white beehives that resemble a graveyard. Also, I remember certain sounds like the distant train and the muted roar of the falls. Those books you gave me spoke of a cascade of memories, once they start coming back. But—I'm in a hurry. Gabe mentioned he rushed out of here without the book on stress you offered him. Can I get it on my temporary card and read some of it to him? Oh, is it that one on your desk about occupational stress?"

"Oh. No, that's one I was looking at, but I have a much better one in the bookmobile parked right out back. I was going to drop it off since the sheriff is so busy. Come on out with me, and I'll get it for you. I'll just put up my out-to-lunch sign and get a bite to eat after I give you that book," she said as she walked to the front door and flipped the open sign. "Well, then, come along."

Taking what looked like a brown bag with her lunch, she left her coffee on her desk and, as ever, walked briskly toward the back of the building. Would the old bookmobile be as much of a time machine as this place was? Tess knew one thing. It would be spick-and-span within and the books would be perfectly in their places.

But the back workroom was a bit cluttered, which surprised her. Boxes and padded envelopes looked partly unpacked. Some sets of large books were stacked on wooden shelves.

"The so-called ebooks and those electronic tablets and phones are making perfectly good sets of encyclopedias and other reference volumes dead as the dodo," Miss Etta said with a shake of her head.

"You know, I had an excellent idea we should discuss," Miss Etta went on. "You'd be the perfect person to help me with groups of elementary students who come to visit the library or go on field trips to my house, where I talk about the Falls County pioneer days. I'll bet you miss working with youngsters."

"Yes, I do. That sounds great, but I'm not sure how long I'll be around."

"I hope you're not getting too close to Gabe McCord, I mean, if you're leaving soon. Ah, here we are."

The old bookmobile was parked so its back door aligned with the library door. Tess realized Miss Etta must have driven it to work, because she didn't see another car nearby. The woman unlocked the door to the old truck and went up a step, clicking on the inside light. Tess followed. The interior smelled musty. The scent seemed vaguely familiar and suddenly overpowering. It reminded Tess of the basement in her house.

"Ah, yes, here it is, far superior to that other book," Miss Etta said. Pointing, she made room for Tess to pass her in the narrow, single aisle.

As she moved farther into the bookmobile, the smell grew stronger and Tess was overwhelmed by a memory. She was in the big, tall room where she was allowed to draw pictures if she was good, the room with all the books along the walls, the room where Mr. Mean lived and terrible things could happen.

Tess gasped and turned. She had to get out of here!

The paper bag crinkled loudly as Miss Etta took something from it and jabbed Tess's neck with a needle. Just like that day in the cornfield.

"No!" Tess shouted, and tried to shove her away, but she was so strong, the rows between the corn so narrow.

"It's all right," Miss Etta said in a crooning voice. "It will be all right...."

Tess felt pain. Had she been stabbed or cut? She swung a fist at the woman but missed. She bounced off a shelf of books, kept in place by a cord in case the road was rocky. Tess grabbed for it to keep from falling, pulled it loose with several books and fell to her knees. Would she be smacked with Mr. Mean for messing up the books?

"I'm sorry," Miss Etta said, in a calm voice as if she were reading to children who had to listen or they would be punished and hurt. She helped lower Tess to the soil in the cornfield. "I needed to do that before you remembered more, my dear. A drink of wine would have been kinder, but you gave me no choice. I must risk taking you now."

Tess tried to hang on to her thoughts. Didn't the drugs in the wine tie in to Dane? She could see the needle on the floor. It had blood on it. Maybe it would explode, because something was exploding in Marva's kitchen and in her brain. However hard she fought it, Tess knew she was going under....

If the leaves hadn't been off many of the trees, they might not even have seen the cabin before they were right on top of it. Gabe was amazed the decent-sized building had no view of the creek, distant waterfall or valley below. But then, he realized, Reese Owens hadn't built it for the view outside but the one inside.

He held up his hand to halt Vic's progress. Instinctively, they both lifted their rifles, despite the fact that they'd found no vehicle parked nearby.

"You go around back," Gabe whispered.

"Roger that," Vic said. He limped toward the upside of the hill.

Gabe was grateful to have Vic with him. He still missed his father. If they had both been law officers at the same time, going out on a dangerous call, it might have been like this. And without Vic, he would have had to pull Jace away from the search for Sandy. But what if he could find her first, bring her back…?

Vic glanced at him before disappearing behind the cabin. Gabe bent low and moved closer to the front door. There was no porch for sitting out, nothing fancy or fine. It was a far cry from the mayor's mansion in town, more like the small house where Reese had been reared.

His rifle ready but pointed down, Gabe put his back against the exterior front wall, crept along and twisted his neck so he could peek in a front window. Blackout drapes of some kind blocked his view. His gut twisted. He was going in.

Vic came around the front. "No back

door or windows," he said to Gabe.

Gabe nodded. "Police!" he shouted. "Come out with your hands in the air!"

Nothing. No sound but the birds and wind in the tree branches.

"That door looks pretty sturdy," Vic said, pressed to the wall between the window and the door. "But I say we go in. We've got cause. The heck with waiting again for a search warrant. He'll find a way to stop it. If it turns out to be nothing, that's the breaks."

"Literally. I'm going to bust out this window," Gabe said.

Vic shrugged. "That or get a downed tree limb for a battering ram."

Gabe broke out the window with his rifle butt. There was no sound but shattering glass, still no reaction from inside. Shoving the heavy curtain aside, he stuck his rifle barrel through, then his head.

"Clear," he told Vic. "I'll climb in, unlock the door. There's all kinds of stuff covered by black drapes in here. On the back wall, I see newspaper articles and pictures of girls, some in strange poses."

"Bingo, if he's still into molesting. And the articles—maybe he likes to read his own press," Vic said, holding Gabe's gun while he climbed through. Gabe tried to avoid slicing his legs up on the jagged glass still caught in the frame.

When he unlocked and opened the door for Vic, in the light, they both stopped and stared. Vic started to swear, and Gabe felt sick to his stomach.

The newspaper articles were all about a TV show called **The Biggest Loser,** where contestants tried to lose a lot of weight. Before-and-after weight-loss pictures were posted. Charts on the wall tracked Reese's weight—down, then up again. The pictures of girls were really of a thin woman who was giving all kinds of tips on losing weight. Wearing tights and a tank top, she was in various poses, demonstrating squats, lunges, scissors kicks on her back with her legs in the air.

And the machines under the drapes included a tread climber, a stationary bicycle, a running track, a rowing machine and a stack of weights.

"Talk about dumbbells and big losers, huh?" Vic said. "Skunked again. There's no evidence of girls here, only a poor, fat sap who wants to get his boyish figure back and isn't going to."

"And now I've got to replace that window, explain to him. He'll really try to get me defeated next month in the election. And maybe he should," Gabe said.

Vic started shuffling broken glass around with his foot, shoving it toward the door. "I suppose he'd never know it wasn't some hunter or that bunch of kids with the graffiti habit. Personally, I can't stand the guy."

"Me neither, but I've got to live with myself. Let's board this up. I'll have to tell him. We need to get back. Thank God Tess is safe at the station and people are pitching in to help with another search. Maybe I was nuts not to take that book from the librarian about stress on the job."

Were the cords the woman was wrapping around her wrists the same ones that kept the books from falling when the library truck made a sharp turn? Ropes around her ankles too, and a neatly ironed linen handkerchief stuck in her mouth. Tumbling, turning, Tess fought the darkness. **Gabe.** Gabe had gone somewhere green when she needed him here in this creeping blackness that was going to drown her under a waterfall.

"You just take a nap right there," a voice said. "We're going on a little ride back home."

It wasn't her mother's voice, was it? Or maybe Char was counseling her to get more sleep.

"It will just take me a minute to completely close up, and you just rest while I drive. You should never have run away, you know, you bad girl! Did you think you could hide from me? Remember, Teresa, if you aren't good, I'll put you underground with the bones."

At those words, at the shift in voice to an even lower pitch, total terror came screaming back at Tess. She saw it all, tried to run, tried to shout for help, but black night covered her.

28

Tess felt groggy, but she was finally getting a good night's sleep. Still, the bed was so hard, and now someone was moving her, dragging her out of bed. Was it Gabe? Was she at his house? She wanted to stretch her sore arms and legs, but they didn't move. The cut on her wrist hurt so much, she was afraid she was back in the meth lab, tied up again. She tried to cry out, but there was something in her mouth, and all that came out was a choking sound.

"Almost there now," a woman's voice said. "Home again, home again, jiggetty jig."

A nursery rhyme about the five little piggies. Oh, she was back at the day care center in Michigan, home again. But no, wasn't Cold Creek home?

She knew that voice, but whose was it? Was there an emergency? Had something bitten her, and she needed shots for rabies?

"You should never have run away, you bad girl. And you owe me for that broken window all those years ago. Broke it out with Mr. Mean, then stacked books to get high enough to crawl out, didn't you? That's no way to treat books! Mama Sybil was so angry when you were gone she hit **me** with Mr. Mean."

Then Tess knew. Jumping out of the dark doors of her mind, pictures poured at her. She remembered Mama Sybil in her wheelchair. She was the one who was mean. She said she loved Tess, but she beat her, scared her every time she cried for home, every time she didn't cuddle up to be read to. Tess breathed slowly and deeply and her gaze cleared. Miss Etta was dragging her from the bookmobile into a building and room she remembered well. Miss Etta had called it the book barn. Yes, that's where she'd broken a window to escape and was found wandering on a road several miles away because she didn't know how to get home.

Tess tried to talk again, hoping Miss Etta would pull the gag from her mouth. It was hard not only to swallow but to breathe because her nose ran and she was starting to cry. She forced herself to continue listening to the woman.

"All I'd done was run to the bathroom the day you got away, but you were so quick, both in movement and in thought. Surprising, since you didn't like to read as your sisters did, but I know you learned a lot hearing books read to you while you were on Mama Sybil's lap. I was hoping to improve your reading. That's partly why I chose you when I drove the bookmobile past your house that day and saw you running wild in your backyard by the cornfield, you naughty girl. Believe me, it was a long trek through that corn to fetch you and get you past that big mower making its passes. I had to carry you clear to the bookmobile parked on the road!"

Gabe! Tess screamed inside her head. **Come find me and maybe you'll find**

Sandy and Jill before it's too late for all of us.

Miss Etta left her on the floor in the middle of a big, worn, hooked rug. The window she'd escaped through was boarded up, as were the others, but the place was lit by four bare bulbs hanging from electrical cords. Fury cleared Tess's mind even more. This was the place, lined with books, where she'd been allowed to play, to draw pictures. And they'd said over and over they were being kind to her! But Mr. Mean lived here as well as in the house attic, where she'd slept. Miss Etta had moved her from place to place after dark. And in the house, Mama Sybil ruled with an iron fist.

Tess blinked back tears and shook her head to force her way through the haze of memories and emotions. Fearful, forsaken. She had to halt the tumble of thoughts right now. Concentrate. Listen and plan.

"Coming alert, Teresa?" Miss Etta asked. "I wasn't sure how much of that drug went into you when you fought like that. Since you're an adult, I'll up the dose later when we go inside to see Mama Sybil. I'll take that gag out for a minute or two, but I have to head back to town, be seen around before I return here. Got to get you all tied up nice and tight until I get back. And they won't find Sandy on their cornfield searches, because you'll both be here, snug as bugs in a rug."

Sandy is here and alive!

It had never occurred to Tess that Etta Falls might be crazy. But she was the one. A librarian. One who was so helpful. One who seemed to be everywhere so no one noticed she had buzzed about in that bookmobile and had taken prisoners.

The minute Miss Etta pulled the gag out, Tess almost dry-heaved. Trying to stay calm, she copied the woman's preachy, almost singsong tone, as if she were talking to a child.

"Miss Etta, you can't keep people prisoner like this. You'll have to let me go, and we won't say another thing about it."

"Oh, we only keep you girls until you get too big for cuddling and commanding. And you're entirely too big and the only one who got away, Teresa. But we can correct that now. Besides, we can't allow your talking to young Sheriff McCord any more than to his father. Oh, we were worried you'd recall things then, just like now, but you cooperated beautifully. That's why I tried to warn you to leave town and keep your mouth shut with the drugged wine and your old drawing, but you didn't cooperate, did you? So you'll have to pay the price. Mama Sybil's rules, not mine, so we all have to obey her."

Tess started to shake. After feeling elated that Sandy was alive, she was so scared she broke into a sweat despite the fact that she felt icy cold. The two old women were disposing of their victims when they grew too big? Then Jill—

"Miss Etta, you know this is wrong."

"People must obey their mothers. Besides, Teresa, some things are only wrong in this big bad world when you get caught. Don't you think we would have been stopped by now if what we are doing is wrong? Mama Sybil loves little girls, just like she loves me. Now let's see about getting you more tightly tied."

"So Jill Stillwell is...gone?"

"Why, yes. She's out back. I told her she should be honored to lie among the pioneer Falls family, but she didn't know what I meant. So I put her to sleep and buried her between two graves."

Oh, dear Lord in heaven, Tess prayed, **please don't let Jill be dead.** But this crazy woman had buried her in that pioneer graveyard Tess recalled seeing from an attic window upstairs. But recalled much too late...

Miss Etta continued to speak as if all was normal. "She would have been entirely too heavy and large for Mama Sybil's lap by now anyway. But Sandy's upstairs in the attic, where I'll take you until we can settle everything, and I can make the final preparations. Oh, dear, you've got blood on your neck from where you moved when I gave you that shot. Here, let me get that off with this handkerchief."

With the saliva-soaked cloth, she dabbed at Tess's neck, then wiped her hands. "Oh, blood on my hands, just like

Lady Macbeth, but then I'll bet you don't know about her, do you?"

She pulled a small bottle of hand sanitizer from her sweater pocket and washed her hands. "This does wonders for erasing fingerprints on bottles and doorknobs, though it's not as good as wearing gloves. You know, in the fifties and early sixties we wore white gloves to shop in a nice store, to church, so much more ladylike and sanitary than all that hand shaking and hugging these days."

Miss Etta efficiently tied Tess's wrists and legs right over her earlier bonds, then took tape from a box labeled Book Cover Repair and wound it around Tess and one of the supporting roof beams. She ignored Tess's pleas as she worked, dumping Tess's cell phone on the floor with the other things from her purse. Positioning the phone, she went into a back corner and returned with another version of the Mr. Mean scarecrow and smashed the phone to bits.

"There!" she declared, clapping her hands free of dust, then digging out the sanitizer again. "It would give me great pleasure to get rid of all of those. You know, people were much better off when they spoke face-to-face. For example, when we chatted at the church service the other night, you told me that you were recalling too much. That's why I left a version of Mr. Mean when I took Sandy, to see if it would jog your memory at all. Then I would know if I had to get rid of you fast, but now will do. I was trying to plan how, and here you came into the library alone."

"How did you get in the house to drug my wine?"

"With a key, of course. I took it from your cousin Grace's coat pocket at the library when she was still living in the Lockwood house, the very day she told me you were coming back to town. You see, I've been buying sleepy-time drugs from Dane for years, but he wanted to charge me more. I said that was immoral and outrageous, but I was afraid he'd tell someone I was using them—I told him I needed them to keep my ill mother calm."

"So you...you shot him?"

"I had to. I left a so-called suicide note, which was really an old excuse he'd penned to me—tongue-in-cheek, obviously—about some overdue books on new dog breeds he'd borrowed from the library. My, he had a big fine for those books. The day he left this world, I had him bring his own antique pistol. I told him I'd buy it for an exorbitant price. But the thing is, I'm not certain that the last batch of sleeping potions he gave me are full strength, and I never was good with an intravenous needle, so sorry about that jab on your neck."

Tess wanted to break down in sobs, but she had the strangest urge to laugh hysterically. Etta Falls should have been committed to the Falls County Insane Asylum in town before it was closed. And her mother must be just as mad.

"Now, Teresa, I can't move you into the big house until after dark, but I'll be back sooner than that," she announced with a pat on Tess's shoulder. "My, you were such a pretty little girl. Mama Sybil's favorite, I really think so, and then you had to sneak away. But not this time. Not this time."

She produced another neatly ironed and sweetly scented handkerchief and pushed it into Tess's mouth. Tess fought to keep from gagging and hyperventilating. While, humming, Miss Etta swept up what had been Tess's phone into a dustpan. She put the other items spilled from her purse back inside it. Then she went out and locked the book-barn door. The sound of the bookmobile driving away faded, but the hushed roar of the waterfall and the piercing shriek of a distant train hovered heavy in the air.

"What do you mean she stepped out and never came back?" Gabe shouted at Peggy.

"She got a cup of coffee. I gave her a little break. I was on the phone with a medical emergency call, and she just stepped out, that's all. You didn't tell me to tie her to her chair!"

"I know, I know. Vic, will you take my gear and stow it? I'm going to call Tess, tell her to get the heck back here." He punched in her number as he went back to his office.

Nothing. He got nothing but voice mail when he knew she kept her phone on during the day. His gut twisted tighter. He rushed back out into the hall.

"She's not answering. I'm going to look for her."

"Look where?" Vic said, still holding both vests and rifles.

"I don't know! I obviously don't know where to look for anyone missing!"

"Calm down. She's probably just at the church helping to set up the search and hasn't recharged her phone or forgot to turn it on. Call Jace."

"I'll walk down there myself."

Gabe strode outside, furious at Peggy, Tess, himself, the world. He scanned the street and sidewalks toward New Town, then walked toward Old Town. Only a few people were on the street, none of them Tess. **Man, I should have locked her up,** he thought. Part of the reason he was having Peggy train her was so he'd know where she was during the day and she'd be at his place at night.

According to Peggy, she'd been gone over an hour. Horrible memories hit him hard. Little Teresa missing in the cornfield. "Well, where is she?" her mother was screaming. "She can't just disappear! You were supposed to be watching her!" His own mother was on the phone, calling his dad to come home. Gabe's panic soared.

He ran across the street and into the Kwik Shop, walked the ends of the aisles. No Tess. He called Jace.

"No, she's not here, Sheriff. I'll keep an eye out. We've got the team leaders set for the search for Sandy...."

Gabe said a fast goodbye. If he didn't spot Tess soon, there'd be a double search to organize.

Creekside Gifts had reopened, but he was pretty sure it was being staffed by friends of the Kentons right now. Still, he went across the street again. Lindell Kenton and Tess seemed to have bonded over Tess's agreeing to read from the Bible at the service. They'd had a long talk on the phone and another at the church. Yeah, she could be here. But when he stuck his head in the door, they told her they hadn't seen Tess.

As he walked toward the library, it hit him. She'd probably come down here to get that book for him. And when talking to Miss Etta, it could be hard to get away. As he reached for the door, he saw a hand turn the Closed sign around to Open. When he opened the door, it almost hit Miss Etta.

"Oh, Sheriff. I just got back from an early lunch. Did you decide you need that book on stress?"

His hopes fell. "I thought maybe Tess Lockwood came down to get it for me."

"Oh, she was here but just to ask if she could keep the books I gave her longer. Just as you had told me, she said they were of some help to her, but she didn't stay long. I got the impression she was going for a walk."

"Thanks, Miss Etta," he said, and ignored her suggestion for the second time to take the book about stress from her desk. He hurried outside.

His phone rang. Thank God. But it was Vic's phone. Tess was really going to hear it from him when he found her. It sobered him to think how much he cared for her, not just as the first victim, not just because both he and his father had lived and breathed these kidnap cases…. He really wanted her, loved her.

"Sheriff McCord here."

"Gabe, it's Vic. Haven't seen Tess, but Pastor Snell tracked down that woman who counseled Tess after she was returned to her family. Melanie Parkinson. She lives in Columbus, but I have her contact info if you want to call her. She works late hours but will be at this number after nine this evening."

"Yeah, I want to call her. You know my motto—any clue will do. Anything. Vic, Tess has vanished into thin air."

Vic read Gabe the phone number, then said, "I'll go into New Town to look for her. Leave Peg on the phones here. Don't panic, okay?"

"Aren't you worried too? Instead of New

Town, how about you drive out to my place, then hers?"

"Because I drove her this morning—remember? She doesn't have a car."

"But maybe she had someone take her out to get it, since you and I were gone. It's a long shot, but—"

"Okay, sure. Stay in touch."

Stay in touch. Gabe felt haunted by the past. What he feared most in all this was losing Tess a second time.

It was just after dark when Miss Etta returned to the book barn, gave Tess another shot—this time in her upper arm—and cut the bonds around her feet. "That drug is for people, not an animal drug, and doesn't take long to work, believe me."

She pulled the gag from Tess's mouth. Tess gasped for air and moved her tongue, trying to get some saliva going so she could speak. She had to talk this woman out of whatever her warped brain had planned. And facing Miss Etta's mother, whom she recalled now as scary and sadistic, would be a trial too. Why was Miss Etta, at her age, still so completely under her mother's thumb? Tess remembered how Sybil Falls had demanded hugs and kisses and complete obedience or Miss Etta would beat her as the old woman called her bad and evil. Was there some strain of dementia in this family, or had the entire world gone mad?

But then a thought hit Tess. She'd been just about ready to tell Miss Etta that Gabe knew about Dane's drug source and that he'd found a list in Dane's house of who bought drugs from him. She was hoping the lie would scare the woman, but suddenly realized it might make her move quicker to get rid of her—maybe put her out in that graveyard with Jill.

But, especially since Miss Etta didn't know how much of a dose to give an adult and was worried Dane had been giving her weaker doses, Tess wondered if she could pretend to be under the influence of the drug and wait for her chance to stop this woman? If it was the drug she and Gabe had researched, she knew it made a person cooperate with a doctor's commands. Maybe she could shove Miss Etta, hit her—something. Mama Sybil must be frail, wheelchair-bound, a paraplegic, so, unless they had more old pistols loaded here, Tess hoped she'd have a chance. She had to fight the effects of the drug, keep telling herself that she could get away from this woman, only pretend to obey her, to stay alert. But she had to find and save Sandy too.

"Upsy-daisy, little Teresa," Miss Etta said, and helped her to her feet. Tess gasped. **Upsy-daisy,** just like the word **smackings,** triggered a flood of terrible memories. Tess longed to shake off the woman's hands, but, pretending to be just a bit slow, she let Miss Etta lead her from the book barn. They shuffled past the bookmobile, across the dark yard, up onto the porch and through the back door of the big frame house. Though her hands were still tied behind her, she was desperate to flee. She only felt a bit groggy and thought she could do it. But she had to keep telling herself to comply with this woman's orders until she could find Sandy.

Miss Etta led her up a set of back stairs that must have once been used by servants. How familiar the house seemed. Her ankles burned, and her legs were sore from being tied so long. Her cut wrist pained her. She had to pretend to be subdued, out of it. Her thoughts rampaged when she needed to keep calm.

If Sandy was upstairs, how Tess wanted to comfort the girl. If only Gabe would realize who had taken her, what had happened. Tess tried to recall what she'd said to Peggy when she left the sheriff's office. She'd been on the phone with that call about a raccoon bite. Tess couldn't remember if she'd told Peggy that she was going to the library or not.

Gabe would kill her for walking into a trap—if Miss Etta didn't kill her first.

29

Gabe took Sandy Kenton's mother aside in the church parking lot being used as the base, where scores of volunteers had fanned out for the search. Some were already reporting in—that they'd found nothing.

"Lindell, I need to tell you something."

"You've found her?" she demanded, grabbing his arm.

"No, though we keep eliminating possibilities. Tess Lockwood's gone missing. I just wanted you to know that my deputy and I notified the groups before they left to look for Tess too. I know you've talked to her lately. Any unusual hints about where she could be?"

The woman's face went blank for a moment. She'd aged so much in the six days since Sandy disappeared. Stringy hair, no makeup, the ravages of little sleep. The torment of not knowing what was happening to her only daughter—if she was still alive.

"Tess?" she asked, her voice shaky. "Like, the kidnapper's taken her again? An adult this time?"

"Around noon today, she walked from the sheriff's office to the library, left there and disappeared."

Her eyes widened. "Oh, no! Oh, no, no!" She lifted her clasped hands to her mouth, clenching her fingers. "But wouldn't that mean the same person who has Sandy and Jill wants to harm her—shut her up? Gabe, I know you've lived and breathed this."

"I— Yes, all over again, times three."

"I hear Tess is special to you. Don't look so surprised. This is Cold Creek, you know. Word gets around. I felt close to Tess the few times we talked. She helped me so much, not only that she came back, but just that she understood my pain. We have to find her and the girls."

"You and Win did a great job with the

TV plea you made," he said. "It's been running on most channels, some nationwide."

"So the mayor told me. You know, Tess said she'd thought of running home to Michigan, but there was more than one reason to stay here now. She said she had to help you, stay close to you."

Tears stung his eye. "Thanks, Lindell. She hadn't put it like that to me. I'd like to keep her here, but all this has to end. I need to find her—and Sandy—fast."

He touched the brim of his hat and started away, but she grabbed his elbow. "Maybe they're together. Sandy, Tess and Jill. I'd like to think that. Tess helped me, and I'll bet she could help Sandy too."

"Hold that thought. I've got to get back to the search. You'll be the first to know anything," he told her and headed toward his vehicle.

He got in, started the engine and pulled away. He was so focused on Tess he'd forgotten to tell Lindell that the Ohio State Highway Patrol was going to fly a chopper over local wooded areas using FLIR, heat thermal imaging. Vic was keeping him updated on any tips or other information that came in on the sheriff's phone lines or reports from searchers in the field. **In the field**—the standard cop term almost made him laugh, but this time it was literal.

"Hitchetty-hatchetty, up we go," Miss Etta recited as they climbed the back stairs, passed the door to the second floor and kept going toward the attic. Tess was convinced Miss Etta sometimes believed Tess was Teresa, a little girl again.

She had hoped that would help to get the woman off guard, but the librarian from hell had outsmarted her again. She held a cocked antique pistol pressed tight to her ribs as they climbed. "As you know I have not one moment's hesitation about using this!" she'd said, and had given Tess a lecture about the gun's pioneer history. Tess's heart nearly pounded out of her chest and not from the exertion of the climb. What if that old gun went off? It was aimed right at her heart.

Miss Etta chattered nonstop about next

to nothing until she said something that put Tess on alert. "I swear I'm going to have blisters on my hands from all that digging. It's been a while since I dug that much, and my shoulder and back muscles are aching like the very dickens. Interesting that one of the greatest writers in the English language had a last name that's a euphemism for the word **devil.** That's Charles Dickens, my dear, but he did have a mistress and was unfaithful to his wife, so he wasn't lily-white. Your father wasn't either."

However much Tess wanted to scream at this woman, she had to try to convince her the drug had made her dopey. "He's gone," she mumbled.

"Yes, I know, and that is sad for you Lockwood girls that he's so far away, but perhaps best he's out of your lives. In the old days, you know," she rattled on, "these servant stairs were important. The maids and kitchen help slept on the top floor and needed to go up and down without being seen by the family. Speaking of Dickens, servant stairs are very Victorian. Well, times have changed and even my family doesn't have an 'upstairs, downstairs' lifestyle anymore. And this is hardly **Downton Abbey.**"

Tess tried to ignore all that and desperately looked for her chance. She concentrated on what she'd say when she saw Sandy Kenton, the treasure for which Gabe had searched so hard. She was excited that the most recent drug that had been injected into her arm wasn't making her particularly groggy.

Tess prayed she'd be able to keep her head in this. She counted the turns of the stairs, lit by only a ceiling light on each tiny landing. The steps were narrow and steep. Coming down, she could easily fall, especially if she was pulling a child behind her.

"Now, Teresa, I expect you to apologize to Mama Sybil for running off the way you did, when you knew she loved you. It hurt her terribly. Hurt me too in more ways than one. I'm going to leave you with her and Sandy while I finish something outside, but it won't take me long, and then I'll be back. You, of course, will be tied, and Sandy will be on Mama Sybil's lap. Finally, she's learned to obey. Spare the rod and spoil the child, you know. You learned that much slower than Sandy. You were quite an independent little miss when you first came to live with us."

Again, Tess had to force herself not to answer back, to tell this demented woman off. It made her sick to her stomach, but she murmured only, "Yes, Miss Etta."

"Actually that old saying, **Spare the rod and spoil the child,** only takes its inspiration from the book of Proverbs, but verbatim it goes way back to a poem called **Piers Plowman** in 1377, and then the adage showed up in another poem in 1662."

Tess wanted to scream. This seemed a nightmare from which she must surely wake. She longed to tell this woman her trivial knowledge was nothing—nothing!— because she was a monster. But she had to hold herself together. At least Mama Sybil would be in her wheelchair, and she should be able to overtake her when Miss

Etta went to finish her business. Of digging graves? Even if Miss Etta locked them in, even if she tied Tess, surely, with Sandy's help—if she wasn't drugged—she'd be able to get away, break out, rush downstairs with Sandy, or at least get to a phone in the house to call 911. She'd bet her life—which was probably what she was doing—that this house had a landline, maybe with an old dial phone.

The other thought Tess had as they reached the chained attic door was that she was still terrified to face that horrible old lady again. If Mama Sybil had a pistol too, would she be risking a bullet to the brain, like Dane?

Even after all the negative reports came in from the volunteer teams, Gabe had exhausted himself searching. He was running on sheer adrenaline, guts and fear. He'd explored Tess's house, attic to cellar, and about jumped out of his skin when his flashlight had illumined a dummy on the floor of the basement. He remembered that Grace had done sewing and alterations to earn extra money before they moved to the Hear Ye compound. It was an old dressmaker's mannequin, but it had looked like a woman on the floor at first.

He was so desperate that he had requested another search warrant, this one for Bright Star's compound. He was afraid he was getting to be persona non grata with the judge, but he didn't care anymore. Not about his health, his job, his life—he just wanted to find Tess, Jill and Sandy safe. Had someone taken Tess off Main Street outside the library?

He drove to the burned-out site of Marva Green's old house and searched the back buildings again. Nothing but trash, owls and rats. He sat down on an upturned tin tub and tried to think about where else he could search.

He decided to go back to the office, make that call to the church woman who had counseled Tess. His hope was that maybe she'd kind of debriefed little Teresa and could shed new light on what happened all those years ago. He remembered his father saying that Tess's mother thought it best if no one mentioned the horrible experience, but just tried to go back to normal. **Normal?** Nothing had ever been normal again.

Miss Etta unlocked the padlock on the chain holding the attic door closed, and it rattled as it uncoiled itself. Tess was tempted to shove the woman down the stairs, but that pistol could go off. And would it endanger Sandy if she was with Mama Sybil on the other side of that door? If only she could get her hands untied like her feet.

Tess steeled herself for what she'd find within, but she also realized that, if Miss Etta locked them in again, they weren't getting out of this chained door without an ax.

With the pistol still pressed to her side, Tess shuffled into the dim attic. She scanned the length of it, built with a long center section and two wings. A small bed under the eaves, a few toys—and another Mr. Mean leaning against the slanted wall under the eaves. Two bare lightbulbs dangled from the ceiling. Old hump-backed trunks were stored here. Stacks of old-fashioned hat boxes, several old, cracked paintings, bedsprings and a headboard, all suddenly, horribly familiar.

But why would Miss Etta keep her mother up here? Those stairs must be close to impossible for a crippled person in a wheelchair. It was chilly here too, so wouldn't she keep her mother downstairs? Tess recalled that it was the first floor where she'd been forced to climb onto the old woman's lap to be cuddled and petted—and held down to be beaten when she disobeyed, all under the watchful eye of a stag head mounted over the fireplace mantel.

As Tess's eyes adjusted, she saw Mama Sybil at the far end of the room sitting slumped in her wheelchair. And Sandy—she was alive!—sat in her lap.

Miss Etta prodded Tess closer with the gun still in her ribs. Her first instinct was to comfort Sandy, who, thank God, turned her head and moved one leg to show she was alert. She must be drugged or too terrified to speak.

Miss Etta prodded Tess. "Apologize to Mama Sybil for escaping!" She stopped Tess about ten feet from Mama Sybil. "Get on your knees and tell her you are very, very sorry!"

Tess dropped to her knees with the pistol now pressed to the nape of her neck. Before she could speak, a deep voice behind her spoke. "Is this our Teresa come back to us, Etta?"

Tess gasped and jerked.

Sandy stirred on Mama Sybil's lap and sniffled.

"I'm sorry I ran away, Mama Sybil," Tess said. "Can I come closer?"

"All right," the voice from behind intoned. "But you behave or else."

Miss Etta was speaking for her mother. Tess thought maybe the old woman had suffered a stroke and couldn't talk.

"On your knees, forward," Miss Etta said, in what Tess recalled was a perfect rendition of her cruel mother's voice.

Tess scooted forward. She forced a

smile at Sandy and mouthed reassuring words. **Sandy, hello.**

Then she gasped. There was no woman holding Sandy. She—it—had no face except an enlarged photograph of Mama Sybil with stuffing behind it and a nylon stocking pulled over it to which a white wig was tied or sewn. The body was maybe wood sticks, like a scarecrow, wrapped with cloth, or stuffed, with fake arms and legs. The gown was old-fashioned and smelled stale and musty. A crocheted afghan was over the legs clear down to a pair of old black, laced shoes. It was so grotesque, yet so real from a distance, that Tess felt she'd been punched in the stomach. She almost screamed.

"She's not...not there!" she cried. "Is she downstairs? Did she die?"

It was the wrong thing to say. The blow to her head was hard. It stunned her. She heard the child squeal. And then she hit the floor.

30

Tess felt a small, gentle hand brushing her hair from her face. Her head hurt horribly. Where was she?

Then she remembered. She opened her eyes. Sandy Kenton was bent over her, her little face wet with tears.

"Is she gone?" Tess asked.

"Miss Etta carried Mama Sybil downstairs to put her to bed. She said Mr. Mean would hurt me if I talked to you, but I just want to ask one thing."

Tess groaned and struggled to sit up. Her hands were still tied behind her back and her feet were bound again. Only Sandy's hands were tied, but the girl was tethered to the empty wheelchair, which she'd dragged close enough to reach Tess.

"Ask me," Tess said, trying to sound

calm and quiet when she wanted to sob and scream. "I'm your friend. My name is Tess."

"Do you know my mommy?"

"Yes. Yes, I know her, and she wants you to come home."

"I can't go home. I can't even say it or Mr. Mean—"

"I know because they kept me here too once, but I got away from them and Mr. Mean and went home to my mommy. And you can too, if you help me."

"But Mama Sybil is my other mommy now."

"Mama Sybil isn't real. Have you seen her walk and talk since you've been here?"

"No, she's always like that, a big doll. But I have to say she's real."

"Sandy, turn your back to my back and let me try to untie you. Then you untie me so we can both go home. Your mommy and daddy want you to come home with me. Come on now, turn around back to back, okay? We might not have much time."

"We don't. Miss Etta said soon you are

going to go to sleep with someone named Jill and some pioneer people, her family."

Tess steeled herself to stay calm. Jill really was dead and buried out back. "Okay, good job, Sandy," Tess said, as the child got close enough that she could begin to fumble with her ties. But her own hands were bound so tight she couldn't grasp a cord to loosen Sandy's. Maybe she should have studied the knots before trying to undo them. At least Sandy's hands were small and sweaty and not tied quite as tight as her own.

As she tried to loosen the girl's ties, Tess spoke to her about the two searches for her, told her that the police would give back the Barbie doll she left behind. Tess fought the worst headache she'd ever had and prayed that Etta Falls, who must be digging another grave, would not come back in time.

Finally she managed to free one of the child's hands, and then they both popped free.

"Sandy, turn around and see if you can untie my hands."

"I have scissors I cut out paper dolls with, but they don't have sharp points."

"Yes, get them. Try sawing at my ties. Hurry, please."

"But they're in the corner with Mr. Mean."

"Mr. Mean isn't real, and I won't let him hurt you. Let's run away from here and go see your mommy and daddy! Hurry, honey, please!"

She scurried away but was back fast, sawing away at Tess's wrist bonds. "Miss Etta shoots her old guns out in back sometimes. I hear them go **bang!**"

Tess tried to stretch the ropes as the girl cut and sawed. Her hands were completely numb. She heard the slam of a door downstairs—surely not the gunshot Sandy had mentioned. Miss Etta must be back in the house.

"Sandy, never mind that. Try to cut my leg ties. Hurry. Saw at them while I stretch them," Tess urged the child as footsteps echoed on the stairs. Tess knew this sort of scissors well, good only for cutting colored construction paper. This wasn't going to work.

"Listen to me, Sandy. I want you to go over behind the door Miss Etta will come through. Hide behind it and keep really quiet when she opens it. I'll do something to get her attention, and then you run down the stairs and outside. Can you open the downstairs door if it's locked?"

"It's dark outside."

"But if we can't both run, you have to get away. That's what I did and someone found me, took me home to my mommy. Can you do that?"

"I don't want to go without you. Miss Etta said you and me can be next to her pioneer family. I don't want to be there alone."

Tess was not only panicked but furious. She yanked at her fraying bonds in a frenzy. The footsteps stopped and Sandy kept cutting. Maybe Miss Etta had gone to the second floor to visit her mother, if she was an invalid. But Tess had the surest feeling Sybil Falls was dead. Miss Etta had probably buried the old woman out back and told no one. She couldn't bear to let the past go and tried to hold on to it any way she could.

Suddenly the ties around her legs gave way! Jumping up on numb feet, Tess stumbled like a drunk, almost lost her balance. Pulling Sandy tight to her, they huddled together behind the door.

"Listen to me now, honey," Tess whispered. "When she opens this door, don't hold on to me. I'm going to hit the door back into her. Maybe knock her gun away, maybe even push her down the stairs. Then I'll get on my knees and you get on my back like playing horsey."

Wide-eyed, the child nodded solemnly.

"Okay, then. When we play horsey, you try to wrap your legs around me. But if you can't because of my tied hands, you just stand on the ropes between my wrists. But there is just one rule. When you put your arms around me for the ride downstairs and outside, don't grab my neck so I can't breathe. Okay? Promise? And—if I fall, or something bad happens to me, you run fast away from here and hide in the cornfield until daylight when a car comes by. Make sure Miss Etta doesn't find you."

"I'm afraid of cornfields at night. Scarecrows can be in them."

"I know, but don't let her find you again. If you see a car going by, you yell your name to them, say that they should call the sheriff. Okay? Promise?" she repeated as the footsteps sounded on the stairs again.

Making a little X on her chest, the child whispered, "Cross my heart and hope to die."

Gabe thought Melanie Parkinson's voice was calm, almost soothing. He was sure she must have been a comfort to little Teresa years ago. Had his father even known the child had been counseled at church? That information was never recorded, and he wondered if it could have been some sort of help.

"I'm asking you to think back twenty years to the Lockwood kidnap case," he said to Mrs. Parkinson after he explained the situation.

"The so-called Cold Creek kidnapper.

Yes, I remember the events and little Teresa Lockwood well. She'd been brutalized and terrified, so much so it had changed her personality. Inward, shy, afraid, when her mother said she'd been so bold and outgoing before that."

"What would help me now," he said without explaining Tess was missing again—it pained him to even say it—"is if you can recall anything specific she might have said about the place she was held or the person who held her. Anything!"

"Yes, all right. Several of her drawings we did for therapy were of a room with a deer head on the wall and a huge, oversize window. I assume she was wishing she could have gone out it, or that might have been how she actually escaped, because she was iffy on that. Out the window, she drew small gravestones."

"She recently recalled that view. Anything else?"

"She once drew a scarecrow and then crayoned through it with near violence. Oh, and for such a young child, I think she referred to the cemetery once as a pioneer cemetery."

Gabe sat up straight. He knew of only two in the area, one in the very back of the Glen Rest Cemetery outside town, but the only place Tess could have seen that from was the caretaker's house. Clemment Dixon was surely no kidnapper, and he'd been in the hospital in Chillicothe when Tess was taken. And the other such cemetery—a little, old, one-family graveyard—was behind the Falls house on Blackberry Road.

A chill raced up Gabe's spine. It didn't seem possible and yet... The library was just two doors down from the shop where Sandy had disappeared. That old rattletrap of a bookmobile was always parked out back. Tess recalled the sounds of trains and the waterfall...but that cemetery was the thing.

"Sheriff, are you there? I just thought of something else. Teresa's mother told me she didn't like to read, didn't like to be read to, but several of her drawings had rows of books on shelves lining the walls and—"

"Thanks, Melanie. You've been a big help, maybe more than you know. I'll call back later."

Disconnecting his phone, he leaped from behind his desk. It couldn't be, and yet it made horrible sense. "Peg," he shouted as he ran down the hall, strapping on his gun belt. "Call Agent Reingold and Jace. Tell them no lights, no sirens, park on the road, but they need to meet me at the Falls house on Blackberry Road."

"But I didn't get a 911 from her—"

"Now!"

Tess heard the chain rattle loose on the other side of the door. Sandy was holding on to her, but it was too late to remind her not to cling to her when Miss Etta stepped in.

The door opened. "I'm back," she sang out. Tess could see her through the crack between the door and the frame as it opened, as the librarian stepped up to their level.

Tess threw herself against the door. It slammed shut. She heard the woman scream, bounce down the stairs, but how far? And what about the gun?

Tess turned her back to the door, grabbed the old knob, twisted it and opened the door. Miss Etta lay on the second-floor landing, looking stunned. In the dim stairwell, Tess couldn't tell if she had the pistol or not, or even if she was conscious.

"Get on my back," Tess told Sandy, bending down. "Horsey time."

The child obeyed. She was heavier than Tess had expected. At least she could stick her skinny legs between Tess's ribs and her tied arms. Trying to flee, desperate not to fall, Tess started down the steps just as Miss Etta moved, tried to right herself.

Tess kept going. The woman had the pistol, raised it and pointed it. They would never dodge a bullet in this narrow space. At least Sandy was behind her, so Tess would take the shot, but that could still leave both of them buried out back.

Scraping her shoulder along the stairwell wall, Tess rushed toward Miss Etta, tried to brace herself with the extra weight behind her and kicked at the woman. The pistol went off, but the gun fell to the floor. Tess waited for the pain but felt nothing. Leaning against the staircase wall, she kicked at Miss Etta again to get her out of the way, then edged past her and fled.

Down, turn, down, turn. No doubt the back door would be locked. It was, but the old skeleton-type key was in it. "Get down, get down!" she told Sandy. "I have to turn that key so we can get outside."

She nearly dumped the girl on the hall floor, turned her back and fumbled with the lock. But she heard footsteps on the stairs. Miss Etta could still have the gun, or did those old ones only have one bullet?

Her hands behind her back, Tess twisted the key, then the knob. The door opened. Sandy clung to her waist. The storm door was locked, a small sliding lock.

"You come back, you bad girls!" Mama Sybil's deep voice came from above. "I'll have to smack and shoot you both!"

Please, Lord, Tess prayed. **Please get us out of this madhouse!**

She was going to kick out the glass. No running into the house, where Miss Etta could trap them. Tied like this, there was no way she could use a phone or get out another door. She was going to leave this place forever, one way or the other. Miss Etta's footsteps and Mama Sybil's voice came closer. Sandy started to wail. It almost took Tess back twenty years, but she fought the fear. She heaved her shoulder into the glass, but bounced back. She had to get Sandy away, run into the safety of the cornfield...

Miss Etta, bloody and disheveled, stumbled down the last few stairs. It looked like another pistol in her hand as the woman bounced off the wall and almost fell. She raised the gun, pointed it at Tess and fired—but the only sound was a **click.**

Tess turned to the glass door, lifted her foot and kicked repeatedly at it. It cracked, crunched and finally shattered, leaving only the frame. Miss Etta righted herself, came closer and grabbed the screaming child, but Tess shoved and elbowed her away.

"Get outside!" Tess screamed at Sandy.

"I have more guns!" Miss Etta said, in her own voice. "I'll get my other guns!" She didn't run back upstairs but down the hall.

When Sandy seemed frozen in fear, Tess stepped through the opening, then said, calmly, quietly, "Sandy, come out now. We are going to see your mommy."

The girl shuffled to the door. "It's dark and if I run away, Mr. Mean will get me."

"No, Mr. Mean is in the house, and he will get you if you don't come out! Take a big, big giant step out. We are going home!"

The child finally obeyed. Tess yearned to be able to lift her, hold her, but there was no time to even get her on her back again. Tess looked behind them. Miss Etta stood silhouetted by the inside light in the open, broken door, holding another pistol. Tess and Sandy ran toward the field behind the graveyard with its old stones like broken teeth.

The cornfield was a sanctuary, instead

of a site that would have terrified her just a few days ago. They'd made it only a few rows in when the entire area seemed bathed with light.

"Police! Don't move! Put that down, Miss Etta!" Gabe's voice shouted.

There was a gunshot. More men's voices.

"She shot herself!" Gabe cried out. "I'm going into the house to find them!"

"Gabe!" Tess shouted. "Sandy and I are here in the field!"

With the child clinging to her waist so hard she had to drag her, Tess walked from the shelter of the cornfield, feeling free for the first time since she could remember. Three big beams of light lit her way, almost blinded her, but she saw Gabe, Vic and Jace Miller, guns drawn. Tess walked right into Gabe's crushing embrace. "Jill?" he asked.

"Dead, I think. The cemetery—not sure who else, but I bet you'll find Sybil Falls there too, when no one knew she was dead. Miss Etta was digging my grave."

He cut Tess's ties, then kneeled to look

at Sandy with his hands on her shoulders. "We'll take you home," he told the child. "Your mother and father are going to be so happy." He stood and looked at Tess, lifted his hand to finger the huge, tender scab on her head. "Maybe we can be happy too," he whispered before he turned back to Vic.

"Etta?" he asked.

"Self-inflicted," Vic said, pointing to his forehead. "Doesn't quite resemble Dane. You get Sandy and Tess home, and I'll search the house for Etta's mother just in case. I'll call, then wait for the squad and forensics."

"There's a dummy of Sybil inside that Miss Etta carried around," Tess told them. "I think she put it to bed."

Gabe's eyes widened, and his mouth dropped open. He pulled her to him. "Let's take Sandy home while Vic and Jace secure the scene. Then we need to get the forensics team to…to disinter things out here, out back." Again, he put a hand on one of Sandy's shaking shoulders. The three of them huddled for a moment, as if they were a little family.

Tess kept rubbing her wrists and hands as the blood and feeling rushed back into them. But, after Gabe lifted Sandy in one arm, Tess did feel Gabe's free hand clasp hers.

"It's finally over," he said as, holding hands, they turned toward the road. "But for us, if you're willing, Tess, it's a new start."

31

In the sheriff's vehicle, Sandy sat on Tess's lap. They were both in the same seat belt with Tess's arms around the girl. Gabe told Tess how talking to her counselor, Mrs. Parkinson, had been the key to his rushing out to Miss Etta's house. Now Tess hoped to be able to help Sandy get over her terrors. She'd stay in Cold Creek awhile for that—and to see how things worked out with Gabe.

The clock on the cruiser's dashboard read 9:58 p.m. as he pulled up in front of the Kenton house. It had only been about ten hours since Miss Etta took her this time, Tess thought, but it seemed an eternity. Electric candles shone in each window of the house, and a sign in the yard read Bring Sandy Home!! Together, she and Gabe were doing exactly that.

But Jill Stillwell's family would soon face devastation, if, at last, closure. Life was like that, the happy and the horrible all mingled together. Despite that, if Gabe let her, she'd like to face life with him.

Gabe went up to the front door and rang the bell. Tess got out with Sandy in her arms, the child's arms and legs around her as tight as ropes. Lindell rushed out with Win right behind her.

"Oh, thank you! Thank you, Sheriff! And Tess!"

Lindell hugged Tess and Sandy hard as Tess passed the stunned-looking child into her mother's arms while her father hugged them both. Tess saw Gabe's eyes as he tried to blink back tears. She went to stand by him, watching the reunion through shimmering eyes and re-membering clearly her own homecoming with her parents.

Tess realized that her return to Cold Creek had actually been a homecoming. Standing next to Gabe, with his arm around her waist, Cold Creek was suddenly starting to feel a lot like home.

• • •

A week later, Gabe and Tess sat at the picnic table behind her house, eating lunch and watching a big reaper harvest the cornfield. "It will be nice to see clearly again," she told him.

Though it was a long bench, they were sitting close together. He leaned over to plant a kiss on her shoulder, then put his steak sandwich down and wiped his hands. "And can you see clearly—about us?"

She turned to face him and put her cola can down. They both leaned inward. It started out as a little kiss, burned brighter as they squeezed even closer. Despite all the difficult and tragic things that had happened, including the forensics experts unearthing Jill's and Sybil's bodies from the old graveyard, Tess felt almost content.

When they finally broke apart, she smiled. "It's not fair you ask me something like that right before a McCord kiss. I can't think when you do that. But yes—I want to be with you, and I'm not afraid of being here anymore. If I get enough money for this house, this area could use a good day care center. Lindell said Sandy will be my first student, and I know the time I'm spending with her now is helping."

"Then I have a proposition for you."

Her insides cartwheeled. "Such as?"

"Let's sell both of our properties and buy one place on the Old Town side of Cold Creek. Then we'd have enough to build your day care out the side, the front—I don't know—of our home, so your commute would be nothing and mine would be less than now. If you like that idea we will go on from there, and, when we're ready, we can talk about other proposals too. So how do you feel about everything?"

This man in her life—and the town of Cold Creek—had seemed so scary just a few weeks ago. But now it seemed perfect.

"I like the way you think, Sheriff McCord. As a matter of fact, I like everything about you. And I know what I'm getting into with the demands of your job. Yet I believe you are worth the price of that or anything."

They kissed again, harder, longer. And the roar of the big reaper cutting and shredding the past seemed like music to her ears.

• • •

AUTHOR'S NOTE

Shattered Secrets is book one of a trilogy set in Cold Creek. When Tess's very different sisters come home for her wedding, they both become involved in crime and love. **Forbidden Ground** will feature Kate as the heroine, and **Broken Bonds,** Char's story, will follow after that.

I did my undergraduate work in Athens, Ohio (English major, of course!), on the edge of the Appalachian foothills where I chose to set this trilogy, so I do know that fascinating area well. Also, our good friends Dr. Roy and Mary Ann Manning live in Chillicothe, so we have visited there and been given several tours of the area. The mingling of people in this stunningly beautiful region makes a perfect background for conflict in this Cold Creek trilogy.

My ideas for these novels are literally ripped from the headlines. I enjoy writing books where an "average" woman's life is impacted by crime or tragedy. The police may help her, but she also manages to find the strength and courage to solve the crime herself. And rural areas are no exception, unfortunately, for unusual crimes.

I'm grateful for the tour I was able to take of the BCI (Bureau of Criminal Identification and Investigation) headquarters in London, Ohio. The tour included the latest information of many aspects of criminal investigation, which I am using in these novels. Victor Reingold and other BCI agents, however, are fictional and are only based in some ways on actual agents.

Crimes against children have certainly been in the news in horrific ways as I write this novel. Nothing is worse than harming innocents.

The two books I found most helpful about childhood trauma and various types of amnesia as background for this story are both by Dr. Lenore Teri, M.D. **Unchained Memories: True Stories of Traumatic Memories Lost and Found** and **Too Scared To Cry: Psychic Trauma In Childhood.** On Gabe's explosive ordnance disposal unit in Iraq, I consulted

The Long Walk: A Story of War and the Life That Follows by Brian Castner.

Considering the villain in this novel, I must make the point that I do **love** librarians. I would probably not be a fiction writer if it weren't for libraries and their keepers over the years. Nor would much of my education, teaching career or author research have been possible without the help of librarians. My author collection of books and papers is in the care of the Ohio State University Rare Books and Manuscripts Department in Columbus, Ohio, and the librarians there are friends and supporters. Thanks to Dr. Geoffrey Smith and all in charge there.

Happy (and scary!) reading. Please visit my website at www.KarenHarperAuthor.com.

Karen Harper